CAN I STRAY

CAN I STRAY

BY

JENNA ADAMS

This book contains material which some readers may
find distressing including discussion of suicide and suicidal ideations,
statutory rape, depression, substance abuse, toxic relationships,
and description of deliberate self-injury.

This is a work of fiction. Names, characters, businesses, places,
events, and incidents are either the products of the author's imagination or
used in a fictitious manner. Any resemblance to actual persons,
living or dead, or actual events is purely coincidental.

Published by Neem Tree Press Limited 2022
Neem Tree Press Limited
95A Ridgmount Gardens, London, WC1E 7AZ
info@neemtreepress.com
www.neemtreepress.com

A catalogue record for this book is available from the British Library
ISBN 978-1-911107-53-8 Paperback
ISBN 978-1-911107-54-5 Ebook

Printed and bound in Great Britain.

TABLE OF CONTENTS

PROLOGUE

2018

BROOKE, 22

'I would describe your tendencies as codependent,' Sanjay said.

I looked up. He was sitting on one of those big, comfy armchairs in front of the window, silhouetted by the light behind him. I had to squint to try and make eye contact. *All his clients must struggle when the sun comes through,* I thought. *Maybe someone should tell him.*

'Codependent?' I said.

He nodded slowly. All his movements were measured, his words too. There was something reassuring about them, even if I couldn't make out his face. 'Do you know what that means?'

'No. I've heard of it, but not really.'

'It means a one-sided relationship. In simple terms, you've got the needy codependent, and the narcissist or addict. I'm not saying that Charlie is a narcissist or an addict, that's just a typical example. But there's a dynamic, one where you are dependent on external sources of love in order to be okay. Would you say you were dependent on Charlie's love?'

I paused for a second. 'Yes. To an extent.'

I expected him to fill the silence, and as usual, he didn't. *Do therapists get all these qualifications and charge all this money just to sit there and not say anything?*

'But aren't most people in relationships a little bit dependent on each other?'

'Absolutely, otherwise we'd all walk out of a breakup unscathed. There's practical dependence, perhaps where one partner is a homemaker and the other earns the income; take one away through death or breakup and you're left with a person who isn't able to look after themselves properly. And then there's also *emotional* dependence, which I think is relevant to you, Brooke. The goal is to keep things at a healthy level, enough to say, "I love you, but if I had to be alone, I know I'd be okay".'

I looked down at my hands, my fingers twisting around themselves. 'I'd die if Charlie left me.'

'That's what I'd like to work on with you. I'm not saying we have to be in a situation where you *are* alone. But I think it would be useful to work on your self-esteem, and draw it from yourself, rather than from things outside of you.'

I looked up at him again. The sun was blazing. I could just make out his legs crossed lazily, his hands dangling over the arms of the chair. I looked back down at my fingers. 'That would be nice,' I mumbled.

'You said your parents separated when you were young.'

'Ten. Divorced by twelve.'

'And after that separation, how involved was your father in your life?'

'About as involved as he was before they split. Which is to say, not very.'

'That must've been hard,' Sanjay said. 'I wonder if that left you with space that requires filling, so when you enter a new relationship, you already enter needing. Which makes it hard for you to leave, even when it's not working out, because you're relying on this other person to give you love. You're not giving it to yourself.'

More silence. I kept my eyes fixed on my hands. He kept his fixed on me. At least, I thought so. That damn window.

'I would be interested to know about any significant relationships that you had prior to Charlie, if that's okay for you to talk about. Maybe we'll see some patterns emerging.'

I stiffened.

'You seemed to have a reaction to that,' Sanjay said.

'It's just…' I sighed. 'I never… I've never talked to anyone about this before.'

'Therapy is—'

'I've done therapy before. I've talked about… my feelings.'

'An old boyfriend?'

I nodded.

'Would you say you were dependent on his affection?'

'Very,' I said.

Sanjay paused. 'Well, when you're ready.'

I didn't say anything for a long time. *How am I supposed to talk about what happened?* 'I was a teenager. I was fourteen.'

'Uh huh.'

'He was… seventeen, I think. When I first… when we first…'

Sanjay nodded. 'What was his name?'

I looked up. 'His name was Matt.'

ACT 1: 14 | 17

2010

SCENE 1: MATT, 17

'**H**e's gonna get ID'ed,' Fliss whined.

'I'm not gonna get ID'ed,' I said.

'I just don't want to get kicked out. We've drunk tinnies in my living room one too many times now.'

'He'll be fine,' her twin brother Simon said, swinging open the door to The Anchor.

'You won't go up to the bar, will you Matt?' Fliss looked worried.

'I won't go up to the bar,' I repeated.

She led me to a secluded booth in the far corner while Simon flashed his perfectly valid ID at the barman. A minute later, he deposited three ciders on the table. 'So, did you say you had an audition today?'

I nodded and took a sip. 'I kind of want a big part. It'll be my last Stagefright show before uni.'

'I'll never understand how you can do all that without getting nervous,' he said. 'Get on stage, say all those lines and shit.'

'Well, when you put it like that, there's not much to it,' I laughed.

Fliss checked her phone. 'Ellie and Georgia are on their way.'

I glanced at my phone too. I had a new email.

'Oof, cast list is out,' I said. Fliss and Simon looked at me as I opened the attachment. The top line read the words *ROMEO: Matt Williams.*

'What did you get?' Fliss asked.

'I got Romeo,' I said, trying not to sound too pleased with myself.

Simon said, 'Waheeey,' at the same time Fliss said, 'Well done!'

'Thanks.' I put the phone down and sipped my drink.

'Who's Juliet?' Fliss asked.

'Erm…' I picked the phone back up. 'Brooke Tyler.'

'Who? Is she in our year?'

'No, she's a bit younger,' I said. 'She only joined a few months ago. I think her sister's the year below us.'

Simon nodded. 'Amy Tyler.'

'Jesus, you really do know every girl in sixth form, don't you?' Fliss rolled her eyes.

Simon raised his glass quickly. 'Let's toast to the fact that we're gonna have to pretend we don't hate Shakespeare for three months and then pay seven quid to watch Matt die on a church hall stage.'

'Cheers to that,' I laughed.

*

That Wednesday was the first full-cast rehearsal in the Connell Complex, a glorified community hall. In this small town there wasn't a lot to do other than amateur theatre, so Stagefright was just one of many drama groups that had popped up over the years. Several people had already arrived by the time I walked up the stairs and into the rehearsal room. My friend Lewis, a huge rugby player who'd been cast as Romeo's father, greeted me with a clap on the back that almost winded me. 'My son! Congrats, leading man!'

'Hi Lewis.'

'You're officially my child now. Prepare for some serious patronising.'

'You're, like, two years older than me.'

'And don't you forget it,' he grinned, then leaned in so his voice wouldn't carry. 'I've gotta say, I'm surprised at Juliet. Brooke Tyler? Against, like, Tilly?'

'Was Tilly upset she didn't get it?'

'I dunno, mate. I just thought Brooke was an outside shout. She seems so shy. Tilly's older, been in loads of shows, we all know she can act.'

'Yeah, and now she's got to act with *you*. No wonder she's upset.'

Just then, Brooke walked in wearing denim shorts that were a little too large for her. She was tall and slim, with pale skin and long, brown hair. Lucy, a girl in her year, greeted her with a hug. Over Lucy's shoulder I saw her glance at me, then look away quickly.

When everyone had arrived, we pulled up chairs while the directors handed out copies of *Romeo and Juliet*. I glanced around and saw Brooke, safely shielded next to Lucy. Despite being one of the taller girls, she seemed to shrink into herself.

'Do you see what I mean, mate?' Lewis whispered to me. 'She's so quiet. If she doesn't loosen up, she's gonna be a ballache for you to act with.'

'Give her a chance,' I hissed.

'We'll end up doing *Romeo and*,' he went on. 'Just *Romeo and*, no Juliet. I suppose we could have *Romeo and Friar Laurence*—'

'Today,' the director Stephen began, 'we're just going to talk about your characters and build up a background for them. What are their traits? What's their favourite food? Do they have an accent?'

'*Oui oui!*' said Callum, Lucy's older brother, who was playing Count Paris. 'My guy's French, isn't he?'

'Actually, everyone's Italian,' Meg, the second director, explained. 'But you can be French if you want.'

'We'll get to characters in a minute. For now, pair up with someone you're acting with. So Romeo with Juliet, Mr and Mrs Capulet, that kind of thing. You'll be working together a lot over the next three months, so come up with five facts about yourself and get to know each other. Off you go, then.'

I looked at Brooke, but she was avoiding my eyes, watching Lucy wander off with someone else. As I picked up my chair and moved to sit by her, I saw her looking around, looking at her phone, looking anywhere but at me. When I finally put my chair down, her eyes reluctantly slid onto mine.

'Hi,' I smiled warmly.

'Hi,' she said, her voice cracking.

'Five facts,' I said. 'I hate this game. We do it in lessons all the time.'

She attempted a laugh, but it came out more as a cough.

I carried on. 'Normally I just say I was a Christmas pudding in a school play.'

She smiled. 'I normally go with the fact I've never had salt and vinegar crisps.'

'You've *never* had salt and vinegar?'

She shrugged.

'Huh,' I said, and the conversation died. *Lewis was right*, I thought, *this is going to be a ballache.*

Finally, she said, 'Are you doing A-Levels?'

'Maths, Chemistry, and Drama. Does that count as three facts?' I spoke with performed enthusiasm, trying to put her at ease.

'I'm taking Drama too.' She lit up. 'For GCSE next year, with Sociology and Art. That's two facts each. And I'd like to be an actor one day, that's my third. What about you? What do you want to be?'

'Erm,' I sighed, not wanting to think about my conditional university offers. 'Something in Chemistry. That's what I've applied to do at uni.'

'So, a scientist?'

'I have no idea. I just picked something I'm good at.'

'Okay, so your third fact is that you maybe want to be a scientist, but not for definite.' She seemed to have relaxed a little.

'And my fourth is that I'm not very good at explaining things!'

She laughed. 'Yeah, me too. I'm not very good at talking. That's my fourth.' She retreated into herself a little. That confident moment I'd been nurturing coming to an abrupt end.

'I think you're easy to talk to,' I said, even though I didn't.

Her face brightened, and she looked at me for a long moment. I jumped to break the silence.

'And five… um… what's your middle name?'

'Maria.'

'Mine's James. Good! Five facts all done.' I gave her what I hoped was a reassuring smile.

The silence hung for a little too long, and again I saw her look down. I extended my hand. 'Nice to meet you, Brooke Maria Tyler.'

'Nice to meet you, Matthew James Williams.' She shook it, brightening again.

'Now talk about your character's details,' Stephen called out over the volume of discussion. 'Accents, age, family, hobbies, anything you can think of.'

I looked at Brooke, eager to keep her chatting, to keep her from getting shy again. 'So, an accent for Juliet?'

'Probably English. Romeo?'

'English too. I can't do any others.' I laughed, and she smiled. After a pause, she added, 'I don't know how to act older than I am.'

'Juliet's fourteen, well, thirteen, in the real play.'

'Oh, okay. I thought she was meant to be a lot older than me.'

'There's a line where the nurse said she's not quite fourteen, and Romeo could be anything from sixteen to, like, twenty-five. So, you're perfect for the part. Here, I'll show you.'

I opened the script in my hand, flicking through in search of the line. When I gave up and turned back to her, Brooke had been studying my motions and was now looking at me expectantly.

'Family,' I went on, for something to say. 'That's easy, Capulets and Montagues. Hobbies…'

'I guess mine could be standing on a balcony wondering where Romeo is,' she laughed, and I laughed too, a little harder than expected.

'Fun fact: "wherefore" doesn't actually mean "where," it means, "why." So, when she says, "wherefore art thou, Romeo," she's saying, "why are you Romeo, why are you a Montague?" Common misconception.'

'That's what I said!' Brooke was suddenly animated. 'But Callum kept saying I was wrong—he'll believe me now that a *guy* agrees with me.'

'Callum, as in, Lucy's brother?' I glanced over at the lanky sixteen-year-old chatting away in French to his partner, who didn't look impressed.

'Yeah, so he's basically my brother too. A sexist one,' Brooke laughed.

'Don't let him wind you up,' I smiled. 'He doesn't deserve the satisfaction.'

When the session ended, Lewis invited me to Bristol. 'Rugby night out. We're going to Thekla. You wanna come?'

'Can't, mate. They ID everywhere in the city. I'll have to settle for sitting at the back of The Anchor and keeping my head down.'

'Ah, not long now dude. I'm gonna give you an eighteenth to remember—or one you can't remember at all, more like. How was your session anyway, chatting to Juliet?'

'Yeah, it was fine. Y'know, I think you're wrong about her. She just needs a little encouragement to come out of her shell.'

'If you say so. See you next week, bro—unless you want to go out tomorrow night?'

'Still seventeen, Lewis.'

'I'm just messing.'

I followed him towards the door, jacket in hand. Brooke was chatting with Lucy, but turned to me as I passed.

'Nice one, Juliet,' I said, offering her a high five. 'See you next week.'

'Yeah,' she said, 'see you next week, Romeo.'

SCENE 2: BROOKE, 14

'Younger zan she are 'appy mothers made,' Callum was saying.

'This will be the death of me,' Lucy whispered. 'At breakfast. At dinner. In his bedroom. He's always doing a French accent. And not even a good one.'

'What are you girls whispering about?' Callum spun back to us.

'Nothing,' Lucy said quickly.

'*Rien,*' I said, and we both snorted.

We were walking to rehearsal, and I felt my stomach squirm with every step I took. I don't know what it was about Stagefright that gave me... well, stage fright. I'd had big parts in school plays before, but I'd always been one of the oldest people in those casts. At Stagefright I was the youngest, by a long shot. Some of the people there were in sixth form, and a few were even in their twenties. When I'd got the part, I'd been so excited, and started learning my lines right away. But that first rehearsal, I'd walked in and shrunk. They all seemed so confident, like they knew everyone else, and I had barely spoken to anyone other than Lucy and Callum. It felt like a lot was expected of me, but Matt had helped. He'd said I was perfect for the part, he'd laughed at my jokes, and he seemed to like me.

We walked in and I felt my arms close around myself again. Callum shot off to chat to Kyle, and Lucy and I hovered at the edge of the room. I told myself I had to be braver today and dropped my arms to my side.

Matt walked in behind me. When I turned to look at him, we locked eyes, and my heart pounded. He was tall and slim in his T-shirt and jeans, with light skin, bright blue eyes, and messy curls that tickled the tops of his ears. 'Hi,' he said, giving me a big smile.

'Hi,' I said brightly, trying to find my confidence, and before I knew it, he was hugging me. I had to get up on my toes to reach around his neck. As I drew back, he smiled, and my stomach flipped.

The session started as usual with some warmup games, but then Meg took me and Matt over to one side.

'We know we didn't ask you to sing in the audition, but we want you to do *Taking Chances* in the show, when Romeo and Juliet meet. How does that sound?'

We spent the next twenty minutes downstairs with Stephen going through vocal warmups, looking at sheet music, and practising harmonies. Singing in front of Matt made me self-conscious and I was aware that I wanted to impress him. I'd heard him sing in the Easter showcase we'd done right before I auditioned for *Romeo and Juliet*, but I'd never heard him sing so close to me.

I realised how much the lyrics related to us as well as to our characters. I was singing about how little I knew him; he was singing about how his future was unplanned, with his university options and uncertain career. Together we sang about how Romeo and Juliet were taking a leap of faith in pursuing an unlikely romance. And as we sang, as he looked at me with those bright blue eyes, I couldn't help but imagine it was about me and Matt instead. It was just a daydream while we sang, but I was lost in it, imagining some dramatic, passionate love affair against all the odds, against all the people who would say we shouldn't be together, just like Romeo and Juliet.

I looked at Matt, and he smiled as we sang together, and I thought about how it felt when I hugged him, and how he'd managed to get me to open up in our first ever conversation, and how I'd been excited to see him again. I felt so different around him: more relaxed, more confident. He was having an effect on me. *Am I having an effect on him?*

Right then and there, I fell for Matt Williams.

SCENE 3: MATT, 17

On Thursday evening, my friends and I decided to have a night off from stressing about our upcoming exams and went to see a movie instead. I really needed a break, so much so I'd got my shift covered at the corner shop. The five of us were all going to meet at the cinema in Bristol city centre, but Fliss and Simon had to take their mother to the hospital because a frozen leg of lamb had fallen on her foot, and Ellie, who had a thing for Simon, didn't want to go without him. It was just me and Georgia, who had come straight from a shift at a clothing store nearby.

We had been friends since primary school, but I'd always been closer with Fliss and Simon, and Georgia had always been in a pair with Ellie. If we had known it would only be the two of us, we probably would have rescheduled. But it was too late now: we were in the city, so we may as well watch the film.

There was a slight awkwardness about the situation. We had known one another for so long, but in thirteen years, I couldn't have been alone with her for more than ten consecutive minutes. But I smiled and took the lead, like I had done with Brooke, and worked hard to make Georgia laugh as we queued up for tickets. It was a comedy Simon had chosen, and I got two-for-one because of some car insurance website my mum had used.

'I don't really want to see this film, but it's nice to have a break from revision,' Georgia said, as I punched in my PIN.

'We can see something else if you like?'

'You've just paid! Besides, there's not much on. I'm sure it'll be fine.'

It wasn't. The film was boring, plotless, and not funny. Half an hour in she whispered that we should leave and get some food instead. I agreed and followed her out of the auditorium. Laughing about how terrible the actors were, we made our way down towards a strip of chain restaurants and chose a pizza place.

It wasn't until now that I really clicked with Georgia. I knew everything about her, but it was like I was meeting her for the first time. She told me about her A-Levels, and how she was hoping to get into Durham uni. I talked about my exams, and Stagefright. We had more in common than I'd realised. We chatted about our friends, and whether Simon would ever notice how much Ellie liked him, and about the rubbish film we'd just endured thirty minutes of. We spoke about how we rarely spent any time together alone, and why that might be, and to my surprise, addressing the elephant in the room wasn't awkward—it was exciting.

The waiter clearly thought we were a couple, and when we ordered a pizza to share, he said, 'How romantic.' I caught Georgia's eye and her mouth curled into a smile.

By the end of the starter, Georgia's foot was sitting on top of mine beneath the table, which hurt because she was wearing clunky sandals. Her eyes were glued to mine, holding my gaze, as if she was scared I'd look down and realise our feet were touching. I couldn't have *not* noticed, the way her heel was digging into me. But I was enjoying being kind of flirty, so I responded to her questions with enough enthusiasm to assure her I was having a good time. She was already eighteen, so she bought us a small glass of wine each, which I pretended to like the taste of. Everything we shared—the two-for-one tickets, the pizza, the advantages of her ID—was drawing us together. By the end of the main course, we'd somehow ended up holding hands beneath the table, as if it was a secret that our hands were hiding from our eyes. My pulse was racing, but I worked hard not to let on.

I guess this was my first proper date, even if it wasn't meant to be a date in the first place. I'd had one not-very-serious girlfriend for a couple of months when I was sixteen, and I had no trouble talking to girls at concerts or parties, but I never pursued anything beyond a kiss at the end of the night. And now here was Georgia, who'd been there all along, yet was suddenly someone new. Her long hair was up in a ponytail, her skin looked soft and clear, and her eyes were huge. She was cute and petite, and very, very pretty.

When the waiter returned with the dessert menus, we let go of each other's hands and turned to look at him. I ordered ice cream and she ordered some fancy strawberry thing. I wanted to touch her hand under the table once I'd finished eating, but she kept hers firmly on its surface, obviously within my reach. *You want me to hold your hand in sight?* I thought for a moment. I took a deep breath and wiped my hands on my jeans, worried their sweat would betray my calm exterior.

She was talking about something funny that happened to her sister at work. I held her gaze as tightly as I could while watching my hand in my peripheral slowly making its way over to touch hers, while trying to circumnavigate the wine glasses. She took my hand, and I felt a rush of relief, but then I realised we were both silent, not knowing what to do next.

'So, where does your sister work?' I said with an ease that was not genuine, hoping she hadn't already told me.

But she smiled, and said, 'She's a hairdresser on the High Street.'

'Oh yeah? How old is she?'

'Twenty-three. Just.'

Silence.

'Oh, right,' I said, running my free hand through my hair for something to do. 'Cool.'

Thankfully, Georgia was happy to keep talking until the bill came, at which point we argued.

'I'm the guy, I should pay for it.'

'I should pay—you're giving me a lift home.'

'I'm driving myself anyway.'

'But you paid for the tickets!'

'Yours was free.'

'Then I should pay for half of yours.'

'We didn't even watch the film!'

'Okay,' she said, standing up. 'When I get back from the loo, we'll pay half each. Deal?'

I nodded, and she left. I breathed deeply, wondering how a casual cinema night with my lifelong friends had escalated into wining, dining, and date-night-ing. It was exciting, but a small twinge of worry hung in the back of my mind: *how could I backtrack from this if I didn't want another date? How can I do that when we sit together every lunchtime?*

Georgia's brief absence gave me a chance to realise I hadn't done anything to prepare for a date. I hadn't shaved in a couple of days and was still wearing the jeans and T-shirt I'd chucked on for sixth form that morning. I tried to smell my breath to check if it was okay, but all I could smell was pizza. I paid the bill before she got back, and I noticed she'd put some shiny lip balm on, and her breath smelled of Tic Tacs when she spoke. I cursed myself for not having any mints. *Could I ask her for one?*

She rolled her eyes when I told her I'd paid, and we walked to Mum's car as the early summer sun started to fade. When I drove her home, I tried to achieve the ideal balance of driving safely while not looking like a wuss. When we got to her house I walked her to the door, even though I'd usually drop her off at the bottom of her driveway and disappear without a second glance. Our pleasant conversation melted into a tense moment of silence as we both recognised the impending goodbye. Georgia took her keys out of her handbag and said, 'We should do this again.'

'Sure,' I grinned, and joked, 'next Thursday.'

She seemed to take it seriously. 'Okay,' she smiled.

And then she leaned in.

This time I was ready for her, and my hands moved to her elbows while hers sat lightly on my shoulders. Her eyes closed before mine did, and she kissed me lightly on the lips. After a moment, she drew back and smiled.

'See you tomorrow,' I said calmly.

'Bye,' she grinned, and disappeared into the house.

When the door closed, I could finally drop the confident act. I turned, stunned, trying to comprehend what had just happened. I grinned as I walked back to my car, my hands in my pockets, and a little added spring in my step.

Lying on the passenger seat was a twenty-pound note. *Well played, Georgia.* I drove home, elated and amazed that I'd thought I was just going to the cinema, but instead had my first proper date. And got my first proper girlfriend too, apparently.

I was nervous when I walked into sixth form the next day, though I hid it well. I wondered if I should hug her or kiss her or ignore her. But she made the decision for me, greeting me with a peck on the lips. Fliss gave me a thumbs up.

Again, the little niggle was back. I thought we would go on another date on Thursday, and then maybe decide if we were "seeing each other", and then maybe progress to actually being in a relationship. I didn't know if I properly *liked* her yet, since I hadn't even had twenty-four hours to process the whole thing. I mean, if we broke up, it could tear the whole friendship group apart. But Georgia was pretty, funny, and smart. She held my hand and called me her boyfriend, and Simon said, 'Nice, bro— she's super hot.' So I guess we were going out, and it was… well, it was nice.

At rehearsal that night, Brooke sat next to me, and we chatted quietly when other scenes were going on. She seemed to be growing in confidence, complaining about Callum winding her up with sexist jokes and grilling me on every subject she could think of—what I was doing in school, what football team I supported, what TV shows I was watching. It was a little annoying to be honest, but I smiled and answered her questions, glad she was no longer feeling shy with me. I always clapped at the end of her scenes.

When I got home from rehearsal, I checked Facebook to find a notification from Georgia asking me to accept that I was 'in a relationship' with her. I guess that made it official.

SCENE 4: BROOKE, 14

I was going to kiss Matt for the first time.

I had known we'd have to kiss when the cast list came out, but that hadn't seemed like a big deal at the time. Actors often had to kiss each other, and I was priding myself on how mature I was at Stagefright. I told myself it would be fine, I would be calm, I wouldn't be nervous. But by the time I was walking to school on Wednesday morning, I was already thinking about that night's rehearsal. We were scheduled to do the scene where Romeo and Juliet first meet, so I knew we would have to pucker up.

But it was also the first time I would see Matt after he had started dating that Georgia girl, and every time I remembered that I felt a pang of jealousy. I had found myself checking his Facebook profile, memorising the few photos on there, nearly every day in the two weeks since we'd sung *Taking Chances*. When I saw the update on my computer screen, my heart plummeted. I felt like an idiot. *He would have never been interested in you,* I thought.

'Ooh, it's the big kissing scene today,' Callum said, as we walked to rehearsal with Lucy.

'It's no big deal.' My voice was a million times calmer than I felt inside.

'Ooooh, Romeo I looooove you,' he teased, making a bunch of kissing noises. I tried my best to give him a disgusted look as he led us towards the supermarket.

'Can we stop here?' he said. 'I want to grab some chocolate. Anything for you? Lip balm? Breath freshener?'

I rolled my eyes as he disappeared into the shop. Lucy leaned against the glass storefront and looked at me. 'But for real,' she said gently, 'are you nervous about it?'

'Uh,' I swallowed, 'A little. I've never kissed anyone before.'

Lucy could tell I was lying, that I was a lot more than a little nervous. She was my oldest friend and could read me like a book. I usually told her about any fleeting crush of mine, but not this time. I was too embarrassed by how impossible it all was. Matt was older, he was going to uni, he'd never look at me twice, and now, he had a girlfriend.

'I'd be nervous, too,' she said, telling me exactly what I needed to hear. 'Maybe Callum's right about the lip balm. Just remember that you're acting, it's strictly professional. If you stick to that, it shouldn't be too awkward.' I nodded, even though she didn't know that, for me, it wouldn't be professional at all. For me, inside, I'd be melting.

When we got to the Complex, the butterflies were back. I scanned the room and saw that Matt hadn't arrived yet. Callum left to talk to Kyle, Tilly came over to say hi. Everything was normal. *No reason to be anxious,* I told myself.

Then Matt came up the stairs behind me, and before I could get nervous his arms were around me.

'Hello,' he said, hugging me as if it was something normal, something routine that needed to be done. And it did need to be done. I was so happy to see him, to be in his arms for a brief moment. I'd missed him. I missed how he listened when I talked, how he made me feel special when I was with him.

'Are you alright?' he asked, as if he suspected I wasn't.

'Yeah,' I smiled, trying to hide what I would give to be Georgia Russell for a day.

After the warmup we began the scenes. *This is it,* I thought. Lucy winked at me from the other side of the hall and blew me a kiss. Stephen put me and Matt in position, holding hands and facing each other. I could barely look him in the eye.

ROMEO: Oh, then, dear saint, let lips do what hands do. They
pray, grant thou, lest faith turn to despair.

JULIET: Saints do not move, though grant for prayers' sake.

ROMEO: Then move not, while my prayer's effect I take.

They both tense up a little, because they know it's their cue. ROMEO leans forward and JULIET leans forward, and he puts his hands awkwardly on her shoulders, and hers hang limply at her sides, and their lips meet briefly, and they pull back, and it was the crappiest kiss ever.

ROMEO: Thus from my lips, by yours, my sin is purged.

JULIET: Then have my lips—

STEPHEN: Okay, okay, hold up. It was great until the end. Let's do that again, from "Then move not."

ROMEO and JULIET resume their positions. Having just kissed terribly, JULIET is looking down at her feet. That was her first kiss ever. She had been dreaming that it would be romantic, and perfect, but it was a huge disappointment.

ROMEO: Then move not, while my prayer's effect I take.

ROMEO and JULIET lean in once more.

STEPHEN: Brooke, put your arms around his neck.

JULIET tentatively joins her hands together at the nape of ROMEO's neck. His skin is warm against her skin. She is self-conscious, knowing that if she sweats or twitches even the tiniest bit, ROMEO will feel it. She concentrates on keeping her hands as still as possible.

STEPHEN: Matt, put your hands on her back.

ROMEO carefully places his hands on her back, not too high, not too low. JULIET's stomach flips at the touch.

STEPHEN: Much better. Okay, pucker up.

Laughter. JULIET is grateful for the lift in mood. She tilts her head and ROMEO leans in. Their eyes close, and he presses his warm, soft lips gently against hers, and her stomach floods with butterflies, and she hopes he cannot somehow feel her thundering pulse. They hold the connection for just a moment, and she breathes in his scent, spellbound. He pulls away. Her eyelids flutter. She realises she has come up onto her tiptoes and drops back down to her normal height.

ROMEO: Thus from my lips, by yours, my sin is purged.

JULIET: Then have my lips the sin that they have took.

ROMEO: Sin from my lips? Oh, trespass sweetly urged! Give me my sin again.

The room is deathly silent as the star-crossed lovers lean in once more. JULIET is grateful it was only two lines she had to wait to feel ROMEO's lips again, to feel his whole body stepping into hers. She swears to herself she will memorise the feeling this time, but it only lasts a second and then it's over. There's silence.

MEG: Brooke, your line.

JULIET: Oh sorry, mind blank.

MEG: You kiss—

JULIET: You kiss by the book.

NURSE: Madam, your mother craves a word with you.

STEPHEN: Good. Run it again—no script this time, Lucy.

And I couldn't wait to do it again. It had been terrifying the first time, but now every second with his arms around my waist and his lips against mine was magic. He never moved his lips when he kissed me, and he never held me particularly close, and he never let it go on for more than the briefest second, but I yearned for his kiss. In that moment, I wanted everyone in the room to disappear and for us to remain frozen in time, rehearsing *Romeo and Juliet*, forever.

But then rehearsal ended, and we said our goodbyes, and he went home, and I remembered a guy like him would never fall for a girl like me.

SCENE 5: MATT, 17

I'd never had a real girlfriend before Georgia. In the last few weeks of sixth form, she'd plant a kiss on my lips to say 'Hello,' and we would walk around the corridors holding hands, and Fliss grinned her arse off when she saw us together.

We were preparing for our exams, but as study leave approached, everyone became excited for their summer, university, and their freedom—all except me. I was scared. Even though I tried to appear calm and confident, I felt insecure, unprepared for moving away and living alone and being in the real world. I kept worrying about the future, and how I didn't have much "normal" time left.

But when I was with Georgia, I stopped worrying. When we were having dinner, or going to the cinema, or kissing in my car, I felt fine. We weren't talking about exams, or uni, or about any of those stressful things. Georgia slowed everything to a stop.

On our last day of sixth form, we had to dress up as what we hoped to be in ten years' time. My friends ran out of ideas, so we just wore hats and surf shorts and said we were Australians. Most of the sixth formers had known each other since secondary school, so it was meant to be a big goodbye for everyone. My friendship group had been together since primary school, so it would be an even bigger goodbye. Fliss cried, and we promised we would all meet up in the holidays, and we went to The Anchor.

Still not eighteen, I hid in the corner of a booth next to Simon while the girls got the drinks.

'School's over,' he said. 'It's so weird. We're grown-ups now, I reckon.'

'Yeah.' I swallowed the lump that rose in my throat. Simon was scrolling through his phone. I looked at his pale, unbothered face. 'Does it ever freak you out?'

'What?'

'Leaving school. Moving away. The real world.'

Simon shrugged. 'Not really.' He kept scrolling. I couldn't believe how easy he found it; how indifferent he could be to it all.

'Freaks me out a bit,' I said quietly.

'It'll be fine.' He spoke without looking up.

Georgia returned with the drinks. She sat next to me and evaporated my worries with a kiss on the cheek. We drank and chatted, and she made us all get up and dance to the DJ's questionable playlist.

'Do you want to come to my house on Saturday?' she called out over *Teenage Dirtbag*.

I hesitated. 'To meet your parents?' I hadn't meant to sound shocked, but I felt, after not even a month together, it was a bit fast to be meeting parents—though I'd probably already met them at some birthday party or parents' evening.

'No, no,' Georgia laughed, and I eased up. She looped her arms around my neck and spoke into my ear. 'It's their anniversary, and they're going away for the weekend, so I thought you might want to stay over.'

'Stay over?' I repeated, as if she'd spoken another language. She nodded, smiling at me, her gaze telling me something her mouth wouldn't.

'I mean, yeah,' I said.

I hadn't really thought about having sex with Georgia. Well, I had, of course I had. I'd thought about it a lot—but I hadn't actually thought about it as if it was something that could or would happen. I guess she went and did that for me.

'Bro, get in,' Lewis said, when I told him at Stagefright the next day. 'But it's not your first time, though.'

'Yeah, it is,' I said, a little uncomfortably.

'Oh.' Lewis looked surprised.

'What made you think that?'

'I dunno, mate, you just seem,' Lewis punched my arm playfully, 'popular with the *ladies*. Anyway, you nervous?'

'Uh, I dunno. Haven't thought about it. Should I be?'

'No, nononono,' Lewis backtracked. 'You'll be great. Just make sure she's actually down with it, yeah? Sometimes girls change their minds, or only want to go part way, y'know.'

'Of course,' I said.

'And buy some condoms. Obviously.'

After Stagefright, I stopped at the supermarket and picked up some condoms. I didn't expect to be nervous walking to the checkout, but with the box in my hand, I was. My eyes darted around, worried I'd bump into someone I knew. Lots of my classmates worked on self-service, so I went up to an older woman behind the till and hoped she didn't go to Zumba with Mum or something.

'That's ten ninety-nine, please,' she said kindly.

My hands shook as I took the money out of my wallet and handed it to her. I dropped a coin on the floor. *Jesus, what's gotten into me?*

I left without a bag and immediately regretted it, attempting to position the box in my hand with my wrist covering the packaging. I marched out towards the car, got in, and drove away.

When I got home, my phone vibrated. I had a Facebook message from Brooke.

Brooke Tyler: Hey, saw you at the shop.

Fuck. I opened my phone and replied straight away.

Matt Williams: Hiya, yeah I was there, sorry I didn't see you.

I hoped that sounded like I was playing it cool. I kept staring at the screen, waiting for her to reply, praying she hadn't seen me in the chemist aisle. The little speech bubble telling me she was typing kept appearing and disappearing on the screen. I wiped my palms on my jeans. What was taking her so long?

Brooke Tyler: It's cool, I think you drove past us on your way out. What were you getting?

Relief flooded me. I'd been in the car. She couldn't have known what I was buying. I typed back.

Matt Williams: Just some bits Mum asked me to pick up for her.
What about you?

I saw the ellipsis appear and disappear several times before she replied again.

Brooke Tyler: Same, just going with my mum.

Relaxed, I replied quickly.

Matt Williams: Cool! Well have a good weekend.

I put the phone down and went to watch TV with Mum and Dad. When I picked it back up on my way to bed, I had three more messages from Brooke.

Brooke Tyler: You too, you doing anything nice?

An hour later she had sent an identical message. Same words, same phrasing, probably copied and pasted. Then she added: *Sorry, it sent twice.*

I sighed. I didn't mind being nice, or friendly, or even supportive to Brooke at Stagefright, but I knew that if I acted too much like her friend, she might start to follow me round like a puppy.

Matt Williams: Not much, just seeing my girlfriend. You?

The next morning, I saw she had replied again.

Brooke Tyler: Nice! Seeing my mates.

Matt Williams: Cool. Have a good one!

I hoped that sounded conclusive.

Brooke Tyler: Yeah you too x

I spent Saturday morning helping Mum clean the house as I had promised her the night before. In the back of my mind, I kept thinking about what would happen later that evening, and I was surprised once again to find myself feeling nervous. Georgia had been with guys before. This would be my first time. *What if I'm not as good as them?*

We'll talk about it first, I reassured myself. *We'll build it up slowly and take our time. Maybe we won't go all the way tonight.* I pushed away the worries and spent the afternoon preparing for our date. I shaved, showered, brushed my teeth, combed my hair, and put on a nice shirt. Dad saw me inspecting my teeth in the mirror and laughed at me for obsessing so much. I ended up revising to pass the time, which is what I should have been doing anyway.

When seven o'clock finally came, I drove to Georgia's house, feeling much calmer now. She looked gorgeous when she opened the door and gave me a peck on the lips. *See, nothing to worry about.* She led me into her house, pulling me eagerly by the hand, reminding me of an excited child in a toy shop.

She had made pizza from scratch—dough, sauce, all of it. We sat around her kitchen table, a tealight flickering at its centre. For dessert, she put ice-cream in a sundae dish and stuck in two spoons, and I started to feel connected with her as we talked and ate from the same bowl. It wasn't particularly exciting, but it was nice, and she was nice. *Maybe this is what relationships are meant to be like?*

'Do you want to watch a film?' she asked.

'Sure,' I smiled.

The thirty-minute process of choosing something on Netflix showed just how different our tastes were. She ended up convincing me to sit through *Friends with Benefits,* which I immediately regretted once I realised the film was just about the characters shagging. But Georgia was laughing loudly, and I took it as a good sign that Justin Timberlake and Mila Kunis talked about sex before having it. *I suppose I could learn a thing or two from this,* I thought, noting that mouthing the alphabet wasn't deemed good oral, at least by Mila Kunis.

We were an hour into it when Georgia started kissing me. And it was good. I liked kissing her, and I knew what I was doing. Her body twisted so that she was no longer facing the screen but practically climbing on top of me. She pressed into me, and I could feel her breasts against my torso. I caught my breath, and a mixture of nervousness and excitement shot through my veins. I put my hands on her back and pulled her closer to me. We'd made out in my mum's car before, but not like this, not without handbrakes and gearsticks between us. *This is so hot,* I thought, *let's just do this all night.*

We made out for ages, and I felt more and more confident the longer we kissed. The credits were rolling by the time she broke away and turned off the telly.

'Want to go upstairs?' she said, and anxiety dropped into my stomach like a bowling ball.

'Erm,' I said.

She grabbed my hand and led me upstairs, excitement flooding out of me with every step I took. I suddenly felt very cold.

She closed her bedroom door behind me and was on me again, kissing me fiercely, and I was gasping for air. *How do I start a conversation?* I thought frantically. *How do I bring this up?*

Without removing her face from mine, she pulled me to sit on the end of her bed. I put my hands on her back again, but she peeled one of them off and replaced it on her hip. I didn't know if I should move my hand away, or stroke her figure, or just leave it there. After a minute, she took my other hand and put it on her left breast. I felt like I was being puppeteered, my hands and legs manipulated in ways they didn't want to go. I wasn't sure if I could feel her heartbeat through her top or if I could just hear my own pulse in my head. My hand froze with nerves, unable to move at all, just sitting gently on top of her shirt. All the times I'd thought about touching a girl's breast, I hadn't pictured it like this. Something in me was telling me this wasn't right. I'd thought we would go slower; we'd be talking while trying stuff out. I didn't feel calm, I didn't feel connected to her, but I did feel an unwavering sense that she expected me to be really good at something I'd never done before. This was all going way too fast.

She finally stopped kissing me and left me waiting for her as she unbuttoned her blouse. It took a long time; her eyes were focussed on her hands, her neck bent into a double chin. I didn't know what to say or do. I looked straight ahead of me, at a poster of the Eiffel Tower she had on her wall. *You've got to lose your virginity sometime,* I thought.

Georgia slipped her arms out of the sleeves and let the blouse fall behind her on the bed, revealing a plain white bra with a little bow in the middle. She reached over to kiss me again, but I didn't move.

'Matt?' she said.

I didn't say anything. My cheeks were flushing, I was sure of it, and my heart was still pounding. I didn't know what to say but I knew I couldn't let her kiss me again.

'What's wrong?' she asked.

'Nothing,' I said.

'Okay, then.' She reached across me, trying to pull me round to her, but I stayed facing the wall, not responding to her touch.

'Matt?'

'It's just, uh... I feel sick.'

'You feel sick?' she said.

I nodded.

'Do you want some paracetamol?'

'Uh. Maybe. Maybe I should go home.'

'Really?' she said. 'Now?'

I didn't answer. For a moment I tried to forget she was beside me, sat there in her bra waiting for me to... to...

'Aren't you enjoying this?' she asked tentatively.

'I am. I *am* enjoying this. But...'

'But what?'

'I thought we should talk about it first. We haven't even talked about protection.'

'Don't worry about that.' She slid open her bedside drawer to reveal a box of condoms identical to the one in my rucksack downstairs. I wondered if we'd been in the shop at the same time. She had a small smile on her face, as if she thought that contraception was the only problem, and it had been solved.

'I'm just not sure I'm ready,' I said, trying to sound confident.

'But… you're a guy?' She looked confused. I didn't know what to say. I just kept staring at the poster, trying to imagine I was in Paris, trying to imagine I was anywhere else but here.

'It's okay if you're nervous,' she went on, wrapping her arms carelessly around me. 'That's normal for your first time.'

'It's not just that,' I said, but she was slipping her hand under my collar and down my back.

'Look, Georgia, I…' She wasn't listening. I spoke more firmly. 'I said no.'

Her smile vanished. She peeled away from me. 'I don't get it. Aren't I attractive?'

'Of course you are.'

'Don't I turn you on?'

'You do, yeah, of course.'

'But not right now?'

I sighed. My head was spinning, the words weren't coming. The poster had a small rip in one corner.

'Are you gay?' she said.

'No,' I said.

'Then I don't get why you don't wanna.' She clambered off the bed and snatched up her blouse. She turned to me, and when I said nothing, she pulled it across her chest.

'I'm sorry if this upsets you,' I said, 'but I just don't think we're ready.'

'I thought we were,' she whined. She looked both disappointed and embarrassed. That made two of us.

'Maybe we have to wait for, like, our connection to build up,' I said.

'You sound like a girl,' she snapped.

Her words stung. 'I should go,' I said.

'Sure, okay.'

'Maybe see you soon.'

'Yeah, maybe.'

I walked towards her bedroom door and saw she wasn't following me. I guess I was meant to see myself out.

I didn't text Georgia after that night. And she didn't text me. And I didn't get any messages from Fliss, Simon, or Ellie, so I guessed that Georgia hadn't said anything. I was grateful. I was trying to forget that night had ever happened.

At the next rehearsal, Lewis ambled over to me, raising one eyebrow and grinning. He nudged me with his elbows. 'Hm? Hm? How did it go?'

'It didn't,' I said, and felt my cheeks flush.

'Oh, shit.' He stood upright and lowered his voice. 'Why, what happened?'

I shrugged. 'Didn't happen.'

'Oh dude. Uh. Okay. Um. Wanna talk about it?'

I shook my head and looked down at my script.

'Y'know,' he whispered, 'my first time, I couldn't get it up for like, an hour. Too nervous.'

I looked at him.

'It's super common—'

'That's not what happened,' I said, a little too defensively. I looked around to check no one could hear us, then whispered, 'I just changed my mind.'

'What, she did?'

'No, I did.'

'Oh,' Lewis said. '*Oh*. Right.'

I flicked through the script, trying to find today's pages.

'Do you think you're asexual?' he said.

'What?' I turned back to him.

'I mean, like, that's a thing, y'know. One of my mates—'

'I'm not,' I said quickly.

'Not everyone has a sex drive—'

'Dude!' I snapped. My eyes darted around the room, checking no one had heard what he'd just said. I stepped closer to him and hissed in his ear. 'That's not what it was, okay? That night wasn't the night, I felt expectation, I felt pressured—'

'*Pressured?*' Lewis said.

'Not by her. Maybe by her. No, not by her. By myself. I dunno. The vibe just wasn't right, okay? Now, can we stop talking about it?'

I wasn't needed for the first scene, so I sat at the side, still hot with embarrassment. Brooke sat down next to me. 'You okay?' she asked quietly.

I smiled and nodded. As she began her usual chatter, I felt something comforting about the way she saw me: a big brother, calm and confident, taking her under my wing.

'How far away is Lancaster uni?' she whispered, as Callum proclaimed, 'And zerefore, I 'ave leetle talked of love.'

'Like three hours in the car,' I replied. 'I chose it specifically so Mum won't visit every weekend.'

She giggled. 'Why didn't you pick Drama?'

I shrugged. 'It's fun, but it's not my favourite subject. I like science more.'

'Oh. It wasn't because your dad made you choose Chemistry?'

'What do you mean?'

'Your dad doesn't think arty subjects are a waste of time?'

'No, no, not at all. My dad would support whatever I wanted to do.'

She broke my gaze and looked down at her shoes.

'Does your dad think the arts are soft subjects?' I asked.

'Yeah. He doesn't like me spending so much time acting. He wants me to be a doctor or a lawyer or something.'

'Ah, he shouldn't be thinking about that now. That's way off for you. Wish it was further off for me.'

'What, choosing what you want to do with your life?'

I nodded. 'The future is…'

'… scary?' she finished my sentence.

'Yeah.' She'd said what no one seemed to be acknowledging. My parents, teachers, friends, were all talking about leaving school and moving away like it was totally normal, like they weren't all freaking out inside. I was freaking out inside.

Brooke smiled. It was nice to feel like someone else got it.

SCENE 6: BROOKE, 14

If I'm being completely honest, I was thrilled when I found out that Matt wasn't going out with Georgia anymore. I knew I was being stupid, and that his break-up didn't mean he had feelings for me, but I was smiling for hours when I saw he'd changed his relationship status back to 'single'.

I chatted to him on Facebook, saying I was sorry that they'd broken up. He said it was okay because he had exams for the next few weeks to focus on, and it was bad timing from the start. I was a little disappointed, hoping it was more than just bad timing that went wrong, that there was someone else on his mind—even if I knew it was impossible.

Dad phoned, which was rare. He used to call every Saturday evening. Then every other. Now it was somewhere round the monthly mark, with visits even less often since he'd moved to London. Mum answered and insisted we talk to him. Amy went first, then me.

'Hi, Dad.'

'Hi Brooke,' he said in his broad American accent. It used to make him seem warm, but now it was unfamiliar. 'How are you?'

'I'm fine,' I said. 'How are you?'

'Good, thanks.'

'Good.'

There was a long silence. Finally, he said, 'How's school?'

'Fine. Boring. I've chosen my options for GCSE though.'

'Haven't you already started your GCSEs?'

'No. I'll start in September.'

'Oh, okay. What are your options?'

'Drama, Sociology, and Art.'

'Hm. Not the most academic subjects.'

'Well, they make you take French, and Double Science, and all the rest.'

'You didn't want to take Triple Science?'

'Not really.'

'Okay. Is it too late to change them?'

'Yes,' I lied through gritted teeth. *He doesn't call for a month and then has a go at my options?*

'Okay, well. When you get to—what is it Amy's doing, O-Levels?'

'A-Levels,' I corrected him.

'When you get to A-Levels, you'll want to consider the harder subjects. Colleges and employers will prefer science to art.'

'I find drama harder than maths,' I said defensively.

'Well, you're very good at math,' he said. The conversation faltered.

'I'm in a play,' I said, to break the silence.

'Oh yeah?'

'Mhm. *Romeo and Juliet.* I'm Juliet.'

'That's great. Is this at school?'

'Stagefright.'

'What's Stagefright?'

'The drama group I joined. Just after Christmas.'

'Oh, right.'

'You couldn't make it to the Easter showcase because you were working in Sheffield.'

'That's right. Yes, I remember now. I'll try to make it to the next one. I'll make time for it.'

I felt my chest warm up. 'That would be good,' I said.

I began feeling that Stagefright was the centre of my world. It gave me something to look forward to, to save my favourite clothes for. I'd get butterflies before rehearsals, and Matt always seemed pleased to see me. The days got happier and longer and sunnier, and we became friends. He kept talking about his exams, how stressed and busy he was, yet he still came to every rehearsal when others missed sessions to revise. After Stagefright, we would continue chatting on Facebook, and I felt myself opening up to him, and him to me.

We were texting so much I started to worry that I was annoying him. Sometimes I'd send a message, hear nothing back, and my head would spiral. *He's getting sick of you,* I'd think. *Of course he doesn't want to talk to you.* But then my phone would buzz, and seeing his name light up my screen, lit up my smile. I couldn't be *that* annoying if he was replying. I told that part of my brain to shut up and just enjoy it.

SCENE 7: MATT, 17

'We can't give him *Best Actor*, that's way too obvious,' Lewis was saying. He'd spent most of the rehearsal break whispering to Liam in the corner of the room.

'Oi oi,' I said, 'what's happening over here?'

'Go away, we're talking about private stuff,' Liam grinned, jokily pushing my shoulder.

'Specifically about not giving you the *Best Actor* award this year.'

'You're doing the awards already?' I raised my eyebrows. 'The play's not for two months.'

For every show, it was traditional for some of the older cast members to dish out awards. They'd usually present them on the first session back after the performance, which could make things awkward, especially last year when Liam won the award for *Best Kiss at the After Show Party* with Kelly, who didn't stay long after that.

'We're just commencing nomination procedures,' Lewis said, 'and you shouldn't be listening.'

'At least nominate Brooke for *Best Actress,* would you?' I suggested. 'She's worked so hard, and she used to be so nervous.'

'I'll take your recommendation into consideration. Now, *Little Ray of Sunshine* has got to go to Lucy. She's just so happy all the damn time.'

'What about *Most Annoying and Terrible French Accent?*' Liam suggested, typing a list out on his phone.

'Are you doing the awards?' Deepak came over, fiddling with a prop sword. 'Can you put Kyle down for *Best Bum?*'

Kyle, a boy in Callum's year, laughed and joined the conversation. 'Thanks man. Never knew you felt that way about me.'

'*Best Bum* has got to go to Tilly,' Liam said, without looking up from his phone.

Silently I felt all our eyes cross the room until we spotted Tilly, chatting to Meg in tight skinny jeans.

'It's like two moons,' Deepak said, and the boys laughed.

'Nah, Brooke definitely has the best bum,' Kyle said.

'Not better than Tilly's,' Liam remained adamant.

'I stand by my claim that Kyle has the best bum in the group—nay, in England.'

'Put Tilly down for *Best Rack*,' Kyle said.

'I think a *Best Rack* category is a bit much,' Lewis interjected.

'Mr PC over here,' said Kyle.

Liam laughed. 'Alright, we have Tilly, Brooke, and for some reason Kyle up for *Best Bum.*'

'At least it's gender-neutral,' Lewis said, 'Though to keep things equal I might have to nominate myself for this one, too.'

Meg called the session to start again. I looked at Tilly, who was in the year below me. Curvy and tall, with curly dark hair, everyone knew she was gorgeous. But she probably wouldn't have liked us talking about her that way.

The scene started. Brooke got up to act with Lucy, and the rest of us watched.

'We are undone, lady, we are undone,' Lucy began.

Brooke said her lines, moving around the stage with a rehearsed poise, a world away from the nervous girl I spoke to that first session. She was taller than Lucy, and slim, wearing patterned leggings and a loose top. Her pointed sandals extended her legs further, and her dark brown hair shook as she spoke. She turned, and I found myself looking at her bum, and forced my gaze up to the back of her head. *I can see why she was nominated*, I thought.

A few scenes later, it was my turn to act again. I was up there with Brooke, and it was just the two of us. We ran the scene, holding hands, and when I looked at her face, I thought she looked older than she was. She could pass for sixteen, maybe even seventeen.

'Farewell, farewell,' I said, 'one kiss and I'll descend.'

Confidently, she stepped into the embrace we'd rehearsed a hundred times. Up on her tiptoes, she put her hands on my shoulders and I put mine on the small of her back. Her top rode up as she reached for me, and I felt my fingers brush against a sliver of skin as she lightly pressed her lips against mine.

SCENE 8: BROOKE, 14

I got an invitation to a Facebook event titled 'Matt's 18th Barbecue'. Everyone from Stagefright was invited, and I responded quickly to say I was going.

On the day of the barbecue, I walked to the High Street and tried to find something Matt would like. I finally settled on a solid chocolate football boot. It would cost all my pocket money, but I wanted to get him something special. At home I wrapped it up as neatly as I could, picturing his face when he opened it. I showered, shaved my legs, plucked my eyebrows and painted my nails blue. My hair had been twisted up in a bun overnight, so when I took it out, the curls fell down my back. I put on one of Amy's skirts and my favourite top and passed the afternoon by watching TV. Finally, Lucy and Callum rang the doorbell, and we walked to Matt's house together.

'What did you get him?' I asked, pointing at the present in Callum's hand.

'Malteasers,' they said in unison.

'Oh,' I said, fighting my smile. 'I got him chocolate, too.'

My fingers were sweaty against the wrapping paper by the time Matt opened the door. I held my breath as I watched him hug Callum and Lucy, take their present, and put it on the table behind him.

I held out my gift. 'Happy birthday. It's only small.'

'Thanks, nice one.' He took it and put it down too.

'Oh,' I said, half-glancing at Lucy. 'Are you not gonna open it?'

Matt picked up my gift and ripped open the wrapping paper in about half a second. 'Aw. Chocolate? Thanks Brooke.' He gave me a quick smile and a one-armed squeeze.

'It's a football boot,' I explained, 'because I know you like Arsenal.'

'Yeah, I do. Cool, come on through guys.'

My cheeks burning, I followed them into the house. His hallway led on to an open-plan living room that joined up with the kitchen-diner. It was neat and tidy, with everything from the tiles to the teaspoons following a monochrome colour scheme.

'My parents have gone away for the weekend, but I've got to return the house to them in *mint condish*,' Matt said, 'so please don't break anything.'

Sliding glass doors led to a garden where Stephen was cooking on the barbecue, and various people sat on camping chairs sipping drinks.

'Eighteen, Matt,' Lewis said, chucking a can of beer at him. 'Drink up.'

'There are soft drinks over here, girls,' Meg said, pointing to a cool box.

We sat in the empty chairs and opened our cans of Coke. Stephen had brought a guitar with him and led a mashup of musical theatre songs in true drama geek fashion, darting from the guitar to the grill until the burgers were ready.

'Where are your friends from school?' I asked Matt, biting into a quarter pounder.

'Revising. I'm the only one who's finished my exams yet,' he grinned. 'Thought a Stagefright-only barbecue would be nice.'

Late afternoon dissolved into evening. At one point, all the boys squeezed onto the sofa to watch the football, then returned to the garden in various states of elation and disappointment. The empty cans of beer were piling up. Matt had managed to get through a load of them, but I didn't notice any difference in how he acted. I did notice differences in the others, though. I watched the older members of the group slowly become less and less like the people I knew as they finished one box of cider, then another, and another. Their roars of laughter got louder, their jokes less inclusive, their interactions more daring. I started to feel like I was back at that first rehearsal again, shying away from these people who were part of a world I did not belong to. When the first few stars appeared in the darkening sky, Lewis, Meg, and Stephen packed up their camping chairs.

'Do you guys need a lift home?' Meg asked me, as she fished her car keys from her jacket pocket.

'Nah, Callum'll walk us,' Lucy said. 'Brooke's sleeping at mine.'

Several people left and the rest of us went inside. We sat in the living room, some on the sofa, some on the floor. Liam plugged his phone into the aux. They were all still drinking. I scanned the room. Callum and Deepak were both sixteen and everyone else was in sixth form. Lucy and I were the youngest there.

'What time are we leaving?' I asked her.

She shrugged. 'Whenever Callum wants to go.'

Callum had made his way through several beer cans and seemed to be proud of it, slurring his words as Deepak appeared with a measuring jug and a pack of cards.

'I played this before, with ssschool friends,' Callum bragged. 'Liam, do you play five azzz drive or jive?'

'What's jive?' Liam replied, clearly better at handling his booze than Callum, who had forgotten his question already.

I held on to my lemonade as Liam laid cards out in a circle around the jug. I'd never been to a party before, not one where everyone was drunk. *This was supposed to be a barbecue.*

'You can just play with lemonade,' Matt said, detecting I felt out of my depth. 'And if you get the last king, I'll drink the jug.'

Tilly walked in from the bathroom. 'Ring of *fiiire*!' she cried. 'I love this game.' She spilled some of her drink onto my skirt as she clambered across me to sit next to Liam.

'Tilly, didn't you drive here?' Deepak asked.

'Yup,' she said, and Deepak laughed.

'Well, I guess you aren't leaving tonight.'

'I'll drive back in the morning,' she said. 'You don't mind us crashing, do you Matt?'

I expected him to mind, but he just shrugged. 'Nah. It'll be fine.'

I glanced at the clock. It had gone midnight, but nobody else seemed to notice. Liam started explaining the game. I played it with lemonade, and when Deepak loudly protested that it wasn't alcoholic, Matt told him that I didn't have to drink if I didn't want to. I hadn't really considered drinking. Lucy played with a single can of cider, which she sipped obediently when she lost whatever challenge was in motion, wrinkling her nose as she swallowed.

The game was really boring. The challenges were designed to get you drunk, rather than to actually be any fun. Callum was getting really competitive about it, trying to impress the older boys. When I tapped him on the shoulder to try to make him laugh, he didn't listen to me. Instead, he shrugged me off or pretended he hadn't heard me, favouring the conversation between Deepak and Liam. After an hour of playing, Liam had successfully downed the measuring jug full of disgusting-coloured liquid, and we had all clapped like it was some kind of Olympian feat. He seized his phone and changed the music, pushing the volume.

'I *love* this song,' Tilly cried, clambering off the sofa.

Liam hit the dimmer switch and we were plunged into darkness. Matt flicked on the hallway light, which spilled a little into the room, so we could see the outlines of figures as they came to their feet.

Matt, Liam, and Lucy hovered at the edge of the room with me, and we looked on to see seventeen-year-old Tilly, the only other girl left at the party, dancing unsteadily on her feet. The boys circled her like planets in orbit. Callum was too drunk to focus on anything, flailing about like a ragdoll. The other boys seemed to have eyes only for her, taking it in turns to move up close to her and see if she would respond to their brushes on her arm, on her waist. I didn't like it. I didn't recognise them, these guys who I rehearsed with twice a week, who chatted to me and cheered me on after a good scene.

Around two-ish a good song came on and Lucy grabbed me, and we started dancing together, holding hands, and spinning about, and I guess it was fun. Matt was sitting on the sofa, drinking more beer and wiggling his shoulders in time to the music. Callum and Liam kept switching the music and arguing about each other's choices. Callum didn't like his songs being changed mid-way through, especially by Liam, whose approval he'd been vying for all night. He stormed out of the room in a drunken strop, ignoring me when I called after him.

Lucy rolled her eyes and followed her brother upstairs, leaving me on my own. I stiffened, glancing at the boys still dancing around Tilly, awkwardly sidling away from them.

Matt clocked this. He stood up and sauntered over to me, all long arms and goofy dance moves, not quite sober enough to stand upright. He spun me around, steering me with one hand and holding his drink with the other. At least he seemed to be somewhat like his usual self.

I glanced over and saw Liam now among the group of boys, but somehow, he had penetrated their barrier and made his way to dance with Tilly. His hands were on her waist and she had one laced around his neck, the other holding a drink that spilled with every step she took. I hadn't thought Liam and Tilly were really friends, but his hand crept down her back, and his lips somehow found hers and she sipped her drink every time he stopped to take a breath. One boy crashed on the sofa. Matt put a blanket over him. Eventually, Liam took Tilly's hand and led her out of the room and up the stairs.

When the clock hit three, Matt turned on the lights and turned off the music, saying something about the neighbours when Deepak protested.

They all went upstairs and I followed. From the top of the landing, I could see Callum through the bathroom door, kneeling half asleep at the foot of the toilet. Lucy was sat on the edge of the bathtub, eyes red with tiredness.

'I think he's stopped throwing up,' she said. 'Finally.'

Matt went to assist her as they scooped Callum up together, his head lolling as they did.

'Right, there's my room and the spare room,' Matt said. 'I'd say a couple of people could go into Mum and Dad's, but it looks like Liam and Tilly wouldn't be too happy about that.'

I glanced at the only closed door on the landing. Deepak laughed.

I watched as Callum was laid down on Matt's bedroom floor; Matt put him in the recovery position and popped a pillow under his head.

Deepak was arguing with the other boys over the spare room. 'I am *not* sleeping on the floor,' he insisted. Eventually, they agreed that all three of them could fit in the double bed and closed the door. 'Try to resist the urge to spoon me,' I heard Deepak joke.

Matt fished a sleeping bag from his wardrobe. 'Here you go, Luce,' he said, and she laid down next to Callum. Matt saw me standing alone on the landing. He looked in his wardrobe again. 'Hm, no more sleeping bags. You can just share with me.' And with that, he sat on his bed and removed his socks.

I glanced around the room. It was small, and the floor was taken up by the two bodies already on it—there was really nowhere else for me to go. I thought of the three guys in the spare bed together, probably already asleep. 'Okay,' I said.

I guess it was the grown-up thing to do, to go to parties and play drinking games and fall asleep next to someone else and act like that was all totally normal. I took my socks off too without being sure why and climbed into Matt's bed with him.

Matt was still in his jeans and T-shirt, and I was still in my skirt and top. No one had brought pyjamas. No one seemed to miss them.

'Goodnight, kids,' Matt said, switching off the lamp and turning his back on me. In the darkness, I faced him with as much distance between us as the single bed allowed. The room was quiet. I was sure everyone was asleep.

I was in bed with the guy I had a crush on. I guess that was meant to be exciting, but I didn't feel it. The night had been so strange, seeing people I thought were my friends behave in ways that were so alien to me: they drank, eyed Tilly up, and pretended not to hear me when I spoke. *I guess that's just what parties are like,* I thought. *Everyone else had fun. There must be something wrong with me.* Physically and emotionally exhausted, I silently started to cry.

I felt Matt roll over. 'Hey, are you okay?' he whispered.

I opened my eyes and could just make out his silhouette. I'd thought he was asleep, but my shaking shoulders must have given away my tears.

'Yeah,' I whispered back, but my voice cracked.

'Hey,' he reached out under the cover and put his arm around me, scooting closer. 'What's wrong?'

'Just,' I began, and sniffed loudly. 'Just that everyone acted different tonight. It was like I didn't know who they were anymore.'

'It's okay,' Matt said. He peeled up his second arm and slid it between my neck and the bed, hugging me fully now and pressing me clumsily into his chest. 'Y'know, alcohol can make people stupid, but they're still the same people.'

'Callum wouldn't even talk to me,' I breathed back. Tears must've been trickling onto his T-shirt. I hoped he couldn't feel them.

'He's just Callum,' Matt whispered, as if that offered any kind of explanation. 'He was trying to impress Liam. That kind of stuff won't matter to him tomorrow.'

'Did you like the football boot?' I sniffed.

'I loved the football boot.'

He sleepily held me, pressing my neck at an uncomfortable angle into his torso, and my trembling started to subside. We lay there in the dark for a long time, and my neck ached, but I didn't dare move. My breathing returned to normal. The room was so quiet, you'd almost forget there were two other people sleeping on the floor. All I could hear was Matt's heartbeat. My eyelids gave way to their heaviness.

He pressed his lips to my forehead, still cuddling me tightly. 'It'll be better in the morning.'

He kept me still. I was getting tired, wanting to roll away from him and fall asleep, but I was enjoying the embrace, knowing affection like this from boys was a rare and valuable thing that I should savour before it slipped away.

'Thanks Matt,' I grumbled wearily. 'I'm gonna go to sleep now.'

'Okay,' he said, and kissed my forehead again. 'Goodnight.'

'Goodnight,' I said, and went to respond. My lips moved up to find his face and sleepily pressed against his cheek.

Except it wasn't his cheek.

My lips landed on his. In the dark, in my sleepy state, I had kissed the corner of his mouth. In my confusion, I stayed frozen for a moment, our lips pressed together, as it slowly dawned on me what had happened. I was about to draw away, to apologise, but then...

Matt kissed me back.

His lips moved against me, as they had done before, as they had done in rehearsal, but now it was different. Now his lips were slowly and gently massaging mine, and I followed his movements, dancing as he led, and his stubble prickled against my skin. Suddenly I was awake. My stomach was flipping. My heart was pounding.

He kissed me for what must've been several minutes, maybe longer, and half of me wanted it to carry on forever, and the other half was too tired to sustain it, to truly recognise what was happening. He ran the tip of his tongue across my bottom lip and then bit it.

'Ouch,' I said.

Matt didn't seem to hear me. He made a quiet, 'Mmm.'

His grip on me released as his head fell back on the pillow. He curled up, and I could feel his warm breath on my nose.

'Goodnight,' I whispered.

He didn't reply. Maybe he had fallen asleep already. It didn't bother me. The bite didn't bother me. Matt had *kissed* me, and not in rehearsal; he had *chosen* to kiss *me*.

Too sleepy to get excited, I tried to pocket this moment for the morning. *He likes you. He fancies you. He wants to be your boyfriend.*

SCENE 9: MATT, 18

My bedroom door clicked. I yawned, stretching my arms above my head. Light streamed in through the curtains. I wondered who was talking in my bedroom, with a vague memory of some kind of party from the night before.

I opened my eyes. Lucy was trying to stuff a sleeping bag back into its ridiculously small bag. Callum was downing a glass of water. And next to me, sitting up in my bed, was… was…

FUCK.

I leapt out of bed. In a secondary moment of panic, I thought I had slept in my boxers as usual and was relieved to look down and see last night's jeans and T-shirt still on. Instinctively, I backed away from the bed, stumbling over Callum as I did.

'You alright, Matt?' he laughed. 'Looks like you've seen a ghost.'

Brooke was looking at me with some kind of expectancy. I must've looked horrified. I tried to correct my expression, not wanting to freak her out. I attempted a reassuring smile, then regretted it, and looked away.

'Callum, you must be feeling a bit worse for wear this morning.' I was trying to sound normal, trying to act normal, but I could feel Brooke's eyes following me.

'I feel like a zombie died in my stomach,' Callum groaned. I laughed a little too hard. The silence that followed went on for far too long.

'Right, breakfast!' I went on, clapping my hands together. 'Who's having some?'

I went downstairs before anyone could reply. Mum and Dad's bedroom door was open, the sheets askew. In the living room Deepak was shoving plastic cups into a bin liner. Liam was watching TV. Tilly's car was gone.

'Who wants breakfast?' I asked, now with much less enthusiasm than I'd had upstairs. I went into the kitchen and started taking out cereal, bacon, plates, and bowls, desperate to keep my hands occupied. *Has she told Lucy already? Did she hear us kiss?* Surely not… surely, she couldn't've… but I'd been drunk. How could I be sure…?

Brooke walked in. I looked down at the stove. She appeared at my side.

'Need some help?' she said.

'All good, thanks,' I said, not looking away from the bacon as I placed it in a pan with unnecessary precision.

She stepped closer to me, and I had to stop myself from stepping away as she did. She spoke in a low voice. 'Matt, do you think we can tal—'

'Sh… uh… anything you want.' I pointed to the cereal boxes. 'You can have anything you want.' I looked her dead in the eye, hoping to convey a message saying *let's talk about it later*. Apparently, she didn't get it.

'Last night,' she began again.

I seized her hand and pulled her further into the kitchen, around the corner and out of view.

'We can totally talk about it, of course we can. We just have to wait until everyone else has gone.'

'But—'

'We just can't talk about it now.'

She glanced back towards the living room where the others were lounging around, chatting away and nursing hangovers.

'Why?'

'Brooke,' I grabbed her hand clumsily, in an effort to reassure her. 'Please. Let's talk about this later.'

She looked up at me with big, hopeful eyes, and said, 'Okay.' She squeezed my hand.

Fuck. I had to fight my instinct not to let go instantly. If she realised I was freaking out, that I regretted last night, she might get upset, cause a scene, tell everyone…

'Who wants bacon?' I called around the corner, returning to the stove.

'Not me, I'm never eating again,' Liam called back.

'I'll probably throw up if I eat anything right now,' came Callum's voice.

Apparently, no one wanted bacon. I didn't particularly want bacon but kept cooking anyway. *When will everyone get out of my house?* I spotted Brooke across the room, sat next to Callum. *Has she said anything to him?* Eventually Liam walked home and Deepak got a lift from his mum. Finally, Lucy and Callum's stepdad showed up, clearly annoyed that they hadn't walked back the night before as planned.

'Brooke, shall I drop you home?' he offered.

'Oh, it's okay—'

'That would be good actually,' I said loudly.

Brooke looked at me in surprise.

'I probably shouldn't drop you back myself,' I said, pretending we'd had some prior arrangement. 'I've got a lot of cleaning to do.'

Brooke looked confused.

'But I'll message you,' I went on, feeling Lucy and Callum and their stepdad's eyes on me. 'About the rehearsal.'

She still looked confused. *Christ, why doesn't she get it?*

'That extra rehearsal. That Meg and Stephen wanted us to do. The *extra* one. I'll message you about it.'

At last, the penny dropped. She smiled again and said, 'Okay.' She came up and hugged me, tucking her arms beneath mine, slotting her head under my chin. I tried not to let it go on for too long, but she seemed reluctant to let go. I made a point of hugging Callum and Lucy too, performing for their stepdad as if he had some psychic ability that could x-ray my brain and find out what had happened last night.

Finally, they left. I closed the door behind them, leaning against it in complete exhaustion, looking around the room with the bin bags full of rubbish, the napkins and crumbs strewn on the arms of the sofa. My head was spinning. What the *fuck* had happened? How the *fuck* had it got to this?

Mum and Dad would be home soon. I picked up a bin bag to finish the cleaning, wanting to fill my brain with something else, anything that wasn't Brooke. I mean, she had looked pretty yesterday, with her hair and that skirt, and we could talk so easily when we were messaging, and kissing her had felt like...

Stop it. Something about it all felt wrong, though I couldn't put my finger on why. We'd kissed loads of times in front of everyone at rehearsals, and it had been fine. We were friends— everyone was friends at Stagefright—and last night she had just been another girl at the party, fitting right in. But this morning she suddenly seemed very, very young.

To distract myself, I started to vacuum. I put Mum and Dad's bedsheets in the wash. I sprayed air freshener in every room, trying to extinguish the smell of alcohol that burnt the back of my throat. When I finished cleaning, I looked at my phone and noticed three missed calls from Brooke.

For fuck's sake.

I couldn't think straight. I went back to bed and laid there, staring at the ceiling, feeling guilty for some reason. Brooke had laid here next to me, hours earlier, and we'd cuddled and kissed, and it had felt *really* good, and something was telling me it shouldn't have felt *that* good, but it did. That kiss had been completely different from rehearsals and now whenever I closed my eyes, all I could think about was the feel of her lips and...

I needed sleep. I rolled over and tried to nod off, knowing I'd be able to think clearer later. But the pillow smelt of Brooke's hair; I couldn't push away the memory of her sleeping next to me, my arms around her, her face an inch from mine.

Something doesn't feel right about this.

I picked up my phone. The three missed calls were still staring back at me. I sighed and clicked her name, putting the phone to my ear.

'Hello?' came her voice after one ring.

'Hi, Brooke, it's me.'

'I know,' she said. 'I mean... I read it off the screen.'

'Right.' I swallowed the lump in my throat. 'I think we need to talk. About last night.'

'Yeah, we do,' she said.

I took a deep breath. 'I want to apologise to you.'

'What for?' She sounded surprised.

'I shouldn't have… you know… kissed you.'

She paused. 'Didn't you want to?'

I rubbed my forehead. *This hangover!* 'I didn't really plan it. It just kind of happened. I mean, part of me wanted to, I suppose, otherwise it wouldn't have… but I was drunk. I wasn't thinking straight. It was a really bad idea.'

Shit. I'd just blurted it all out. I'd probably hurt her feelings.

'I don't think it was a bad idea,' she said quietly.

'Look, Brooke—'

'I wanted to kiss you. I mean, it was an accident to start with, but I like you, Matt.'

For fuck's sake. This poor girl's heart was in the palm of my hand. *It was just one kiss,* I thought, *surely that wasn't enough to get her hopes up?* 'I just think you're too young,' I tried to say softly.

'Fourteen isn't *that* young.' She sounded defensive. 'We were cast against each other, right? We're both the leads? We're friends. I don't get it.'

I kicked myself. *If you hadn't been a dick and kissed her last night, you'd be swallowing paracetamol by now. What a mess you've made.*

I tried to be as clear as I could. 'I'm eighteen now, Brooke. I'm the year above your sister in school. I never noticed before, but now…' I sighed heavily. 'I'm sorry, Brooke. I don't want to do this.'

There was silence down the phone. *Oh God, please tell me she isn't crying.*

'I just want to be friends,' I said.

'Okay,' she spoke quickly.

'Is that okay?' I said. 'For us to stay friends?'

'Yeah, of course,' she said, her voice hitching at the end. *She's crying. Nice one, mate.*

'Maybe we shouldn't be… quite so close. Offstage.' *Fuck, Matt! Could you say it any harsher?*

'Okay,' I heard her squeak again.

'I'd rather you didn't tell anyone about last night. About the kiss. If that's okay.'

I was picking my words clumsily, and wished I'd planned what to say, wished I'd been gentler. Silence came down the phone.

'Okay, well... okay,' I was saying. 'I guess I'll see you Wednesday.'

'See you,' she said, and hung up quickly.

Mum and Dad came home and were pleased to see the house wasn't trashed. I went for a run to try to sweat out my hangover, but it didn't help. I ended up curled on the sofa, playing video games and trying not to think about last night.

*

My exams were over and one by one, my friends finished theirs. I went round Simon and Fliss' a few times and watched football at the pub with the guys. I did shifts at the corner shop. Mum and Dad were at work all the time, and I was mostly alone. And on Wednesday, I went to Stagefright.

Brooke was already there. She didn't come and hug me. She didn't sit next to me in between scenes. She didn't even look at me. I wondered if I should go up to her and start chatting, try to make things between us seem normal, but I couldn't imagine her responding well to that. She looked sad, quieter than usual.

Lewis came up to me. 'Nice barbie, bro. Bet you were a bit worse for wear the next day.'

'Yeah,' I said, trying not to think about it.

'Heard it went on a bit late after I left.'

'Yeah, people ended up staying over.'

Lewis got closer and lowered his voice. 'I also heard that Tilly and Liam hooked up?'

'Oh. Well, yeah, they did.' I looked around and saw them both at opposite ends of the room, not looking at each other, as if nothing had happened.

Lewis wrinkled his nose.

'What's up?' I asked.

'I dunno,' he said. 'It just seems a bit weird. The younger ones being at the same party as people who are hooking up.'

Christ. This is just what I need.

'Never mind, eh,' Lewis shrugged.

We were getting towards the end of the play, the show date creeping closer. We whizzed through the last few scenes, and a knot grew in the pit of my stomach. *We'll be doing the death scene,* I realised. *Just you and Brooke, with everyone else watching.*

I got up to act and saw Brooke chatting to Lucy. *Has she told her? Does she know?* Brooke wandered into the middle of the room, her eyes looking at anything but me. She laid down on the floor, pretending to be in a coma, her eyes shut.

'Oh, my love, my wife,' I began. I ran through the lines, kneeling next to her, looking at her frame as she breathed slowly and steadily. 'Beauty's ensign yet is crimson in thy lips and thy cheeks.'

'Matt, on that line, can you gently run your thumb over her lips?' Stephen said.

'Um. Okay.'

I said the line again, this time dragging the tip of my thumb gently across her bottom lip. I tried to make the contact as minimal as possible, but I could feel her breath on my skin.

'Eyes, look your last,' I went on. 'Arms, take your last embrace.'

'Just kind of scoop her up with that,' Meg said, 'so she's in a sitting position. Make sure you support her head.'

I slowly slid my hand under Brooke's head, and the other under her back.

'Swap hands, Matt,' Stephen said. 'You're blocking her face.'

I moved my hands carefully, half believing Brooke had actually taken this sleeping draught and would fall if I let her go. My heart was pounding, trying to push away the thought of the last time we'd been this close.

'And lips, seal with a righteous kiss…'

I slowly leaned in.

'Wait till the end of the line, Matt,' Meg said.

I looked at her, confused.

'A dateless bargain…' Meg prompted me.

'A dateless bargain to engrossing death,' I said. Slowly and delicately, I pressed my lips against Brooke's, and time stopped for a moment, and all I could feel was her lips on mine. I pulled back suddenly. Her eyes fluttered open to catch my gaze for a split second. I placed her down carefully on the floor.

'Here's to my love.' I mimed taking a bottle from my pocket and chugging it. 'Oh, true apothecary. Thy drugs are quick, thus, with a kiss, I die.'

Slowly I got down on the floor, awkwardly. I'm sure it wasn't a convincing death. I wasn't thinking about that, though.

'Romeo,' I heard Brooke say. 'What's here closed in my true love's hand?' I felt her soft fingers on mine, which fell open at her touch.

'Left no friendly drop, to help me after? I will kiss thy lips.'

I opened my eyelids a sliver. I could see her face coming closer, her hair hanging over me and brushing my chest. My heart raced.

'Haply some poison yet doth hang on them,' she said.

And when she kissed me, I felt fire.

SCENE 10: BROOKE, 14

I left rehearsal that night without saying a single word to Matt that hadn't been dictated by William Shakespeare himself. I saw him looking at me on my way out, but I ignored him.

I had been choking back tears during that phone call. I'd never had a boyfriend. I'd never even liked a guy who'd liked me back. I thought I was finally *so close*. And yet, there I was, embarrassed and heartbroken again. How stupid I'd been to think I stood a chance with him. How stupid to think I'd been chosen, that it was my turn to be happy. *Of course he'd never want you. You're nothing to him. You're nothing to anyone.*

Lucy fell into step with me on the walk home. 'Are you okay?'

'I'm fine,' I sniffed.

'You haven't seemed yourself. Since the barbecue.'

'It was nothing. I just felt weird, everyone being drunk.'

'It was a strange night,' she said softly.

'Yeah.' I looked at my feet, walking in rhythm with hers. 'Yeah, it felt a bit weird, when I... kissed Matt.'

Lucy's jaw dropped. 'You *what?*'

She looked horrified, though I didn't know why. 'Yeah, I—'

'You kissed Matt at the party?'

I hadn't expected this reaction, and I instinctively back-tracked. 'I mean, in rehearsal.'

Lucy's face instantly relaxed. 'Oh, right. You mean today.'

'Yeah,' I said.

'I thought you meant at his birthday, and I was about to be like, "Wow, that's really weird!"'

I looked at her. 'Would it be weird? If we kissed outside of rehearsals?'

Lucy shrugged. 'I mean, a bit. He's older, right? He's older than Callum.'

I looked at Callum, trailing behind us with his eyes on his phone. I didn't know what Lucy meant. I felt like I'd done something wrong, though I wasn't sure what it was. I didn't tell her the truth.

'How was rehearsal?' Mum asked when I got home.

'Fine,' I said.

'Did you have fun? What scenes did you do?'

'I'm tired,' I said quickly. 'I'm going to bed.'

Mum looked at me for a long moment. 'Okay, love,' she said.

I went upstairs and laid out my uniform for school the next day; it was almost summer, but I still had a few weeks of term left. I got into my pyjamas and scrolled through Facebook, trying to think about anything other than the party. Then my phone buzzed.

Matt Williams: Hey

I grabbed it. *Ohmygod.* He was messaging me! I sat up and tried to suppress my initial excitement, reminding myself that he was probably just messaging to be nice, to clear the air. I typed back.

Brooke Tyler: Hey

It took him a couple of minutes to message again. *Come on, come on!*

Matt Williams: How are you?

I replied instantly.

Brooke Tyler: Not bad thanks
            You?

Matt Williams: I'm okay
            Sorry about rehearsal
            I felt like I made things awkward between us

I sighed. He *was* just clearing the air. It wasn't the change of heart I'd been hoping for.

> *Brooke Tyler: It's okay*
>> *I just didn't really know how to act*
>> *You said you didn't think we should be as close anymore*
>
> *Matt Williams: I know*
>> *I'm sorry*
>> *Maybe that was a bit much*
>> *We can still be friends, can't we?*

I smiled a little sadly at my phone. This wasn't what I wanted, but it was better than before.

> *Brooke Tyler: You don't think I'm annoying?*
>> *Or weird?*
>
> *Matt Williams: What? Of course not*
>> *I want to be friends with you*
>> *Can we be friends?*

My smile grew wider. Maybe all the bad things I thought about myself weren't true. Maybe I was okay.

> *Brooke Tyler: Of course* ☺
>
> *Matt Williams: OK, good* ☺
>> *How was your day?*

I'd always chosen my words carefully when texting Matt, trying to keep the conversation going, to make him laugh, but that night it became effortless. We were friends again, and suddenly I felt like I could tell him anything.

Matt told me he was freaking out about moving away. I would love to be leaving school forever, but he seemed to find the idea really scary. I listened, and it felt special to be the one he confided in.

Matt Williams: I'm worried I'll screw it all up
        I'm worried it'll be too hard
        At uni, I mean

Brooke Tyler: You have good predicted grades, though
        Surely that means you're smart enough for the course?

Matt Williams: I suppose
        But that's another thing
        Everyone expects me to smash my exams, but I had to work really hard for them. I'm shitting myself about the results
        But I'm the only one, none of my friends are freaked out
        About any of it, moving away, making new friends
        And it's like, everyone expects me to be this confident guy who life is effortless for
        And sometimes people say stuff like they expect me to be really experienced with girls, or that I find it easy to get good grades. It's like they have this idea about who I am
        I know I come across as like, calm and chilled and stuff, but I worry a lot.

Brooke Tyler: And when people have high expectations, you have twice as far to fall

Matt Williams: Exactly.
        It feels like no one else gets it

Brooke Tyler: I get it.

The conversation lasted hours. I saw the clock at midnight, but ignored it, telling myself we'd only be five more minutes. Then it was ten. Then fifteen.

Matt Williams: Oh God, it's 1AM!
               You'd better go
               Have you got school tomorrow?

Brooke Tyler: Oh shit
              Yeah I do
              ☹

Matt Williams: Haha, sucks to be you
               I'm living that sweet study leave life

Brooke Tyler: Haha
              Okay
              Speak tomorrow?

Matt Williams: For sure
               Sleep tight
               Night x

Brooke Tyler: Night xx

We went back to normal after that—no, even better than normal. Matt was making a real effort with me. In rehearsals, he'd come over and give me a massive hug. He'd chat with me every chance he got, and we'd carry on our conversations well into the evening on Facebook. I felt like we really clicked. Maybe this friendship was even better than the relationship I'd wanted.

Dad phoned the next Tuesday, more than a month after his last call. Mum answered the landline and made me speak to him.

'Hi Brooke,' he said. His accent never failed to take me by surprise.

'Hi, Dad.'

Silence.

'How's school?'

'Fine. Nearly over for summer. Are we going away this year?'

'I'm not sure. I'll have to look at the calendar. Is your mom taking you on vacation?'

'She doesn't think so,' I said.

'Okay.'

Silence.

'Next time you come and visit, I'd like to introduce you to someone,' Dad said.

'Okay.'

'It's my girlfriend,' he said.

'Oh,' I said, 'right.'

'She lives here. In London. With me.'

'Cool,' I said.

'Your mom knows,' he said.

'Okay. Okay, well, maybe you can bring her when you come and see my show.'

'What show?'

I sighed. 'I *did* tell you. *Romeo and Juliet*. I emailed you the details.'

'Oh, right, yes, right. Yeah, I'm not sure if I'm going to be able to make that one, honey.'

My heart sank. 'You said you'd make time for it.'

'I know, but something came up.'

'Why did you say you would come, then?' I whined, tears queuing up behind my eyes.

'Don't snap at me. I'll come to the next one. One when you've got a bigger part.'

'I'm Juliet!' I cried. 'As in, *Romeo and!*'

'Calm down, Brooke. I know you're disappointed. I'm sorry I couldn't move things around. I tried.'

'Try harder,' I said, and hung up.

'Brooke, don't hang up on your dad,' Mum told me off, but I ignored her. I ran upstairs and the tears started falling. *Standard Dad. Why did I expect he'd be different this time?*

I was there for a few minutes, gripping my pillow with anger and disappointment, before grabbing my phone. I opened my Facebook chat with Lucy, ready to complain about Dad as I usually did—but then I saw Matt's name above hers in my inbox.

I typed a message.

Brooke Tyler: Hey, can I talk to you?

I expected him to be a while, but he replied almost instantly.

Matt Williams: Of course.

Brooke Tyler: I just had an argument with my dad

Matt Williams: What happened?

Brooke Tyler: He told me he'd come to see the show
And now he's telling me he won't
He said he'd make time
He always does this

Matt Williams: I'm so sorry

Brooke Tyler: It's not your fault
It's just shit
He always does this
You think I'd be used to him disappointing me by now

Matt Williams: When was the last time you saw him?

Brooke Tyler: Christmas
We did Boxing Day at his

Matt Williams: Jesus, that was ages ago

Brooke Tyler: Yeah, he moved to London after the divorce
Now he has a girlfriend
Soon he'll have a replacement family

Matt Williams: He wouldn't replace you

Brooke Tyler: You don't know him

Matt Williams: True
What about your grandparents? On his side
Do you see them often?

Brooke Tyler: Nah
They're all in America
He's American
Moved here in his 20s, met mum, got married, had me,
fucked off to London
Sorry for ranting
I'm just really upset

Matt Williams: It's ok
You can rant to me
I don't mind ☺

Brooke Tyler: Thanks
Sorry
How are you?

He made me feel better without even trying, and once again, we were talking until the early hours of the morning. I had to stifle my giggles when he said something funny, so I didn't wake Mum up. When I walked into Stagefright the next day, he marched over and scooped me into a hug. 'Hey Brooke,' he said into my hair.

'Hey Matt,' I giggled. It was like the awkwardness from a couple of weeks ago had never happened. When he released me, he smiled like he was really happy to see me. I was happy to see him, too.

The show date was gradually approaching, and today was the first run through of the entire play. Every time I turned to face the audience, I looked at Matt, and he was looking at me. Even when I was standing at the side, and even when it was someone else's line. When I turned away, then looked back, he was still watching me. I felt a smile creep across my face, and my cheeks blush. I couldn't help but think—hope—that he might have changed his mind.

He hasn't changed his mind, I told myself. *He's just being supportive. A good friend.*

SCENE 11: MATT, 18

*S*hit. *I think I like her.*

She finished her scene. I forgot to clap. She came over and took her seat next to me. 'You okay?'

I snapped out of it. 'Oh yeah. You were great.'

She smiled and ran her fingers through her hair, the glossy brown streaks falling neatly into place. *Oh no. I properly like her.*

'Guys, I can't keep calling out the scene names,' Meg was saying. 'You need to be following the script and getting ready to go on.'

Deepak and Liam got up to act. Stephen came over and knelt in front of Brooke to quietly give her some notes. He said something to make her laugh, and her eyes creased, and her lips curled into a smile. *Oh, fuck.*

'Matt, that means you,' Meg said.

'Oh, right.' I jumped to my feet. I had no idea which scene we were doing, but ambled into the middle of the room all the same.

'Nay, gentle Romeo, we must have you dance,' Deepak said.

Got it. 'Not I, believe me. You have dancing shoes…' I went on, running my lines, only half aware of what I was doing. I felt my eyes move back onto Brooke. She flipped her hair behind her shoulders and her gaze moved across the room until it locked with mine.

I quickly looked away, stumbling over my words as I did. *Fuck, man,* I thought, *you've caught feelings.*

Of course I'd caught feelings. I'd texted her more in the last couple of weeks than I'd ever texted anyone. I'd found myself thinking about her when she wasn't around: wondering what she thought of the show I recommended, or remembering how she'd made me laugh when we talked about football, and the kisses in rehearsal, the kiss in my bed…

'For my mind misgives,' I said, 'some consequence yet hanging in the stars shall bitterly begin his fearful date with this night's revels.' We moved onto the next scene, when Romeo first sees Juliet at the ball. Brooke got up, already in character, miming a conversation with Tilly.

God, I really like her. But what about all the reasons I'd said no before? What about all the reasons we shouldn't be together? What was I supposed to do now? Push her away, keep her at arm's length? I'd tried that already, and with all this acting and kissing, it had been an uphill battle. But what else could I do? Tell her? She'd told me she liked me, only a couple of weeks before, but what if I'd missed my chance...

'Did my heart love till now?' I said. 'Forswear it, sight. For I never saw true beauty until this night.' I approached her, and offered her my hand, and she took it, and we started singing *Taking Chances.* I spun her around, her hair spinning out, her hand soft and small and warm in mine. As the song came to an end, my heart started thundering. I'd kissed her a hundred times before, but suddenly it felt like I'd never kissed anyone. *Am I sweating?*

'They pray, grant thou, lest faith turn to despair,' I said.

'Saints do not move, though grant for prayers' sake,' she responded.

'Then move not, while my prayer's effect I take.'

I kissed her. My hands on the small of her back, hers on my shoulders, our lips lightly touching, my heart racing, my stomach churning...

What if this is all a terrible idea?

There were three more kisses in the show after that: one just before Romeo's banishment, and two in the crypt. My heart pounded ferociously before each one, and it took all my strength to release her after only a second.

When we'd run through the whole show, Meg and Stephen got up to give us their notes. We sat in a circle, Brooke next to me, far too close but also much too far away. *This is all wrong,* I thought. *She's too young. People would say things. People would think things.*

'Brooke, you aced your lines,' Meg was saying. 'Matt, yours need a polish. You stumbled a couple of times.'

'You two were great, though,' Stephen chimed in. 'You remembered all your blocking; your chemistry was on point. Nice job.'

Everyone was looking at us. I didn't know what to do. I was sure she was looking at me, but I couldn't meet her eyes. I just stared back at Stephen until he moved on to the next note.

At the end of the session, I was the first out the door.

Of course, Brooke texted after the rehearsal. Three times.

Brooke Tyler: Good feedback tonight!

Brooke Tyler: I can't believe it's only a month till the show

Brooke Tyler: Are you ok?

I groaned. She could tell something was up; it was unusual for me not to respond.

'Want to watch a movie, Matty?' Mum said, remote in hand.

I shook my head. 'I don't feel well. I'm going to bed.'

I made the same excuse to Brooke as to why I wasn't going to be texting until 1AM tonight. I heard the buzz of her reply, but I couldn't look at it. I flopped onto the bed, my phone on the floor, wondering what the fuck had happened. She'd robbed me of all my calmness, my confidence. She saw me, she saw me for real—she may have been the first person who ever had. And she made me feel like what she saw was okay—good, even. *If only there was a way...*

You can't do this, mate, came a louder voice in my head. *It's weird.* It took me a minute to realise it was Lewis' voice. I could picture his face with the same concern he'd worn when he heard that Tilly and Liam had hooked up.

He's right, I thought, *I'm just going to have to get over her.*

*

She was at school the next day, so I wasn't bombarded with texts. And I eased up. I had a kickabout with Simon, then ate lunch with him and Fliss. I went to work in the afternoon. I didn't think about Brooke, running her hands through her long brown hair, stretching up on her tiptoes to reach me. *Maybe it was just a little crush*, I thought, as I refilled the Starburst on the shelf. *Maybe it was all in my head.*

I closed the shop at ten and took my phone out of my locker. She hadn't messaged all evening, which surprised me. Maybe it was fine—we were just friends, and she didn't need me to be texting her all the time.

An hour later I was at my desk, deep down a YouTube rabbit hole, when my phone rang. My stomach flipped as I read her name off the screen, out of dread or excitement I couldn't tell. I put my headphones in to answer.

'Hey,' I said slowly.

'Hi, Matt,' she said, and I realised she was crying.

I sat up immediately. 'What's wrong?'

'I'm r-really sorry to b-bother you, I just, I had a big fight with my m-mum, and I did something stupid…'

'What did you do?' I said quickly, and realised I'd come to my feet.

'I stormed off and g-got the bus into the city—'

'Where are you?' I cut in.

'B-Bristol Bus Station.'

I raced down the stairs and grabbed my shoes. 'I'm coming. I'll be like half an hour. Tell me what happened.'

'We had a f-fight over something stupid. I can't even remember what it was. But there isn't a bus home until six in the morning, and I don't have any money, and I'm on like twelve percent—'

I opened the door to the living room where Dad was still up reading.

'I'm going to Simon's. Movie.'

'Okay, have fu—'

The door was closed before he finished his sentence. I grabbed Mum's keys and got into the car. 'Okay, Brooke, I'm coming. Stay inside the station and don't talk to anyone.'

'I'm sorry for dragging you out. God, I'm such an idiot,' she was saying.

'Did you say you're on twelve percent?' I put my phone in its holder and started the engine.

'Yeah.'

'Okay, make sure you put your headphones on so no one will talk to you. I'll be there in half an hour. You should probably hang up to save your charge, but if anyone makes you feel unsafe, call me immediately, okay?'

'Okay.'

'I'll see you soon.'

I drove, my mind focused, gripped only by the need to get to my destination. *Left at the lights. Right on the roundabout. Onto the M32.* I couldn't think about my stupid crush on her or trying to keep my distance. All I could think about was the fourteen-year-old girl alone in the city at eleven o'clock on a Thursday night.

At the speed I went, it only took twenty minutes to get there. I parked badly and hurried into the deserted station. She sat alone at the furthest bay, her headphones on like I'd told her, and relief washed over me. She spotted me and came to her feet as I approached her, then pulled her straight into a hug.

'God, Brooke,' I said. 'I'm so glad you're okay. You are okay, aren't you?'

She nodded and gave me an embarrassed smile. Her eyes were red. 'Sorry I made you… sorry you had to…'

'It's fine,' I said, putting my hand on her shoulder and steering her back towards the car.

On the drive home she was quiet. I glanced at her in the passenger seat, her head slumped against the window.

'So, what was the fight about?' I finally asked.

'Can't even remember,' she mumbled.

'It must've been big, for you to come all the way into the city.'

She didn't say anything, just readjusted her posture.

'Why did you... um... get the bus?'

She hesitated. 'I was trying to get to Dad's.'

'In London?'

She nodded.

'Take the coach, you mean?'

'Or the train,' she said. I wondered if she even knew how to get to Temple Meads from the bus station. She'd have probably had to walk there, through the city, in the dark, on her own. I bit back a shudder.

'But you didn't have enough money,' I said, rather than asked.

'I wasn't thinking clearly. I was upset. It wasn't like I *planned* to go.'

'But why would you want to go to your dad's? I thought you were mad at him.'

She shrugged. 'I just wanted to get out of here, y'know.'

I didn't know. 'Here,' I said, handing her my charging cable.

When she plugged her phone in, it vibrated incessantly. She opened her messages and I saw she had seven missed calls.

'Your mum?' I asked.

She nodded. 'She thinks I'm at Lucy's. That's usually where I go when we argue.'

'Do you guys fight a lot?'

She shook her head. 'No. It's just sometimes I can't handle my feelings and I need to get out of there. But she's starting to worry. It's super late and I have school tomorrow.' Then she said quickly, 'I don't want her to know what I did, please don't tell her—'

'I won't tell her,' I said.

Brooke directed me to her house, and I pulled up at the bottom of the drive. She reached across to give me a hug from her seat. 'Thanks Matt. You're a good friend.'

I caught her arms as she retracted them from around my neck. 'Brooke, if you're ever stuck like that, please call me. Or if you're upset, please text. I don't want anything bad to happen to you.'

I wasn't sure she'd understood the seriousness I'd been trying to convey, but she thanked me again and hurried out of the car. I turned around further down the road, and as I drove back past the house, I saw her mum had met her halfway down the driveway, looking panic-stricken in her dressing gown.

*

I was exhausted the next day and slept in till eleven. I worried about Brooke all afternoon, wondering if she was still upset, or if she'd even realised how much danger she could have got herself into. But when I saw her at Stagefright that night, it was like nothing had happened. She was her bubbly, smiley self, giving hugs to everyone as they walked in. I held her extra tight for a really long time.

'Was your mum mad?' I whispered to her in between scenes.

She shrugged. 'A little. But she doesn't know what happened.'

I looked at her and felt a strong urge to hold her, to pull her close to me, to press her into my chest. I couldn't tell if it was driven by a protective need or affection. Were those even two different things?

None of the scenes tonight had us acting together. Not one kiss. She watched me do my scenes. I watched hers as she spun around on her feet, her eyes ablaze, her face glowing. *You're in trouble*, I thought. *This isn't just gonna go away.*

But what could I do? I'd promised myself I'd keep away from her, and the second I did, she needed my help. And I'd told her to text me if she was upset or call me if she needed me. How could I retract that when I'd sworn it less than twenty-four hours earlier? But if I didn't push her away, how was I supposed to get over her?

If I could just talk to her…

I spotted Lewis across the room. He was scrolling on his phone, waiting for his next scene. He didn't have a clue what was going on in my head, but I knew, if I asked him, he'd say: *Dude, you can't do this.*

*

After rehearsal, I went to the pub with Fliss and Simon and forgot about Brooke. We bought drinks and laughed and chatted and played pool. Fliss ran into some friends from her hockey team; Simon quickly got talking to one, and I introduced myself to the other, Zahra. She asked me to teach her how to 'shoot like a pro,' and I did, leaning over the table and holding her hands in place. She laughed at all my jokes, even the shit ones. She let me buy her drinks and threw peanuts into my mouth and giggled when she missed.

When I woke up the next day, Fliss had messaged: *Zahra wanted me to give you her number.*

I groaned at the eleven digits on the screen. I'd felt normal last night, just another guy at the pub on a Friday with my mates. And Zahra was pretty, and fun, and had made me laugh from what I could remember. But this morning I had the overwhelming feeling that I did not want to text her, that there was only one person I wanted to text, and the very desire to do so meant that I was not normal.

You can't keep going on like this, I thought.

If I could just talk to her, we could talk about the weirdness, the worry, the what-would-people-think of it all. We could decide together if this was a bad idea, we could figure out where we both stood.

Do you want her, or do you want to be normal?

I dragged myself out of bed. It was nearly lunchtime. Mum was gardening. Dad was reading the paper. I took ham and cheese out of the fridge and started making a sandwich.

'How do we get tickets for this thing?' Dad said.

'What thing?' I slathered butter onto bread.

'That play you're in. *Romeo and Juliet.*'

This was the last thing I needed. 'I can probably just get them at rehearsal.'

'Okay, well, make sure you get enough for your aunties.'

Suddenly, I was no longer hungry. 'Need a shower,' I mumbled.

I forced my tired face under the water, cold at first, then soothingly warm. I hoped it would clear my head, push out the thoughts swimming in there: her dark eyes locking with mine across the room, the long-legged steps she took, her hair strewn across my pillow—

The water wasn't helping. I switched it off, took a deep breath.

I threw on shorts and a T-shirt and lay on the bed, scrolling through my phone. I ended up binge watching episodes of *How I Met Your Mother* for a few hours, which successfully distracted me until the credits rolled, and I felt sick again. The sun burned through my window. The room suddenly seemed too hot, too small.

'Going for a walk,' I muttered to Dad as I headed out. I needed air, I needed to think. I wandered through the town, mindlessly following my jogging route down the back of the corner shop and towards the park. *What am I supposed to do with these feelings? What am I supposed to do with these thoughts? How am I meant to get rid of them?* The harder I pushed away the image of her face, the more intently it stared back at me. I could feel the tension in my stomach, the knots, the nausea. The anger at myself. The confusion. But all those feelings evaporated the second I saw Brooke across the park.

Her hair was up in a bun, which I'd never seen before. Her headphone wire trailed down to the pocket of her denim shorts. She was carrying a blue plastic bag. And for a second, I thought my knees were going to give way.

She saw me, and instantly undid the bun, putting the elastic on her wrist and shaking her hair out with her fingers. She was still walking towards me. I realised I was still walking towards her. *What do I do?* I thought. What *do I say? Do I say anything?* She was taking her headphones out, putting them in her pocket, preparing to smile. *Is this the moment? Is this a sign?*

'Hi,' she said, when she got close enough.

'Hi,' I said stiffly.

We'd stopped in the middle of the path. We didn't hug, which I guess wasn't normal for us, though we'd never run into each other unexpectedly before.

'Going somewhere?' she asked when I didn't say anything.

'Um, yeah, well, no, not really, just a walk. You?'

She indicated the blue bag. 'Mum's making a roast and we were out of gravy. They didn't have any at the corner shop, so I had to go to the High Street.'

'Yeah. Yeah, we don't do gravy. Maybe I should… maybe we should fix that.'

She laughed politely at whatever had just come out of my mouth. My mind was whirring. *Do I do it now? Do I say something?*

'You going this way?' I said, pointing behind me.

'Yeah.'

'I'll go with you,' I decided.

We walked away from the openness of the park, back towards the shop. My stomach was churning. After a few seconds, she filled the silence.

'Amy tried to make a roast all by herself once, but it was such a mess. Now Mum is kind of giving her lessons.'

'Makes sense,' I said. I was only half-listening. *Do I say it, do I say it, do I say it…*

'Are you okay?' she asked.

Now or never. 'Um, actually, there was something I wanted to talk to you about.'

'Okay.' She looked at me expectantly.

'Um.' *Where to start.* 'Okay, so, um. It's about the kiss. At my party.'

Her cheeks went red. She looked away.

'I've been thinking,' I went on. 'About that. And about how close we are. I mean, I think it's fair to say, we get on like a house on fire.'

'We… yeah, we get on well,' she mumbled.

'And on the phone afterwards, you said you liked me.'

'I thought we were going to forget about that and be friends,' she said quietly.

'But it's about that…'

'You aren't going all cold on me again, are you?' she asked, and when she looked at me, I could see she was scared.

'No, it's not that. I…' I fell silent as a man with a dog passed us. We kept walking, our footsteps echoing. Brooke was looking at her feet. *How do I say this? What do I even want to happen?*

We were approaching a short alley down the back of the shop. I glanced over my shoulder at the dog walker's retreating figure. 'Can we go down here?'

'It's longer that way—'

'Just for a minute.' I grabbed her hand and led her into the alley, checking there was no one around. I held her other hand too and looked into her eyes, taking a deep breath.

'They pray, grant thou,' I said, 'lest faith turn to despair.'

She hesitated for a second, but then said, 'Saints do not move, though grant for prayers' sake.'

I squeezed her hands. 'Then move not, while my prayer's effect I take.'

The last word had barely left my mouth before I was leaning in, and she stood still, and I kissed her. She was surprised but then she was kissing me back, and my hands were in her hair, and she was up on her toes, and I forgot everything I was supposed to say. All I could think about was her lips against mine, her hands around my neck, how good it all felt—

Her phone rang. We broke apart.

'Sorry,' she said. She took it out. 'It's Mum. She'll kill me if I don't…'

'Yeah, go on,' I said, running my hand through my hair and trying to think straight.

She put the phone to her ear, not looking at me, unsure of what to do with her hands. 'Mum, I'm nearly home. I've got the gravy. Five minutes.' She hung up. 'I have to go.'

'Yeah, okay,' I said, as we retraced our steps out of the alley. 'Um. I'll message you.'

'Yeah.' She was fighting a smile. 'I'll message you.'

'Bye,' I said, and walked the other way.

SCENE 12: BROOKE, 14

Did that actually freaking happen?
My cheeks hurt from smiling. My head was spinning. Nothing like that had ever happened before, not to *me*. As I rushed home, I took out my phone and instinctively went to message Lucy.

Oh my god, you won't believe what just happened, I typed, but as I looked at the cursor, I hesitated. Lucy had said it would be weird if we kissed. Matt had asked me not to tell anyone about the party. My finger hit 'delete' instead of 'send'.

When I walked in the door, Mum gave me a cold look for being late. I tried to keep a straight face as I handed over the gravy.

'No mobiles at the table,' she said, when she saw me check my messages (nothing yet). I put my phone in my pocket and ate fast, chatting to Amy and Mum, every nerve in my left thigh waiting in anticipation for the vibration that meant he had texted.

Mum was saying she definitely couldn't get the time off work for us to go on holiday this summer. I didn't mind. It was better that way.

Buzz. I felt my whole body jump at the sound. Mum glowered at me and I knew I couldn't check it right then, but *he had texted.*

I excused myself as quickly as I could and raced upstairs to look at my phone, but my heart sank when I saw it was just a Facebook notification; Lucy had changed her profile picture. I dove on the bed and shut my eyes, remembering the feel of his hands in my hair, his arms wrapped around me, his lips—

Buzz. I seized my phone.

Matt Williams: Hey you

I replied instantly.

Brooke Tyler: Hey

Matt Williams: Soooooooo

Brooke Tyler: Yeah
            Good kiss btw
            Great kiss
            10/10 would recommend

Matt Williams: Haha
            Glad it got a good TripAdvisor review

Brooke Tyler: Haha
            But I'm a bit surprised
            After what you said
            After the party
            What changed?

Matt Williams: Can I call you?
            Don't want to type it all out

Brooke Tyler: Sure

'I'd thought it was a bad idea,' he was saying on the phone. 'After the party. Because I'm a little older than you, and I'm going away in September…' My heart dropped momentarily at the reminder. '…but since then, we've really clicked. It's hard to stop talking to you.'

He was saying all the things I'd been wanting to hear for *months*. For years, really, from boys who never gave me a second look. Finally, this was happening for me.

'I just feel you really get me, like no one else does,' he went on.

I grinned. *Is this real?* 'Yeah, I mean, I feel like we have a strong connection. And I can talk to you about anything.'

'And I knew, like, I mean, I wanted to talk to you about this, because we were texting so much and acting together, it kind of felt like we'd have to do something about it eventually.'

'Is that what you want?' I asked. 'For us to do something about it?'

'I mean,' he said, 'I er… well, I guess we could go back to just being friends.'

'I don't want to go back,' I said quickly.

'Yeah, I mean, I don't really want to either.'

I couldn't believe it. *He likes me!* 'Okay,' I said, struggling to keep my voice steady. 'Then let's do it.'

'But can we… can we keep it between us?'

I detected the plea in his voice. 'Of course,' I said.

'So, no telling your mum, or Amy.'

'No, no, only people I *really* trust.'

'No, Brooke,' he spoke seriously now. 'You can't tell *anyone*. If we are going to be… if we are going to do… be a thing…' I grinned so hugely at this it made my mouth ache, but I couldn't fight it. His tone seemed so serious in comparison, I felt I had to hide my exploding joy. '…then you can't tell any of your friends. Not a single one. Not Lucy, or Callum, or any of your school friends.'

'They wouldn't tell anyone—'

'Someone would find out, Brooke. Maybe they wouldn't tell, but it always gets out. Please—we can't be together if you tell anyone. I'm not trying to give you an ultimatum or anything, I just… people would say things, think things, if they found out.'

I didn't care about any of it. All I cared about was the fact that he said there was a chance we could… we could be…

'Is that okay?'

It was so incredibly hard not to squeal with delight. 'Yeah,' I said, trying to control my voice.

He asked me to come over on Saturday while his parents were at some salsa festival, which was a whole week away. The time without him seemed to stretch out, and it felt like everything I did was just part of the long waiting game before I could see him again.

'What's got you so smiley?' Lucy asked me in Maths on Monday.

'Nothing,' I said, and turned back to the textbook. My secret was like a warmth that spread throughout my chest, but as Lucy shrugged and went back to her work, I longed to be able to tell her. To share my excitement with her. To be able to change my relationship status on Facebook. All the little things I'd looked forward to about getting my first boyfriend. *But it's worth it for him,* I told myself.

On Tuesday, she caught me giggling at my phone. 'What's so funny?' she piped up.

'Oh, just something Matt said,' I replied. 'It's nothing.'

She looked down at her sandwich. 'Lately it feels like we don't tell each other everything anymore, y'know?'

My heart sank. I knew exactly what she was talking about.

'It's nothing, really,' she went on. 'Just that, with you playing the lead role and being friends with Matt and the older ones… I feel a little left behind. Like you guys have in-jokes you don't share with me.'

'We don't have in-jokes,' I said, biting my tongue as I put my phone away. 'And I still tell you everything. There's nothing going on. What wouldn't I tell you?'

'I don't know,' Lucy said. 'It just feels like there's something. But it's probably nothing. I believe you, B.'

It didn't feel good to lie to my best friend. And she was right—as we walked to rehearsal on Wednesday, I knew I couldn't tell her about the butterflies swelling in my stomach. Lucy always made me feel better when I was nervous, but I had to handle it alone while appearing engaged in her rant about Mr Gilbert's fondness for full-class detentions.

My legs were like jelly as I walked into the rehearsal room that night, but when I saw Matt smiling at me from the top of the stairs, my chest burned with warmth again. He hugged me as usual, and we chatted quietly as usual, and we acted together as usual. But every touch, every moment of eye contact, was charged with something deeper, something unspoken between us: *we know something that no one else knows.* Sitting a metre apart at the edge of the room felt more like acting than actually doing the scenes; less natural than being up there, dancing together, holding hands. The session was over too quickly, and we texted until I couldn't keep my eyes open.

High on having seen him, the next couple of days passed in a blur. I saw him again at Friday's rehearsal, and when he hugged me goodbye at the end of the session, he whispered, 'See you tomorrow.' With only one more sleep to go, it was like Christmas Eve.

I came home from rehearsal to find Amy getting ready for a party that didn't begin for hours. I wondered why she had started so early.

'Because *Tom* is going to be there,' she said.

Tom Wallis was Amy's newest victim. She met him at some Battle of the Bands gig and hadn't shut up about him since.

'He plays bass,' she'd gone on. 'He has blond hair…brown eyes…and the *cutest* smile…'

And now, three months, two parties, and one cinema trip later, she was getting ready for yet another occasion where he *might* kiss her. I went to my room and spent another night messaging Matt until the early hours, too excited to sleep, desperate for dawn.

I woke up far too early for a Saturday and spent a long time choosing my clothes, playing with my hair, trying to make myself pretty. I realised why Amy had spent so long on her makeup the previous night.

I told Mum I was meeting friends at the park and left earlier than planned, too excited to wait around any longer. I tried to slow my steps to make the walk last longer, so I didn't show up half an hour before I was meant to. In the end, I was only ten minutes early and I thought it best not to sit suspiciously outside his front door.

With a shaking finger, I rang the bell, butterflies fluttering in my stomach and my heart pounding. What if I didn't know how to act, now that we'd finally be alone together? Would it be awkward? What if he'd changed his mind?

Matt, in contrast, seemed remarkably cool. He opened the door and said, 'Hiya,' and stepped back to let me in.

I was disappointed by the fact he didn't immediately kiss me. We had kissed before. Weren't we boyfriend and girlfriend now?

As I stepped over the threshold into the house, I thought that might be like crossing the line between friends and lovers, and he might spin me round and kiss me and tell me how he'd been craving it. But no, he just smiled at me.

I thought maybe he would wait until he closed the door, then seize me and press his lips against mine, or even just give me a sweet peck. I slipped my shoes off as he firmly pressed the handle down until the door clicked closed. All he did was take my jacket.

'Can I get you a drink?' he said.

I didn't really know what to do with myself, so I just said, 'Yes.' He led me into the kitchen and got me a glass of orange juice and asked about my week, as if we hadn't been texting for six hours every night. We sat on the barstools sipping, both a bit stiff, and I started to worry that it was not playing out as romantically as I'd hoped.

Then Matt said, 'Right, shall we talk about us?'

I said, 'Okay.'

'So, like we said on the phone, do you still want to be a...a thing?'

'Um,' I smiled, 'what exactly is a "thing"?'

He leaned back. 'Well, I don't know, really. Whatever you want it to be.'

'Like, boyfriend and girlfriend?'

He hesitated. 'Like seeing each other.'

'Same thing, isn't it?' I blurted. This was not how I'd imagined this conversation going.

'Um. Basically. Yeah. Just without the label.'

'Labels don't matter to me,' I said, hoping that would relax him. If it *was* the same thing, as Matt had said, then it made no difference to me.

'Is that still what you want?' he asked.

'Um, well, is it what you want?'

He paused. 'Yeah. Okay. Yeah.' He ran his fingers through his hair which fell back perfectly, tickling the tops of his ears. 'Now, you haven't told anyone about us?'

I shook my head.

'Not Amy?'

'No.'

'Your friends?'

'No.'

'Not Callum or Lucy or anyone?'

'I said no, Matt,' I giggled. It was so silly, the seriousness with which he spoke. I had no idea what he was worrying about; I was ecstatic.

'Brooke, please take this seriously.'

I stopped laughing. 'I am taking this seriously.'

'And you're sure you won't tell anyone?'

'I'm sure.'

'Because we…this can't work if we…if other people…'

'Matt, I get it,' I said. 'I'm not going to tell anyone.'

'Okay.' The silence stretched out a bit.

'So, is there anything else we need to sort out?' I asked.

'I…erm, well…I'm not sure.'

I giggled.

Then Matt said, 'Can I kiss you?'

I blushed. 'You don't need to ask.'

'I do. Because how would I know if you wanted me to, or not?'

'Okay,' I smiled shyly. 'Well, I do. Want you to.'

He smiled back, and leaned in, and my heart pounded. He pressed his lips gently against mine, but I was scared again, scared of screwing it up, and my mouth was glued shut, and my body was frozen. I felt him part his lips against my firmly closed ones. The moment stretched on for too long.

He leaned back. 'You okay? You look…um…not okay.'

'I'm okay, I am,' I insisted in a panic.

'Do you not want to kiss with open mouths? Just peck?'

I wanted his linoleum floor to swallow me whole. 'No, I do, I mean, I just don't know—'

I moved my arms, fumbling with my words, and the barstool wobbled. I gasped, but before I could fall, Matt seized it and steadied me.

We started laughing, and his hands took mine, and I could tell he was trying to relax me. We tried kissing again, and he went slower this time, and I followed his lead, and it was nice. It wasn't fiery and passionate like in the alley, or awkward like that first kiss in rehearsal—it was sweet.

We kissed for a while, and then he said, 'What do you want to do now?'

'Um,' I paused. 'Not sure. Show me your house?'

'You've been here before,' he said.

'Yeah, but I didn't have a tour guide!'

Matt took my hand and led me round; the downstairs was pretty self-explanatory. Upstairs, he showed me the spare room, his parents' room, and finally his room. I'd been in there before but had been so caught up in the party that I'd barely taken it in. It was small, plain, and tidy, with creamy walls hosting several framed pictures.

I looked closer at one. It was a tall, triangular building. 'What's that?' I asked.

'The Flatiron building, in New York.'

'And this?'

'The Space Needle, Seattle.'

I spotted the piano keyboard in the corner of the room. 'Whoa. Can you play piano?'

'Not really,' he grinned, 'just chords.'

He sat on his bed while I spent the next fifteen minutes opening drawers and asking questions and generally being a nuisance. He was patient, answering a bajillion rounds of 'What's this?' and 'Where's this from?' Gradually he lay down while giving me his life story in objects.

When my curiosity had worn out, I fell onto the bed next to him. He put his arm around my shoulder and I put my head on his chest. I loved the feel of his shirt on my cheek, the sound of his heartbeat, the way he smelt. His arms were warm and secure, and I felt so blissfully contented, like there was nothing else in the world I could possibly want, like I could stay there forever.

As long as no one found out about us.

SCENE 13: MATT, 18

I know I said that being with Brooke was a bad idea. But it was too hard to keep away from her. The way I felt was like nothing I'd ever experienced before; it was completely different to my relationship with Georgia. There was a force that pulled me towards her, like my own personal gravity. She understood me in a way that no one else could. When we were together, I forgot her age because she was so mature, and she looked and acted older. She told me she wanted to be with me, so I let her be with me, because I wanted to be with her too. It felt impossible to do anything else.

The next week at rehearsal, Stephen and Meg announced we were going to have to learn *another* song.

'The second half needs some padding out,' Stephen said. 'So, we're going to have Brooke and Matt sing *Dangerous Game* from *Jekyll and Hyde*, right when Juliet finds out that Romeo killed her cousin.'

Brooke and I went downstairs with Stephen to the piano to learn the song, then came back up to run the choreography—mostly simple steps and a lot of near-embraces. There were also parts where I had to spin Brooke around, or practically waltz with her, and she smiled at me shyly as I sang my lines.

Brooke's voice surprised me too; I didn't know she could even reach those high notes, let alone belt them out. As the song progressed, our movements became more vigorous and our singing became more intense, and by the time we were finished, we were panting. I downed my bottle of water.

Stephen was grinning. 'That was brilliant! You picked that up so quickly.'

Brooke and I looked at one another, and I put an arm loosely round her shoulder, giving her a friendly squeeze.

'We'll go over it a few more times next week, just to be sure you remember it…' Stephen went on, but I wasn't listening.

Over his shoulder I saw Meg, notebook in hand, observing me sternly. She wasn't smiling. I retracted my arm.

By the end of the session, I really needed the bathroom after drinking all that water. Stephen was giving some announcements. I crossed my legs, listening for the end of his speech, waiting for the 'See you next week,' that never came. Eventually I had to dart out the door while he was mid-sentence, hearing Lewis say, 'Oh, he's off,' as I went. When I came back, I'd somehow managed to miss all the goodbyes—the only people left were Stephen and Brooke, who were talking about the song.

'Yeah, I see what you mean,' Stephen was saying, 'but I wouldn't worry about it. You managed fine today.' He picked up his bag and headed for the door, waving to us as he went. I heard his footsteps echo down the stairs and Brooke turned to me.

'Is he going to lock us in?' she said.

'Mum's a keyholder, she can let us out,' I laughed. 'Though it wouldn't be so bad, would it?'

Without saying another word, we walked towards one another. She wrapped herself up inside my arms and I kissed her gently, like I'd been wanting to all night.

'Do you want to meet up soon?' I asked.

'Yeah,' she said, 'it'll be easier when school ends next week.'

'How about after the session next Friday? My parents have this dinner thing. We could have our first proper date—'

Over Brooke's shoulder I clocked Meg, standing in the doorway, her eyes burning into me with a ferocious look.

Shit. How long had she been listening? How much had she heard, or seen? I was certain she'd only just appeared there. But she saw us now, our arms still round each other, and my heart was pounding, and I knew I was in trouble.

Instinctively, I tried to pull away from Brooke, but she held on tightly to me. Hadn't she seen Meg? I was sure she had, or at least she'd noticed my face turn white.

'What's going on?' Meg's voice was like thunder.

I moved my mouth, but no words came. My heart was no longer pounding against my ribcage—it had stopped altogether.

Without letting go of me, Brooke turned her head to look at Meg and said, very calmly, 'The spinny bit in *Dangerous Game*. Last time I thought he was going to drop me.'

Meg looked confused, but Brooke didn't wait for her to react. 'Try it again,' she said.

I seemed to wake from my stupor and remember which part Brooke was on about. I leant forward and she leant back and, being very sure to support her weight, we moved our parallel bodies in a circular motion.

'Yep, that felt a lot better,' Brooke said, 'Thanks.'

'Sorry I nearly dropped you last time,' I said, stepping away from her and half-laughing.

She went to collect her bag. 'Well, you didn't, so it's all good. See you, Matt. Bye, Meg.'

'Bye,' Meg said, watching her leave but remaining unsmiling. She closed the door at the top of the stairs, and I didn't understand why. The door was never closed, not even in winter, and it made the room look alien, unfamiliar. I zipped up my jacket despite it not being cold. Meg turned on me like a viper.

'Matt, you're eighteen now,' she began, as if I hadn't been at my own birthday party.

'Uh huh,' I agreed. I wasn't sure where she was going with this, but I knew it wasn't somewhere good.

'I just want you to be careful, because while a lot of things are legal for you now, that means you will also be tried in an adult court if you commit a crime. And you'd go to proper jail, not some young offenders'.'

I was confused. 'What do you think I've done?'

'I'm a child protection officer for Stagefright, *and* I'm a primary school teacher. If I think someone is a danger to the children under my protection, it's my job to report it. If I didn't, I wouldn't be able to live with myself, not to mention I'd risk my job.'

'I don't understand—'

'I'm not threatening you, Matt, I'm just warning you. We knew there'd be an age difference when we cast you and Brooke in these roles. I told Stephen I didn't like it. But age gaps aren't uncommon in drama groups and we chose you partly because we know you're reliable. If we find out you've been abusing your position with Brooke—'

I winced at the word "abusing". 'You think I'd hurt Brooke?'

'No, that's not what I was suggesting,' Meg said. 'I just mean that someone else might *think* something. When you were seventeen, you counted as one of our kids, too. But now, someone might worry that you're not *just* acting, because you two seem close even when you're not rehearsing.'

'We're friends—'

'I get it, she was shy, you took her under your wing, and we're grateful for that. All I'm saying is, act your socks off in the performance, but for rehearsals, maybe tone down the romance.'

I wanted this conversation to end as fast as possible. I'd never felt so uncomfortable in my life. 'Got it. Only acting.'

'I know that, but not everyone else does. You're an adult, she's fourteen. She's *not sixteen yet. Do* you hear what I'm saying? Someone could misinterpret your actions, and you could get into all sorts of trouble. I'm talking assault charges, Sex Offenders Register—'

'Okay, okay, *IknowIknowIknow*,' I almost hissed. I didn't want to hear her say those things. I didn't want to feel guilty. I had to remind myself that I'd done nothing wrong…right?

'Then don't give them anything to misinterpret,' Meg said. 'Remember, if you never let yourself be alone with a child, you're never putting yourself in a position where you can be accused of something. Alright?' She lightened her tone, trying to restore her friendliness.

'Alright,' I said miserably.

'Okay, see you next week. Get those songs learnt,' she said, and I marched out the door without looking back.

I hadn't done anything wrong, I kept telling myself. I hadn't made Brooke do anything she didn't want to—we'd only kissed—but Meg had made me feel guilty. Our parents, our friends, they wouldn't see what Brooke and I had. They wouldn't see that there was nothing wrong with us, that she was mature, that I wasn't pressuring her into anything. It was innocent, sweet, and there was a connection between us, and it was real, and it blew my mind. They wouldn't understand, so we had to keep this from them.

It certainly was a dangerous game we were playing.

SCENE 14: BROOKE, 14

The last day of year nine meant three things: first, the last day of wearing blue polo shirts, so everyone was getting them signed; second, a half day; and third, the beginning of summer. At break time, I signed each of my friends' shirts before giving them a hug and wishing them an amazing holiday. Some were going to the beach, others were going abroad, but when I looked at my summer, all I saw was Matt.

I walked home from school to an empty house; Mum was at work and Amy, who had just had her last day of year twelve, was out with her friends. I had a shower and got into some of my favourite clothes, ready for rehearsal and my first proper date.

At the end of the Stagefright that evening, Lucy grinned at me. 'Off to the bus stop!'

'I'm not going to the cinema,' I said, and her face fell. My friends had been planning this movie trip for weeks.

'Oh, why not?'

'I have a family thing,' I lied.

'Oh no,' she said. 'Okay, well, we'll miss you.'

As I watched her hurry off, I felt a rush of affection for her, and wished that I could just tell her about me and Matt, wished I didn't have to lie to her. But he'd said he would only be with me if I kept it a secret, and I wanted to be with him more than anything.

Matt and I had to execute our departure carefully. We'd planned it in advance the night before: he would leave immediately and go to his car, which was parked a little walk away, and I would leave later with whoever was locking up. I'd take the longer route there, round the shops, to make sure that everyone had driven off before we met.

The streets were almost deserted, so it was easy enough to get to Matt's car without being seen. He kissed me quickly and started driving.

'Good session tonight,' he said. 'Only a couple of weeks till the show.'

'Will you miss Stagefright when you go to uni?' I asked.

'*If* I go. I haven't got my grades yet.'

His emphasis on the word "if" made my stomach flip, and I felt guilty for hoping he would fail his exams. But still—he could be here for another year...?

'But yeah, I will. I'll probably join the drama society at uni. And I'll come back to sessions in the holidays. I just won't be able to be in shows. I'll run the lights or something.'

I tried to imagine Stagefright without Matt. It suddenly seemed very empty. 'I love this play. I wish we could keep doing it.'

'What's your...' He tapped his fingers on the steering wheel. '...favourite scene?'

'Um, probably the last one of ours. It's the most romantic double teen suicide ever,' I joked. 'Yours?'

'Hm...probably our first one, where we meet. I just think it's sweet.'

I smiled to myself. *My boyfriend is so romantic!*

'Favourite song?' he asked.

'*Dangerous Game*, easily.'

'Really? I don't like that one very much.'

My heart sank. I'd thought it described our secret relationship so well, the mention of danger, of forbidden pleasures. 'What's yours, then?' I asked, a little defensively.

'I really like *Taking Chances.*'

My heart rose again. He liked our original, optimistic duet. I suddenly wondered why I liked *Dangerous Game* so much. 'Really?'

'Yeah. I kind of feel like it...sort of describes us.' His slight nervousness in admitting it was adorable.

Matt made a stir fry when we got in, and we put on the *Les Misérables Concert* DVD because we both knew most of the songs. He pulled me close to him, positioning my head against his chest in a way that didn't make it easy for me to see the screen, but I didn't care. Being close to him was my favourite thing in the world. It was a fairy tale, singing along with him and laughing at each other when we got the words wrong. Then we were kissing, and his hands were on my shoulders, and my lips were endlessly exploring his, and it was pure magic, neither of us wanting anything else, anything more than to just stay here, in this moment, breathing the same air—

He pushed me off. I blinked, and he turned back to the TV. 'Are you okay?' I asked.

He nodded. He crossed his legs and put a cushion on his lap.

I leaned in to kiss him again, but he pointed at the screen. 'This is a good bit,' he said.

I looked at the TV: *One Day More* was starting. 'Oh yeah, this is the best one,' I agreed, and started singing. He didn't join in this time, just stared at the screen.

'Are you okay?' I asked again, and he nodded without looking at me. He wasn't touching me at all now, not even holding my hand. The warm glow I'd been feeling before was evaporating quickly. *You did something to piss him off,* I thought.

I crossed my arms over myself, a full foot away from him on the sofa. He was completely still, his hand resting on top of the cushion, his eyes fixed on the TV. The singers went on without our accompaniment. *He's annoyed at you. You're annoying.*

'Need the bathroom,' he mumbled. He came to his feet, turning away from me and chucking the cushion down as he went.

SCENE 15: MATT, 18

Well, that was fucking inconvenient, wasn't it?
I stood in the bathroom and waited for it to go down. I looked in the mirror. My hair was messy. This morning's stubble was growing back. *Just think about football.*

It had surprised me, when it happened, and I'd panicked. I didn't want her to see it, or accidentally feel it. I was sure it would freak her out. It felt kind of gross to be with her, and then for *that* to happen. But it wasn't like I chose for it to happen. It wasn't like I thought about her in that way. I just thought she was cool. And she was pretty, with her long brown hair that she'd tied up in a ponytail, exposing her shoulders, the column of her throat, skin that would be so soft against my lips—

Football. Arsenal. Wayne Rooney. Just kissing. We were just kissing. I wasn't pressuring her into anything more. She was okay with kissing, and I was okay with kissing, so what could be wrong with that? But a wave of guilt washed over me. I pressed my forehead against the mirror.

I looked down and realised the problem was long gone. Now able to, I peed and went back into the living room. The sight of her long brown hair trailing over the back of the sofa was like an instant painkiller, and I relaxed. How could this be bad if it felt so good?

I slumped down next to her. Éponine was singing against a rainy backdrop. I leaned forward and took a slug of water.

'Are you mad at me?'

I turned to look at her, and she looked so small, so fragile, like her face would crack any second.

'No,' I said. 'Why would I be mad at you?'

She looked down at her fingers, twisting them up in each other.

'Brooke.' I leaned back and looped my arm around her, pulling her close. 'What happened? What made you think I was upset?'

'You just,' she said into my chest, 'you just seemed off with me. Before.'

'Oh.' *Shit.* 'Oh, Brooke, I'm sorry, I just…I had a weird moment. I thought I felt a migraine coming on. I'm so sorry, it wasn't about you. I was just caught up in my own head.'

Feeling her tearful sobs under my arms caused a surge of guilt that eclipsed whatever I'd been feeling in the bathroom. I paused the DVD and held her, wishing hard that I could go back to before and undo whatever I'd said that had resulted in her crying into my chest. Eventually she quietened, and we chatted about something else. I cracked some jokes, and only when she was laughing loudly again did I restart the DVD, making sure to keep my arm tight around her.

SCENE 16: BROOKE, 14

Matt and I established a pretty good routine for dates once my summer holidays started. His parents were at work all week, and so was Mum, but Amy would be in and out unpredictably, so we only hung out at his house. I wanted to spend every day together, but Matt had shifts at the corner shop, and sometimes he'd have plans with his friends, so it was more like every few days. The ones without him dragged by, as did the weekends, when our parents were home and we were forced apart.

The evenings dragged, too. I started to dread four o'clock, which was the time Matt started suggesting I should go home. His parents worked until five and commuted, so I thought he was overreacting. We would push it to quarter past, then half past, then twenty to five, but one time he heard a car pull up in the driveway and panicked. Turns out it was a delivery, but by that time he'd already rushed me into the garden and towards the back gate. We went back to four o'clock after that.

At the end of one afternoon together, I found myself lounging on the sofa with Amy. In honour of the upcoming show, she had put on *Gnomeo and Juliet*, and related to me her unsuccessful encounter with Tom Wallis at a party the night before.

'I was *this close*,' she hissed, holding her fingers an inch apart. 'The playlist went to *I Don't Wanna Miss a Thing*—you know, that Aerosmith song—and we started slow dancing, and we were leaning in, about to do it—and then someone put the Macarena on.'

'You'll get your chance,' I said, turning up the volume. Amy ignored this.

'I don't know, he might've given up…'

'He liked you enough to dance with you, didn't he?' I said.

'But boys are more complicated than that!' she groaned.

I think I might know a little more about boys than you, Amy, I thought. Instead, I said, 'Maybe you'll learn something about them from these gnomes.'

She curled up grumpily. 'I only get these Shakespeare references because of A-Level English.'

'I only get them because of the play,' I said.

Her phone dinged. She seized it and beamed.

'It's Tom!' she cried. 'And he wants to know if I'm free tomorrow!'

'Told you.'

'I'll wait a few minutes to reply. I don't want to seem too available…'

She texted him back after precisely seven minutes, and ten seconds later, we heard a buzz. She leapt for her phone and was disappointed by the blank screen.

'Sorry,' I smirked, and looked at mine.

Lucy Haines: Want to hang out tomorrow night?

I sighed. I hadn't seen Lucy outside of Stagefright for weeks, and it felt bad to let her down. I typed back: *Really sorry, I have a family thing.*

Amy's phone dinged. 'He's invited me over for dinner tomorrow night!'

'Nice,' I said, putting my phone down. 'That's exciting.'

'Thanks. My first date! Wow. What are you doing tomorrow? Out with Lucy again?'

'Uh,' I swallowed, 'Yeah.'

*

I'd told my family I was with my friends, and my friends that I was with my family, because Matt and I had the opportunity to spend a rare Saturday evening together while his parents were at a wedding reception. We'd been a bit stuck with what to do, since we didn't usually see each other two days running, and ended up googling games you can play with only two people. There weren't that many, so we mostly just cuddled. Being in his arms felt like the only thing I needed.

At ten he took me home, and it was impressive to watch him drive. Not like Amy, whose second lesson ended abruptly when she backed into a lamp post. Matt was smooth and calm and in control. *My boyfriend has his own car!* I thought. *How many of my friends can say that?*

'It's not *my* car,' he corrected me, when I referred to it as such.

I shrugged. 'It's as good as.'

My phone buzzed with a message.

Mum: Home soon? x

Brooke Tyler: On my way. Went back to Lucy's after cinema x

Matt turned off the main road into my street, but continued past my driveway.

'It's the second one in,' I said.

He kept going.

'Matt, you missed it,' I repeated.

'I know,' he said. 'I just…we can't be seen. I'll park further down.'

'Why can't you park outside my house?'

'Well, what if your family sees us together?'

'I can just say we've been practising lines,' I smiled, dishing out an excuse I'd thought of earlier.

'Is that where you said you were all evening?' Matt suddenly looked panicked. 'With me?'

I hadn't expected this reaction. 'No.'

'Where did you tell your mum you were today?'

'At the cinema with school friends. And then back to Lucy's.'

'So would it make sense that we'd been rehearsing lines?'

'I…guess not.'

Matt sighed. 'You have to think about these things, Brooke. If this is going to work…'

The 'if' caught my attention.

'…we have to be really careful. Is there any way your mum could find out you were lying about where you were? Would she come by Lucy's house, or call her parents?'

'No,' I said. 'She trusts me. I've never…lied to her before.' The excitement of it all gave way to a long moment of guilt. I hadn't thought twice about lying to Mum that morning.

'We have to keep this really quiet, Brooke.'

'I get it.'

'Because people might think—'

'I said I get it, Matt,' even though I didn't. It felt like he was telling me off.

'Okay. So, I'll stop down the road and you can walk over.'

Matt turned into a cul-de-sac round the corner from my house, our words still hanging in the air between us. He parked up.

'I had a really good time tonight,' he said.

I seized the opportunity to lighten the mood. 'Me too. I really like spending time with you.'

'I'll text you about when we can next see each other.'

'Okay,' I smiled, and leaned over to him.

He glanced around warily before kissing me, cutting it short and leaving me hanging. 'See you soon,' he said.

I guess that was my cue to go. It had all been a bit abrupt. 'Bye.'

I closed the car door and walked towards my house, glancing back at him from the street corner. He was still there, looking at me, and I waved to him as I went. But the evening had turned sour, leaving me feeling miffed.

Amy came home ten minutes after me and flew into my room, where she jumped onto the bed.

'You okay?' I said, buttoning up my pyjamas.

'I'm fantastic,' she said breathlessly. She'd just come back from Tom Wallis' house where they'd finally made the step from 'friends' to 'seeing each other' and he'd finally, *finally* kissed her.

'Brooke, it was amazing.' She sat up now, looking ecstatic. 'Finally kissing him after I'd wanted it for *so long*. And he introduced me to his parents. They seem really nice.'

'Oooh, Amy's got a boyfriend,' I said teasingly. I expected her to retaliate, but she just lay back on my bed, grinning at the ceiling.

SCENE 17: MATT, 18

It's not like I never felt weird about the age thing. Spending an afternoon with Brooke and then going to the pub made it feel weird. Laughing over pints in a room where under-eighteens were not allowed made it feel weird. And Simon asking how snogging a twelve-year-old in rehearsals was going made it feel really weird. I'd feel guilty, stressed, and mad at myself. I'd wonder what the hell I was doing.

But when I saw Brooke, those feelings disappeared. When we were together, I'd forget about the age thing, and all I saw was her. I felt happy. We would lounge on the sofa and the weight of her head on my chest slowed the world to a stop. But A-Level results day was fast approaching, the day I'd find out if I got into Lancaster University. As that Thursday crept closer, my anxiety was building, and I picked up extra shifts in the shop just to distract myself.

The night before, I had my usual Wednesday rehearsal. Brooke and I had been messaging about my results, so she knew I was nervous. When she hugged me goodbye, she whispered, 'Good luck for tomorrow.'

From rehearsal, I drove to Fliss and Simon's house. They'd invited us over for a movie to calm our nerves before the big day. I was relieved to hear that Georgia was working and wouldn't be joining us.

'It's the end of an era!' Ellie kept saying on repeat as we tried to pay attention to *The Hangover*. She was sitting next to Simon and kept glancing at him. Perhaps she thought this was her last chance to win him over before we all went our separate ways. He was too busy laughing at the screen and stuffing his face to notice.

'How you doing, Matty?' Fliss leaned over and whispered to me.

'I'm pretty nervous. Just trying not to think about it. You?'

'Shitting myself,' Fliss said. 'Tomorrow, I find out if I move to London for the next three years and if Simon will get his apprenticeship in Liverpool. I can't imagine being that far away from him. We haven't gone more than a week apart since we were in the bloody womb!'

'Are you worried about missing him?'

'So much. He can be a bit of a pillock, but he's the best. I can't imagine leaving this tiny little town, can you?'

For the first time, I tried to imagine it. Living in a house I'd never seen before, in a city I'd visited twice, with people I'd never met. Saying goodbye to Ellie, Simon, Fliss, Mum, Dad and Brooke. I'd been trying not to think about what it was going to be like, but it was becoming harder and harder to ignore. Would my school friends meet up between semesters? Would they come and visit for the weekend? What would happen to me and Brooke?

I was up at six the next morning, refreshing the UCAS web-page. They said university offers would be confirmed at eight, but there were rumours every year that the results were visible early, and even worse rumours that the UCAS server would crash when everyone logged on at the same time to see if they had got in.

At seven, Dad was by my side in his dressing gown, armed with two cups of tea. Sip, refresh, sip, refresh, sip, refresh. Mum came in and made us eat toast.

At seven forty-five, the page updated. I scrambled towards the screen and looked at my result, spilling my cold tea as I did. *Congratulations,* it read, *your place at Lancaster University for Chemistry F100 has been confirmed.*

'He's in!' Mum cried, and threw her arms round me. 'He's done it!'

Relief flooded through me. I'd got in. Plan A was on track.

'So you must've got at least AAB?' Dad said.

'Guess so. I'll find out when I go to sixth form.'

'We ought to celebrate,' Mum said, and her smile wavered momentarily.

'Mum, don't be sad,' I said. 'I'm not moving away for another month yet. And I'll be back in the holidays.'

'I know, I know,' she said, blinking rapidly. 'And we have so much to sort out. We have to pay your halls deposit, and work out how to get all your stuff up there—mind you, if you don't get into halls, we'll have to go up there and find you a flat…' It sounded like the next month would be non-stop university prep. She wouldn't be able to forget I was moving for even a second. She beamed again, trying to put on a brave face. 'How have your friends done? Text them to find out. You're going out tonight, aren't you?'

We did go out that night. At eight, I found myself at Fliss' house again, armed with prosecco and cider.

Fliss had got into her London uni, Simon was off to do his apprenticeship, Ellie had gone through clearing but was happy to be going to Swansea, and, when Georgia arrived late having clearly already started drinking, I found out that she was going to Durham. Her tipsy state made our first reunion since breaking up a lot less awkward than I'd imagined.

'Maaatt,' she said, and gave me a bit of a loose hug. 'I'm going to Durham!'

'You are,' I replied, patting her on the shoulder.

'Two A-stars and an A. I beat you! Woohoo!'

As she traipsed off, my phone vibrated.

> *Brooke Tyler: Sorry I haven't messaged all day. Thought you'd be too*
> *busy to talk.*
> *How did you do? xxx*

> *Matt Williams: AAB. Got into Lancaster! Going out tonight*
> *to celebrate xxx*

A while later, my phone buzzed again.

> *Brooke Tyler: Congratulations! That's amazing, well done. Have a*
> *great night! xxx*

At ten, the taxi came to pick us up and take us into Bristol. There was a huge results day event at a club that most of our sixth form was going to, and Fliss had written our university names on our arms in glow-in-the-dark facepaint. Getting into uni had been a relief, but it brought with it even more anxiety about moving away. Tonight, I would ignore that. Tonight, I would just have fun.

As we stepped out of the taxi, my phone vibrated again.

Brooke Tyler: ☹

What? Why did she send a sad face? Was she was upset about something? Was she trying to tell me *I* had upset her? I scrolled back through our conversation, looking for anything that could explain the emoji. Nada. She'd sounded fine up until this point. So what had I done? Not texted early enough about my results? Was she jealous that I was going on a night out, and she was stuck at home? I couldn't help but feel annoyed. Brooke was making this about her.

'Coming, Matt?' Fliss said, as she joined the line outside the club.

I looked again at the sad face on the screen. *This is* my *night*, I told myself.

'Coming,' I replied, and switched off my phone.

SCENE 18: BROOKE, 14

I cried all day when I heard about Matt's results. He had gotten into his first-choice uni, and I knew I should be happy for him. If a degree was what he wanted, and Lancaster was where he wanted to be, I knew I should be supporting him. But it was hard not to be sad.

We hadn't talked about what would happen when he went away: if we would do long-distance or break up. I'd sent him a sad face, hoping for reassurance that he'd want to stay together in September. Even if he did, it was going to suck. He would be miles up north, and I wouldn't see him at Stagefright, and we wouldn't get to spend lazy afternoons cuddling on his couch in front of the TV.

I saw Matt for a few hours when his parents were at work on Monday. He made lunch and we played video games, and I smiled and acted normally and laughed at his jokes, but my mind was still reeling with too many unanswered questions. I couldn't stop worrying about what would happen when he moved away. How often would he come back and visit? Would he still want to be my boyfriend? Or would he want to be single and get drunk and be with other girls? I was too scared to ask and came away from his place feeling sick.

Performing in the play distracted me, and that week led up to the show. Rehearsals intensified, and on Friday night we all met at the Complex for the dress rehearsal. The actual performance was going to be in the downstairs auditorium, with a proper stage and dressing rooms. We ran the play from start to finish without pausing, even when things went wrong, which happened a lot. Stephen was visibly stressed by all the mistakes we made, and at one point snapped at Deepak for forgetting at least half of his lines.

The next day was the real thing: three months of work coming to a head. We all met at two to run it again before the actual performance at seven. I pushed Matt's results day to the back of my mind, just enjoying the last few times I'd be able to kiss him in front of everyone, the last few times we'd be running these lines and singing these songs.

The evening crept up on us quickly, and soon every seat in the auditorium was taken. I spotted Mum chatting to Stephen's boyfriend, and Amy sitting hand in hand with Tom Wallis. A few of mine and Lucy's mates from school had made it and were giggling together in the front row. There was a guy and a girl I recognised from Facebook as Matt's friends—twins, I was sure, though I couldn't remember their names. I didn't know what his parents looked like.

I stopped peering around the corner of the doorway and went backstage. There was a hum of nervous energy in the dressing rooms. Meg put lipstick and eyeliner on me. Stephen had a clipboard and an earpiece. 'Break a leg,' someone said.

Callum came over. 'How are you doing, Brookers? Nervous?'

'Yeah,' I breathed, wiping my sweaty hands on my skirt.

'It's gonna be fine,' he said, leaning against the wall. 'Haven't seen you round our house in a while. Everything okay between you and Luce?'

'What?' I said suddenly. 'Yeah, everything's fine. Did she say something?'

'No. You just usually spend half your life at our place. I thought you might've fallen out or something.'

I looked across the room at Lucy, who was giving her monologue a last scan.

'Everything's fine between us,' I said. 'I've been busy.'

'Just wanted to check. Honorary big brother, and all.' He gave me a one-armed squeeze. 'You're gonna be great tonight. Although I think Shakespeare had the right idea sticking with all-male casts—less of a liability.'

At five to seven, Meg and Stephen hushed everyone to give us a pre-show pep talk. They said something about putting in energy and having fun, 'plus there's cake to look forward to in the interval.'

I made sure to catch Lucy at the end of their speech, and I gave her a massive hug. 'Break a leg,' I whispered.

'You're gonna smash it!' she said into my hair.

We all waited with bated breath as she went on to open the show. The silence buzzed around us as we listened to her voice through the wall: 'Two houses, both alike in dignity; in fair Verona, where we lay our scene...'

Matt caught my eye across the room and gave me a thumbs up. I returned it just as applause erupted at the end of Lucy's prologue.

'Alright, scene one,' Stephen said, and the boys headed off. *Months of rehearsing all pays off tonight*, I thought.

I got up to do my first scene with Tilly, which went well, and soothed my nerves. Being on that stage was so different from rehearsing upstairs; my voice seemed louder somehow, as it rang throughout the room. My actions all felt purposeful, and my nerves seemed to drive me. It wasn't till I got back to the dressing rooms that I realised my heart had been thundering.

My second scene was with Matt: Romeo meeting Juliet and singing *Taking Chances*. I hovered at the side until I heard the music for the song to begin. Matt and I met centre stage, and he spoke over the piano.

ROMEO: If I profane with my unworthiest hand, this holy shrine, the gentle fine is this: my lips, two blushing pilgrims, ready stand to smooth that rough touch with a tender kiss.

JULIET: Good pilgrim, you do wrong your hand too much, which mannerly devotion shows in this, for saints have hands that pilgrims' hands do touch, and palm to palm is holy palmers' kiss.

ROMEO: Have not saints lips, and holy palmers too?

JULIET: Ay, pilgrim, lips that they must use in prayer.

The piano swells. The rest of the cast exit the stage as JULIET sings first, then ROMEO. Slowly they clasp hands, and as they break into the chorus together, they begin the choreography, and it's all acted, all rehearsed, but it's also the realest thing in the world. JULIET drinks in his blue eyes, the way his hair sways with his motions, and she is sure he must be the most beautiful thing she's ever seen. When the song comes to an end there's applause. JULIET is disappointed it couldn't have lasted longer.

ROMEO: Oh, then, dear saint, let lips do what hands do. They pray, grant thou, lest faith turn to despair.

JULIET: Saints do not move, though grant for prayers' sake.

ROMEO: Then move not, while my prayer's effect I take.

ROMEO gently brings JULIET into his arms and kisses her. JULIET's mother in the audience shifts in her chair. ROMEO's dad coughs loudly.

We got through the first half without any massive screw ups, which was a big relief. Meg put her hand on my shoulder to ask how I was and told me I was doing awesome. Matt gave me a friendly hug. Lucy handed me a cupcake and made conversation. I smiled and ate, and answered when she spoke, but I was quiet. Being onstage was such a thrill. Being Juliet, being the lead, hearing all those people clap, was like nothing else. And tonight, months of work would all be forgotten in two short hours.

The second half started, and to everyone's relief, Deepak remembered *nearly* all of his lines. Romeo and Juliet got married. Romeo killed Tybalt, who came offstage covered in fake blood. Soon it was time for *Dangerous Game*.

JULIET: Oh serpent heart, hid with a flowering face! Did ever dragon keep so fair a cave? Beautiful tyrant, fiend angelical! Dove-feathered raven, wolvish-ravening lamb!

JULIET tries to concentrate on the acting, to feel the loss of her cousin, the anger at ROMEO, but all she can think about is the fact this is the last time they will be singing together.

JULIET: When thou didst bower the spirit of a fiend in moral paradise of such sweet flesh? Was ever book

containing such vile matter so fairly bound? Oh that
deceit should dwell in such a gorgeous palace!

*ROMEO enters. JULIET turns away. The piano slowly begins
the song. ROMEO approaches JULIET from behind, tentatively
placing a hand on her shoulder. She starts singing. The song is slow
at first, then picks up into something powerful, sinister. ROMEO
joins in after the first chorus, and they run through the movements,
repeatedly approaching each other, and then turning away. The
music builds up, the choreography gets faster, and JULIET is looking
at ROMEO as they dance together, trying to remember this moment,
this harmony, this feeling. They belt out the climax of the song and
end up forehead to forehead, panting for breath. Applause erupts,
and one of JULIET's friends in the audience whistles loudly. The
star-crossed lovers take hands and exit the stage.*

Callum hugged me when I got back to the dressing room. 'You
were awesome!' he said. 'That's a song to remember. You belting
it out like that.'

I smiled politely at him, but I felt a weakness in the corner
of my mouth. *It's over. Both songs are over. Soon the whole show
will be over.* I think Callum noticed, because he looked like he
wanted to say something, but then Stephen called him to the
stage and he was gone.

It was all so quick after that. We did the crypt scene for the
last time. I kissed Matt in front of everyone for the last time.
And then we were bowing for the last time. We stood in two
lines, and the audience applauded; some even came to their feet.
And I guess I was happy, and proud—I mean, this was what
three months had all been for, right?

Backstage was wild. Everyone was whooping and cheering,
and everyone hugged one another. Meg and Stephen looked
happy, or at least relieved. Matt picked me up and spun me
around in front of them all. Meg closed the door between the
dressing rooms, and we all got changed, wiping off our stage
makeup and heading out to meet our families.

When Lucy and I stepped outside, our school friends leapt
on us with hugs and showered us with praise. I hadn't seen

any of them for weeks, but Lucy clearly had—they talked about sleepovers and barbecues that I could vaguely remember declining invitations to without a second thought. My heart sank a little.

I spotted Matt across the auditorium, chatting with the twins. I wanted to talk to him, but him being with his school friends and me being with mine felt like a barrier keeping me from crossing the room. His friend glanced around and met my gaze. I looked away quickly.

Eventually, our friends joined the flow of people leaving the auditorium. Mum came over and gave me a big hug, and so did Amy, trailing Tom behind her. 'When did you get good?' she said, which was the best I could have hoped for.

Matt was heading out with two people who could only be his parents, and for a second I thought he was going to leave without saying goodbye. But he came over and gave me a friendly hug. 'You were amazing,' he said.

'Not as amazing as you,' I replied.

When we got home, Mum told us to go to bed, but not before saying how proud of me she was. I could barely hear her. My head was swimming with thoughts. *That's it. It's over. Show's over and now you have nothing to look forward to.*

I brushed my teeth with Amy. She told me about her day with Tom, and how much she liked him, and how special he made her feel. I nodded along, barely able to meet my own gaze in the mirror. *All that's left of the summer is waiting around for Matt to leave for uni. Then you'll be alone again. And he'll forget about you.*

I rinsed my mouth. She said goodnight and I mumbled back. I got into my pyjamas and laid down, staring at the ceiling. Three months of work, gone. Three months of rehearsals, over. And all that was left in front of me was September.

He will leave and you'll be stuck here, and no one will love you. Again.

SCENE 19: MATT, 18

'You were great,' Mum said on the drive home. Dad, half listening, grunted in agreement. I think he might've drifted off in the second act. Shakespeare wasn't his thing.

'Thanks, Mum.'

'How old was she? Juliet, the girl who played her.'

'Um,' I said, 'she's fourteen.'

'Really? She looks older.'

'Mm,' I said noncommittally.

'I do think, though, they could have paired you up with someone closer to your age.'

'Didn't you think she was good?'

'Oh yes, her acting was fine. But you had to...you know... kiss her. I didn't realise how much you had to kiss her.'

I felt my cheeks go red. 'It is *Romeo and Juliet*, Mum.'

'I know, I know, I just think it's a bit strange, for parents and all. She's so much younger than you.'

'She's fourteen.' I felt defensive. 'At rehearsal, you forget we're all different ages, because we're all friends.'

'I know, I know.'

My stomach churned. 'Do you really think fourteen's that young?'

'Well, I mean,' Mum said, as she turned onto our driveway, 'remember when you were fourteen. Think how grown up you thought you were back then, and how much you've changed since.'

We went into the house. Mum and Dad repeated that the show had been good and that I'd done a great job, then went to bed. I sat on the sofa feeling sick. I took out my phone, went onto Facebook, and flicked back through my profile pictures.

Fourteen-year-old me. Matt in year nine. I was significantly shorter and skinnier, with a face full of acne and a big, goofy grin. In one picture, I had one arm round Simon and the other round Fliss. She looked younger than she did now, much younger; her choppy side fringe and heavy eyeliner set her back several years. I could imagine her looking at the photo and saying, 'Oh, God, what was I thinking?'

I swallowed the lump in my throat. When I was fourteen, I barely knew how to speak to girls, and had certainly never kissed one. I looked at my current profile picture. Much taller, more muscular, with stubble that required daily shaving. Ten times as confident. Practically unrecognisable.

I tried to imagine an eighteen-year-old Brooke: a bit taller, a bit curvier, totally gorgeous. Someone who could stand her ground. Someone who could own the room. Someone whose neck I could press my lips to...

So far, I'd been pushing away the thought of doing anything with Brooke beyond kissing, but I could definitely see this older version of her in a sexual way. I was an eighteen-year-old guy who'd never gone further than kissing, and yes, I got turned on at times, and yes, I thought about sex. But I kept that separate from Brooke, thinking instead about the faceless women in videos I only watched on incognito mode.

I knew Simon had had sex a couple of times, and Lewis had a long-term girlfriend. Sex was something all us boys had obsessed over since we first found out what it was, and when we were younger, we'd all lied and said we'd done it already. I could remember being fourteen and feeling like two years was a *really* long time to wait to reach the legal age. Then when I'd hit sixteen, I hadn't had any luck anyway. So I'd waited. Of course, sex was something I was interested in, something I wanted to do—just with Georgia, it hadn't been right, it had all been too fast. Now I was eighteen, and Brooke was fourteen. I could wait two more years for her—more like a year and a half. But then I'd be nearly twenty, I realised. A man in his twenties, a real adult. And something felt very wrong about a twenty-year-old man and a sixteen-year-old girl.

Eighteen-year-old Brooke. Would she still want to be with me? Would she remember her younger self and agree she made good choices, or would she regret them? Would she look back at a picture of me and say, 'Oh, God, what was I thinking?'

SCENE 20: BROOKE, 14

I knew it was over as soon as Matt said, 'I've been thinking…'
He was holding me in his perfect arms, on his perfect sofa, on another perfect afternoon. Then he ruined everything.

'No,' I said blankly. I closed my eyes and prayed that, when I opened them, I'd realise I'd imagined it.

'You can't just say "no", Brooke.'

'I don't know what else to say.'

'Well, then,' he said.

The seconds passed in silence and I clung on to the moments prior, the moments before he'd said anything at all, almost as if I could wish myself back there.

'I just…I think this whole thing…might not be good. For us both,' he added quickly.

'How?' I said, sitting up. 'I love…'

His face went white.

'…being with you.'

Colour flushed his cheeks, but, strangely, he looked almost disappointed.

'And I don't want it to end,' I concluded.

'I don't want it to end either.'

'Well, then,' I said.

Silence.

'I just think it's what's best,' he said.

'For you?' I asked, not bothering to hide the accusation in my tone.

'For us both,' he said again.

'Well, nothing in this relationship is bad for me, so it must just be that you want to go to uni a free man.'

'That's not true,' he said, and I heard him sound defensive.

'Well, why do you want to end it, then?'

He sighed. 'I feel…when I'm with you…'

'Yes?'

'You—'

'How do *I* make you feel?'

'Horrible!' His voice snapped, and so did my heart.

After a stunned pause, I said, 'I'd better go, then.'

I got up to leave, but he grabbed my hand.

'I didn't mean it like that!' he exclaimed, speaking rapidly. 'It came out wrong…let me say…let me explain. *You* don't make me feel horrible. I make myself feel horrible, because of what I do to you.'

That freaked me out. 'You haven't…you aren't *doing* anything to me,' I whispered, knowing my voice would shake if I spoke louder.

'You think that now. But in a few years, you'll realise. Your perspective will change.'

'Oh, so you know me better than I know myself?' I demanded. 'So, what exactly is this enlightening revelation I'll get when I'm no longer just a stupid little girl?'

'I didn't say that.'

'What, though? What will I *realise*?'

'That I'm…I'm being irresponsible.'

'How are you being irresponsible?'

'You're fourteen!' he cried. 'I'm eighteen, I'm an adult, you're a child, I'm moving, and this whole thing is fucked.'

I tried to hold back the tears. 'Fucked,' I repeated.

'This isn't what I want, Brooke, but I'm just trying to do the right thing. Meg said something—other people would think it's weird—'

He gave up trying to explain, but I didn't need to hear his excuses. I knew why he was breaking up with me. He wanted to go to uni and have one-night stands and be with other, older girls.

'Fine,' I said, biting back tears. He didn't let go of my hand as I tugged my arm away. 'Since I'm just a *child*, I'd best be off.'

'Brooke—no—let's talk—'

'Let me go, Matt.'

'We don't have to break up, we can just talk—please don't leave like this, Brooke.'

'You're hurting me,' I lied, pulling my hand back; he let go instantly. I picked up my bag and looked at him.

He opened his mouth to speak but had nothing to say. My face was about to crack from all the pain I was pretending not to feel. With that, I swung my bag on my back and left.

SCENE 21: MATT, 18

I wasn't happy with how I left things with Brooke. She'd been so angry, so stubborn, determined not to hear my side of the story. If I could get her to listen to me, maybe she would get it. Maybe we could be friends. And maybe she'd understand why I was so scared of people finding out about us. She had seemed so mature before, but when we broke up, she'd been such a brat. And now I didn't trust her to keep our secret like she'd promised. I didn't trust her not to go crying to Lucy. And I didn't trust Lucy not to tell Callum, who would tell Meg, who'd go to the police. They would talk to me and realise I never did anything illegal. But everyone would still find out we'd been together, would still think differently of me, maybe not even speak to me anymore. So, yeah, I was scared.

I thought about ignoring the whole thing: quitting Stagefright, moving to Lancaster, cutting off all contact. Maybe she'd forget me. Maybe she'd let it go. But I couldn't be certain, couldn't be sure that one day, months, maybe years from now, I'd get a call from Mum crying down the phone about a rumour she'd heard, about something her son might've done with an underage girl.

I asked to meet up as friends. I asked to talk about what happened. She didn't reply to my Facebook messages, she didn't reply to my texts; she seemed to have completely disappeared from my life. Her invisibility was impossible to ignore.

After a week off, Stagefright was back to just Fridays now, doing workshops rather than rehearsing a play. Brooke was already there when I walked in, talking to some new joiners. We didn't hug. She didn't look at me. I wondered if anyone would notice that we'd suddenly stopped talking to each other. My head was spinning with worst-case-scenarios—she'd cause a scene, scream at me, tell everyone what we were, or tell Meg.

What if she already had? What if Meg was waiting to pull me aside in a quiet moment before…before…

The session started, some new people were introduced, we did warmup games. Stephen gave us some scene work to do. We had the break. People bought snacks. Lewis, Liam, and Deepak chatted to me. Tilly hadn't come back. Meg didn't pull me aside. Brooke didn't look at me. I stared at her eyes, willing her to meet mine, to catch my gaze so I could convey some sort of plea.

The session resumed. Meg split us in half; Brooke was in my group but made an excuse to stick with one of the new kids and switched. She really was avoiding me. *God, I need to talk to her.* Why was she so mad at me? Georgia had been quite laid-back about our breakup despite the embarrassing end. If Brooke was angry, I had to get her on my side, or else I'd be waiting for the day that this all came back to bite me.

When the session ended, I marched straight up to her before I could chicken out. I said her name and she twisted on the spot to face me, her hair spinning, her eyes dark. I felt a knock to my stomach: that familiar pull towards her, those lips that mine knew so well. I had to compose myself before muttering, 'We need to talk.'

'No, I don't think we do,' she said.

'But Brooke—'

'I think you've said all you needed to say,' she snapped, and her eyes blazed.

She was being a dick—stubborn and fierce, the things I loved about her used against me—and yet I still felt drawn to her, like she was a giant magnet that only affected me.

'Why won't you answer my messages?' I said in a low voice.

'Because,' she said, as if that was an answer. I waited for the rest of the sentence, but she just kept looking at me, her eyes intense, and then her lip shook. She blinked hard, and then Lucy called her and she turned away.

SCENE 22: BROOKE, 14

All summer I had deserted my friends. I had neglected my family. I had abandoned everything I cared about, everything that defined me, to run around with a boy. After the breakup, I tried to repair the friendships that had faded. I arranged to go shopping with Lucy, but she had to cancel for her great-great-somebody's bajillionth birthday. I tried to spend time with my family, but Mum was always at work and Amy was out with Tom. I tried to focus on the things I used to do by myself—painting, singing, daydreaming—but every colour, song, and fantasy led my thoughts right back to Matt. And at Stagefright, I had to see him.

Every Thursday night I prayed that he would be ill, or have plans, or go on holiday, but every Friday he was there, and I hated it. I hated that unmistakable rush of hope when he walked into the room. I hated catching his eye and missing how we used to share stolen glances. I hated how I knew that if I was just willing to be a little less stubborn, maybe things wouldn't have ended like that.

'Hi, Brooke,' he said gently one week. 'Please can we talk?'

'No,' I snapped. If we talked, I knew I'd start crying in seconds. If we talked, he would patronise me again. If we talked, I'd end up telling him how much I adored him and I'd beg him to stay with me, and he wouldn't. He wouldn't stay.

He looked hurt by my tone. 'Am I bothering you? Do you want me to leave you alone? Do you want me to stop texting you?'

No. I didn't want him to stop. I didn't want him to leave me alone. It was the only thing that made me feel like some part of him still cared about me. Maybe still had feelings for me. I sure as hell still had feelings for him. He was my everything. But even if he did still have feelings for me, that wouldn't stop him from leaving. And I couldn't let him leave me a second time.

I didn't say anything. Meg called the session to start. At the end, I saw Matt looking at me, wanting to try to talk to me again, so I made an excuse to Lucy about needing to dash off and left without saying goodbye to anyone.

Then came the texts.

Matt Williams: Brooke, please, we need to talk.

Matt Williams: Brooke, come on, let's talk this through.

Matt Williams: I'm sorry for upsetting you. Can we please talk so we can fix this?

Matt Williams: I miss you.

Matt Williams: I miss you.

Matt Williams: I can't leave things like this between us.

*

The days passed, all the same. Saturdays to Thursdays: texts and Facebook messages, all begging me to quit ignoring him. Fridays, quiet whispers to check I'd got those messages, to check I hadn't changed my mind. One time he passed me a note saying, 'I miss you.' I didn't know what to do with it, so I stuffed it in my pocket. I couldn't bring myself to chuck it out and instead spent the night reading and re-reading those words in his handwriting, tears spilling onto that little scrap of paper.

The holidays came to an abrupt end, and I went back to school to start my GCSEs. The first day of term was miserable. It was not until I was at the lunch table with Lucy and our other friends that I realised I missed them, missed being able to tell them how I felt. A distance had grown between us. I still couldn't open up to them about what had happened that summer, about why I was feeling so down, because I still adored Matt and I would keep our secret. I felt so alone.

Matt gradually gave up texting me, and on the second Friday after term started, he wasn't at Stagefright.

'He's at some leaving thing with his school friends,' Meg said, when I hinted at the subject. 'He probably won't be here next week either because he goes to uni the next morning.'

That was it. He was gone. No texts, no goodbyes, and no one to blame but myself. The school days were routine, passing like clockwork, already counting down to the next half-term break with no word from him. Just as Meg had said, he was not at Stagefright the following week. Without my Matt, my Romeo, everything was dull.

Mum wondered why I was slow, quiet, lost in thought, but she knew better than to ask. I went to bed unusually early that night, feeling doubly shitty. It was over. He was going to uni. He'd forget me in a week. I may never see him again.

I was seconds from falling asleep when my phone vibrated. Snatching it up instantly was now a habit, and my heart pounded against my ribs when I saw it was from Matt.

Matt Williams: I'm leaving tomorrow.

Not a question, not an invitation. No requests or demands or pleas. No kisses. Just a fact. I wished and wished it wasn't true.

I clicked to type a reply, but I couldn't think of anything to say. *I miss you. I don't want you to go. I wish we were still together.* But I couldn't admit these things to him. No words would make him stay.

I switched off the phone, turned off the light, and cried myself to sleep.

SCENE 23: MATT, 18

I checked my phone. She hadn't replied.

'You should take your GCSE certificates,' Mum was saying, having emptied the contents of a drawer onto the kitchen table. 'You might need them if you apply for a part-time job. But remember, your studies come first.'

We had spent the day playing suitcase Tetris, squeezing boxes and bags into the car. It had been a struggle to keep the back window clear enough to see out of while also giving myself enough legroom to drive, but, at ten at night, we had finally locked the car doors.

Mum was anxiously checking and re-checking the house for anything we could have forgotten while Dad went to bed, exhausted. I sat on the sofa and tried to relax, but all I could feel was a pang of sickness, thinking about moving to Lancaster the next day.

'Do you think you'll need your birth certificate?' Mum said. 'I'm sure that can stay.'

'Maybe you should take it. Two forms of ID, you know.'

Eventually she went to bed too, though not before unlocking the car to squeeze some extra knives and forks in. I promised her I wouldn't be up late, but I was stuck on the sofa, looking around the house that had been turned upside down from packing, wondering where I'd be this time tomorrow, who I'd be with, and what I'd be doing.

I checked my phone again. Still no answer and it was one o'clock now. Brooke wasn't going to reply. I was leaving and she was staying, and she'd probably never speak to me ever again. So far there was no sign she had told anyone our secret, which was a relief. But I hated how we'd left things between us. Thinking of her made me ache.

I lay down on the sofa, remembering a month earlier when she'd lain here with me. Back when uni had seemed distant.

Back when all I thought about was her. Her head on my chest. Her hand wrapped up in mine. How we could talk about anything. How proud I felt when I made her laugh. How her presence alone dispelled all my worries, my fears, and filled me instead with a feeling like no other. It was like nothing I'd ever experienced before. She was like nobody I'd ever met. Was this really how things were going to end for us?

I went out the front to check the car full of stuff hadn't been stolen. The streetlights were still on. I walked to the end of the driveway, my eyes adjusting to the dim light; the end-of-summer night air was surprisingly warm, and the tops of the trees were swaying overhead. I walked back to the house, took a deep breath, grabbed Mum's keys, locked the front door, and started walking.

SCENE 24: BROOKE, 14

A tapping noise woke me up. I checked my clock, glowing against the dark: twenty past one. I rolled over. Maybe I imagined it.

Tap. Tap. Tap. My head was heavy on my pillow and my brain too exhausted to try to figure out what the sound was. It was close, I could tell that much.

Tap. Tap. Tap. I groaned and switched on my bedside lamp. As my eyes adjusted to the brightness, I realised the sound was coming from my window. Between taps, I could hear lower thumps too, as if something was hitting the wall…as if someone was missing the glass.

I opened my curtains. The orange burn of the streetlights flooded the back garden: Mum's perfectly tended flowers, the old swing, the rusty garden furniture…and a boy. Matt. In my back garden. Tossing pebbles.

A rush of excitement shot through me. *He's here.*

He went to throw another one, then saw me, and failed to suppress his smile. I forced a stony expression and opened the window.

'Matt,' I hissed, so as not to wake up my family, 'how did you get into my garden?' My voice cracked a little with excitement, and I hoped it seemed like it was more just from weariness.

'Climbed over the gate,' he hissed back.

'What are you doing?' I ran my fingers through my hair to subtly check for bedhead.

He stood there, almost pathetically, with nothing to say, nothing to offer. Apparently, he hadn't planned this part. Then he looked around cautiously.

'Is your mum asleep?'

'Yes.'

'Is Amy?'

'Yes,' I groaned.

'Hold on, I'm coming up,' he said.

'No, Matt!'

'Why not?'

'Well…what if they wake up?'

He paused for a second. 'Well, you come down then.'

I sighed with false reluctance. 'Fine.' I closed the window and grinned. My heart was pounding and adrenaline was pumping through me. The thrill was back. He was back.

I threw on a top, shorts, and sandals, and was grateful I had shaved my legs earlier. Our floorboards were unforgiving. Over the years I had figured how to minimise creaking: move slowly, spread out your weight, avoid that loud spot at the top of the stairs. I headed out the back door and slowly approached the boy in the garden.

I stood there, holding myself, rubbing my arms even though it wasn't cold. I didn't know if I should look at him, or how to act. He kept staring at me, smiling stupidly, saying nothing.

I glanced at him nervously. 'What do you want, Matt?' My gaze dropped to the ground, and I was almost tearful. The mask I'd been maintaining was slipping away, and the fact he was leaving was killing me.

'I'm sorry,' he said.

I looked up at him. 'I'm sorry too,' I whispered, and a tear rolled down my cheek.

He spotted it, and soothingly said, 'Hey.' He stepped closer to me, touching my chin with one hand and wiping the tear away with the other. 'Don't cry. Why are you crying?'

Helplessly, childishly, I whispered, 'Because…because this is breaking up all over again. You're leaving, and you're gonna go and get drunk and meet other girls, older, prettier—'

'Don't say that,' he said softly, pulling me into him, and it was all I had been wanting for a whole month, but it was so much sadder than I'd imagined. He kissed my head and spoke softly into my ear. 'That's not true. That's not going to happen. I promise.'

'How can you be sure you won't change your mind?'

'Because I love you,' he said.

What? I stepped away, tears frozen halfway down my face, searching for a sign of recognition in his expression that he had said anything of significance.

'I love you,' he said again.

I smiled and wiped my face. 'I love you too.' The words felt big and unfamiliar in my mouth, but they didn't sound wrong, and this night had suddenly become a fairy tale, and I didn't want it to stop.

The release from the past few weeks of loneliness left me with a sudden need, and I had to have him, to feel his lips on mine. I flung myself at him, and he was ready for it, and he picked me up at my waist and I wrapped my arms around his shoulders and kissed him.

We kissed for what felt like only moments, but with hindsight, it was probably much longer—until he probably felt like his arms were going to fall off. He set me down on my feet with a gentle *thud*. 'Come on,' he said, and took my hand.

'We're going somewhere?'

'Unless you want to stay here.'

I didn't.

I had never snuck out before. But it was my last night with Matt before he moved, and he had just told me he loved me, and, right then, I would have done anything for him.

I took the spare key that we kept hidden in the barbecue and locked the back door. 'Where shall we go?'

'I have an idea,' he grinned, and started walking with purpose, pulling me along. I was anxious now, but he seemed so sure of himself, and I didn't want to ruin whatever he was planning by asking questions. He was so focused, leading me down the empty roads as the streetlights started to switch off in front of us. The night air was cooling, especially on my bare legs, but Matt seemed not to feel it. His hand held mine tightly, leading me behind him, and I tried to memorise the feeling of his palm against mine. Our last few hours together.

Suddenly he said, 'Do you remember the first time we met?'

'Um...why?' I asked.

'Just tell me,' he said. His hand dropped mine and his arm came up around my shoulder.

'Well, my first day at Stagefright, I suppose.'

'No, I mean, when did we first speak?'

I realised we were heading towards the Connell Complex. Was he expecting it to be open?

'Are we going to the Complex?' I asked.

He nodded silently, still waiting for the answer to his question.

'But won't it be locked?' I continued.

He shook his head and took out some keys from the pocket of his jeans.

'How did you get those?'

'These are Mum's keys. She's on the Stagefright committee. She always has a copy.' He grinned at me cheekily, the thrill of it all. I was a world away, petrified of getting into trouble.

Matt moved ahead and went to unlock the door, activating an automatic light. I hurried over to his side in a panic, gripping his arm.

'What's wrong?'

'We could be seen!'

He smiled. 'It's two in the morning, Brooke. The only people around are too drunk to remember.'

That didn't reassure me. I kept looking round as he tried several different keys before getting the right one. He saw my worried expression as the door swung open. 'Don't you trust me?'

What was I supposed to say to that? Yes, I trusted him. I trusted him to be nice to me, to treat me well. I didn't trust him not to have an over-inflated confidence in how his 2AM schemes would turn out. I didn't trust him not to go to uni and find someone better than me.

'Yes,' I said awkwardly.

Matt led me into the dark hallway and went straight for the alarm. Here, with a door between us and the rest of the world, he was so confident. He wasn't glancing round like he would when he dropped me home. He wasn't sneaking me in through his front door, as quickly as he could. He was big, bold, brave

Matt, with nothing to be ashamed of. I could see it in the force of his fingertips as he punched in the alarm code, then turned to me with those bright blue eyes and said, 'You still haven't answered my question.'

'Sorry,' I said, 'what was it again?'

He placed his hand between my shoulder blades and started steering me through the building, turning on lights to guide our way. 'When did we first speak?' he said.

His hand was gentle on my back, but it felt like it exerted a powerful force over my body, and I shuddered. I hoped he hadn't noticed, in case he thought it was because I disliked the contact, but he must have done because he moved his hand down to hold mine.

'It was probably the showcase before *Romeo and Juliet*,' I said. Matt smiled and nodded.

He wasn't steering me up the stairs to the rehearsal room; instead, he led me through the corridors until we were outside the auditorium. He pushed the door open, and the house lights flickered on, illuminating rows and rows of red chairs facing a bare stage.

He squeezed my hand. 'What did I say to you?'

It now struck me that I had never tried to recall when I'd first spoken to Matt. I had seen him when I first joined Stagefright in January, learnt his name indirectly, possibly spoken to him when we were put in groups to devise little scenes, but I'd never tried to pinpoint one precise moment where we *met*. With Matt, I'd always been looking forward. Looking back was something I was saving for when he left.

'I have no idea,' I told him.

He took me up the steps and onto the stage. 'Yes, you do.'

Standing where we'd performed a month earlier, I looked out at all the empty seats staring back at me. The auditorium was gloomy, ghostly, and lifeless without an audience. It looked almost abandoned, its emptiness weighing down on me. Matt made everything better with another squeeze of my hand. But what would I do when he was gone?

'Brooke?'

'I don't know, Matt.'

'Try to,' he said.

I felt like he was a teacher, struggling to help me get to the right answer on my own, and I didn't like the feeling. Why was he wasting our last night together with these questions? 'Can't you just tell me?' I asked.

'I want you to remember.'

'I can't!' I snapped.

His smile vanished. He sat on the edge of the stage, his long legs dangling over the orchestra pit. 'You think this is stupid, don't you?' he asked.

I realised that I was disappointing him, that I was not playing the character he'd planned for me when he'd rehearsed this scene in his head. 'I don't,' I said. 'I just don't see why…' Then I remembered. 'Was it the Austin Powers dance?'

He grinned at me over his shoulder, and I didn't have to tell the story to remember it, because we were both playing it through in our minds.

It was a gawky sixties style dance to the Austin Powers theme song. The whole group was doing the routine, and there was a bit where Matt and Liam joined hands, and everyone did a conga line beneath their arms. In one rehearsal, I tripped over Matt's foot and went flying into the back of Lucy, who fell into the back of Callum. I ended up on the ground, clutching my nose behind the pile-up.

Matt had rushed over to my side and apologised. I apologised back over Callum's roars of laughter, and really, I wasn't hurt. It was a very unromantic way to speak for the first time, and likely that we didn't exchange any further words until we were cast as Romeo and Juliet.

'I knew you'd remember,' Matt said, coming to his feet. He started humming the Austin Powers theme song, taking my hands and dancing round shamelessly.

'Dun, dun dun, dun dun…dun!'

'Matt…'

'Doo do de doo, doo do de doo…'

'Matt…'

'I won't stop until you dance!' he said teasingly. He looked so silly, waving his arms about and doing the sixties moves. By no means was this the actual routine; he'd forgotten it, and so had I. But he was going away. I rolled my eyes and let him spin me around the stage. Maybe it could have been romantic, had it been a different song and had I not felt like such an idiot in front of all the empty seats.

He waltzed me clumsily around the stage, making up the moves as he went along. I felt like we were two kids being immature together rather than two lovers dancing at midnight, or 2AM, or whatever. It seemed like a waste of our last few hours together before he left, mucking around rather than being sincere and serious like we'd been in my garden. But he seemed to enjoy it, so I went along with it.

Matt forgot the end of the song and finished with an abrupt 'Dun, dun…dah!' He wiggled me round in time, leaning over me on the last beat, and we laughed. Then he was suddenly silent and pressed his forehead against mine. And in that moment, we both seemed to remember he was leaving.

'We should go,' he said.

I didn't want to go. Not yet. I wasn't ready for this night to end, for our time together to be over. My hand crept up to his chest to feel his heartbeat, to remind myself that he was here, that this was real, but I couldn't feel it through his shirt. So I slid my hand beneath it, moving it up until it was in the centre of his chest. I'd never touched him under his shirt before, and we both watched my hand move, as if I hadn't been controlling it, as if it was something happening *to* us. It was strange, but then I could feel his heartbeat, and I felt like I needed that. Because soon he would be two-hundred and nine miles away from me.

His top rode up over my arm, exposing a sliver of his stomach, so I pressed my elbow flat against him to let the shirt fall and cover him again. I felt his heart beat faster as I did, my arm stretching from the middle of his chest right down to just above his belt, skin on skin, uninterrupted by layers of fabric. His eyes bore into mine, and his hands moved from my back to my shoulders, stroking my arms up and down. His lips came at me and I saw his eyes close before mine did.

Beneath his shirt, my hand slid up to his collarbone, his top stretching up again, and I felt its resistance at my elbow. My free hand looped around his back, slipping down under the neck of his shirt. I loved the feel of his skin. Warm and alive in this dead, empty theatre.

His hands seemed to be as restless as mine, but not nearly so brave. They moved up and down the small of my back until they rested at the hem of my shirt, and finally, they moved under, stroking the bare skin just above my shorts. His hands moved no higher and mine moved no lower for a long time, just repeating the same safe strokes. Our bodies were pressed against each other, my arm crushed between us, and we were as close as we could possibly be. But he was leaving. No matter how present he was now, the inescapable fact that he would soon be gone dangled above us like the flickering house lights. He'd told me he wouldn't forget me. He'd told me he loved me. And he was pulling me closer, ever closer...

SCENE 25: MATT, 18

One baby step. Two baby steps. Intermittent. Alternating. A kiss on the shoulder. A shirt on the ground. Neither of us sure how far we'd take it. Both waiting for the other to say, 'Let's stop now.' But neither of us said it. Neither of us.

What the fuck just happened?

SCENE 26: BROOKE, 14

*D*id that really just happen?
 We had left the stage and moved to the dressing rooms, daunted by the two hundred empty seats, the four hundred invisible eyes that stared at us. And now I found myself on the sofa, tangled in Matt's arms, our clothes strewn all over the floor like confetti.

You had sex. You had sex for the first time. You're not a virgin anymore. I hadn't expected us to go all the way, and maybe he hadn't either. I thought we were just trying stuff. It wasn't something I'd actually considered doing. Had I actually wanted it to happen? I must have, because I didn't stop it, and I guess I'd felt okay about it at the time.

But it had hurt. I hadn't expected it to. Matt had seen me flinch, but I dismissed his worries. I had told him I was fine, and bit my lip.

'I love you,' he had said, and he'd kept saying it, over and over again, as if he thought I hadn't heard him before. 'I love you. I love you. I love you.'

He pressed his lips to my cheek for a long time, and I could hear his breathing in my ear, but I couldn't look at him. I stared at the ceiling, holding down the feeling that something was wrong, terribly wrong. Shamefully, my eyes started to fill with the tears I had held back when I'd felt the sting between my legs. I pulled away from him, standing up, and was surprised to feel my knees trembling.

I was naked, and he could see all of me, parts of me I'd never even seen. Suddenly frantic, I was desperate to get my clothes back on, struggling to find my underwear. As I clipped on my bra, I felt his eyes on me, not looking at my body, but at my face. I couldn't meet his gaze. Out of the corner of my eye, I saw him slowly following my lead, putting his boxers and jeans back on. But he still kept his eyes on me.

I now had my underwear and shorts on but couldn't find my top. He picked it up and held it. 'Brooke,' he said, and I was forced to meet his gaze.

Without his shirt on I could see his shoulders were wide, his arms big and hairy. He didn't look like the boys in my year at school, skinny and pale; he looked like a man. *What do I look like?*

Slowly he approached me. He put his arms around my shoulders and pressed my body into his, and for a brief moment I was possessed by the urge to push him off me and run into the street in my shorts and bra, run so far that he could never find me again. It passed, and I reminded myself that he loved me, and that meant he could never hurt me, so I rested my head on his chest as the tears defeated my efforts to hold them back.

'Everything's okay, isn't it?' I asked.

Silence.

'Matt?' I said, reaching for his reassurance. 'We're okay, right?'

He didn't say anything for a long time. When he finally spoke, he said, 'What have I done to you?'

'What?' I asked. My tears stopped in their tracks, and I pulled away to look at him. Now he was the one who couldn't meet my eyes. He turned away, dropping my shirt on the floor. 'Hey,' I said urgently, taking him by the wrists and bringing him back to face me. I touched his cheeks with both hands and said, 'Look at me.'

He did, and I saw a vulnerability in him that I'd never seen before. He looked helpless and frightened, and it scared me. 'What are you talking about?' I asked.

After a long pause, he said, 'I've hurt you.'

I felt a lurch in my stomach, thinking he had seen through my lie, that it hadn't hurt, that it felt good. 'No, you haven't,' I insisted, a little unconvincingly.

'Not physically,' he said, and I realised he had believed me. 'I've...I've done something terrible.'

'What do you mean?' I asked, but I knew what he meant, because I felt it too: the feeling that something bad had just happened, and that the whole night was ruined, the whole summer spoiled.

'I've taken your virginity, haven't I?' he said. 'I've taken it and now I'm pissing off to uni...and you're so...I should have been...'

He fell into silent sobs. I couldn't let this happen. I couldn't let this be the way the story went. I took a deep breath. 'You haven't taken anything. I gave it to you. Just like you...' I drifted off.

'What?'

'I mean, was it...did you give me yours, too?'

He seemed confused. 'What do you mean?'

'I mean, was that your first time, too?' I asked slowly, tentatively. He nodded, and I felt relieved for some reason. Maybe the score was even between us.

'Then...then we're just two people who did something... something good, and special...but nobody else would get it. That's all.' The words felt awkward as I said them, but they were comforting, so I chose to believe them.

'They...wouldn't...understand...' Matt was speaking disjointedly, as the words came to him one by one. '...what we have,' he finished.

'We were responsible about it. We used a...we used protection.'

'Yeah,' he said, and we were both reminded of the condom he had taken from his jeans pocket and put on. It suddenly struck me that he had been prepared for this. *Did he plan for this to happen?*

'No,' he said, when I asked him. 'Of course I didn't. Simon gave it to me today when I said goodbye to him. A leaving present for uni.' He saw my worried face. 'A joke present.'

I wasn't sure if I believed him. An hour before, I would have believed anything he said to me. 'It's a bit convenient,' I said tentatively.

'Honestly, Brooke, I wasn't expecting this to happen. I'm sorry if I made you feel...I'm so sorry...'

His head fell into his hands again, and I felt a rush of guilt for doubting him. *He loves you,* I reminded myself. *He loves you and he's crying. You only just got back together. You've got to fix this.*

I reached for his hand. 'Let's not be sad,' I said. 'You're going soon. Let's enjoy this time. Tonight was special. It was romantic. Wasn't it?'

He looked up at me and nodded half-heartedly.

'I love you,' I said.

'I love you,' he said back, and we wrapped our arms around each other and held each other tight.

It wasn't how I had hoped my first time would go. But I had taken a piece of him to keep forever, and he had taken a piece of me. Maybe it had hurt, maybe we were careless, and perhaps we weren't quite ready. But I was fourteen and in love, and an older boy had wanted to have sex with *me*.

Matt picked up my top and put it on me, pulling it over my shoulders. He located his T-shirt and handed it to me, and I realised he wanted me to put it on him. Since we had undressed each other, it seemed to make sense to re-dress each other. He had to get onto his knees for me to fit the shirt over his shoulders, and we laughed, and from his kneeling position he put his hands on my legs and kissed me.

Silently, he took my hand and led me out onto the stage, down the steps, and through the corridors, turning off lights as he did. He locked the door and looked at me, as if we'd just locked up our secret. It was ours now, and it could never be stolen; ours until we died.

He checked his phone. 'Shit,' he said, 'let's get you home.'

'Why? What time is it?'

'Nearly four.'

He snatched up my hand and we started running, the silence of the night broken only by the pounding of our feet, the cold broken by our sweat. Our adrenaline was pumping and suddenly we were smiling, and I loved this feeling, as if I was running away with my impossible lover; Juliet running away with her Romeo.

We arrived back home far too quickly and had to say goodbye far too soon. From the back garden, my house seemed peaceful, and no one seemed to have noticed I'd gone. I went to the barbecue to grab the spare key again and unlocked the door.

I looked at him and wanted to speak, but the right words weren't there and I feared the wrong ones would ruin what we'd just stitched back together. He took me in his arms and looked down at me.

'I'll be back soon,' he promised. I nodded, blinking away the tears that stung in my eyes for the third time that night. He kissed me for a long time.

'I love you,' he said again.

'I love you too,' I said back.

'Go,' he whispered, but didn't let me go. I ended up having to push his hands off my forearms. I stepped inside, looked back at him, and didn't blink until the door was closed.

Inside the house I sighed, full of sadness and exhilaration and misery and joy all at once. But now he was gone, the adrenaline crashed, and I realised how tired I was, and how badly my stomach ached. I knew I'd regret not spending every second I could with him, but I couldn't go out and see him again. We had said goodbye and now we had to learn to live without each other.

Just before I slumped beneath my bed covers, I went to the window and looked out. He was still there. He was sitting on the swing, looking down at the ground, slowly hovering back and forth. I thought about trying to get his attention, but he didn't know I was watching, and he might not want me to see him like that. I just stole a few moments, staring at the back of his head, his hair, his clothes, memorising how he looked. Then I fell into bed and tried not to think of how hard it would be to get up in a few hours' time.

SCENE 27: MATT, 18

I sat on that swing in the cold for ages, maybe hours, thinking about the messy night just gone and the daunting day ahead of me. When I realised the sun would be rising soon, I got up and went home. I walked in through the front door at six, and there was a horrible surprise waiting for me: Mum was up.

I stopped myself from actually swearing aloud.

'And where *exactly* have you been?'

'I…Mum…'

'I've been up for *two hours*,' she said slowly, allowing every word time to settle firmly on my eardrum. 'Your phone was here. You didn't take it with you.'

'I—'

'Can you *imagine*,' she went on, 'how terrified I was to wake up to your lack of snoring? It is *every mother's nightmare* to find their child's bed empty—'

'Mum—'

'—even if you are *legally* an adult,' she continued, and I tried not to think about what I'd been doing three hours earlier. 'But if an adult is how you want to be treated, then that's how you ought to start behaving. You better have a bloody good reason for giving me the shock of my life.' Her voice wavered on the last word.

'I'm sorry, Mum. I just freaked out about…about leaving. I went for a walk.'

She hesitated, then said, with less scolding now, 'A walk?'

'A walk,' I repeated. 'I couldn't sleep. I didn't mean to scare you. I'm sorry.'

Mum looked at her slipper-clad feet for a moment. 'Yes, well…' she drifted off and forced her disciplinary mask back on. 'You'd better go back to bed for a while, since you're driving. And you probably won't be sleeping again until this time tomorrow.'

Grateful that she dropped it, I wandered upstairs, suddenly aware of my weariness. Mum was right: today would be filled with a lot of driving, unpacking, and no doubt partying. Moving to university and leaving Brooke was scary, but I pushed her to the back of my mind, knowing that if I thought about any of that I'd never fall asleep.

*

University was wild. I'd visited Lancaster on open days before, but that Saturday morning felt like I was seeing it for the first time.

I drove up the road from the real world onto the campus, thinking *I'm going to take this route every time I go into town.* I introduced myself to my housemates, thinking *I'm going to see these people every day.* I hung my clothes in the wardrobe, thinking *I'm going to call this home for the next year.*

I hugged Mum and Dad goodbye, not knowing when exactly I'd see them again. It wasn't the same as when they went away together; I'd have my familiar house with familiar friends and Brooke to invite over. Now I was alone in a strange city with strange people, and I had to look after myself.

Freshers' week was unlike anything else. It was a week to get to know the campus, meet new people, and get very, very drunk. My halls were the 'townhouses', three floors of four bedrooms, each sitting atop a kitchen with a living area. Lancaster University was one of the few in the country that was split into colleges, and I was in one called Grizedale. The flats opposite us belonged to Pendle college, who, we were told, were our rivals.

'Whenever you see a girl from those flats,' our freshers rep Natalie explained, 'you have to shout, "Pendle girls have STIs"!'

The campus was like a mini city, with little roads and shops and cafés. There was an expensive chain bookstore, a posh coffee shop, and the greasiest pizza place I'd ever seen: Pizzetta, open twenty-four hours a day in term time! I learned that the main reason for its opening times was the fact that the food was too gross to eat sober, and you had to be coming home from a night out to stomach the place.

I kept busy that first week, going to talks on university life and introductions to Chemistry. Every night my housemates would cook dinner together at six, start pre-drinking at eight, go out to the local bars or clubs at eleven and come home at four. Then we would wake up at noon the next day, eat, attend welcome talks, and do it all over again. I was having so much fun, I couldn't remember what it was that I'd been so scared of. Talking to people and making friends was easy. I forgot all about home. I didn't even reply to Mum's texts asking if I was still alive. I only had a chance to check my messages the Wednesday after I'd arrived, and I realised Brooke would be at school.

Thursday was the main student night at the union bar, Sugarhouse. It was a little place crammed with freshers, all bright lights and loud music. I sat at the bar chatting to my new best friend, Mike.

Mike was a massive metalhead, with big tattoos and hair down to his waist. His girlfriend from secondary school had ended up in Bowland college, and at about midnight she showed up with a gaggle of girls. She stayed for a drink but then took him off to dance, making me promise to join them in a minute.

My head was gone. The cumulative hangover of six nights of drinking was catching up with me, and I was pretty sure I was coming down with Fresher's flu. I decided to call it a night and was draining my lager when a voice rang out behind me.

'You haven't ordered another one, have you?'

I slammed my glass on the bar and twisted round.

The girl was beautiful. Not just beautiful, but hot, too. In a translucent top with a black bra visible beneath it, she was heavy on the necklaces which tumbled over her chest as naturally as her thick, dark locks. Her skin was tanned, but not as if she'd been to a spray place—more like she had been to the beach every day of her life. She came and sat on the barstool that Mike had vacated, her cool green eyes scanning me with a casual curiosity. From her bag she withdrew a tenner.

'Two of whatever the beautiful boy just had,' she said, in a voice that was delicate and like thunder simultaneously. It took both me and the barman a second to realise she was referring to me. I was too busy staring at her to speak. She didn't seem to mind.

The barman handed her the change. 'Thank you,' she smiled at him.

'Letmegetthat,' I suddenly blurted out, waking from my stupor and remembering my manners.

'Too late,' she grinned, pulling the strings closed on her bag and resting it on her knee. I noticed her legs, how they seemed to glisten, how smooth and long they looked beneath her black shorts.

She stuffed one lager into my hand and clinked the second against it, saying 'Cheers.' She had a long slurp, then said, 'Bleurgh. Awful stuff,' before taking another gulp.

'Why did you order it, then?' I asked.

She shrugged. 'A little game I play. Kind of like a bucket list. Try every kind of booze there is. Lager's easy; it's the cocktails that get you. Trouble is, I often can't remember which ones I've had the next day.'

She smelled of sweat, coconut, and cigarettes—like a beach party in human form. She was totally unfazed and sat in silence, observing me with her penetrating gaze.

'What's your name?' I asked.

She rolled her eyes and groaned.

'What?' I said, more curious than defensive.

'It's always that question first, isn't it? "What's in a name? Would a rose by another name not smell as sweet?"'

I smiled, briefly thinking of Brooke. '*Romeo and Juliet.* Theatre student, are we?'

'English Lit.' She took another sip of her drink before saying, 'So are *you* one of those geeky Drama students then?' I thought that was a bit harsh, and it must've shown, because she said, 'Sorry, it's the pisswater talking.'

'I'm not studying Drama. I'm Chemistry—'

'Much less geeky.'

'—but I guess you could call me a drama geek,' I said jokingly, trying to keep it light.

'Hey, don't be offended,' she said. 'I called you "beautiful boy" earlier, remember?'

I laughed, unsure if I was meant to thank her, compliment her back, or deny it. She went on before I had to figure it out.

'So, beautiful boy—'

'It's Matt.'

'—I don't care. Tell me about yourself.'

I hesitated. 'Um, alright.' I sat upright on my stool and turned to face her a bit more. 'I'm from Bristol.'

She looked at me, in an *is-that-it* kind of way.

'I'm studying Chemistry.'

'You already said that,' she said, deadpan.

'But, like I said, I'm a theatre geek—'

'Oh my god, then *please* give me some drama!'

'Well, what do you want to know?'

'Tell me *real* stuff about you. Whether you ever broke a bone, or your childhood best friend died, or if you smoke or not, or if your lifelong dream is to climb Mount Everest. Stuff that actually counts. You know.'

I didn't. 'You think that stuff really counts?'

'Of course! Do you have a disconcerting fondness for liquorice allsorts, have an unhealthy obsession with Vaseline, overuse the word "basically" or struggle to spell "favourite"?'

'Look, I—'

'Are you a cat or a dog person? Where's somewhere you really want to go? What's the long number on the front of your debit card?' she smirked.

I looked at her looking at me expectantly, and broke down laughing, literally knocking my head on the bar and nearly spilling my drink. It would've probably hurt a lot more without that second lager, and suddenly I was grateful towards… towards… whatshername.

More like whatsherlegs. Her hips. She had an hourglass figure and a half, and throughout my conversation with her I found my eyes moving to the outline of her body, at how masterfully it curved in and evened out in all the right places.

'I'll go first, then,' she grinned, and I noticed that, on her bottom jaw, one of her front teeth overlapped the other: an imperfection which made her seem all the more perfect. 'One. I've never broken a bone, had a blister, nor a nosebleed.

'Two. My dad ran off when Mum got pregnant, and she died when I was little. My Aunt Lyd brought me up until she got a new boyfriend when I was thirteen, and then I brought myself up really.' She drained her glass.

'Whoa,' I began, 'that sounds—'

She held up a finger to silence me as she swallowed. 'Three. I don't do sympathy. Can't take it, can't dish it out. Even if you tell me that your parents had a rough divorce and your pet cat died in a plane crash. Gonna be ziltch, beautiful boy.

'Four. I'm a lightweight.' She seized my drink and took a large gulp, then slammed the glass back down on the bar and said, 'Not sorry.' I had to laugh.

'And five, I sleep in the nude,' she finished, and I wished she'd said anything else. She smirked, knowing full well the image she'd put in my head. 'Your turn,' she said after a second.

'Okay,' I twisted my stool so I was facing the dancefloor, my ankle brushing against hers. 'I was once a Christmas pudding in the school play.'

'Nice,' she said. 'Good start. Two?'

'God. Jeez. Um…I love The Elder Scrolls—'

'NOPE. Generic. Not factable enough.'

'I'm a big fan of—'

'BORING.'

'Salt and vinegar—'

'Mark!'

'It's Matt.'

'You can do better than that.' She reached over and trailed her fingertips over my wrist.

'Okay. Okay,' I sat up. 'Alright. I've never watched the *Star Wars* films.'

'Eh! There we go. Something to be ashamed of!'

We sat there for twenty minutes, her touching my arm at convenient intervals and me shielding myself with my empty glass, until she'd dug deep enough to find facts worthy of sharing.

'Three, I thought "vinegar" was pronounced "viligar" for the longest time. Four, I'm scared of snakes.'

'And five?'

'Er…can't think of anything.'

'Can't think of anything, or can't *stop* thinking about me sleeping in the nude?'

I laughed awkwardly, and took a sip of my drink, before realising there was nothing left in it. She let the silence drag on, and I knew I'd have to be the one to break it.

'What can I say?' I said slowly. 'It's a nice image.'

'KAYYYYYLEEEEEEEIIIIGHH!' A very drunk girl with a nose ring that was half falling out came over and looped her arm around who I now assumed was Kayleigh. 'Can we go to Pizzetta? I want cheesy chips!'

'Where's Miriam?' Kayleigh said.

'She went home with some hairy Grizedale guy.' Kayleigh's friend was swinging on her heels; her eyes fell on me. 'Unlike this fella! You taking him home, Kay?'

'Not tonight,' Kayleigh said. 'Let's go to Pizzetta.'

'Meet me in the smoking area,' her friend said, tripping over herself as she went.

Kayleigh got up to leave, and I noticed that I didn't want her to. She turned to me with those piercing green eyes. 'Want my number?' she said.

I gulped. 'I mean, sure.' *This is friendly, right? She's just being friendly. I've added a million people on Facebook since I got here. This is the same thing.*

I handed her my phone. She typed in her number and gave it back. 'Message me,' she smiled, 'we can grab a drink.'

'Ooh,' I said suddenly, 'not sure about that one.'

'You don't want to go out?'

'Well, I imagine my girlfriend might be a bit miffed if I did.' Kayleigh glared at me. 'Your *girlfriend?*'

'Um,' I gulped, 'yeah.'

'Is she here?' She indicated the room.

'No. Back in Bristol.' I cleared my throat. 'Year below.'

'So, to be clear, you've let me sit here and chat you up for twenty minutes while you have a *girlfriend?*'

'Um,' I said.

'You're hitting me with all this flirty banter, me sleeping naked.'

'I mean—'

'And then you save my number in your phone?'

I sighed. 'It doesn't look great.'

'No, it doesn't.'

'I thought you were being friendly.'

'Sure you did.' With a twist of the head, she was gone, her brown locks swaying down her back as she marched off.

Nice one, mate, I said to myself, flopping back on my barstool. I looked at the screen. *Kayleigh Sugarhouse*, she'd saved herself as. I figured I wouldn't be texting her anytime soon. I checked my notifications. One new message. From Brooke, hours earlier: *Miss you. How's it going? xxx*

I felt a surge of guilt. I had been so busy I'd hardly thought of Brooke since I'd got to Lancaster. I'd certainly not been thinking of her for the last half hour. But I hadn't been flirting—well, not deliberately. And whatshername—I mean, Kayleigh—must've been less sober than she acted, or else she would never have shown interest in me. She was way out of my league.

SCENE 28: BROOKE, 14

I missed Matt so much. That summer, all those days we had been lying on his sofa, we'd never talked about being in a long-distance relationship. We'd never planned how to make things work when he went away. I was figuring out how to cope with it all. It was much harder than I thought.

He was so busy at university, and I understood that, but it didn't make it any easier. He could keep busy, but I couldn't go clubbing, drinking, or to lectures. He had all these new people to meet, new activities to distract himself with, while I was stuck in the same boring school with the same boring people doing the same boring subjects.

Despite his reassurance, I was always scared he would find another girl there. Someone taller, older, prettier. The teenage boys in my year were hardly a threat Matt had to worry about, but the first-year girls at his university would be confident, sophisticated, and so much less insecure than I was. They were there with him, and I was here alone. Surely he'd forget about me.

'What's up?' Lucy asked me, when she caught me looking sad. I wished I could just tell her the truth, how I had fallen in love and had sex and coped with the pressure of keeping it all a secret. If I could just tell her I was missing someone who was so far away and who I thought had forgotten about me, then maybe she and I could reconnect. Maybe she could support me, and I could feel like I still had friends. But everything that had happened with Matt felt like a huge, invisible barrier between us.

'Not much, you?'

I was checking my phone constantly, waiting to hear from him. I didn't want to pester him and was trying to let him get on with his fun. But still, I found myself staring at my lock screen, willing a message to tarnish its blankness.

'Stop checking your phone,' Mum berated me at dinnertime. I dropped it on the table and turned sadly back to the spaghetti

I was twirling around my fork. I saw Mum exchange a look with Amy in my peripherals.

'Everything okay, Brooke?' she said, gentler this time.

'Mm hm,' I nodded.

Even Callum could tell that something was up with me. 'What's got you so quiet, Brookers?' he said as we walked to school together. 'Someone bothering you? Need me to beat them up?'

I finally heard from Matt at the end of Freshers' week.

Matt Williams: Hey, Brooke, how are you?

I was so excited to see the notification come through on my phone. I typed back right away, wanting to catch him while he wasn't busy.

Brooke Tyler: Good thanks, how about you?

It took him a while to reply.

Matt Williams: Good thanks
            Been really busy
            Sorry I haven't had a chance to speak to you, it's all
            been so hectic

Brooke Tyler: Don't worry about it
            I've missed you

Matt Williams: I miss you too!

Brooke Tyler: Awh ☺ What's it like there?

Matt Williams: It's great, just so busy
            So many new people, my housemates are cool though

Brooke Tyler: Found a pretty girl yet?

Matt Williams: I have, but she's back in Bristol
            What's her name… Brenda? Brooke? Something
            like that

Brooke Tyler: Awh ☺
        You're really slow at replying, is your WiFi bad?

Matt Williams: Don't think so, sorry Brooke
        I'm trying to sort myself out for the first day of
        lectures tomorrow

Brooke Tyler: Oh, okay
        Don't let me distract you ☺

Matt Williams: Thanks for understanding
        Gotta go, dinner's ready
        My flatmate Mike made us toad in the hole

Brooke Tyler: Oh ☹ *Okay*
        Speak tomorrow?

Matt Williams: Yeah, I'll try
        Love you xxx

Matt was gone before I could say goodbye. I had tried to keep it light; I hadn't wanted to let on how much I was missing him. He seemed to be doing just fine without me.

A few days later, he messaged again. The conversation seemed like a repeat of the previous one, two actors reciting lines.

Matt Williams: Hi, Brooke, you alright?

Brooke Tyler: Yeah ta, you?

Matt Williams: Yeah, thanks
        A little hungover 😵
Brooke Tyler: Oh, my ☺

I pretended the thought of him going out and getting drunk didn't bother me, but it did, like at his birthday barbecue, when everyone started acting differently. Matt had seemed mostly himself that night. But that was before we got together, before he moved away. What would he be like now that he had this new grown-up life that I wasn't a part of?

Matt Williams: Been up to much?

Brooke Tyler: Meh, school.
          Stagefright
          We're just doing random workshops at the moment
          You?

Matt Williams: Lectures, going out
          That's it really 😄

Brooke Tyler: Found a replacement for me yet?

Matt Williams: Don't be silly, I'm not looking for a replacement ☺

Brooke Tyler: Just checking 😄

Matt Williams: Sorry Brooke, I have to go to class, speak soon ♥

Gone again.

I used to delete his messages in case Mum went through my phone and found out about us. But now I saved every one of them. I needed reassurance that what we had was real. I needed to read 'Love you xxx' over and over again. I'd fall asleep re-reading our texts, or else flipping through the same one hundred and thirty-seven photos of him on Facebook, trying to remember the feel of his arms around me.

He finally messaged again at the end of his second week away.

Matt Williams: Hey, Brooke

Brooke Tyler: Alright Matt?

Matt Williams: Yeah, alright thanks
          Tired
          And I've had so much to do

Brooke Tyler: Awh, what are you busy with?

Matt Williams: Chemistry! Haha
          You been up to much?

Brooke Tyler: Not done much really
          Missing you

Matt Williams: You too beautiful ☺
    Sorry Brooke, I've got to go to the library

Brooke Tyler: To meet some chemistry girl you had chemistry with...?

Matt Williams: Come on Brooke
    This is getting old
    Don't you trust me?

Brooke Tyler: I do trust you
    I'm sorry

Matt Williams: It's okay
    I just can't have you worrying all the time

Brooke Tyler: I know but it's hard not to
    You're so busy with your new life but nothing's changed
    for me
    And I just spend so much time worrying that I'll lose
    you

Matt Williams: I'm sorry Brooke
    I really have to go
    But just remember that I love you and you're not
    going to lose me
    ♥ *xxxxxxxxxxxxx*

Matt used to be my distraction from school. Now, school was my distraction from him. The feeling of missing him filled the gaps between seconds and was heavy in my chest. When would I see him again? Was he ever going to come home and visit? By the time he came back at Christmas, would he have forgotten about me? He'd said that he loved me, but it was no comfort. I didn't feel he meant it, or I would convince myself he'd changed his mind. I wondered when a night would come that I didn't cry myself to sleep.

SCENE 29: MATT, 18

The first week of lectures was a big kick in the balls courtesy of real life. I'd definitely caught Fresher's flu and was sniffing all the way through my lecture.

'9AMs should be illegal,' Mike said later when I came home for lunch.

'Mate. Just send me the change.org petition. I'm with you.'

'Miriam's cooking at hers tonight. You should come. It'll just be a chill one.'

'Your girlfriend won't mind her boyfriend bringing along his visibly ill housemate for free food?'

'Nah. Come on mate, she's really cool. You should get to know her. You'll be seeing a lot of her from now on.'

So, armed with tissues and paracetamol, Mike and I walked through the rain across campus all the way to Bowland college, and Miriam let us in. We perched on the unmistakable cheap plastic of university halls furniture, in a kitchen that would never quite be warm enough. *I guess my coat's staying wet.*

'MIRIAM, I'm *hungry,'* her flatmate whined as she walked into the room. I thought I recognised her nose ring, but her present sobriety made her hard to place.

'Ten minutes,' Miriam chimed.

The flatmate's eyes fell on me, and then Mike, and a rush of recognition flooded her face. 'Mir Mir, you've invited the hairy Grizedale boy you hooked up with to dinner!'

'Hairy Grize—that's my *boyfriend,* Priyanka.'

'Hi, I'm Mike,' Mike said, getting up and offering a handshake.

'The guy you hooked up with four days ago is now your *boyfriend?'* Priyanka said.

'We didn't hook up Pri, we've been together two years.'

Mike was still standing, arm extended, hand still unshaken.

'I told you I had a boyfriend,' Miriam went on. 'Did you think I was just cheating on him at Sugarhouse?'

'I guess I thought you'd broken up—'

'And not mentioned it?'

'I dunno Mir, I can hardly remember that night!' Priyanka finally clocked Mike's extended hand and shook it. 'Hi, hairy Grizedale boy.'

She looked at me, and I knew she was wondering if she was supposed to remember me too. 'I'm the less hairy Grizedale boy,' I introduced myself, throwing a glare at Mike; I realised now that he'd dragged me here so he wouldn't have to face Miriam's flatmates alone. He smiled weakly.

'Alright, Mir, I'm ready to meet your boyfriend.' A second flatmate walked into the kitchen, making the boyfriend-meeting sound like a chore she wanted to get over and done with. She was tall and tanned with thick brown hair…she was… she was…

'Hi, I'm Kayleigh,' she said much more sweetly now, pulling Mike into a hug. She turned to me and her green eyes registered recognition.

'Hi Kayleigh,' I said nervously.

She looked less sexy but more human in her combat-print T-shirt and jeans, her hair lazily wrapped up in a bun. She had a lot less makeup on, but her eyes were just as piercing as the first time I saw them.

'Mark,' she said coldly.

'It's Matt,' I corrected her.

'How's the GF?' She snatched up a chair and sat opposite me.

'Yeah, fine,' I said stiffly.

'Picked up any more numbers from Sugar recently?'

My stomach churned. 'Nope,' I said.

'Pleased to hear it.' And with that, she turned her attention to Mike, being super friendly to him while blanking me for the rest of the meal. I resigned myself to eating quietly. The food was actually really good. 'I've converted four people to veganism with this curry alone,' Miriam beamed when I told her as much.

'I can't believe I didn't realise you were her man,' Pri said to Mike. 'I was sooo drunk. Though Kay, weren't you talking to a guy, too?'

'I chatted to a few people that night. Can't remember who.'

'Did you hit them with the five facts move?' Priyanka said.

'You know it,' Kayleigh replied.

'Kayleigh's such a nerd. She goes all in wanting to get to know the guy on an *intellectual* level. I'm like, just tell him he's hot and take him home!'

My heart sank. *It was a move.* A flirting trick she kept up her sleeve. It was stupid of me to have felt like it made me special in some way, even though she'd come in all confident and well-rehearsed. She must use the same five facts on everyone.

'It was so funny,' Pri was explaining to Mike, 'on the first night of Freshers, she was chatting to this Irish guy, she kept calling him "beautiful boy"!'

'Drunk me is a hopeless romantic, okay?'

'Like it was a movie or some shit! He looked so confused.'

'Hey. Fifty percent of the time, it works every time,' Kayleigh giggled. Priyanka roared with laughter. I shovelled down more curry.

Priyanka went upstairs to ring her parents and 'make sure they know I haven't died.' Mike and Miriam got on the sofa, flicking through Netflix on her MacBook. Kayleigh went out for a cigarette. I followed her through the rain to the designated smoking area, a patch of concrete under a plastic canopy.

'Want one?' she offered begrudgingly, after I had stood next to her for a few seconds.

'No thanks,' I cleared my throat. 'I wanted to apologise. About the other night.'

'The one you should be apologising to is your girlfriend,' she said. 'Did you tell her what happened?'

'No. And I don't think she needs to know. I don't want to blow it out of proportion.'

She scoffed.

'I'm sorry, but you came over and started chatting me up and I had no idea what else to do except let you. I didn't want to be rude. You were laying it on *thick*.'

Kayleigh considered this for a moment. 'Okay. That's fair. Drunk Kayleigh does like to flirt.'

'It was more than flirting. That stuff about you sleeping naked.'

'And that's not even true this far north,' she said, more to herself than me. She took a puff of her cigarette. 'Alright. I take responsibility for that. But you were enjoying the attention.'

'That's fair. I guess, er…I guess I found it flattering.' I glanced at her, her green eyes burning over the tip of her cigarette. 'But I shouldn't've let it go on.'

She gave me half smile and shrugged. 'There you go.'

'And if my housemate is going out with your housemate, we'll probably be seeing a lot of each other. It'd be good for us to be friends.'

'The famous five,' Kayleigh smiled. 'I suppose we could be friends. Providing you're not a cheating asshole.'

'I have no interest in being disloyal to my girlfriend.'

'If I found out you were, I'd have to track her down and tell her. Girl code.'

'That won't happen.'

'And if what happened at Sugar happens again—not me, but someone chatting you up—then you'll tell them you have a girlfriend, immediately. Or walk away.'

'I will walk away,' I repeated.

'Because I don't like cheaters, okay?'

'I can promise I'm not a cheater.'

'Alright.' She stubbed out her cigarette and binned it. She offered me her hand. 'Friends?'

I shook it. 'Friends.'

SCENE 30: BROOKE, 14

Every Thursday morning, first period, we had 'Learning' lessons. 'Surely every lesson is learning,' was a common criticism of the subject.

As it turned out, 'Learning' was just PSHE. This term we were beginning Relationships and Sex Education. The first week was as expected, watching videos made twenty years ago of people discussing their first times. I didn't need this.

The next week focused on contraception. This was where I was not so informed. When the subject came up, I told myself that we'd used protection, that we were fine, and I brushed it aside. Miss Johnson handed out information sheets about how to put on a condom to giggling boys whilst rolling her eyes. I hadn't even looked at how Matt had put it on. But surely he knew how to do it properly.

We learnt about a common type of contraception known as 'the pill' which could be taken to stop pregnancy. 'But,' Miss Johnson emphasised, 'it won't protect you from sexually transmitted infections, and you have to take it correctly for it to work.' I wondered how you could take a pill incorrectly.

We progressed to the A-Z of Sex and Relationships, which involved video clips of experts and doctors and almost-celebrities boring us with personal experiences and scientific opinions on everything from 'Asking Out' to—get this—'Zones'. Miss Johnson then led what was meant to be a group discussion but, when the boys showed no intention of taking it seriously, turned into a lecture.

'The *most important thing* to know about sex,' she said, 'is consent.' She had told us many times before that she used to be a prison officer, and now she showed it, listing off memorised laws. 'Manual or oral sex without consent is sexual assault. So is kissing, touching of buttocks, and touching of the female breast. Penetration by a penis of a mouth, anus, or vagina, without consent, is rape.' The word 'anus' caused a huge roar of laughter from the boys at the back of the class.

'Consent is characterised by a verbal, enthusiastic, continuous "yes." You should have no doubt in the world that what you're doing is what your partner *wants* to do. Remember, it's not their responsibility to stop you—it's your responsibility to ask. A simple, "Are you alright with this?" will work just fine. And you need consent for every single different activity you do. Just because someone consents to one thing doesn't mean they consent to another. And just because they consented before doesn't mean they consent again. Check, check, and check again—*verbally.*'

I swallowed the lump that rose in my throat. Matt hadn't checked in with me. I hadn't checked in with him. Of course, we would have stopped if either one of us had wanted to. But neither of us said anything. Neither of us asked. What would he have said if I'd asked him? What would I have said if he'd asked me?

'There are times that someone can't give consent, even if they give you a verbal "yes",' Miss Johnson went on. 'For example, if they're drunk.'

I thought of Tilly at Matt's barbecue, upstairs in his parents' room with Liam. She'd said she was too drunk to drive. She'd been spilling her drink.

'If they're unconscious or asleep, then they certainly cannot consent. If they give consent and *then* fall asleep, you have to stop. Even if you're in a relationship. Even if you're married.

'The age of consent is sixteen. Therefore, people below the age of sixteen cannot give consent to sexual activity of *any* kind. If someone has sex with an underage person, then that is always statutory rape.'

I sat up. *Was that true? Was it rape if I was too young?*

'If someone has power over another person,' Miss Johnson went on, 'then sex should not be involved in their relationship. For example, a therapist and a client, a doctor and a patient, or a teacher and a student—' The boys laughed again.

It hadn't been rape. I had consented—maybe not in the opinion of the police, but I'd been okay with it, I hadn't stopped it, and it had been magical, romantic lovemaking, it wasn't...

'A person in a position of trust cannot engage in a sexual relationship with someone entrusted to them, regardless of age.'

Was this why Matt had been so afraid of anyone finding out about our relationship? Was this why he'd tried so hard to keep it a secret? Surely he hadn't known this stuff. He would have told me.

'Even between famous celebrities and their fans, that's a dangerous relationship to bring sex into...'

Was Matt a rapist? Could he go to prison? Would it matter if I said I was okay with it?

'...because the fan may find it hard to say "no" to someone they look up to.'

I looked around the room. Was it a room full of people who'd never had sex, except for me? I looked at the popular girls. Some of them had sixteen, seventeen-year-old boyfriends. Surely they had already...but maybe not. Maybe I was the only one.

The lesson went on, but I wasn't there anymore. I was back in the auditorium, my hand under Matt's shirt, neither of us knowing just how far we were about to go. I couldn't help but wonder, if we'd stopped then, and we'd talked about it, maybe we would've made a different choice.

*

The next Thursday, Miss Johnson wrote on the whiteboard in all-capitals *WHY IS CONTRACEPTION IMPORTANT?*

She then tried unsuccessfully to get the class to make sensible suggestions as to what the answer could be. She ended up resorting to a lecture again.

'You can get pregnant—or get someone else pregnant—your first time.'

We used protection. I was fine.

'That goes for STIs as well.'

We used protection. I was fine.

'Even with contraception.'

I was not fine. My hand shot up too urgently.

'Brooke?'

'I…well, if…what's the point…' I didn't even know what I was going to say. What I really wanted to ask was, *is there a chance I could be pregnant? Or have an STI? How can I tell?*

'…what's the point of contraception if it doesn't work?' I finished.

She looked at me strangely, and I wondered how out-of-character I was acting. I glanced at Lucy, who was staring at me, and I glanced away.

'Contraception methods, when used correctly, will usually work in stopping conception. Barrier methods—we're talking condoms—are the only way to stop STIs. But condoms can split and leak. When used correctly, they're about ninety-eight percent effective, but the average use makes them only about eighty-six percent effective. People keep them in wallets and the like, where friction causes them to wear down. The correct way to store a condom is in a tin, like a mint tin, which will protect it from wearing down.'

Shit. Matt had kept his condom in his pocket. Could it have gotten worn down in his jeans?

'Sexually active people, or people who think they may soon become sexually active, should always carry at least two condoms in a tin with you in your bag. In case the first one breaks.'

One of the boys raised his hand. 'Miss, doesn't that just make you look really horny?' His friends giggled.

'Some people think so, but the truth is that it's just responsible.'

Yes, Matt having the condom had been responsible—not horny—

'People often use a combination of contraceptives, such as condoms and a hormonal method, to ensure they have effective protection. It's a good idea to take your sexual health into your own hands, and not rely on your partner for contraception.'

Miss Johnson started reading from her lesson plan, but I wasn't listening. All I was thinking was *I'm not safe. We weren't safe. We were careless and unprepared and* so *not ready.*

I had to ask another question. I had to know if this meant I should take a pregnancy test—or an STI test, which seemed like less of a big deal for some reason. I wondered if I should stay behind and speak to Miss Johnson, or tell Lucy that I was worried I might be pregnant, or subtly sneak the question into conversation with Mum, or go to the school's guidance centre. But no doubt one question would lead to another and another and another right up to the fact that Matt was eighteen. Then he'd get into trouble, and the school would find out, and my parents...

I raised my hand. 'Miss, when should you take a pregnancy or STI test?'

She looked at me, funnily again, and I felt my cheeks go red. 'There's no *time* you have to...'

'No, I mean—what situation would mean you should?'

'Well, you should get STI tested with every new partner you have, before you do anything with them. Remember, STIs can be passed through manual and oral sex, too. And you wouldn't necessarily know if you have one—unless you get tested. If you've had unprotected sexual contact with someone, you should get a test from your doctor. There are sexual health clinics you can go to, as well.'

Did that mean I ought to go? We'd used protection, but what she had said earlier made me think it might not have been good enough. Should I get tested? If Matt had never had sex before, could he have given me anything? Could you be born with an STI?

'Likewise, if you've had penetrative sex without contraception, you should get the morning-after pill, which can be taken up to three days after sex, or five days for some pills. But the earlier you take it, the safer you are. The morning-after pill is free for people aged sixteen and under if you get it from a chemist, or you can get it on prescription from your doctor. If you skip more than one period in a row, you should take a pregnancy test, though missing periods doesn't definitely mean you're pregnant—it can also indicate stress, or a change in diet.'

Fuck. My periods were irregular enough as it was. I had never worried about them because I knew I didn't have to yet. How would I know if I missed one? All this information, these rules, seemed so complicated. How could I keep track of all these 'ifs' and 'whens' and 'hows'? Didn't Matt know about any of this? Couldn't he…shouldn't he have warned me?

I couldn't sleep that night. My head was aching with too many thoughts. *What if I was pregnant? Would I get an abortion? Put the kid up for adoption? Be a mother?*

Brooke Tyler, fourteen-year-old mum—well, fifteen by that time. Big difference that would make. I could already hear the rumours at school. What would my friends say? What would Mum, Dad, and Amy say? What would Matt say? I'd have to tell people what'd happened. I'd have to tell people about us. Would he have to drop out of uni? Would he go to prison?

What would I name the baby? It hardly mattered, but it sprang to mind. How would I tell Matt? He seemed so far away, so grown up at university with his big dreams, too busy moving forward to turn back and look for me. I felt like an afterthought in his life. No matter how many cute texts he sent or how many times he swore he loved me, it felt like he didn't. Like I was kidding myself. Like we had never done *Romeo and Juliet* or had a secret love affair or spent that night together at the Connell Complex. When he left, something had broken between us while neither of us was looking. And now we could have a baby.

Lying in bed, I started crying. I missed him. I needed him. And I was scared shitless at the thought of how crap a mother I would be.

SCENE 31: MATT, 18

I had been at university for three weeks when I came back to Bristol for the weekend. I had a few short calls with Brooke in that time, and she'd sounded strange—perhaps a bit sad—so I decided to surprise her. I was there when she walked into the rehearsal room on Friday night, and she immediately lit up. For a moment I was struck by how young she looked, small and skinny in her school uniform. She was so excited to see me though, so I shook it off, putting it down to the fact I hadn't been around anyone younger than eighteen for the best part of a month. We were early for the session and, to my surprise, Meg left us alone together. We snuck a kiss, and she looked so happy, and it felt amazing to be reunited, but then we heard Meg's footsteps and our embrace had to end.

We were put into groups to work on sketches that night, and Stephen made me play Brooke's father, which was awkward, but we did it. At least we were acting together. At the end of the session, I gave her a friendly hug and whispered that I'd text her to arrange to meet up.

She clearly thought I meant meet up *that night*. She texted me asking what the plan was, if she should walk over like she used to or if I'd come and get her. By this point, I was already in a Chinese restaurant with Mum and Dad, who were gushing about their empty nest and asking all about uni. I told her I'd see her tomorrow, and she seemed disappointed, but agreed anyway.

The next day at noon, we met up in the fortunately empty car park outside the Connell Complex. We kissed in my car for a long, long time, awkwardly reaching for each other across the gearstick. I had missed her, the feeling of hugging her, my arm draped around her shoulders as we lounged on my sofa—but as it was Saturday, Mum and Dad would be roaming the house. Instead, I drove Brooke into the city centre, away from the people we knew in our little hometown, and took her to lunch at an Italian place.

'If anyone asks,' I said to her, 'you're my cousin.'

She looked at her feet for a moment, then came back with a smile. 'Either that, or we don't speak English. Parlez-vous le francais?'

'Er…nein,' I laughed. Over pizza she asked me how university was, and I launched into detailing everything that had happened since I last saw her. I told her about my flatmates, my halls, my course—though I deliberately left Kayleigh's name out of it. Brooke smiled and nodded along, asking about Lancaster right up until dessert. When I asked her what she'd been up to, she shrugged. 'Not much.'

I took her to see a movie. She picked a comedy, rated twelve, and I looked at her. She was tall, but was wearing bright green converse shoes, and I worried she would get asked for ID. The thought made me feel sick. *Don't be stupid,* I thought, *she's nearly fifteen.* In the queue I was self-conscious, keeping a modest distance between us, but once we were safely shrouded in the darkness of the cinema, I put my arm around her. I felt her stiffen at my touch, but then she relaxed and leaned her head on my shoulder.

As the movie started, I looked at her. She had been quiet today, looking at the floor and not talking much about herself or how she had been. Her apparent sadness on the phone was evidently more than just my imagination. I held her tighter in my arms, and she snuggled up to me, but it didn't feel like love was pulling us together; it was more like something was pushing us up against each other. I hoped that having sex had not changed things between us. Since that night, I had tried to think of it as special and romantic, but I still felt a pang of guilt about it. I promised myself that we would wait until she was sixteen before trying that again.

Two years is a long time, I thought, but pushed it away.

After the movie, I said, 'I should probably get you home.' Brooke seemed reserved, almost grumpy, and didn't say anything as we walked out of the cinema and back to my car.

'What's wrong?' I broke the silence on the motorway.

'Nothing.'

I knew I risked her exploding, but after a pause I said, 'I can tell when you're lying.'

'Now's not the time, Matt.'

'When is the time, then? Who knows when we'll get to see each other again?' She didn't say anything, so I pressed on. 'Why won't you tell me? I'm supposed to be your boyfriend.'

'Yeah, you're *supposed* to be.'

'Why are you sulking?'

'Don't patronise me!'

Silence.

'I'm sorry,' I said. I was scared of losing her again, of upsetting her.

'No, I'm sorry,' she said, touching my hand, which was resting on the gearstick. I moved it away from her and held the wheel. I didn't mean to reject her—I just wanted to focus on the road. She looked put down.

'What's bugging you?' I asked, trying to sound warm.

She responded by slumping against the passenger window.

'Brooke.'

She ignored me.

'Please talk to me.'

She sighed. 'I thought I was pregnant.'

Try not to crash the car. 'But you're not?' I asked, working hard to keep my voice calm.

She looked at me, disgusted. 'Don't sound *too* hopeful, Matt.'

'It was because you said you *thought* you were,' I said slowly, with a newfound firmness in my voice. 'And forgive me for not wanting to be a father right now. Are you telling me you're ready to have a kid?' Her silence told me her answer. I went on, trying to keep it light. 'So, why—what happened?'

After a loud sigh, she began. 'I thought...I thought that, because we used a condom, we'd be fine.' Her voice was shy and shaky. 'And in school we were doing sex education, and I freaked out when I found out that you can get pregnant even if you use defence.'

'Defence?'

'Er…protection. And then I missed my period—not that it's very regular anyway, and to be honest sometimes I can't tell if it's the real thing or if it's just spotting—'

I shuddered. 'Brooke!'

'What! I get periods! Get over it!' She was getting more and more worked up. 'So I went to this sexual health clinic which was the most humiliating experience of my life, and I couldn't bring a friend because I had to keep you secret, and I took a pregnancy test which involved handing the nurse a pot of my piss and it came up negative and I cried in front of her. And then I got my period a week later, and she told me I didn't need an STI test because you were a virgin, but that I should do one anyway because I shouldn't take your word for it.' She hid her face in her hands. She didn't say if she ended up doing one. 'I didn't know…I thought, a condom meant…you can't get pregnant.'

Relief washed over me. It had all been sorted out. 'I see. Well, yeah, you can, but it's a small chance.'

Her hands fell away from her face. 'You knew? You *knew* and you didn't tell me?'

I glanced at her briefly. 'Huh? Knew what?'

'That condoms aren't one-hundred percent effective?'

'Yeah. Everyone knows that.'

She scoffed. 'I didn't! *I didn't!* I can't believe you didn't tell me before you—before we—'

She looked injured, as if I'd betrayed her. I couldn't understand why she was so upset.

'Well, most people are confident that it's good enough. No contraception is one hundred percent effective.'

She sighed, and went back to sulking, arms folded. I tried to appease her. 'I'm sorry, Brooke.'

'You should be.'

That was it. I swerved and stopped on the hard shoulder, making her cry out. For the first time, she looked frightened of me, but I couldn't deal with her being such a brat.

'For what?!'

'Well…' she started uneasily, with forced conviction. 'You… you did this to me.'

That wasn't fair. 'No, actually, I recall *you* being the one to put your hand under my shirt. And *you* were the one to take off my jeans. You wanted to do it.'

'Didn't you?'

'Yes. I wanted to, *too*. That doesn't make me the bad guy. I didn't force you.'

She was crying now, jumping from hurt to angry to defensive to apologetic. 'You were irresponsible, though,' she sobbed. 'I'm underage. You should have been the responsible one!'

'I thought we were on the same page!' I yelled. 'I thought you felt the same as me!'

'I do—'

'Shut up,' I snapped. I was angry and she was upset, and it was sad to see, but I had to stand up for myself. She had been fine with what happened. She was just changing her mind *now* to pick a fight.

'I—I'm s-sorry, Matt,' she sobbed.

'No you're not.'

'Well, it's st-statutory rape!'

I felt like I'd been kicked in the stomach. She'd actually said it out loud. I looked at her with burning eyes. 'You don't really think that's what it was?'

'It's not what I think, it's what the law says it is!'

I sighed. 'Sex ed?'

She nodded.

I rubbed my eyes. 'I thought you'd had more sex ed than that.'

'Why? Are you telling me *you* knew it was statutory rape before now?'

'It wasn't rape!'

'In the eyes of the law!'

'Yes!' I screamed. Not at her, but at the situation, at the windscreen, at the cars whizzing past. 'Yes, I knew it was illegal! But I thought you knew too, and you didn't care! I thought we both agreed. We said shit like the rest of the world wouldn't get it, that it's different for us. I thought you knew…' I drifted off.

She was silent. I barked at her, 'Are you telling me you wouldn't have done it if you knew?'

After a pause, she said, 'Maybe not.'

'Don't lie to me.'

'Out of fear for you! You getting into trouble, getting arrested! And don't tell me that's a lie. Out of consideration for you,' she said again, quieter now.

'I could only be arrested if *you* pressed charges,' I said, and instantly regretted it, because then we were both thinking the same thing. The silence went on and on like the end credits of a film.

Then she said, 'Who's Kayleigh?'

I wanted to punch the wheel. 'She's my friend!' I exploded. 'We're just friends! What's your problem? Why don't you trust me?'

'I do—'

'Again with the lying! We're going round in circles. We're getting nowhere!' The cars speeding past seemed to echo my shouting. I had never been this angry before.

'I saw the photos on Facebook,' she went on.

'What photos?' I snapped.

'The Freshers' ball.'

'So what? What's wrong with that?' I was tired of her paranoia, her constantly bringing up irrelevant things just for something to throw at me. 'It was only a ball. She's my friend. What did you think? I'd drive down and pick you up and dance with my fourteen-year-old girlfriend in front of everyone?'

Her sobs had dissolved into silence.

'It was only a ball,' I said again.

'I can't believe you just said that,' she said.

The credits dragged on. She unclipped her seatbelt and got out of the car.

'Brooke,' I said, frantically unbuckling myself and rushing out after her without closing the door behind me.

She was standing at the edge of the hard shoulder, the wind whipping her hair around violently. Her fingers scratched at her face, trying to push the hair out of her eyes.

I raced to her side. 'Brooke, get back in the car.'

'No,' she said stubbornly. She gave the cars that zoomed past a thumbs up, apparently hoping someone would pull over on this seventy-mile-an-hour stretch and let her hitchhike her way home.

I reached for her shoulder, but she shook me off. 'Get off me.'

'I'm not letting you get in a car with a stranger.'

Silence.

'Brooke, please get back in the car.'

'*No,*' she said again. She was edging closer and closer to the lanes, and my heart dropped as I dove for her wrist to yank her back. She tugged her arm away from me as a car sped past, its horn screeching.

'Don't touch me!'

'*You're too close!*' I yelled in her face.

I let her go, and she turned to the road but stayed back. I stood and watched her as she stared at the cars, my whole body numb except for my thundering heartbeat, ready to grab her if I had to, if she launched herself forwards.

Eventually, she got back in the car, slamming the passenger door behind her. When I got in the driver's seat, she wouldn't look at me. We drove in silence, both of us wondering if we were breaking up, but neither of us brave enough to ask. For once, I dropped her off at the bottom of her driveway. The sky was darkening. As soon as the car had stopped, she unclipped her seatbelt and opened the door without looking at me.

'Wait, Brooke.'

She stopped on the pavement but didn't turn back to face me.

'We're still…we aren't…are we still?'

'No,' she said, slamming the door behind her.

I watched her as she stormed off, the very image of a stroppy teenager. Maybe the problem was that we both were.

SCENE 32: BROOKE, 14

When I stepped out of the car, I instantly regretted breaking up. Having some of Matt was better than having no Matt. Better than being on my own.

But as I stood at the bottom of my driveway, something kept me where I was, watching the car go as tears stung in my eyes. Something told me that it wasn't meant to be this hard. Something told me that my fairy tale had ceased to exist, maybe had never existed. He drove off, and I knew a boy would never toss pebbles at my window again.

SCENE 33: MATT, 18

It was finally over.

It had been stupid to try to be with her, and then to try to get back together with her, and then to try to do long-distance with her. She was a kid, for God's sake. What the hell had been wrong with me, to think any of this would be a good idea?

Mum dropped me at the train station on Sunday night. She looked just as sad as she had done when she'd left me in my university halls.

'I'll be back soon, Mum,' I said, but I wasn't sure if that was true. Without Brooke, there was little reason for me to return before Christmas.

Breaking up had come as a relief. At the start, things had been good. I'd liked Brooke, and she'd seemed so mature. But recently our relationship had felt like a burden, trying to keep her happy while getting on with my life. I had felt guilty that she missed me, I had felt guilty for being so far away, and I had felt guilty for what had happened in the auditorium. But *she* had been the one to convince *me* that the night had been special, and romantic, and far from something terrible. And then, to spite me for moving away, she tried to make me feel bad about it. Now she seemed so young, naïve, and bratty.

Mum gave me a watery smile as I passed through the barriers and waved goodbye. Once I was on the platform, I could breathe. The mess was over now. I could go to uni and talk to whoever I wanted and be like everybody else. Brooke couldn't make me feel guilty anymore. She had been the one to initiate things that night, anyway. She had touched my chest.

But as the train arrived and I stepped on board, I wondered if, when she had touched my chest, she had only wanted to touch my chest.

SCENE 34: BROOKE, 15

I got used to Matt being gone. We'd been apart for so long already, and I felt like I'd only been convincing myself that he loved me, so breaking up wasn't that hard to accept. Something had felt wrong about it all, the secrets, the hiding. But I still missed him, and I still thought about him a lot.

Time in my mind was marked from our relationship. For instance, Christmas was six months after we first got together. Three months after the night at the Complex. Two months and one week after we broke up. I'd hoped my first real relationship wouldn't be so messy or as short-lived as this. I'd wanted it to be special.

Matt didn't come back for weekends after we broke up— or, if he did, I never heard about them. Every time Stephen or Meg mentioned his name at Stagefright, I felt a burning in my stomach. *Romeo and Juliet*, which we started studying for English GCSE, was a nightmare. There were times I looked back on how much we'd been intoxicated by one another and the ecstasy that came with our stolen moments, and I was enchanted for a second, and then I remembered him driving away, and I came back to reality, and I carried on.

I focused on the days. On school. On rekindling my relationships with the people I used to call my friends. Things got a bit better with them, even if we weren't as close as we used to be. Every Stagefright session, I held my breath and hoped that when I walked into the room he wouldn't be there. He never was. It was a relief, if a sad one.

It didn't help that Amy was bringing Tom round all the time. They couldn't keep apart for more than five minutes. He was always coming for dinner, making polite conversation with Mum and being overly enthusiastic about her broccoli. Then they'd go upstairs, and Mum would shout after them, 'Keep that door open!' If they weren't at home they were going to the cinema, or Nando's, or driving round in Tom's car, enjoying an openness I'd never experienced.

I auditioned for Stagefright's next play, a comedy version of the Trojan war. It felt kind of juvenile after *Romeo and Juliet*, and I was struggling to concentrate. I forgot my lines in the audition. Lucy got the lead. I didn't get a speaking part.

November arrived quicker than I had anticipated, and I turned fifteen. There was cake and Amy was happy and I was okay. Mum offered to let me have a party, but I didn't want one. She had been worrying about me. I'd been quieter, she said. She invited some of the girls from school over as a surprise. We had a takeaway and watched a film. I didn't think about Matt.

Then Christmas. The obligatory call from Dad. My grandparents round for dinner. The tree was up and Amy was happy and I was okay. I didn't think about Matt. As the days passed, I started to believe I was over him. I didn't miss him anymore. My feelings had gone.

Then what on earth led to the events of New Year's Eve?

SCENE 35: MATT, 18

I t was New Year's Eve, and I was in the bathroom with my lips glued to Brooke's.

She was just fifteen, but seemed a world away from fourteen. Her mouth was soft, and she was warm, and I couldn't get enough of her. She was wearing a strappy top and a black skirt, her high heels kicked off. She looked gorgeous, beautiful, much older than fifteen.

I was in a T-shirt and some old, ripped jeans. I'd left my jacket in another room. God knows where; Callum and Lucy's house was so big, and everyone from Stagefright was there, along with a bunch of their school friends.

The clothes didn't matter. The fact they were still on did. We were just kissing, with no intent to go further. It was like when we first got together, like we'd never kept secrets or seen each other naked or had huge fights or broken up.

I remembered walking in and seeing her there, four hours earlier. I'd arrived with Stephen and Meg—we'd been late, and I'd been nervous. Everyone was in the lounge watching *Dreamgirls*, and when we walked in they all turned to greet us except for her. I could hear Callum next to her saying, 'Brookers, you okay?'

The party had progressed as the movie ended and people started drinking and music started blasting. The lights went off in the living room, making it the official dancefloor. The soberer people, including me and Brooke, seemed to get cornered together in the kitchen to make polite conversation. She was mature, and confident, and it kind of surprised me. How had she grown up so much in only a couple of months?

One by one, the sober people got picked off by the crowd and went to drink and dance. They attempted to lure both me and Brooke away, but their only success was the lone beer in my hand. Eventually, it was just the two of us.

'I've missed you,' I said, just after eleven. It was risky but true.

'I missed you too,' she replied brightly, as if it was friendly, nothing more. But the look in her eye had told me otherwise.

I'd asked her to come with me and we climbed the two— no, three—flights of stairs, and with every step her smile grew. Halfway up she took my hand and we both realised what was going to happen and neither of us wanted to stop it.

So there I was, in the middle of the bathroom, bending down to reach Brooke, my arms surrounding her like a fort. I hadn't realised how much I'd missed her, missed this. Every time she'd crossed my mind since we broke up, I'd thought our relationship hadn't made any sense, and now that I was with her, she was the only thing that made sense.

I remembered Mum picking me up from the train station at the start of the holidays. She'd flung her arms around me and smooched the side of my face.

'Hi, Mum,' I said, my voice muffled by her shoulder as she wrapped her arms around my neck.

'Never go away from me again!' she grinned, pulling back and patting me on the cheek. As she scooped up one of my bags, she said, 'Gramps is coming for Christmas. You don't mind sleeping on the sofa for one night?'

My bedroom had already been usurped. I had to laugh. 'No, I don't mind,' I said.

I was now sitting on the cold floor, my back against the glass shower door, my body twisted to face Brooke, our lips joined. I kept my hands firmly on her back, her face, her shoulders. I avoided above or below her waist, steering clear of her legs or her neck or her hips. Sleeping together had been a brilliant mistake, but we would not make it again. We were starting over.

I remembered leaving university to come home for Christmas. Mike, Miriam, and Pri had already gone, but I stayed a couple more days. Kayleigh had stayed, too. We'd hung out in her flat in Bowland, watching films and catching up on assignments. It was like we were housemates living together; she'd take a bath while I watched Netflix on my laptop and did the washing-up.

'Where are you going for Christmas?' I asked her once.

'Nowhere,' had been her response.

'Not to your aunt's?'

'Nah,' she said, and then she'd gone to boil rice for our dinner.

One morning, I had been going up to her flat and I'd picked up the post for her, as I always did. Among a few cards and takeaway menus, there had been a 'Christmas Cruise' postcard. I flipped it over.

Hey Kayleigh,

The cruise is fantastic, we've been to loads of places and I've got a tan. Jack's been enjoying the golf. I'm so sorry I won't be home for Christmas but I'm sure you'd rather stay on campus with your new friends. If you fancy coming home for a bit, the house is all yours. Jack sends his love.

Kisses,

Auntie Lyd x

That was why she wasn't going anywhere for Christmas. I felt a rush of sympathy for her, despite the fact she hated that. Or so she said.

When she came out of the shower, she spotted the post on the table. 'Did you read my postcard?'

'No,' I lied, 'I just picked it up.'

She flicked through the letters, put the cards on the window-sill, and tossed the postcard and menus in the bin.

I felt so bad for her and couldn't sleep that night. I wanted to invite her to spend Christmas with me, to not be all alone, but Mum would probably say no. So instead, I scoured the internet for the perfect present—two tickets to see her favourite band.

Kayleigh had her own car and was nice enough to drop me off at the train station to go back to Bristol. We stopped in front of the platform barriers, next to a little flower stall selling wreaths and last-minute gifts.

'I got you a present,' I said, remembering the tickets.

'A Santa snow globe?' she replied, glancing at the stall.

'No,' I laughed. I reached into my coat pocket, but she stopped me.

'Wait,' she said. 'You're early. Go to the loo now, so you don't miss your train.'

I did as she said and, when I returned, I saw her gleefully skipping over to me from the stall.

'Present time,' she smiled. 'You first.'

I hadn't been aware that she'd got me one. From my coat pocket I withdrew the envelope and handed it to her. Like a child, she snatched it off me and tore it open.

'Ooohmygod,' she cried, 'ohmyGOD!'

'Do you like it?' I asked, as if it'd needed answering.

'Yeah! I love it! Twin Atlantic—they're coming to Manchester? I had no idea—you're coming with me!'

'Nah,' I smiled, 'you should take Pri.'

'God, she'd hate them.' She proceeded to momentarily throw her arms around me before leaping back and thrusting the second ticket in my face.

'You'd better keep hold of it,' I said, 'in case you change your mind.'

'I won't,' she said, but put it in her bag anyway.

'Well, you might want to take that guy you've been seeing,' I said awkwardly. 'Owen, right?'

'Greg,' she corrected me. 'Owen was the one before. But we're not dating anymore.' She gave me a long look. I was sure I was red.

'Your turn,' I said, hurriedly changing the subject. 'What have you got me?'

'Oh,' she said, looking downwards. 'Well, it's not as good as yours, but…here.'

From her coat pocket she withdrew a single, slightly crushed strand of mistletoe. I took it, not sure what to make of it.

'Hold it above your head,' she said, moving my arm until I was dangling the mistletoe between us. And still it did not hit me, not until she placed her hands on my cheeks, her thumbs on my jawline, and her face came towards mine.

Then I realised. And I didn't know what to do, whether to back out or lean in or smile or speak, and all I could do was look at her, how she looked less hot but more beautiful in her waterproof jacket and skinny jeans, compared to how I'd first seen her in that see-through blouse with her long, tanned legs, and I wasn't thinking and I leaned in and we kissed.

My first kiss since Brooke. And she didn't even cross my mind. I was single and Kayleigh was awesome and she wanted me, so I kissed her. When she pulled away, she smiled and said, 'Merry Christmas,' and walked back to her car. I watched her go, stunned, still hanging the mistletoe over my head like an idiot. It was not until she'd got halfway across the station that I woke from my stupor and shouted, 'Merry Christmas!'

She heard me and turned full circle without stopping, flashing a grin at me and continuing on her way.

But it wasn't like Kayleigh was my girlfriend. It wasn't like I was cheating on her now. How could I have known what would happen tonight?

Brooke and I were now standing against the white tiled wall, and she had her heels back on to reach me. Her hands were on my collarbone and mine were on her back. Kissing Kayleigh had nothing on kissing her.

My phone beeped and we broke apart. 'Five to midnight,' I read out. 'We'd better get back.'

'You set an alarm?' she smirked.

'I missed it last year! I was in the loo.'

She laughed, then gave me a long look. 'But this is…' she said, 'not over?'

I heard fear in her voice, anticipating that I was going to say it was. But no way was I going to say that. I'd forgotten that pull, that gravity she held over me. She was a black hole right through the floor and I had no choice but to fall towards her. 'Not over,' I said, and she grinned.

I poked my head out of the door to check the hallway was empty; everyone was downstairs. I told Brooke that the coast was clear, and we laughed at how the situation was like a film, only I didn't have a twisted tie and she didn't have smudged lipstick. We held hands down to the second floor, and then dropped them cautiously.

'I'll go into the lounge first,' I said. 'Come in in a minute, okay?'

I walked into the dimly lit room. Callum was pouring bucks fizz into cups, decidedly more sober than he had been at my eighteenth (probably because his mum and stepdad were in the next room). People were moving around, saying goodbye to the year, keeping an eye on the TV screen that hung on the wall. Images of the London Eye, crowds of people, the countdown to 2011 projected on the side of a skyscraper. People were pairing up. 'Kiss me at midnight,' they said to each other.

Thirty-two seconds. Tilly wobbled drunkenly over to me. 'Matt!' she cried, waving her arms and spilling her drink down herself. I'd heard that she'd broken up with her latest boyfriend, and tonight was the first time since then that she'd managed to drink without crying. She flung her arms around me and shouted, 'I've missed you!'

'Really?' I asked sceptically. Twenty seconds.

'Count down with me?' she instructed more than asked. She was definitely not my first choice of people to start the New Year with, but I glanced around and couldn't see Brooke. Maybe she was looking for me over the other side of the lounge. Maybe she'd found Lucy and would catch up with me later. Twelve seconds.

'Kiss me at midnight,' Tilly said, slurring her words.

Ten.

'What?'

Nine.

People were shouting the countdown with the telly, and I wondered if Brooke was looking for me, and if she would find me, and if I could steal a kiss from her when nobody was looking.

Eight.

'Come ooon, Matt,' Tilly said, taking a step and stumbling. I caught her at the waist to stop her falling over.

Seven.

Tilly took me by the shoulders and looked at me with weary eyes. 'Are you ready?' she asked, with sloppy seductiveness.

Six.

I looked around frantically for Brooke, or for someone to push Tilly on to, or for anything at all that urgently needed my attention.

Five.

'Because I'm going to give you the beast—the bestest—the bestedest ever kiss you've *ever* had,' she said, stumbling again, and I held her tighter, keeping her upright.

Four.

Everyone was smiling, holding hands in a pair or else with arms around friends. Nobody met my desperate gaze.

Three.

Tilly closed her eyes.

Two.

She pursed her lips.

One.

SCENE 36: BROOKE, 15

It was not until I heard the countdown reach eight that I went back into the living room. I didn't think people would notice me, too distracted by hugs and kisses to see my lips briefly meet Matt's in the darkness. I scanned the room for him, but I couldn't spot him, and everyone's arms were around someone else.

As cries of 'Happy New Year!' erupted all around me, I spotted him, across the room, wrapped around Tilly.

Her hands were draped around his shoulders and his were on her waist and she was kissing his neck seductively. My heart plummeted. I'd thought, now that I was older, and more mature, and had let go of this fairytale version of how love was meant to be, maybe he could take me seriously. Maybe we could have another shot.

Callum wandered over as my limbs went numb. 'Happy New Year, Brookers,' he said softly.

'Happy New Year,' I said back.

'You okay?' he asked, knowing full well that I was not.

'Tired. I feel ill.'

'Do you want to go home?'

I didn't want to stay. I nodded wearily and he put his arm around me and, in silence, walked me all the way to my front door.

'Is your mum in?' Callum asked as I took out my keys.

'No, she's staying at my aunt's till the morning.'

'Amy?'

'She's at her boyfriend's.'

'Oh. Are you going to be alright on your own?'

'Yeah, it's fine. You go back to the party.'

'I can stick around for a while, or sleep on the sofa—'

'Seriously, Callum,' I said, forcing a smile. 'Go back to yours. I'm only gonna go to bed.'

He left, but I didn't go to bed. I was lost, drowning in the space of the dark, empty house. I decided to shower, wanting to wash the night out of my hair. *He just wanted a snog. He's probably snogged loads of girls at uni.*

I stepped into the tub and turned on the showerhead, barely registering the water on my skin. I poured a dollop of strawberry shampoo onto my hand and mindlessly kept pouring. The thick red liquid overflowed between my fingers and bled down to the bottom of the bathtub. I rubbed it into my hair as an automatic response, only half aware of my movements, my mind not here nor back in Callum's living room—it was somewhere else entirely. The shower wasn't warm enough. I turned up the dial, and hot water flowed over me. The scarlet shampoo suds rinsed from my hair, over my skin, down to my toes. *Of course he doesn't want you. Who would ever love you? Are you stupid as well as worthless?*

Hotter still. I twisted the dial up to maximum. Soon, the hot water would run out and I'd be left to wash in the cold, but I didn't care. I could barely feel the heat burning through my chest, thawing the numbness inside me. The skin on my arms and shoulders reddened. *Stupid and ugly and needy and boring and worthless.*

Water from the shower and water from my eyes washed over my face, and soon the echoes of my sobs filled the air along with the steam. I cried for a very long time. I turned to reach for the conditioner. The mirror had steamed up and the air was thick with water vapour. As I reached for the bottle, my hand slipped onto the razor. My breath hitched as I felt the blade against my skin for a split second before it fell to the bottom of the bathtub with a thud. I looked down. My palm was bleeding, a thin red line at the heel of my hand. I noticed how it stung. I also noticed that I wasn't thinking about Matt anymore.

The razor had landed between my feet. I picked it up and saw small droplets of condensation on the metal blades. I must've stared at it for a long time, because the air got cloudier and cloudier. My racing thoughts had ceased, and it was all I could see.

I placed the razor against the skin on my wrist. *I'm just trying something*, I told myself. I blocked every thought, every feeling.

Two little red lines appeared, light. Two more. Still light.

My body was too numb to feel the pain, but I still noticed my breathing quicken sharply as I did it. There was something heavy at the bottom of my stomach. How unnatural it was to fight your most primitive instinct to protect the body. How treacherous to attack it.

I wanted to get the blades out of the plastic to be able to cut deeper. It was like some new, untapped part of my brain was moving my limbs while the rest of me just watched, too tired to stop myself. Somehow, I managed to force the blades out, cutting my fingers in the process. The plastic was tough, but not as tough as holding the small strip of metal, free in my hand, and trying to figure how to put it to my skin again.

I'm just trying something.

The water flowed with a seemingly endless supply of hot water that stung the four little cuts I'd already made on the underside of my wrist. I hadn't noticed the pain when I'd been trying to get the blades free, but I was still crying. I raised the blade, closed my eyes, and swiped it down against my wrist. One long line, deeper this time. Beads of blood started forming along its seams, like the droplets of condensation that were trickling down the mirror. I cut again. And again. And again. Quick and sharp and deeper, always deeper.

Blood was trickling from my arm and water was bursting from the shower and tears were streaming from my eyes. And then the numbness melted, and I couldn't breathe, and I felt the pain in my arm and the heat on my skin, and the steam was choking me, and all I felt was the slam of my body and all I saw was darkness.

SCENE 37: MATT, 18

I turned my face at the last second and Tilly's lips landed on my jawline. I pushed her off me. 'Uh, happy New Year,' I said, wiping my face on my sleeve. She wasn't listening. She'd already sauntered off to find another pair of lips.

I looked around the room but couldn't spot Brooke. As I moved through the crowd of people, I was launched upon with hugs from friends stopping me to wish me a happy New Year, and Meg saying goodbye as she and her boyfriend took off. I decided to go back to the top floor bathroom, thinking that Brooke must be waiting for me there, but she wasn't. Her coat wasn't in the hallway and her bag had vanished. I'd seen her not five minutes earlier. Where had she gone?

I asked around, trying to be subtle about it. I even braved the cold of the garden to ask the smokers, but there was no sign of her. I locked myself in the toilet and rang her phone. Twice. It went straight to voicemail both times: off or dead.

I started to worry. Things had finally seemed okay between us. We'd been kissing and smiling, and now she'd taken off without explanation. *Why would she leave the party without saying goodbye? Did she see me with Tilly and get the wrong idea?* I needed to talk to her, to explain that it wasn't what it looked like.

I went back into the party and continued to ask around. Nobody had seen her and nobody seemed to care.

'Stephen,' I said, catching the eye of the only other sober body in the room, 'have you seen Brooke?'

'No? Why? Is she missing?'

'I don't know. Nobody's seen her and she didn't say goodbye to anyone, so I'm starting to worry.' The image of her, small and alone in the bus station, flashed in my mind. 'Want to...y'know...check she's okay.'

'Hmm,' he said. 'Have you called her?'

I nodded. 'No answer.'

'Hang on, I think I have her home number from the emergency contacts. It would be good to check she got back safely.'

He dug out his phone, found the number, and I was grateful that he was the one ringing. I checked the time. Twenty-five past.

He shook his head. 'No answer,' he said.

Right on cue, Callum came in through the front door.

'Where've you been?' Stephen asked.

'I walked Brooke home. She was feeling sick. She's fine though, she's gone to bed.'

Shit. If she left without saying goodbye, after the night we'd had, she *must've* seen me with Tilly. And she must be upset. I needed to talk to her, tonight, to make things right again.

'You made sure she got in safe?' Stephen asked Callum.

'Hey, I'm her adopted big brother, okay, I take that responsibility seriously.'

Stephen ignored this. 'You saw her go into the house?'

'I saw her go into the house,' Callum repeated.

Stephen shrugged. 'Sounds like she's fine.'

She'd tried to get to London, alone, at night, after a fight with her mum. What would she do after I kissed her and then kissed someone else five minutes later? 'Yeah,' I said. 'Yeah, awesome. Cheers Cal.'

I had to get over there. I had to make sure she hadn't done something stupid. I fake yawned. 'Never been good at staying up on New Year,' I chuckled with a bit too much enthusiasm. I looked at my phone: half past midnight. 'I'd better head off.'

'It's still early,' Callum said. 'Mum said the music doesn't have to go off till two.'

'Won't stay awake that long, mate,' I grinned, putting my hand on his shoulder. I pulled him into a hug and then Stephen, too. 'Thanks for a wicked night. I'm gonna walk home.'

I didn't walk. I ran, taking off my jacket as my feet fell to the ground with heavy thuds. Her house was only ten minutes from Lucy and Callum's, but every second it took to get there was too long. I could see her on the side of that motorway again, her hair whipping around her face, willing to get into a car with a stranger—or jump out in front of one.

When I finally arrived at her house, I had to put my head between my knees to catch my breath. I climbed over the back gate and grabbed some gravel, like the last time. Her bedroom, the one on the far left with the *Romeo and Juliet* flyer taped to the glass, was dark. But a light was on in the middle room. The window was smaller, slightly ajar, steam pouring out of it. When I listened, I could hear running water. Someone was in the shower.

It could be her—or else she could be asleep, and her mum or sister could be in the bathroom. I rang her mobile again. Still no answer.

I threw the stones at her bedroom window. They'd woken her up last time, surely they would again, if she was sleeping? But I heard nothing; the shower was still running and steam was still flooding out the window.

If she wasn't waking up, it must be her in the shower. I threw the gravel at that window instead. Still no answer.

'Brooke,' I hissed, quietly to start with. 'Brooke?'

No answer. No movement audible inside the bathroom.

'Brooke!' I was louder this time. 'Brooke! *Brooke Brooke Brooke!*'

I was practically yelling. Why couldn't she hear me? Even over the shower, she should've been able to. I started to panic.

I opened the garden gate and went back onto the driveway. No cars. Maybe she was home alone. Either way, I had to check. I took my chances and rang her doorbell, prepared to come face-to-face with her pyjama-clad mother. No one answered. I rang the bell again. Still no answer. I rang it three times in a row, enough to piss anyone off at quarter to one in the morning. Nothing.

Why was no one answering? I went back into the garden, looking up again at that bathroom window. The steam was pluming out like smoke from a factory chimney. My heart pounded. *No one showers for this long.*

I went to the barbecue and scoured the grill for the key I'd seen Brooke use last time. I had to turn on my phone torch, but there it was, icy to the touch. I unlocked the back door and kept my torch on to navigate through the garage, the kitchen, and the living room. There was nothing to signal anything being out of sorts, nothing that looked ransacked or robbed. I had never been in Brooke's house before, but I managed to find the bottom of the staircase. A horizontal line of light cast against the wall of the upstairs landing.

'Brooke!' I called from the bottom of the stairs. Still I heard nothing except the sound of the shower. I made my way up, so very aware that I wasn't supposed to be here, and scared of what I would find.

The light was coming from the crack beneath what had to be the bathroom door. I knocked on it loudly, dropping my jacket on the floor.

'Brooke, it's me, Matt.'

No reply.

'Please open up.'

Nothing.

'I need to talk to you, Brooke, but first I need to know you're okay.'

Nothing.

'Brooke, if you don't open the door, I'm going to come in to make sure you're alright.'

Nothing.

'I need to know you're alright. Say something?'

Nothing.

'Okay, I'm coming in.'

I was nervous. She might slap me if I walked in on her in the shower, but she wasn't replying and I had to know she was safe. I fumbled in my pocket for a penny to twist the lock backwards and slowly opened the door.

I was met with a wall of burning-hot steam, and I coughed, choking on the vapour. Alarm bells rang in my head. *If she's in here, she's in danger.*

I felt my way to the bathtub, pushing the curtain aside and getting a faceful of spray. I scrambled for the showerhead through the scalding hot water; my hands fell on boiling pipes, but I soon found two dials. I turned the first all the way to one side and the water went instantly icy. The second turned the water off. The steam was clearing out into the hallway and I saw a figure lying in the bathtub.

She was on her side in an inch of water, naked, the heel of her foot blocking the plughole. Her eyes were closed and her lips were parted, the water flowing around her nose and into her mouth a little. One arm was draped across her chest, both sides of it covered in glowing red lines. A trail of blood trickled from her wrist into the water, mixing with the soapy suds and diluting into nothing. I thought she was dead.

I tried to move as quickly as I could, but my arms were shaking and every second was slower than the last. I scooped her from the water, refusing to tear my gaze away from her closed eyelids, as if I could stare at them fiercely enough to force them to open.

'Brooke,' I sobbed, 'Brooke, wake up.' I cradled her in the bathtub, holding my forehead against hers, crying and crying and crying. Water dripped from her limp hair, blood from her limp arm. I honestly thought I was holding a corpse. I put my ear to her lips. She was breathing.

'Thank you, God,' I said, despite never having believed in one. My eyes flooded with relief and I wiped them on my sleeve, but it was wet from the shower.

Pull yourself together, I told myself. I had to keep her alive. I laid her out on the bathroom floor. 'Brooke, can you hear me? Can you open your eyes?' She didn't move.

I looked at the cuts on her arm. They were deeper than they had first looked and were now bleeding faster. I seized a towel from the rail and wrapped it round the wounds. I held her arm upright like I thought I was meant to do, and squeezed it tight, my arms wrapped awkwardly around the towel, trying to press down with my elbows, my forearms, across the whole stretch of cuts.

'Brooke, can you hear me?' Nothing. Why wasn't she waking up?

I looked at the towel again. A large red patch was growing across it, leaking onto my shirt. *Fuck.*

I placed her arm on her stomach, keeping the towel around it, and stood up. I tore my phone from my pocket and dialled.

'999, what service do you require?' A deep voice answered, much slower and calmer than I felt.

'Ambulance.'

'What's the address?'

'Um...' I knew the road, but not the house number. I had to rush down the stairs and look at the front door to check it.

'What's the emergency?'

'Um...' I said, as I ran back up the stairs, taking them two at a time. How could I explain this? 'My...my friend. I found her unconscious in the shower; it looks like she's cut herself.'

'Is she breathing?'

'Yes,' I checked again, placing my ear above her mouth, looking down at her stomach which was rising and falling. 'Yes, she is.'

'But she's not responding to sound, or touch?'

'No.'

'How deep are the cuts?'

I dared to move the towel. 'I don't know, they could be deep. I can't tell, there's a lot of blood.'

'Is she losing colour in her face?'

I checked. 'No.'

'What direction are the cuts on her arm, vertical or horizontal?'

'Um,' I forced myself to look again. 'Mostly horizontal. Some diagonal.'

'How long are the cuts?'

'I don't know!' I cried.

'Try to stay calm. Can you wrap the wounds in something, like a towel or clothing, and apply pressure?'

'Doing it,' I said, putting the call on speaker and wrapping her arm back up in both of mine.

'Hold it upright, above her heart, and apply pressure. Did she say or do anything to indicate she may have been suicidal?'

The weight of his last word dropped into my stomach like a bowling ball. 'Not that I noticed.' My voice trembled as I spoke.

Shitshitshit. Was Brooke trying to kill herself because of me? Because I kissed Tilly? Because I had fucked her about and broken up with her and gotten back together with her and kissed someone else? Had I messed with her head that badly?

'What's your friend's name?'

'Brooke Tyler. This is her house.'

'How old is she?'

'Fourteen. Fifteen, sorry, just turned fifteen.'

'And yourself?'

I stopped. I hadn't even considered my own involvement in this, and now, here I was, on the phone to 999. 'Seventeen,' I lied. Was that any better than the truth?

'Is there an adult around who can help you?'

'No. There's no one else here.'

'You say you found her in the shower?'

I hesitated. I could see now how bad it looked. 'I was worried. She wasn't replying. The water was still running, really hot. And the room was full of steam, it would have been hard to breathe.'

'Does she have any burns, from the water?'

I looked at her. 'I don't think so,' I said.

'Have either of you consumed any alcohol this evening?'

Why was he so interested in me? 'She hasn't. I had one beer.'

'And she made the cuts herself?'

What was he suggesting? That I had cut her? 'Well, there's no one else here.'

'Can you see anything in the room she used to cut herself with?'

I did a quick scan. On the edge of the bathtub I saw the plastic handle of a razor with the blades removed.

'Yeah,' I gulped, nausea rising in me. 'Yeah, looks like she used a razorblade.'

He asked me more questions, like the length and width of the blades, and if the blood flow was slowing down, which it seemed to be. 'The ambulance is blue-lighting to you. It'll be fifteen minutes. Keep checking her breathing and her pulse at regular intervals, keep putting pressure on her arm, keep her arm raised above her heart. Stay on the line.'

Fuck. What would the paramedics say when they saw me, hovering over a naked girl with a bleeding arm?

I saw Brooke's clothes, the skirt and top she'd been wearing at the party, piled up in the laundry basket. I dropped her arm and picked up her underwear, sliding them over her feet and lifting her legs up to get them on her. Then the skirt. The fabric clung to the moisture from the shower on her legs, and I had to awkwardly lift her torso up to get it on her. I ignored the bra and tights and rolled up the neckline of the strappy green top.

'The ambulance is eleven minutes away. Stay on the line.'

I picked up her head, then slid one of her arms through the strap and tried to pull the shirt down over her, without having to move her injured arm. It didn't work, it just pulled her arm tight to her body. I removed the towel and held her wrist gently as I pulled her injured arm through the other strap, trying to avoid staining her clothes. Blood dripped on the shirt and the floor and ran over my fingers. I quickly wrapped her arm back up in the towel and pressed hard on it.

'The ambulance is six minutes away. Stay on the line.'

Fuckfuckfuck. They were almost here, and I had no idea what to tell them when they found us like this. I checked Brooke's arm, bleeding much slower now, and looked around for something to tie the towel on with. There were no hair bands, I wasn't wearing a belt. I ended up grabbing her balled-up tights from the wash basket and using them to feebly secure the towel around her arm.

'The ambulance is three minutes away. Stay on the line.'

'I'm sorry, I have to go.'

'You need to stay with your friend and apply pressure to the wound.'

'I have to go. I'm sorry.'

'Stay on the line—'

I hung up. I looked at Brooke, my head hanging above hers. 'What have I done to you,' I said.

Her eyelids fluttered.

I caught my breath. 'Brooke? Brooke, can you hear me?'

'Matt?' she breathed.

'I'm sorry, Brooke, I have to go. The ambulance will be here in a second, you'll be okay. I'm sorry.'

I stood up.

'Matt…Tilly…' she groaned.

'I know, I know, I'm sorry Brooke.' I wanted to explain, wanted to tell her that I hadn't wanted to kiss Tilly, but the words wouldn't come out. I could picture the paramedics, could hear their questions. My phone rang, and when I looked at it, it was 999 calling me back. 'I need to go,' I said, and rejected the call.

I tore my gaze away from her, seized my jacket, hurried down the stairs, turning on lights to guide the paramedics as I went. I couldn't hear sirens, couldn't see lights flashing through the windows yet. I left through the front door, being sure to keep it open and on the latch for the ambulance. From the top of the driveway I scanned the area; the streetlights were still on and nobody was around.

I rushed out of the street and over to the pavement of the adjoining main road. Surely the ambulance would have to come that way—there was no other direction to get to Brooke's house. I walked and walked, till I was far down the path, a hundred metres from her house, and I stood, and watched, and waited.

My breathing was rapid, and my arms were still shaking, aching, from the strain of squeezing the towel tight. I turned my back on her house, then back to face it, checking the road in both directions. There were no people, and no cars. No sirens. No lights.

I checked the time on my phone, but didn't know when the operator had said it would be three minutes. Was that one minute ago, or five? Had he actually said three minutes, or had I misheard? I zipped up my coat. If the ambulance didn't arrive soon, I'd have to go back inside to check on her.

With my back to the house, I finally saw flashing blue lights. The ambulance whizzed past me, and I followed it with my eyes and watched it pull onto Brooke's road. I turned and walked.

I wandered the streets numbly, aimlessly, and wound up at home. I let myself in to find Mum in the living room, her heels chucked on the carpet, watching Jools Holland and eating Hula Hoops.

'Matthew!' she cried when I came in, waving her arms about and almost knocking over a vase. 'Happy New Yeeeaaarrrrr!'

'Happy New Year, Mum,' I said, shoving my hands in my pockets and sitting down next to her.

'Wazzerparty any good?'

I shuddered. 'Not really.'

I stared at the screen as a group of twenty-odd people sang together, wrapping up the show. Mum crunched her crisps. I tried to feel normal, tried to remember what life was usually like.

'How was Katie's?' I asked.

'Really good. Amazing food,' she said.

'Dad in bed?'

She nodded.

Jools was looking down the camera, singing into a microphone. He wished everyone a happy New Year as the credits rolled. Mum turned it off.

'Night night, sweetie pie,' she said, planting a clumsy kiss on my head.

'Night, Mum,' I said.

I waited till I heard her bedroom door close before following her up the stairs. I went into the bathroom and looked at myself in the mirror. I was a mess. The bags under my eyes were huge, my hair was a state, and somehow, I looked older.

I unzipped my jacket and realised Brooke's blood was all over my shirt. I saw it, then saw my reflection, and I wept. I looked like I'd killed someone. I'd come close. The tears streamed down my face, and I took the shirt off and balled it up and threw it in the bin. Crappy New Year.

SCENE 38: BROOKE, 15

Mum hadn't stopped crying since she saw me. I was just sitting there when she came in: my wounds were stitched, my arm was bandaged. I didn't look that bad.

Mum had tried to leave my aunt's house immediately when the hospital called, but no one there was sober enough to drive, so she'd had to wait an hour for a taxi. By then, a doctor had examined my wounds and told me I had been very selfish to do this. As if I didn't feel bad enough. Someone else had cleaned, stitched, and bandaged my arm. A nurse had taken some blood and urine to check I hadn't overdosed. I sat there, waiting to be allowed to go home. A psychiatric nurse with a clipboard gave me a mental health assessment. He asked me loads of personal questions right in front of Mum, and she sobbed harder with each answer I gave. He referred me for counselling at a service with a twelve-week waiting list. He looked at Mum, as if I wasn't even there, and said, 'Make sure she gets an appointment with her GP this week to talk about medication.'

It was after four o'clock in the morning that we left the hospital. We got a taxi home. Mum was still crying, silently now.

'They said there was a boy with you,' she said finally.

Matt. Matt had been there. He had called the ambulance. By the looks of things, he'd dressed me, too, and tried to stop the bleeding. How had he gotten into my house? 'No one else was with me,' I said.

'They said it was a boy who called the ambulance. Or a man.'

'I called the ambulance.' I didn't know if she would believe me, but I couldn't think of a way for her to check.

'No one came home with you from the party?'

'Callum walked me home, then left. Then I went in the shower. Then I called the ambulance.'

'Callum didn't call the ambulance?'

'No.'

Silence.

'Were you drunk?'

'No.' I wondered if it would have been easier for her if I said I was drunk. Maybe that would make her feel less like a failure.

'I wasn't trying to kill myself,' I said. I wasn't sure what I'd been trying to do. She didn't say anything.

At school I covered up the bandage with long sleeves, but some of the popular girls saw it when I was changing for PE. I got called an attention-seeker, a drama queen, a suicidal bitch. Boys would dare each other to pull up my sleeves, or joke that I was going to use a compass in Maths to scratch myself under the table. These things hurt, and I would cry about it, and I withdrew. Lucy must've heard the rumours because she tried to talk to me, but I would steer the conversation away. I still sat with her and the others at lunchtime, and went with her to Stagefright, but we didn't talk anymore. Not about real stuff.

For a while, Dad started phoning more frequently. Every other night for a few weeks. He never mentioned what happened, though I knew that was why he was calling; checking I was still alive.

Mum threw money and fake smiles at the problem. She bought me new clothes, girly and colourful, and got herself a bunch of parenting books. She never spoke about what happened or asked how I was feeling. She was too scared of the answer. Everyone was, so no one asked, except the counsellor.

After the twelve-week wait, Mum cheerily drove me to the appointment. I hated the boring grey walls and hated the woman sitting opposite asking me questions. I told Mum I hated it, so she tried another counsellor, one at a charity. It wasn't on the NHS, and it wasn't free, but I liked the lady. I didn't tell her everything—I didn't tell her about Matt—but I tried to engage with her, and the stuff she was saying about learning to like myself.

Matt didn't contact me, and I guess I didn't really expect him to. Maybe he wanted to. I wanted him to, but more so, I wanted him to want to. But neither of us seemed to have anything left to say to each other. I had hoped he'd at least check I was okay, but I guess the lack of obituaries spoke for me. I had selfish thoughts of cutting myself again and telling him, just to see if he would care, but I never lived up to them. I may have been a brat, but I was growing out of it.

SCENE 39: MATT, 18

I worried about Brooke, of course I did. But I couldn't bring myself to get in touch with her again. We'd broken up and got back together and broken up and got back together, and I was getting tired of it, and she was getting hurt. I concluded that I was bad for her, and she wasn't good for me, and I had to let her go. I wanted to evaporate from her life. I tried to.

I gave her no messages to read, no calls to answer, and I considered deleting her from Facebook. But I needed to see her profile. When she commented on posts and appeared in pictures, I knew she was safe.

I waited for someone to call me about that night. The police, the hospital, the 999 guy, her mum, but no one got in touch with me. I guess she hadn't mentioned I'd been there. Maybe she didn't remember.

I returned to university early after New Year, deciding that the more distance between us, the better. Mum was sad about me going, but she understood—well, she was understanding. I took the train back to Lancaster, where Kayleigh met me at the station.

She did not kiss me, which was a relief. She instead hugged me, then pulled back slowly, giving me the chance to kiss her if I wanted to, which I didn't. It was unlike her, creating opportunities rather than seizing them herself. Perhaps she wasn't as confident as she made out.

'How were your holidays?' I asked as she drove me back to halls.

She groaned. 'Shitty. I was working. Yours?'

'Yeah, it was fine,' I lied. I didn't ask about what she was doing the night Brooke almost died.

I didn't 'almost die,' don't be silly, I imagined Brooke saying. I pushed her voice away.

January was bad, really bad. I went through the motions, going to lectures and sitting with my flatmates, but I wasn't really there. I was in my head, replaying the moment where I'd left her bleeding on the bathroom floor. I should have stayed; I should have prioritised her life over my future. Instead, I'd been a coward, and I hated myself for it.

Mike noticed something was up and knocked on my door one night to ask about it. 'You've stopped coming to Sugar. You don't seem as chatty. I'm worried about you, mate.'

I dismissed him, saying that I was just stressed, but I knew he was right. I wished I had the balls to tell him, someone, anyone, about what had happened, just to ease some of the pressure in my head. I considered going to the university's counsellor, but I couldn't face admitting what I'd done.

But I knew I had to stop moping and pick myself up. I made more of an effort to go out with Mike and the girls. Hanging out with them was a relief, and Kayleigh made me feel better. When she laughed at my jokes, or took my hand, or snuggled up to me on the sofa, I let her, because if someone like her liked me, then I must be normal. I initially told myself it was platonic, friendly, but came to realise I liked it in a definitely-not-platonic, much-more-than-friendly way.

As the term progressed, she would talk about us getting together. I told her I liked her (true), I liked her a lot (true), but I wanted to take it slowly because I had just got out of a relationship (true) and was scared of commitment (lie). She sounded pretty happy with that, and suggested we just go on some dates and 'have fun' as she put it. Soon it was clear that we were a thing, whatever that meant.

What surprised me about dating Kayleigh was that she seemed so adventurous in so many ways, and said she'd lost count of how many guys she'd hooked up with, but she was so sensible when it came to sex. She made us get STI tested together, and then to the pharmacy to buy some condoms. I remembered, months earlier, how I'd gone and got condoms for a night with Georgia that never happened. I'd been nervous when buying them alone, but with Kayleigh I was confident, relaxed, laughing with the shop assistant. As we walked out of the pharmacy, she said, 'So this is just in case. For when—if ever—we decide to use them. This isn't pressure to go home and get it on.'

We went home and had some pressure-free getting-it-on. I think we were both surprised by how little I'd actually experienced. I'd only had sex once before, and I'd never built up to it properly. When this became clear, Kayleigh took the lead, offering me guidance and checking I was okay. She knew what she liked, and how she liked it, and she wasn't afraid to ask for it.

There was a stark contrast between my previous experiences with sex, and what was happening now. With Georgia, I'd felt expectation, and I'd freaked out when we didn't talk about it first. With Brooke, it had been too unexpected to talk about. If I'd done things right, none of that would have happened at all, and what was happening now with Kayleigh would be my first time with my first *real* girlfriend. With Kayleigh, I felt comfortable. She was always checking that I was okay, reminding me that we could slow down or have a break or stop altogether. I didn't want to stop. She was so, so sexy.

One night we were lying together in my single bed, and I asked her if, during her first time, she'd been with someone who guided her through it like she had done with me.

'God, no,' she laughed. 'I was fifteen, and it was in a bush. Well. Behind a bush. He took me in there, did it, then got out. Quick and dirty.'

At least with Brooke it hadn't been in a bush. 'How old was he?' I asked.

'Uh, dunno. Maybe a year or two older.'

I twisted the corner of the duvet round my finger. 'Did he ask if you were okay with it?'

'Not really,' she shrugged. 'Didn't matter to me. I know *now* that he was meant to actually ask, but it didn't bother me at the time. I thought I was cool.'

The duvet cover was frayed. I pulled at a thread. 'Did it hurt? It's meant to hurt the first time, isn't it?'

'No, it's not *meant* to hurt. It did for me, though. I'm not sure the dude had any intention of being slow or careful—we were in a bush, for Christ's sake. But no, first times—well, no time is meant to hurt, or bleed. You're meant to go really slow and gentle and use lots of lube.' She pointed at the bottle on the bedside table.

I was quiet, my eyes on the threads splaying out. She looked at me. 'You okay?'

I couldn't tell her what I was really thinking: *another terrible thing I've put Brooke through.* After everything, after all the trouble I'd caused her, I hadn't been careful enough to make sure the sex we'd had—the sex we shouldn't've had—was painless. She had said it was fine. But I could remember a few drops of blood on the condom as I threw it away.

'What's up, baby?' Kayleigh said.

'My…my first time, it must've hurt. For her.'

'That's what it's like usually. People don't know how it's meant to be.'

When I didn't react, she added, 'Hey, don't beat yourself up about it. How could you have known? They don't teach this in school.'

'I should have been more responsible,' I said, sitting up so she couldn't see my face. 'I should have taken better care of her.'

'Hun, honestly,' Kayleigh said, wrapping her arms around my shoulders. 'Don't blame yourself. There's no way you could have known better. Look, if you wanted to do it, and she wanted to do it, then that's the main thing. That's what really matters.'

'What, consent?'

'Yeah, consent.'

Kayleigh leaned back and puffed on her vape. She was oblivious to the fact Brooke was underage. But then, Kayleigh had been underage, too, and she seemed fine now. Maybe in four years Brooke would be leading some clueless eighteen-year-old through his first proper relationship, like Kayleigh had done for me.

'Do you mind that you were underage?' I whispered in the darkness.

'Nah. It wasn't a great decision, but hey. Things turned out okay.'

Things did seem to turn out okay. We became official, and I loved holding her hand through the corridors, showing off this woman that could get any guy she wanted and had chosen *me*. What was weirder, she seemed to enjoy showing me off, too. She even pushed for us to update our relationship status on Facebook. I wanted to, but I was also scared that Brooke would see it and react badly. I mean, she'd reacted pretty badly the last time she saw me with someone else. I made the excuse that I didn't go on Facebook much, but one time I was scrolling through it while she sat next to me in the library. She suggested we update it, and I couldn't really say no. If I said, 'I'd rather not, because of my ex,' that would have sounded like I wasn't over Brooke. I was over Brooke…well, probably. I'd been thinking about her much less, and I really liked Kayleigh. We updated it, and my friends from home sounded pleased, and I didn't hear from Brooke.

And because I didn't hear from her, I stopped worrying. I saw her in April, because Stagefright was doing a play and Meg insisted I run the lights. We didn't talk at all, didn't even make eye contact. She was up there on the stage we'd sung *Taking Chances* on, and then she'd disappear backstage and maybe even sit on the sofa we'd been naked on together. Part of me wanted to talk to her, but then she'd go home, and Kayleigh would call, and I'd forget Brooke completely.

After the Easter holidays I returned to Lancaster for the exam term, after nearly a month at home. When Kayleigh picked me up from the train station, I gave her the flowers I'd bought from Tesco. We went out for dinner and split a bottle of wine. It was all very romantic, and mature, and natural. When we went back to her flat, I undressed her, and the light from the streetlamps outside illuminated the curves of her tanned skin. I felt her fingers caress my face. It was good to be adored and to adore someone like her, someone beautiful, sexy, and so grown up. This was how it should have been all along.

ACT 2: 18 | 21

2014

SCENE 1: BROOKE, 18

'I know how to do laundry,' I said to Mum.

'Yes, but you don't know how to do laundry at a laundrette!' She had on her bright-voice and big-smile, trying to excite me with the prospect of clean clothes.

For months, she had been preparing me for university. She'd left prospectuses stacked up outside my bedroom door. She'd taken me to open days, hovered over my UCAS application, and now she was trying to teach me to look after myself.

'You won't have a washing machine in your halls,' she explained, 'and you might not have one in your second-year house.'

'I haven't got in yet,' I said.

'You could suggest to your housemates that you all do laundry together. Good way to make friends!'

Mum had been worried about me ever since that night at the hospital. She had noticed I'd stopped asking to go to Lucy's, or for lifts to the park, or if I could go to the cinema with friends. They weren't close with me, and I wasn't close with them. Sure, I still sat with them at lunchtime, but I rarely spoke. I'd become quiet, reserved, someone I never thought I'd be. I stopped arranging to meet up with them outside of school, and when I did go along to some party or whatever, I sat in the corner, isolated.

I'd been sleeping more. On some days, I would come home from school and go straight to bed. Living was exhausting, and pretending to be okay was even more so. Sleep was an escape, and I didn't want to wake up again in this dark, unforgiving world, inside my dark, unforgiving mind.

I'd begun crying every night. Over what, I didn't know. I would cut myself, too, but never bad enough to have to go to hospital again. I lost all my confidence, walking through the school corridors with my sleeves pulled down, my head bent low.

When I would close my eyes, I'd see ways I could die. I'd hear news reports about stabbings and shootings in London and

New York, and would pray that could happen to me, or else a car would send me flying, or I'd slip through an open window on the seventeenth floor, or a meteor would hit me, or I'd suddenly get terminal cancer.

Mum made a project out of fixing me. I wouldn't talk to her about much because I wouldn't talk to anyone about much. She'd beg me to open up to her, and when I wouldn't, she'd scream and yell and then slam the door and cry in her bedroom.

'There's nothing to say,' I'd tell her, over and over again.

Amy had done well in her A-Levels and had gotten into Birmingham uni to do archaeology. Mum couldn't shut up about it. Amy was the perfect child. I was the failure.

I kept going to the counsellor, but it didn't help much. I was diagnosed with depression, given therapy and tablets, and I'd do what she told me to do—go to this party or talk to that person—but nothing got better. I was numb.

Mum had suggested I get a job, to give me a sense of purpose. I said, 'Okay.' I became a kitchen porter at a restaurant on the High Street. They offered to have me as a waitress for a bit more money, but I couldn't stand the thought of having to smile at people all evening. I worked a few nights a week and some weekends, and saved up.

When I was sixteen, I told Mum that I wanted to leave Stagefright with the excuse of focusing on my GCSEs. She said, 'No, that's "losing an interest in activities you used to enjoy," and that's a symptom of depression,' which wasn't surprising, since I had depression. She told me to stay. I said, 'Okay.' I didn't audition for any big parts, though. Much better to disappear into the background.

Staying at Stagefright meant I saw Matt. He'd come home from university in the holidays: Christmas, Easter, and summer, regular as clockwork. The first few times I was nervous before sessions, but after a while he became part of the scenery, just another face in the crowd. We said 'hello'. We chatted politely. We'd work together in groups. We acted as if we'd forgotten everything that'd happened between us. Maybe we had.

SCENE 2: MATT, 21

After one maddening year when I was eighteen, everything went back to normal. I dated Kayleigh all through uni, and we religiously went to Sugarhouse on Thursdays. She tried to cut down on smoking throughout our relationship, but failed repeatedly. I didn't really mind.

I worked part-time at the union bar while studying and saved up enough to get my own car. For second year I moved to a flat in the city centre with Mike, but we were always round the girls' house anyway. That Christmas I convinced Mum and Dad to let Kayleigh come and stay with us since her aunt was off on a Caribbean getaway. Mum was a bit nervous about meeting her, since this was the first time I'd had a girlfriend come to stay. But everyone got on well, and Kayleigh managed to hide the vape she puffed on every two minutes. Mum was initially iffy about letting her sleep in the same bed as me, but she soon realised I was an adult. I realised it, too.

Mike and Miriam broke up in third year, and she quickly moved on with some skinny, tattoo-less guy from the football team. She still lived with Kayleigh, and I still lived with Mike, so that made things awkward. I started going to Kayleigh's a lot so she wouldn't come over and remind him of Mir. He was a bit of a mess about it all for a while. I even had to talk him out of shaving off his beard.

We worked our arses off, and both graduated with firsts. Mike stayed at Lancaster to do his master's and I moved back to Bristol to do mine, which meant living with Mum and Dad again. Kayleigh went back to St Albans and waitressed while figuring out what she wanted to do with her life. We tried long distance for three months, but it was really shit. When she came over for the weekend, Mum and Dad were always around, and when I'd visit hers, I was always tired in lectures on Monday. The distance came between us, and we started fighting down the phone. She decided to take a year out to go travelling, and we broke up. I was pretty down about it for a couple of months.

When I moved back home, Meg and Stephen begged me to help them run sessions. 'People never come back after uni,' Meg had moaned. 'We could really use the numbers, and your help.' I'd been back to Stagefright every time I came home in the holidays, at her insistence, and while I dreaded it, part of me needed to be there. I needed to see Brooke, alive and okay, to undo the image of her on that bathroom floor. But she wasn't her old self anymore. She seemed permanently sad.

The first summer was the hardest. I was so nervous about seeing her, scared she'd slap me or kiss me or tell people about us. But nothing happened. We didn't speak. Nor that Christmas. Or Easter. By the second summer, we were talking to each other in group discussions. By Christmas, we could speak politely at the end of the session. At Easter, we even said hello. Things were as back-to-normal as they could be. We chatted. We had occasional banter. And sometimes I still felt that pull towards her, but I wrote it off as memories, as first love. We'd learned from our mistakes, and we'd grown up, and neither of us tried to initiate more than a polite conversation. After all, we were only friends—if that.

SCENE 3: BROOKE, 18

'**A** duet?' Matt said uneasily.

'Yes,' Meg said, giving him a stare which told him there was to be no arguing. I looked at him and he looked at me, but I quickly glanced away.

'We've got a bunch here you can choose from, or else you can pick your own,' Meg continued, indicating Stephen, who was waiting eagerly at the piano.

'I...don't know,' I said stiffly.

'You've both sung before. I don't see why you suddenly have a problem with a duet. The show is in July and we're not even close to being ready. I'm not asking for much from you!' Meg and Stephen had left it too late to choose a play for the summer term, and so had settled for putting various scenes, songs, and dances together into a showcase. The trouble was, they'd left it too late to find enough material for that, either.

'It's just...my A-Levels start this week—' I began, but Meg turned on me with a piercing glare. She was a little edgy when she was stressed.

'Are you going to be in the showcase?'

'I—'

'Well?!'

'—yes.'

'So I'm sure you can cram learning one song in between your exams. Half a song each.'

'I...okay,' I said.

Matt and I walked silently over to the piano. I could hear the boys on the other side of the room rehearsing a scene from *Richard II*: 'Now no way can I stray, save back to England, all the world's my way.' I glanced at Matt's shoes—green vans—but couldn't look at his face.

We practised the song with Stephen, *All the Wasted Time* from *Parade*. It was a historical musical about a Jewish man who was imprisoned for murder and later lynched, and then pardoned after his death. The musical made a love story out of it, about him and his wife, and the song was about the wasted years they could've had if they'd known how to love each other properly. Standing next to Matt, I struggled to concentrate. I tried to focus on the character, but thinking *this is the last time you will see your husband before his death, you just don't know it yet* didn't help. We bore through it, oddly united, yet entirely disconnected.

We sang together, and everyone in the room who had been practising their own scenes and sketches stopped what they were doing to listen. As Matt belted out the final note, the room clapped like they had done when we'd practised songs for *Romeo and Juliet*, only this time we didn't look pleased or even smile. We just stared at the sheet music and waited for the session to end, then left without a word.

SCENE 4: MATT, 21

Brooke was coming over. Just to practise the song. But it would be the first time we'd been alone together in years and, well, it was awkward.

She came in, and I took her jacket, and we exchanged pleasantries. It was like the first time she'd ever walked into my house, only now, nobody was smiling. I could see the ghost of her, smaller, happier, moving through the rooms with a brightness that was nowhere to be seen in the woman before me.

I led her up to my bedroom and turned on the piano keyboard. When she stepped over the threshold, she looked awkward and out of place, her shoulders stiff beneath her baggy jumper. I saw her looking at the picture of the Space Needle and remembered how fourteen-year-old Brooke had ransacked my room, picking up objects and holiday souvenirs and asking where I'd got them. It probably looked exactly the same as it did back then, except for my master's notes all over the desk. She looked at me, then looked away. Was she pretending she hadn't been here before?

'*All the Wasted Time*,' I said, for something to say. 'Oh—we should warm up our voices.'

'I already did,' she said.

'Oh. Well, I should.' She stood there, staring into space, while I breathed and hummed and did scales. Vocal warmups never sounded good, and it was worse when someone else was there to witness it. I gave up early, stopping before I got to the high notes. 'That'll do.' She was looking out the window.

When I started playing the song, it was clear I was out of practice. I probably hadn't touched the keyboard since school and I stumbled a few times, but eventually picked up the chord sequence. I sang my verse, and she was still looking away. She barely moved, just stood on the spot, breathing. It was like she wasn't even awake. Did she notice the song had started? I finished my chorus and kept playing, half-expecting her to miss her cue, to keep standing there motionless. Without shifting her gaze, she came in when she was meant to and sang her verse. She didn't look at the sheet music. Her voice was so warm and full for a person who looked so empty. The song was kind of sad, and she looked sad, and I wished I could wake her up, breathe life back into her and see the bright, fiery Brooke again.

She finished the chorus and the key changed, and my fingers fumbled. She stopped, still not looking at me, but I found the keys and she sang again. We sang against each other, and I stared at her, but she was *still* not looking at me. I was desperate to see some flicker of a flame that used to drive her, to see her passionate about something or even angry about something rather than just hollow. She stopped when she was meant to stop, and I carried on with the last line. I tried to belt it out, but it was too high, and I hadn't warmed up properly. My voice wobbled, then cracked. Brooke looked at me and fell about laughing.

I stared at her, stunned, and I laughed, and she laughed harder, and I couldn't believe she was laughing properly. 'Should've warmed up better,' she giggled.

'I should have,' I laughed back.

She caught her breath. 'I forgot you can play piano.' It was the first time either of us had acknowledged there'd been a *before*.

'I can't really,' I said, 'just chords.'

Her smile actually lasted this time, and for a second, she looked bright and pretty.

Then I said, 'Why do you never do that?'

'Do what?'

'Laugh for real. Why do you always fake laugh?'

'I don't—'

'Yes you do.'

For half a second I thought she was going to get angry, going to say that I was claiming I knew her better than she knew herself, like she used to. But her smile faded. 'Let's run it once more, then,' she said.

I had to keep the old Brooke here, to remind her how she used to be stubborn and bold and sarcastic and warm. So I did the only thing I could think of and played *Taking Chances* from when we did *Romeo and Juliet*, and without saying anything, she just started to sing. My heart was pounding, and I sang my part, though I'd forgotten the words a little, and she laughed and reminded me. Then we both came in with the chorus and she was smiling, actually smiling, and my stomach flipped, and I felt that pull again. I was looking at her and we only got about halfway through when I abandoned the keyboard and turned to her. She looked like she knew exactly what I was going to say.

'Can I kiss you?' I asked.

'Yes,' she said without hesitating, and I wrapped my arms around her. She put her hands on my face and we kissed.

It was magic and there were years of unspoken words pressed between our lips and to hold her again was amazing. I was on fire, but then I felt wetness on my cheeks and pulled back to find that she was crying.

'Brooke?'

She sat on the floor, leaning against my bed, sobbing into her hands. I knelt down next to her, stunned, and tried to touch her shoulder.

'Brooke—'

'Don't!' she cried and squirmed away, as if my warm skin burned her cold body. I just knelt there, looking at her for a long time, trying to figure out what had just happened. She looked so pathetic, so feeble and hopeless, slumped in her jumper and jeans. Strange clothes for early summer.

I said, 'Do you want me to take you home?'

She said, 'Okay.'

In the car she cried silently until her tears subsided, and occasionally I glanced at her, at how thin she was, her bony face and baggy clothes, how her skin and hair looked dry and dull. She couldn't have been eating properly. She wasn't taking care of herself.

I parked around the corner from her house like I used to, and she said, 'Thanks,' without looking at me. I wanted to say something, but I had no idea what. As she got out and walked to her door, I wondered if it was me, if I'd ruined her life.

SCENE 5: BROOKE, 18

On Tuesdays at two I had counselling, and I always felt queasy as I walked in. Even though I'd come here every week for more than three years, I could never shake the anxiety I'd felt before my very first session.

The charity that provided my counselling rented a side office in a pre-school, so I had to weave my way through toddlers to get in, and their screaming offered a background ambience to my sessions. The room had several soft chairs, boxes of art supplies, and a toddler-sized table.

'How are your exams going?' my counsellor Carrie asked.

'Alright, I think. I'm halfway through now.'

'And whereabouts are your stress levels?'

'Medium. Not too bad. I'm just tired. Looking forward to them being over.'

'The end is in sight,' she smiled. 'Good to hear you're keeping things under control. You've got all your university offers. This is just the last hurdle to power through.'

I smiled politely.

'Now, is there anything in particular you wanted to talk about today?'

Carrie had been helpful over the years, working on my self-esteem and dealing with my difficult feelings, but I'd never opened up to her about how this had all started. How I'd fallen in love and fallen apart at the same time, and never really been able to find myself again. I'd vaguely described some events, and gone into detail about my dad, but I'd never told her about Matt.

'I kissed someone this week,' I said.

'Oooh,' Carrie said. 'And was it someone you like?'

'It was someone I used to like a lot.'

'And that person must like you back, if they kissed you.' Carrie leaned forward in her chair, smiling. She probably thought a boyfriend was just what I needed.

'I guess. I can't tell. It might've been more to do with how we used to like each other.'

'Was it that you both used to like each other and never got to act on it?'

I shook my head. 'We did act on it. At the time. We were kind of...together. For a bit.'

'How did things end between you?'

I sighed. 'Badly. We broke up. During an argument. And then got back together. Then we had another fight, and broke up, then ended up kissing. And I guess I thought that was us getting together again. But he didn't.'

'Was this a while back?'

'Years ago. I was a lot younger. Too young.'

'That must've been hard,' she said, 'to break up without getting real closure.'

'Yeah. There was a lot left unsaid.'

Carrie let the silence drag on. She did that a lot, to see if I would add anything else. I had found these long silences awkward at first, but got used to them over the years. 'What about this kiss, then,' she said eventually. 'Do you want it to happen again?'

'I don't know. Kind of. Yes. But...'

'Wait a second. Do you like this guy? Do you still have feelings for him?'

I didn't say anything.

'When we experience a lot of pain, we can go numb, so we don't have to feel it anymore. But that means we're numb to other emotions, too, like joy, and love.'

'Mm,' I said.

'We can do a visualisation to find out,' Carrie said. She sometimes made me picture scenarios or dreams I'd had, to try to get answers.

'I don't need to,' I said. 'I do still have feelings for him.'

'Well, that's great,' she smiled, a slight gap between her two front teeth that I'd always noticed.

'But, me and him…we don't have a future.'

Carrie looked sympathetic. 'Brooke, you are allowed to let yourself be happy. Just because things were bad in the past doesn't mean your future has to be that way.'

'But I'm leaving.'

'I'm not saying you must have a full-on relationship with this guy, or work out all the details right now. I'm just saying, if you like him, you can give yourself a chance. You can let yourself have hope.'

I imagined some future in which I could be with Matt, one where our past hadn't been so disastrous. Now I was eighteen, I could go with him to the pub, or out for dinner. I could introduce him to Mum and Amy. People could see us together, and it would be fine. I could imagine it. I could imagine myself being happy again.

'Besides, Cardiff uni is only, what, an hour away?'

Matt wasn't the only thing I hadn't told Carrie about.

SCENE 6: MATT, 21

'The showcase is only three weeks away...' Stephen was wrapping up the session with his usual reminders. Meg stood next to him, nodding along. I looked at Brooke. She wasn't looking at me. She hadn't looked at me all night.

'Alright, learn your lines!' Stephen finished, and as everybody stood to leave, I walked straight up to her.

'Brooke,' I said.

She looked at me, and her eyes were sad, but not in the way she always was. It was like looking at me *made* her sad.

I lowered my voice. 'Please, Brooke, would you let me take you for one drink, just to talk? And then I'll drop you home. And I won't ask for any more of your time.'

She looked at her shoes. 'Um, okay.'

I was surprised. 'Great. Alright. Is The Anchor okay?'

'Sure. That's fine.'

Stiffly, we walked out of the rehearsal room. 'Get that duet learnt,' Meg said as we passed her; I responded with a half-laugh. It was unnatural, walking side by side with Brooke in front of other people, and not trying to hide it.

'How are your exams going?' I said awkwardly, as we wandered from the Connell Complex over to The Anchor.

'Fine. Only one more to go now.'

I looked at our shadows, stretching out in front of us in the early evening sun. 'When's that?'

'Friday. Prom night,' she sighed heavily. 'One week left. Then I'm outta here.'

'Yeah, you'll finally be done with school,' I said, for something to say.

Brooke had her hands in the pockets of that hoodie she always wore. I held the door open for her, and she passed through it without looking at me. I had never imagined taking Brooke into a pub.

'Where do you want to sit?' I said, trying to act like a gentleman. She slouched in the nearest chair. I went to sit opposite her, then remembered the drinks. 'What do you want?'

'Just a lemonade.'

'You sure? You've got ID with you, right?'

'Yeah, but y'know. Exams.'

'Right, okay.' I went up to the bar and ordered a lemonade and a half of cider. I showed my ID, then got asked for hers.

'She's the lemonade,' I said.

'No under eighteens allowed on the premises after eight.'

I went back to the table and told Brooke that she needed to show her ID. She came up to the bar and handed over her drivers' licence. The man looked at it sceptically. 'When did you pass your driving test?'

'January sixteenth. This year.'

He gave it back to her. Brooke didn't seem annoyed that he hadn't believed it was a real licence. She just seemed tired. Every move she made, every word she said, had no energy to it. Even putting her purse back in her bag looked exhausting.

She took the lemonade, and I followed her back to the table. We sat opposite each other and she sipped her drink, eyes down.

'Talk to me, Brooke,' I said.

She swallowed. 'What do you want to talk about?'

'What happened the other day. What happened...before.'

'Go on, then.'

'Okay.' I adjusted my posture. 'You...you haven't seemed yourself. Your old self. Since we...like, since we broke up.'

She shrugged. 'I got ill. Not your fault. No one's fault.'

'You got depressed?' I asked.

She nodded.

'But do you think, us breaking up, do you think that's what caused it?' My hand shook as I sipped my drink. Did I really want to hear the answer?

'No,' she said, and I didn't feel relieved. 'I guess it all kicked off around that time, but there was stuff going on with me before. Stuff with my dad, and just general self-esteem issues, I guess. It's still going on. Everything that happened was probably just stressful.'

'Don't you think if we hadn't…if, er…if we didn't do what we did, maybe you wouldn't be ill now?'

She shrugged. 'If it wasn't one thing it would've been another that kind of…triggered it. But they say it's chemical. Well, they don't really know why it happens.' She took a sip.

I looked at my drink. 'Brooke—I'm sorry. About everything. That happened. Before.'

She shook her head and swallowed again. 'Don't be. It's okay. We were both being stupid. Neither of us asked, before we, y'know—I mean, I don't think either of us knew we were going to go that far.'

'But even so, I was the adult in the situation. I mean, I was the age you are now. I should have—I was meant to be the responsible one, and there were things I shouldn't have done. I shouldn't have done any of it. I wanted to say that I'm sorry.'

'Don't be sorry,' she said again.

'But that night—'

'You saved my life.'

'I didn't mean New Year's…' I pushed away the image. '…I meant that night, at the Complex. I did something terrible to you. I regret it, and I wish it hadn't happened. I'm sorry.'

She looked blankly at me. 'I forgive you,' she said calmly.

I expected to feel a weight lift from my chest, but it didn't. I couldn't look at Brooke, all dull skin and dry hair, and not feel guilty for what I'd done to her. It didn't matter if she said it wasn't my fault.

'What about the other day then?' she said, and I was surprised that she was volunteering anything.

'Um. Well. I was worried. Afterwards. That you—that it hadn't been okay to kiss you. And so I wanted to apologise for that, too.'

'It had been okay.'

I looked at her. 'Really?'

'Yeah. I…' She looked down, but not sadly, like she usually did. She stared at her glass and said, 'I wanted you to kiss me.'

'Then why—why were you crying?'

She sighed heavily. 'I dunno, Matt. I was upset. Old feelings. I was all depressed, and then I felt happy, and if I risk that…' She drifted off.

'If you risk being happy, you risk being disappointed when it ends,' I said.

'Yeah! Especially when—you know, we broke up and got back together so many times. I just can't…couldn't get my hopes up again.'

I knew she was right. The last time I saw her happy was back when we were together. Before she got sick. Before that night in the auditorium. Before I broke her heart three times over.

I looked at her, running her finger along the condensation on her glass, her movements slow and dreary. There'd been a glimpse, though, of the old Brooke, the other day in my bedroom when we'd laughed together. She couldn't be gone completely.

'So…what if—this is going to sound stupid,' I said. 'But that kiss. It was real, I mean, I felt something. Did you feel something?'

Again, she looked shy. 'Yes,' she said quietly.

'What happens the first minute we're alone together—we kiss, right? I don't want to ignore that. Everything that happened, it wasn't smart, but it wasn't nothing. We did everything too soon, but maybe this is a sign that we're…'

'…compatible?' she suggested. She could always finish my sentences.

'Exactly. And if there was a chance that we could…y'know… start over. If we could make it work. Would that be something you wanted?'

She smiled weakly at me, but her eyes were sad again. 'It doesn't matter. Because it can't happen.'

'But if it could, Brooke.'

'I'm ill, Matt. You can't love me better, and you definitely don't want to date a depressed person. We're no fun,' she added with half a smirk.

'But what if I did, and what if I didn't care that you were ill?' I pushed on. 'What if I just sat through it with you? And things could be like they used to be, but better, without all the mistakes?'

'I gave up on fairy tales a long time ago, Matt. Tossing pebbles at my window is a nice gesture, but it's not real life.'

'But forget real life for a second. If it *could* happen. Would it be something you wanted?'

She sighed. 'I…well, yeah, maybe.'

My heart pounded. 'Really?'

'Yeah, but it doesn't matter. Because it can't happen.'

'But what if we just gave it a go? I won't fuck you around like before. You don't have to worry about getting your hopes up, because I won't let you down this time.'

She was smiling again. 'It sounds really, really nice, Matt. But we don't have a future.'

'But I'm saying we can,' I persisted. 'We can have any future you want. I just want to…be with you.'

'I'm moving away.'

'Uni doesn't matter. I'll follow you anywhere. Or we could do long distance.' It hadn't worked out before, but this would be different. This would be us starting over, doing what we should have done all along. 'That doesn't matter—that's miles down the line—all I'm asking for is one date. Just to try.'

She picked up her bag and gave me another sad smile. 'I'm sorry, Matt,' she said. Her eyes were welling up. Why was I always making her cry?

'Brooke—'

'Thanks for the drink.' With that, she was gone. Again.

SCENE 7: BROOKE, 18

I hit my pencil on the desk. *Tap, tap, tap.* The invigilator at the front coughed loudly, and when I looked up, he was staring at me. I put my pencil down and rubbed my eyes. My sleeve rode up, exposing week-old cuts on top of older scars; I shook it back down. At the start of my exams I'd been so stressed. It'd proved easier to cut for five minutes and then study for fifty-five, rather than sit through the bad feelings for an hour. Carrie wanted me to sit through the bad feelings; she said my health was more important than my exams. I said if I didn't pass my exams, I basically had no reason to live. I couldn't retake. I couldn't spend another year in this place.

I triple-checked every answer. This was my last exam. After this, I was finally free. *Do I have everything ready?*

'Time's up, pencils down,' the invigilator said. I felt a weight lift from my shoulders. Finally, it was over. He dismissed us row by row and we went into the library to get our bags.

'You coming tonight?' said Finn. He was one of the few people I sat with at lunch who still made an effort to talk to me.

'I dunno,' I said. 'Not sure I'll feel up to it.'

'Come on, Brooke, it's the last time we're all going to be together. You've got a ticket, right?'

I nodded. Mum had insisted that I buy a Prom ticket weeks ago. She'd even sent me links to dresses online, but I hadn't chosen one. I'd never actually considered going.

'Tell you what, if you come, and you make a thirty-percent effort, I'll be your gay prince charming. I'll bring you a corsage and everything. Pick you up at six?'

I think I have everything ready. 'Alright,' I said, 'but I'm driving.'

I washed my hair and shaved my legs and ransacked Amy's wardrobe for anything long-sleeved that she hadn't taken to uni. There was a black dress, a little tighter than I'd have chosen myself, but it would do. Mum offered to curl my hair, so I let her, and she put a little makeup on me.

Finn arrived at six, wearing a navy-blue suit and holding a lily corsage. 'Whoa, Brookers,' he said when he saw me. 'Thirty percent effort? More like a hundred and thirty.'

'What do you mean?' I said.

'Losing the hoodie works wonders on you.' *Oh God, a compliment.* I was suddenly self-conscious, regretting having let Mum curl my hair. It was too much. If only Amy had left a different dress behind.

'Have a good time, then!' Mum said brightly, handing me her car keys. For a moment her smile wavered, and she compensated by beaming even wider. I wrapped my arms around her for a long moment, which seemed to surprise her, because she said 'Oh!' loudly, before hugging me back.

'Bye, Mum,' I said into her shoulder.

Finn and I got into the car and drove to a function room in the city. The year eleven Prom had been all spray tans and ballgowns, but this one was more like short dresses and alcohol. Some people did give me a double take, not quite recognising me at first, and I pulled my sleeves further down. We put our coats in the cloakroom and greeted the closest people I had to friends. There was a buffet, a photo booth, and a teacher got asked for ID at the bar. We laughed, and we danced.

'You look gorgeous,' Lucy said, in the queue for drinks.

'Oh,' I said, 'thanks.'

Lucy had never stopped being nice to me, and never stopped inviting me to group things, but we didn't spend time alone together anymore. We didn't talk properly. She had left Stagefright when she turned sixteen to join a different drama group, one in the centre of Bristol that cost a lot. No more walking home together.

'Can't believe it's over,' she said, 'all those years at school.'

'Yeah, thank God,' I said.

'I'm sad to be leaving. But we'll all still see each other, at Christmas and stuff.'

I didn't say anything. Lucy put her arm around me and gave me a squeeze. 'I reckon you're my oldest friend, Brooke. D'you know that?'

I worked it out in my head for a second. 'Yeah. You're right. Thirteen years.'

'To thirteen more,' she said, and giggled. I looked down.

Around ten, my friends were talking about going to some club for the rest of the night when we heard raised voices at the door. Our heads turned: a small crowd of people stood around, blocking our view. I walked over to see what was happening. In the doorway, dressed in a suit and tie and holding a bunch of roses, was Matt. My stomach flipped in a way I didn't know it still could.

'I'm not trying to gate crash,' he was arguing with a teacher. 'I just need to talk to one of the guests…'

His eyes found mine and his expression softened. I squeezed through the crowd to get to his side. 'It's alright, Mr Wilson, he's a friend of mine.'

'He's not coming in,' Mr Wilson snapped.

'I'm not trying to—' Matt started.

'It's okay, he just wants to talk to me.'

Mr Wilson glared at him before moving away. I looked at Matt and couldn't fight the smile that crept across my face, a genuine smile. *He'd come.* He smiled, too, looking nervous. 'Can I talk to you?' he said.

We stepped into the corridor and I could see he was choosing his words. He handed me the roses. 'These are for you.'

'Thank you,' I said, and took them.

'Okay, so,' he began, 'I know you said no to going on a date with me. But you did say it would be something you wanted if… if what, I dunno, but it seemed like part of you still…' He caught himself stumbling over his words and started over. 'If I've got this all wrong, I'll fuck off.'

'I don't want you to fuck off,' I grinned.

He grinned back. 'Okay. I know you said you didn't believe in fairy tales anymore, but all I'm asking for is one chance to try to prove to you that romance isn't dead.'

'Okay,' I said.

'Okay?' he repeated. 'You'll let me take you out? One date?'

'One date. Tonight.'

'It doesn't have to be tonight,' he said. 'If you wanted to stay with your friends—'

'It has to be tonight,' I said.

'Okay. Are you sure you don't want me to fuck off?'

'Please don't fuck off,' I laughed. 'I've just got to talk to my friend.'

I went back into the room, past Mr Wilson, who was standing at the door and glaring at Matt. My heart was hammering against my ribcage. The one thing I thought would never be real, the one thing I thought I could never deserve, had happened: someone still wanted me.

Too late, though. The thought made my stomach drop, and I had to stop, grab the back of a chair and catch my breath. People rushed around me, crowded around phones to plan the rest of their evenings. They were just going to enjoy their last night. *I guess I should, too.* Tomorrow could wait.

I got my jacket from the cloakroom and went to check Finn was alright for a lift home.

'Oh yeah, everyone's going out after. We'll just share a taxi back,' he said.

Lucy joined us. 'Is that Matt at the door? From Stagefright?'

'Um,' I said, 'yeah.'

'Why is he at our Prom?'

'Oh, well, um,' I said sheepishly. It was weird to tell Lucy the truth, though now there was no reason why I shouldn't. 'We've been talking, a bit, recently. And he wants to take me on a date.'

'*Ohmygod*,' Lucy said. 'On Prom night? That's so romantic!'

'I guess so,' I grinned.

She pulled me into a hug and squeezed me tight. 'Have the best time. We can have another night out soon!'

I didn't say anything, and just let her hold me for a moment, before releasing me and smiling sweetly. 'Oh, one sec,' she said, and went into her bag. She took out a little tin and handed it to me. 'In case you need it later.'

'Jesus, what's this? Cocaine?'

She laughed. 'Condoms! Remember what Miss Johnson told us, keep 'em in a tin, stops them wearing down.'

'Oh, I don't think I'll need these…'

'Just in case,' she said. 'Have them.'

I returned to Matt and snatched up his hand and he grinned. Maybe there was a little fire left in me.

'You sure you don't mind leaving early?' he said, as we walked down the stairs.

'Hell no,' I said, with an exhilaration I hadn't felt in a long, long time. Maybe this was the feeling he'd been trying to give me that night we walked through the empty streets to the Connell Complex, two kids running away together. I'd been too nervous to properly enjoy it, but tonight I would let myself. 'Where are we going?'

'You'll see,' was all he said.

It hadn't been dark for long, but the streetlights reflected off his car windows like stars. He turned to me. 'Okay, so. If it's alright with you, I want to take you on a first date. But I mean, a real first date. As if we've just met. So, m'lady,' he offered me his hand. 'Matthew Williams, but you can call me Matt. Pleased to meet you.'

'Brooke Tyler,' I shook his hand. 'Pleasure.'

'I'll have her back by nine,' he said to nobody, and I laughed, and I was happy and excited, and I tried not to think about tomorrow.

He opened the passenger door for me like a gentleman, and I dumped my jacket and bouquet in the back seat, and when he turned on the engine, *Taking Chances* came on the speakers, and I looked at him and he returned my gaze sheepishly.

'So Matt,' I said, as he drove through the city. 'What do you do?'

'I'm doing a master's,' he said. 'Chemistry.'

'Oh my. I'm not sure how I feel about going on a date with someone who's still a student.'

'You want someone with a proper job?' he laughed. 'Someone who can provide for you.'

'Exactly. I've got high standards.'

He left the car in the multi-storey on Trenchard Street, sliding his parking ticket into his wallet. Hand in hand, he led me up Park Street, past the people spilling their way out of the pubs and towards the clubs. I got breathless with the walk, and he offered to give me a piggyback, and when I got on his back, he only lasted a few seconds before he had to put me down. At the top of the hill, he headed for a fancy restaurant, the fanciest I'd ever been in.

'Are we going to eat?' I asked.

'Well, I imagine you've already had dinner, right?'

'Right.'

'I've got something better in mind,' he said.

He'd made a reservation and they took our coats, the restaurant mostly empty, candles burning out on the tables.

'I should tell you, sir, that the kitchen will be closing in twenty minutes,' the waiter said, as he sat us down.

'That's alright. Can we jump straight to the dessert menus, please?'

I looked at Matt and he smiled at the brilliance of his plan. I got a giant chocolate brownie, and he got the strawberry cheesecake. We kept swapping questions as we swapped forkfuls of dessert, as if we didn't already know the answers, and it was silly, but it was also eye opening, to see him as I would have done if we'd started here. If only we'd started here.

After dessert, he took me to a very posh hotel, a wedding party roaring loudly from the function room. We sat in the bar and sipped champagne, and he held my hand, and I put my foot on his stool so my ankle was between both of his. It was effortless: the little touches, the magnetism between us. I felt like a real woman, grown up, happy and alive and in love. I could hardly remember anything from before tonight, how tired and sad I was hours earlier, how I'd got the scars on my arms.

Midnight came, and my heart sank. It was tomorrow already. I pushed away the thought and tried to stay in the moment, stay here with him, letting myself feel happy for the first time in a long, long time. Matt drained his glass and silently took my hand. He led me out to the bar's stone balcony, overlooking the gardens, which were massive and colourful with explosions of flowers lit by flame lamps. The wedding party had moved down onto the lawn, gathered around the bride and groom. A firework shot from the horizon and into the black sky.

'Just in time,' Matt said, removing his suit jacket and placing it lightly over my shoulders. I removed it and put it on properly with my arms through the sleeves. He laughed.

'What?' I asked, taking off my heels.

'It's the old you,' he smiled. 'You're back.'

If only for a night, I thought, then blocked it out.

If all he'd wanted was some fireworks, then we could have stayed at Prom, but it was better here. He stepped behind me and wrapped his arms around my waist. I ran my hands over his sleeves, his knuckles. His face was next to mine, the smell of him enveloping me, and every now and then he would press his lips against my cheek or my neck, and every time he did, I'd bite my lip, forcing back the thought of tomorrow.

We stayed there for God knows how long, and I wished every moment would just stop so I could just stand there barefoot, my toes pressed against the cold stone, with Matt's arms holding me upright, stopping me from collapsing and crying and falling apart. Tomorrow didn't have to come. What was wrong with just tonight?

'Shall I take you home?' he said, after the sound of the last firework had fizzled away into the sky.

'Was that it?' I said quickly, turning to face him. 'Wait, I didn't mean—tonight's been lovely. I just don't want to go home yet.'

'I'd only planned up to here. And it's late.'

'Can't we…' I bit my lip. The words felt big and unfamiliar on my tongue. 'Can we get a hotel room?'

Matt looked surprised. 'Really?'

'Yes,' I said.

'Okay. Well, to be honest, I don't think I can afford a room here.'

'Honestly. Anywhere. Travelodge.'

'Okay.' He took out his phone and looked on Google Maps. 'There's one near Millennium Square. Are you sure?'

I nodded.

So we went, him in his socks and me in his too-large shoes with my heels in my hand. We walked down Park Street and all the while I was clinging to him, clinging to the smile on my face, trying to make it last, trying to make tonight the only night. The lights reminded me of London or New York or other bright, beautiful places where Matt and I could run away to and start again entirely. If only that was what tomorrow could be like.

We got to the Travelodge. It was almost one o'clock and it was completely deserted, minus the teenager behind the reception desk. Matt booked a room and steered me through the hallway. He smoothly slipped the keycard into the door and held it open as I went inside.

'Now, just because we've got this room doesn't mean anything has to happen,' he said, closing the door behind him. 'We can just go to sleep. Or I can get another room—'

I shut him up with kisses. Seizing the collar of his shirt, I pulled him towards me and led him to the bed. I lay down, pulling him on top of me.

'Is this okay?' he asked.

'Yes,' I said, looking up at him. 'Is this okay?'

He nodded, and smiled, and started kissing my cheek, my neck, my shoulders. His lips were hot on my skin and I caught my breath. He asked before he touched a new part of me, and made me new with his touch. I asked before I touched him, too, and we undressed each other, as if seeing each other for the first time, and I opened the tin Lucy had given me and tried as hard as I could not to think about tomorrow.

At the end of it all, I started shedding silent tears as he held me tight, stroking my hair, thinking that I was crying because it was the start of something beautiful, when really, it was the end.

SCENE 8: MATT, 21

Things are going to be better this time.

I looked to my left, at the woman sleeping next to me. Her body rose and fell slowly, her brown hair splayed across the pillow. I moved closer, so that I could feel her breath on my face and draped my arm over her thin frame. She didn't look healthy. And she was different. She was quiet now, subdued, and sad all the time. But things were going to change. That old, burning person I knew was still in there. I'd seen her tonight, and I was going to bring her back. I was going to look after her. We would fall in love all over again and we'd do it right this time.

I looked at her bare arm, at the tally chart of white and red lines that criss-crossed her wrist. Gently enough not to wake her, I pressed my lips against the scarred skin.

'Things are going to get better,' I whispered.

SCENE 9: BROOKE, 18

I only pretended to sleep that night. I waited until five o'clock—the plan had been to wait until four, but I didn't want to leave. Of course I didn't. So why did I? I don't know.

But at five, when dawn was only moments away, I slipped out of Matt's weary arms and put my underwear back on. I dressed as quietly as I could, all the while hoping he would wake up and make me stay. He didn't stir.

I took all the freebies from the room—shampoo, conditioner, shower gel, soap, stuffing them all into my little strappy Prom bag. I would need them where I was going.

Then came the hard part. I didn't know whether to kiss him goodbye, leave a note, or climb back into bed with him and forget the whole thing. I'd been so happy last night. But I knew that happiness couldn't last. I took the notepad and pen on the desk and wrote *SORRY*.

As I opened the door to leave, I gave him one last look. He was deeply asleep. His breathing was slow and regular, his face turned away from me. I closed the door.

It was then that I realised I had no way of getting home. I cursed myself for not insisting we take my car the night before, too swept up in the moment to think about it. *Don't you see?* I berated myself. *Things go wrong when you let yourself be happy*. The bus would be too slow, so I got an Uber. The driver was annoyingly chatty for half past five and I had to tell him I was exhausted to get him to shut up. He dropped me at the Prom venue where my car was waiting, proudly bearing a parking ticket. I swapped my heels for my worn-out Vans that I'd kept in the boot and drove home, keeping half an eye on my phone, hoping it would buzz, hoping would call. Mum had left me a bajillion voicemails the night before, then realised I was either at a club, or staying with a friend, or hooking up with a stranger, and had gone to bed smiling at the thought of me having an actual interaction with another human being.

When I got home, I crept around as quietly as I could. If Mum woke now, I had no idea what I'd do. Probably just go to bed or call Matt and not do what I'd planned. But she didn't wake.

I had already stuffed the clothes I would take into plastic bags, hidden inside my wardrobe, and I chucked them into my suitcase. A toothbrush, toothpaste. Both of my passports. Snacks from the kitchen cupboards, anything that would keep. I checked the time and realised I couldn't shower or change, so I shoved a jumper on over the top of my dress.

People would wonder how I did it, but it was easy. I'd been planning this for a long time. It had started as a daydream. Then it became a possibility. Then a probability. Never definite, not even now. It would only be definite when it happened.

I'd been preparing for it over the past couple of years, just in case. I'd asked for cash for my birthdays and saved every penny I was given. Mum would hand me two tenners to go shopping with my non-existent friends, and instead, I'd go to work at the restaurant. With all the extra money she'd given me as a deposit for university halls, to buy books, to pad out my loan, I had plenty. And without her knowledge, I had turned down all my university offers.

I had to leave before she woke up. I was going through the motions, numbly following all the steps of a plan that was now running more smoothly than I had ever imagined. My hands barely felt the pressure of Mum's car keys as I placed them on the kitchen table next to the note I'd written months earlier. Tears stung in my eyes as I double checked my passports and documents. I didn't know if I even wanted to do this anymore, but it was the only future I could see ahead of me. I had no backup plan. I breathed my last breath of home air and left.

I hadn't been sure which would be harder, leaving Matt or leaving Mum, but I had been certain one would be more difficult than the other. Matt's broken-hearted face was not etched in my mind as deeply as my mother's. I blocked it out. *Everyone will be better off without you,* I reminded myself.

I had booked a taxi days before, and there it was. 'Bristol airport, please,' I said as I slid onto the back seat and watched my childhood home disappear from view.

We drove back into the city and I coughed up far too much cash for the fare. I had my passports and I'd booked my tickets, but that was it. I didn't know what would happen when I landed. Maybe I'd never really believed this day would come.

I found my flight's check-in desk and joined the queue of sleepy travellers, families with children, all travel pillows and colourful rucksacks. I must've looked like shit. I felt like shit too. My anxiety started to build. Was I really going to go through with this? I guess I could get in a taxi and go home, or back to the Travelodge. But I couldn't picture what tomorrow would look like, or the day after that. I had no future here. I had to leave.

I got to the front of the queue. 'Morning,' the woman said.

'Morning,' I grumbled back.

'DL4348 to Seattle?'

'That's right,' I said, and handed over my US passport.

SCENE 10: MATT, 21

I rolled over and looked at my phone. Ten past nine. I rolled back with heavy eyes and tried to bury my face in her hair, but I couldn't find her. I reached blindly over to touch her, but she was gone.

I opened my eyes and saw her side of the bed was empty, but I wasn't frightened. The bathroom, I told myself, but there was no sound of a shower, and when I opened the door, she wasn't in there either.

I noticed her dress and shoes were missing. Perhaps she'd gone out, to get breakfast or something. I put on my trousers and shirt and went to the Travelodge's reception.

'Hi—sorry—did you see a woman in a black dress come through?' I asked.

He shook his head. 'Sorry, mate, I've just started. I'll check with the guy who was on earlier, shall I?'

He disappeared into the side room, returning with the teenager from last night who had on a rucksack, and looked exhausted. 'Can I help?' he said tiredly.

'Did you see a woman in a black dress? The woman I checked in with last night?'

He thought for a moment, then said, 'Yeah, uh, she left.'

'When was this?'

'Maybe five, five-thirty.'

'Thank you.'

Flying back to the room, I jammed the keycard into the door. As I entered, I realised I wasn't sure what my target was, so I went for my phone to call her. And that's when I saw it. The notepaper on the desk reading one word: *SORRY*.

Fuck.

SCENE 11: BROOKE, 18

'Last call for flight DL4348 to Seattle. Any passengers intending to travel on this flight, please make your way to gate sixteen. This is the last call for flight DL4348 to Seattle.'

I downed my coffee. It burnt my throat, but I didn't react. I'd waited for the last call before boarding.

I'd been out of the hotel room for four-and-a-half hours. I thought he'd be up by now, or at least woken briefly to see that I was gone. I had arrived at the airport well before my flight. There had even been a delay. I had waited as long as I possibly could, but no one came. No one messaged or rang. They'd called my bluff. I'd called my own. And now my only future was on that airplane. I had to get on it.

'Bye, Matt,' I whispered, my eyes finally succumbing to tears. I dropped my phone into a bin, took my bags, and walked to the gate without looking back.

SCENE 12: MATT, 21

Wherever her phone was, she had three missed calls from me.

I rang her again and this time I left a message. 'Brooke. Hi. It's me. I'm worried about you. You disappeared. Please let me know you're okay?'

I sat on the end of the bed, my breathing rapid, my heart racing, trying to make sense of the million thoughts in my head. The only thing I could see clearly was that bloody image of her on the bathroom floor, from the last time she vanished on me.

But she'd left, and she'd taken all her stuff with her, and I'd read that suicidal people leave behind or give away their things because they know they won't need them. She could have left to go and kill herself, but why? Where would she go? Maybe she didn't want to do it here. Maybe she didn't want me to find her like I did the last time.

But the last time was because she'd thought I'd been kissing Tilly. We'd just had the best night of our lives—or my life, at least. Why would she want to kill herself after that?

Maybe she hasn't gone to die, I told myself. *Maybe she's gone home. Maybe she had to get back, for her mum. But why would she just disappear? Why the note? Why isn't she answering her phone?*

I tried to calm my breathing. I had to go to her house and let her answer the door, and be all embarrassed that I'd shown up when her mum was home. She would laugh and tell me I shouldn't have worried, that she just had to get home and didn't want to wake me, that she wanted to go out again and everything was alright.

I got up and grabbed my wallet and keys, trying to keep my hands steady. I stuffed the phone in my pocket and dashed out of the room. Down the hall, into the foyer, out through the main doors.

'Mr Williams!' called the receptionist. 'Are you leaving?'

'Yes,' I shouted, without looking back, 'but I'll be back later.'

'But check out is—' Too late. I was gone.

Don't run, she's fine, I told myself, but still my pace increased from a powerwalk to a jog and then a sprint as I rushed across College Green. I got back to the car park, sweaty and gasping for breath, and paid the parking ticket. *Fuck, where did I leave the car?* It took me a minute to remember. I got in and stuck my phone in the holder; I was on fourteen percent. I grabbed the cable with the dodgy wire from the glove compartment and stuck it in the cigarette lighter.

The satnav app automatically routed me home, which was close enough. I started driving, trying to stay calm. *She's fine,* I told myself, *she's definitely fine. You're overreacting.*

I was stuck at a red light just before the Bearpit when my phone rang. The vibrations gave me a start, and then a rush of relief: Brooke must be calling. But when I looked at the screen, it wasn't her; Amy Tyler was ringing me through Facebook. My stomach dropped.

I put it on speakerphone just as the light went green and I entered the roundabout. 'Amy?' I said.

'Matt, hi, God, okay, is Brooke with you?' Her voice was high and fast.

'No, she's not,' I said, fear rising inside me. 'She was with me last night.'

'Shit, fuck, okay. Mum rang me, and I rang Lucy, and she said Brooke left Prom with you.'

'Yeah, she did—she's not with you?'

'I'm still in Birmingham, but she's not at home, she's not in London with Dad, we don't know where she is,' Amy said.

'Fuck, okay, fuck—well, let's not assume the worst. She could be on her way home.'

'She's been home. She left a note.'

My heart stopped. 'A suicide note?'

'No, it wasn't that—I can't remember it word for word, but it was like, I'm moving abroad, don't miss me, you'll never see me again—Mum said she took her passports and suitcase. I really think she's leaving.'

I indicated right and swerved into the lane. The car behind me honked. I turned round the roundabout and started going back the way I came. Another red. 'I'm in town. I'm at the Bearpit. I'll go to the airport, see if I can catch her, talk some sense into her.'

'She could be flying from London.'

'I have to try!' I said, scrambling to change the satnav's destination. 'Where would she go? If she was leaving permanently, where would she move to, do you know?'

'I've got no clue. We're half American, so we've got dual citizenship, but we've only been there once. It's not like we know anyone there. She could go anywhere—'

'Can you keep calling her, maybe call the airport?'

'Yes, of course.' Amy's voice went quiet for a moment. 'Matt, why was Brooke with you last night?'

'We…we'd been talking. About dating. We went on a date. Stayed in a hotel. She was gone when I woke up.'

'Okay. Okay, call me back later.'

She hung up. I was laser focused now, gripping the wheel hard as the light went green. The satnav said eighteen minutes, but I was speeding. Every second seemed to drag by, and I tried to keep calm, tried to focus on my destination instead of every other thought that was going through my mind.

When I finally got to the airport, I parked in the drop-off zone and ran inside. There were dozens of desks, each for different flights. Which was her airline? Where was she going? It would be pointless to guess. I decided to try security instead, racing up the escalator two steps at a time. The entrance was gated; people scanned their boarding passes to get through. There was a uniformed security guy hovering in front of the barriers. *No way is this gonna work,* I thought, as I approached him.

'Hi, sorry, hi, I was wondering if you could help me. My… girlfriend is in here, and, uh, I need to speak to her. Can you make an announcement or something?'

He didn't buy it for a second. 'Can't you just call her?'

'That's the thing,' I said, making it up as I went along. I took my phone out of my pocket and waved it in front of him. 'She left her phone. It's her work phone. She needs it, it's really important.'

'I'm not sure we're going to be able to help you with that.'

'Please, is there anything you can do? Can't you just go on the tannoy and ask her to come back for it?'

'Can you tell me which flight she's on?' he said blankly, knowing full well that I couldn't.

'No, I er…lost the details,' I said.

He shrugged. 'You won't be able to get through security without a boarding pass.'

'Please can you—fine,' I said, unlocking the phone and going straight to EasyJet's website.

'Her work phone,' the guy snorted.

'I know her code, okay.'

I booked the cheapest flight, the next one to Edinburgh, and did the online check-in. After a full five minutes, I had my boarding pass and went through. The security guy pointed me out to his colleague, who proceeded to keep a very close eye on me as I joined the infuriatingly long queue. I took off my belt and shoes and put my wallet and phone in the tray. When I got through the body scanner, to no surprise the alarm beeped, and the colleague did a very thorough pat down of me. My tray also beeped, and I had to wait for them to wipe down the inside of my wallet until they were satisfied it wasn't lined with cocaine. Then I raced through the duty free, the shops, the restaurants, until I saw a sign with all the gates listed.

Fuck. Where to start? There were a few cities I recognised as America, others going to Europe, and then places I'd never even heard of. At random, I picked gate thirteen for New York. That seemed like a good place to start a new life, if that's what she was planning to do. I raced to it, darting between suitcases. *God, I'm unfit.*

Boarding hadn't begun when I got to the gate. I ran up to the desk and gasped, 'Excuse me,' to the man behind it, who looked a lot calmer than I was.

'Yes, sir?' he said brightly.

There was a poster on the wall behind his head: a woman watching the sunset from an airplane window. My eyes moved to the caption at the bottom: *326 destinations. 60 countries. 6 continents. 1 airline.*

I looked back at the man and spoke rapidly. 'I can't find my girlfriend—she's got our bags. Is it possible to make an announcement for her to come and meet me?'

'Are you on this flight, sir?'

'Er…not sure. She's got the boarding passes.'

'But you're flying to New York?'

'Um. I don't know. She's surprising me. Birthday trip.'

He didn't question what was becoming an increasingly dubious story. 'What's your name, sir?'

'Matthew Williams.'

I heard him type it in. 'You're not on this flight. Or any flight on Delta.'

'Her name is Brooke Maria Tyler. Can you search her name?'

'Mm, I'm not sure she'll come up if you're not flying Delta…' he said, but typed it in anyway. The computer took a long time, and my heart was racing, and I couldn't keep still. *Can he take any longer?*

Finally he said, 'Oh.'

'Oh?' I asked. Was that it? Oh?

'She is on this airline, but her flight's already left.'

Oh no. 'Where did she go?'

'Excuse me,' an older man appeared behind him. 'David, can you open the gate?'

David looked sheepish as he shuffled off. His supervisor turned to me with fierce eyes. 'Can I help you, sir?'

'That man was helping me find my girlfriend,' I reverted to the original lie. 'I have her work phone. I was trying to get it to her.'

'You can't be here without a boarding pass.'

'I have one, I have one.' I flashed him the EasyJet one on my phone.

'This is Delta.'

'We're not travelling together.'

'But she didn't tell you where she was going?'

'She's had a lot of trips this month. Work.'

He peered at me suspiciously. 'Are you sure she's your girlfriend?'

'Yes!' I lied. 'Where did she go, please?' The desperation was audible in my voice. He saw through me. He looked at the computer, and I heard him click the window closed.

'If she is your girlfriend,' he said dryly, 'I'm sure she'll call from the hotel.'

I looked again at the poster, at the woman looking at the sunset. Was that Brooke, looking out of a window, hoping for something better? Three hundred and twenty-six destinations. Sixty countries. Six continents. I would never find her.

'Please,' I said slowly. 'Please, can you tell me anything?'

'Sir,' he said, clicking a button under the desk. 'I find your story very suspect, and I'm calling security.'

'Don't bother.'

I put my hands behind my head in defeat and wandered off, just as a security guy started tailing me. He put his hand on my arm and I let him, because that was it. It was over. She was gone. She was so frightened of me that she had to escape to another country to feel safe. What did that make me? A monster? Had she even wanted to sleep with me last night? The old guilt crept in. Had I really made the same mistake twice, even though I'd tried so hard to be considerate, to give her everything I'd failed to last time?

That couldn't be it. She'd wanted to be there last night. She'd wanted the hotel room. She'd been the one to kiss me, and I'd told her we didn't have to. I'd checked, and asked her a hundred times, and she'd said yes, she wanted it, she wanted me, and it had been amazing, and she'd left that note, she apologised for leaving. Well, now it was my turn. *Brooke, I'm sorry, I am so, so sorry and I will never stop being sorry. I will be sorry forever and ever until the day I die.*

The security guy chucked me outside somewhere. I found my way back to my car, miraculously ticketless, and got in.

I put my phone in the holder and sat there, breathing hard. The adrenaline of the last hour was slowly seeping out of my bloodstream and left me physically and emotionally exhausted. Just as I felt the first few choking sobs coming, some uniformed guy tapped on my window. 'This is drop off only, mate,' he said.

I nodded, sniffing back the tears for now. I opened the satnav app and set it to take me back to the Travelodge to no doubt pay for a late checkout. Then I opened Facebook and called Amy on speakerphone.

'Hello, Matt?' she said quickly. I could tell by her voice she'd been crying.

'I'm too late, Amy,' I said, as I pulled onto the road. 'She's gone.'

SCENE 13: BROOKE, 18

When I got to my seat, I had a panic attack.
The woman next to me seemed to think I was scared of flying and helped to manage my hyperventilating as the plane left the ground and I saw England disappear from view. As soon as the seatbelt sign went off, I locked myself in the bathroom and looked in the mirror, trying to slow my breathing. *Oh, God, what have I done?*

It was never meant to get this far. Or maybe it was. I couldn't separate the part of me that wanted to destroy me, and the other part that wanted to keep me safe; warring factions that blurred together in the fight to control what I did or didn't do. Which part had decided to leave? The part that wanted to destroy my past or the part that promised a better future? It was true that I couldn't picture a life in England. I had to get out of there. They'd all be better off without me, they'd soon realise. I couldn't believe that anyone would want me to stay. But maybe I'd wanted someone to want me to stay.

When someone knocked on the door, I returned to my seat and wrapped myself in a blanket, still freaking out internally. *It's okay, I just need a plan*, I told myself. *I just need to decide what to do when I land.* I'd been fantasising about leaving for years, but the image always ended with me getting on the plane. I'd never considered what would happen after.

Seattle. I'd picked it because I liked *Grey's Anatomy*, and that picture of the Space Needle in Matt's room, and the weather didn't get too hot or too cold. It was far away from Indiana, where Dad grew up before he moved to England, and where a grandmother I'd only met once still lived.

Okay, so when I land, I'll just use Google Maps to find the nearest motel—fuck! I'd ditched my phone in England, as planned; I couldn't have people contacting me, and I couldn't be tempted to contact them. But I'd never thought about managing without a phone, or getting a new one. *Shit.*

Okay, so when I land, I'll ask at the airport where the nearest motel is, and they'll have a restaurant nearby so I can get some food—shit. Money. I hadn't thought about money. I mean, I'd been saving up, but I didn't think to get any fucking *dollars.* Fuckfuckfuck.

Okay, so when I land, I'll change my cash at the airport and also ask where the nearest motel is, and they'll have a restaurant nearby so I can get some food, and then after that, I'll…I'll…

I started hyperventilating again.

I guess I could kill myself.

I pushed the thought away. Surely I'd moved across continents to do more than off myself? I just needed a plan, and then I'd be fine. *I'll have to get a new phone, and a bank account, and then I'll need a job and a flat. Then I'll make some friends and find a boyfriend and all my problems will be left behind in England and I'll be fine.*

I started to take deeper breaths to calm myself down, like the woman next to me had said to do. She was asleep now. I pulled the blanket tighter around me.

New phone—the motel reception will be able to help me find a shop. American bank account—I can google how to set that up once I've got the phone. Then I can ring the English bank and close that account. For jobs, I can apply online once I've got my phone. I can also hand my CV in to offices. I've got the right to work in America, and I'm really smart, so I'll get hired. I've always had good grades. I got into Cardiff uni. I'll be fine, I'll find something I want to do. And then I can find a flat online, once I've got the job—maybe a one-bed, so I don't have to live with other people. And then I'll make friends at work and I'll meet someone who really loves me, and I'll be happy. That's the plan.

When we landed, my legs were trembling. The lady next to me smiled and said, 'You did it. It's over now.' I smiled politely back.

We got the 'people mover' to the main terminal, then got to the passport check. I'd never thought of myself as a US citizen in my life, but I joined the queue that read as such. The man didn't ask me anything when he looked at my picture.

Then out into the real world. I found the bureau de change and changed all the pounds I had for dollars. I asked about motels and was directed to a bunch that lined the main road outside the airport. The summer sun was hot and the wide streets provided no shade as I dragged my massive bag up the pavement. There were lots of tents pitched on the streetside, shopping trolleys and makeshift shelters. I'd never seen so many homeless people before, not in Bristol. I kept my eyes down and swept past them, knowing I had to keep hold of every penny I had until I was settled. I ended up going for the first motel I found, Baker's Motel, and booked the cheapest room for one night.

I sat on the creaky bed. The mint-green walls loomed over me, the skirting board marking the edges of my chartered America. The big, unexplored expanse of the rest of the country stretched out around me. *Now what?*

I realised I was exhausted, and hadn't slept since before Prom, before my exam. That felt so long ago now. I also hadn't eaten all day. I figured I'd better get some food.

Across the motel's car park was a dingy bar. It wasn't until I saw the signs about IDing that I remembered the drinking age here was twenty-one, but I had a feeling they wouldn't care. I was the only woman in the place, and all the men smelled of cigarettes and booze. I sat at the bar and ordered a burger and 'french fries'.

'Going someplace nice?' a man said, perching on the barstool next to mine.

'Huh?' I said.

'Your skirt.' He touched the fabric just above my knee. I realised I was still in my prom dress, a baggy jumper lazily chucked over it.

'Don't ask,' I said, and he didn't. He was super tanned, and ruggedly handsome. His eyes were glossy, he had a stubbly thing going on, and there was something sweetly shy in his smile. I was flooded with hope. *My first day in America, and this guy starts*

*talking to me. Maybe this is a sign that I made the right decision.
Maybe he'll make it all worth it.*

'Harry,' he said, offering his hand.

'Brooke,' I said, shaking it and wishing I'd showered before eating.

'British Brooke. Nice to meet you. So, what brings you to the States?'

'I live here,' I said, before another bite.

'Oh, right. How long have you lived here?'

'About forty-five minutes,' I said.

Harry laughed, his glossy eyes gleaming. 'So am I your first American friend?'

'You are indeed,' I smiled back.

He bought me drinks. I was pretty inexperienced with alcohol, seeing as I wasn't meant to have any when I was on anti-depressants. But those meds had never agreed with me, and now I was in America I probably couldn't afford them. I drank up, and he chatted about himself, which may have seemed selfish but I didn't want to talk about me. The drinks made it easier to flirt, to be smooth and charming in the arms of this handsome stranger. I told Harry how I needed to find a flat and a job. He promised to help me, to show me round the city and introduce me to his friends. I got properly drunk for the first time in my life, and the next thing I knew I was waking up to the sound of knocking at my door.

Bloody hell, was my first thought. *Are hangovers always this bad?*

For a moment I'd forgotten everything that'd happened, everything I'd done in the last couple of days, and it hit me like a punch in the stomach. I guess I deserved that. The room's mint walls towered over me, the bedsheets cold and rough on my skin. I rolled over to reach for Harry, but he wasn't there.

I sat up. Where was he? My first American friend, my only friend in the world, had vanished.

There was another knock, and I realised it must be him: he must've gone out to get us coffee or something. I wrapped myself in a blanket and went to answer the door, but then I heard Mr Baker's voice coming from the other side.

'Miss, check out was at ten,' he said.

'Right, right,' I said, 'sorry.'

I grabbed the knickers and prom dress from the floor to cover my naked body, and opened the door. Mr Baker did not look pleased to see me in what was clearly the night before's outfit—or, really, the night before the night before.

'I'll be ten minutes,' I said.

'Now. Sorry. Cleaner's waiting.' He pointed to the man at his side.

'Right,' I said, 'okay.'

I chucked the jumper back on and put the few things I'd unpacked back into the suitcase. I could see Lucy's tin was open and there was a wrapper in the bin, a good sign that Drunk Brooke had been smart enough at least to use a condom. I grabbed the tin and lugged my bags out of the door, scanning the car park for some sign of Harry on his way back from wherever he went.

'Mr Baker? My…friend stayed over last night.'

'That guy left around eight. Your *friend* isn't coming back, sweetheart.'

'Oh.' I cleared my throat. 'Right.' I'd been hoping Harry would help me, like he'd said last night. I was hoping he'd bring meaning to everything I'd done. My cheeks went red.

'Mr Baker,' I said, 'Is there somewhere round here I can buy a phone?'

He sighed, like it was a real inconvenience, before telling me to get the red line and then a bus to Southcenter Mall. It was confusing, and I knew I'd struggle to find the right bus stop without a phone.

'Right,' I said, hoping a burst of chivalry would possess him. 'You don't know anyone who could give me a lift, do you?'

He looked at me like I was stupid. 'No,' he said.

'Okay,' I gulped, 'thanks.'

I would have got an Uber if I'd had more than cash, but I couldn't have my British bank card tied to my journeys. I walked back to the airport, trying to remember Mr Baker's directions and feeling stupid for hoping Harry was going to be someone special. I used cash to buy an Orca card at the airport's tube station, then took the red line to Tukwila Boulevard. I wandered around for twenty-five minutes before figuring out which of the crowded buses to squeeze onto, then travelled to Southcenter Mall. All the while my eyes were wide with terror, taking in America like a lost little kitten in last night's clothes.

At Southcenter, I talked to the guy at the phone shop, but I only had cash so he couldn't set me up on a contract. I hauled my bags to a bank to set up an account, but they couldn't help me as I didn't have an address. I went back to the phone shop on the verge of tears and begged the guy to help me out. He managed to get me some overpriced pay-as-you-go data thing that I'd have to top up in corner shops like it was 2005 or something. After two hours I wound up at Panda Express, gorging on orange chicken and trying to stifle sobs from the failures of the day. How had I left England with so little preparation? How had I not planned ahead about a phone, a bank account, a place to live? Why hadn't I applied for jobs ahead of time, why hadn't I looked at flat listings and at least made some enquiries?

I considered buying a ticket home. Making some excuse as to where I'd been, apologising for scaring them all, for making Mum cry...God, when she read my note, she probably called the police—

I blocked it out. I opened my new phone and got on to the mall WiFi, choosing to save the data for later. Now I had the phone, I had a lifeline. I could download CityMapper to get around town, SpareRoom to find a flat, and Indeed to apply to jobs. But first, I needed a place to sleep tonight.

What did other people do when they moved away, or went travelling? They got drunk and made friends effortlessly, fell in love and had adventures. They left all their problems behind. They stayed in hostels. Maybe that'd be a good idea: stay in a hostel for a week, apply for jobs, make some friends. If I could establish a friendship group, they'd help me find a place to live. They'd make everything better. The trouble was, I hadn't made a new friend in years, and had barely kept my old ones. But it was easy to meet people in a hostel, right?

I went onto the HostelWorld website and found a place that was close to the city centre, so hopefully I could find a job near there. I tried to book online but remembered the bank account, and again the thought of the exact hostel I was sleeping in coming up on my British bank statement freaked me out. I prayed that they'd take cash if I just rocked up.

CityMapper told me to get a bus there. My arms were aching from dragging the suitcase, my legs hurting from walking so much, and I was desperate to shower. The app directed me to the right bus stop and I made it to the hostel. They did take cash, thank God, and I checked into an eight-bed dorm. There were lockers, and I bought a padlock from reception, which made me feel safer; that bag was all I had in the world. The room was empty, as it was mid-afternoon, except for one person who seemed to be napping.

They've got the right idea, I thought, and fell asleep without changing out of my clothes.

I woke up to someone switching the lights on. Some girls came in, chatting away in French and starting to put on makeup. I checked the time on my new phone: nearly ten at night. *You're not doing your jetlag any favours,* I thought.

I sat up in bed and rubbed my eyes. The plan was to make friends, but I was too nervous to speak. I got up and went to find a bathroom. I looked like shit. My hair was greasy and my face was screaming for a wash. I went back to my room to grab my toiletries.

Now there were two guys in the room as well who, from their accents, seemed to be Australian. I looked down at the French girls, cross legged on the floor in front of the mirror, and knew that if I went too long without saying anything, I'd miss my chance. I dug deep for my courage and managed to squeak out a 'Hi.'

'Hi,' they said back, then continued doing their eyeliner.

My cheeks were hot. I made a beeline for my bunk, wishing I'd been born without a voicebox. I dug into my suitcase and took out my shampoo, shower gel, towel, and hairbrush. It was best I didn't make friends when I looked like this anyway. I could shower and sleep tonight, and try again tomorrow.

The French girls left, and the Aussie guys tailed out behind them, though one of them stopped and looked at me on his way. 'Hey,' he said effortlessly.

'Hey,' I replied, my voice cracking.

'Are you doing the bar crawl?'

'Umm,' I said.

'We're pregaming downstairs. You should come.'

'Okay,' I said.

'See you down there.' He left. I put the towel away. I guess no time for a shower; Aussie guy had handed me an olive branch that I was going to grip on to with all my might. I quickly put on some deodorant and perfume, and tied my hair up so it wouldn't look so greasy.

I wandered downstairs, passing strangers and looking at my feet as I did. In the lounge I saw a lot of people around my age sat around a table, cups and cans in hand. *This is where I'm meant to make friends. How do I do it? Do I just join the group and say hi?* I clocked the Aussie guy talking to his mate and squeezed onto the arm of the sofa next to him. 'Hi,' I said.

'Hi,' he replied. 'We're playing Never Have I Ever. You got a drink?'

'No,' I said.

He handed me a can of something from the pack between his flip-flopped feet. 'Here you go.'

'Thanks.' I took a sip of the horrible drink.

He turned back to the game, and I felt a desperate urge to keep his attention. *Got to be less boring, Brooke!*

'I'm Brooke,' I said to him.

'I'm Brian,' he said.

'Are you from Australia?'

'Nah, New Zealand.'

'Oh right,' I said, 'cool.'

I chatted to him, and to people around me, but it became clear I was the only one stopping in Seattle for more than a couple of days. Everyone else was doing the great North American road trip, in pairs or small groups, leaving tomorrow or the day after. No candidates for long-term friends here, then.

We got tipsy, some mostly sexual confessions came out, and eventually we left for the first bar. A few of us were ID'ed and didn't get in, but the crawl organisers promised that the second place wouldn't check. It was loud and we clutched bottles and stepped from one foot to the other. Brian was looking at me and getting closer, brushing my arms and waist. I drank loads and we kissed. I thought that maybe Harry was a mistake, but Brian would be different. Brian would make everything fall into place and he'd stay with me and help me and it would be okay again...

I woke up in my hostel bed, still in the jumper and prom dress. The French girls were packing up their stuff. The curtains were closed but the main light was on. I turned over and tried to go back to sleep, to escape the banging in my head.

The girls talked loudly which I thought was rude so early in the morning, but when I checked my phone, it was almost noon. I sat up and saw that there was nobody else here. Brian's bunk was empty, but his stuff was still on his bed. I'd been in there with him hours before, stifling giggles as he quickly and quietly fucked me, pulling up the skirt of my dress without taking my shoes off. It couldn't've lasted more than a couple of minutes before he asked me to go back to my bunk so he could sleep.

I got up and went to the kitchen to see if he was there, but it was empty. Everyone had gone out already, sightseeing on their gap years and summer holidays. I looked at the five phone numbers I'd added last night. None of their owners staying in the city. Brian was leaving for Portland the next day, but maybe I could go with him. I didn't have to stay in Seattle. Maybe that could be the new plan: backpacking with the Kiwi guys, spontaneous and fun. Maybe that would make everything better. I messaged him: *Hey, I'm up. Whereabouts are you? Maybe I can catch up x.*

I closed my messages and looked at my phone screen, its generic background tarnished by only a few apps. In England, I'd checked social media multiple times a day; now I couldn't risk logging on. I downloaded Reddit, which I'd never used before, but I knew it was anonymous and I needed something to keep me occupied. Brian still hadn't replied. I had some of the free cereal the hostel offered and scrolled through the Reddit homepage. After thirty-five minutes, my phone dinged.

Brian Hostel: Heya, just out and about with the guys. Have a good day!

The polite sting of you're-not-invited plunged into me. Brian was not going to rescue me. Brian was not going to stay in Seattle, and I was not going to follow him across America. I felt hope fading away, remembering that all I had were two more nights in that hostel bed.

That sole conversation sat in my inbox, my isolation staring back at me. I couldn't remember Mum's mobile number, but I'd memorised the landline years ago. I could call her if I wanted to. It was two in the morning there, or maybe three, I couldn't remember. Maybe I could call Amy through Facebook. I could download the app, but what would I see when I opened it? Posts on my profile asking where I'd gone, asking me to come back? Messages of anger, wondering how could I leave and not tell anyone, not even say goodbye? Or worse—nothing at all? Would anyone care that I was gone? Had anyone even noticed? My chest tightened and I put my phone down.

The benefit of the hostel being empty meant all the showers were available, and I was three days overdue. I washed three men from my hair, six hands from my body, and a hundred kisses from my lips. When I got out, I picked up that effing prom dress and shoved it in a plastic bag which I dubbed my new laundry bag. I shoved my bra in too, but the knickers had a one-way ticket to the bin. Three bedroom floors those knickers had laid upon, three men who'd got their itchy little fingers inside them. This was not how I thought this would go.

I felt a little better after the shower, so I went onto the hostel's shared computer to put together a CV. It fit on one page, without any A-Levels or experience outside the restaurant to pad it out. I printed it and saw the whiteness of the page staring back at me. *Is this little piece of A4 all I have going for me?*

I started applying for jobs. I went for anything entry-level, hoping that the cultural difference in qualifications would mask the fact I'd never know my A-Level results. I applied to be a receptionist, a PA, a waitress, a dog walker, a sales assistant. I wrote cover letter after cover letter, but I had no references, no LinkedIn, and very little experience. I kept telling myself I was smart, I'd been good at school, there was no reason anyone wouldn't hire me. I spent the whole afternoon at that computer, typing until my fingers ached.

That night I went to Trader Joe's to get something easy to cook, then sat in front of the TV in the lounge, refreshing my email and watching reruns of *The Bachelor*. People started filing in, in pairs or small groups. Brian came in and gave me a quick smile and a 'Hey,' before ignoring me and going to an Indian restaurant with his friends. I went to bed at a normal time that night, trying to get into a decent sleeping pattern, but I was silently crying for hours about how I'd ruined my life. I didn't realise there was any part of me that still cared about myself. How wrong I'd been to think getting on a plane would be fine, that I was too numb to feel anything anymore. Landing in another country without a plan or a friend in the world had certainly thawed any numbness in me, replacing it with a deep, gnawing fear. At least I'd discovered I still had some will to survive. But this wasn't what I'd imagined. Did I really think this was better than home?

Don't call it home anymore, I told myself. *You can never go back.*

The next day, I woke up pretty early and the first thing I did was pick up my phone and check my email. Nothing. I'd been hoping for a few responses, maybe an interview. My chest tightened. Why wasn't anyone getting back to me? I was more than qualified to work in a store, or in an office—hell, anyone could walk a dog. Why wasn't I getting anywhere? *Maybe they just need a few more days,* I thought.

Back at the computer, a big old machine that looked like it should run Windows '98. More applications. Most of the vacancies from yesterday had closed already, and I kept glancing hopefully at my phone. Brian came into the lounge to check out and left without a word. I kept typing.

I'd exhausted the job sites, but was still desperate to keep going, to take some action towards my own survival. I looked on Google Maps at nearby businesses. Then I went upstairs and put on the nicest clothes I had, a blouse and a pair of trousers.

After a second helping of cereal for lunch I walked around the city, knocking on office doors and approaching reception desks. I shook hands and smiled, handing in my CV and asking about entry-level jobs. I assured them that yes, I did have a right to work in the US, then felt my stomach twist uncomfortably as I told them no, I didn't have a college degree. They all said there was nothing at the moment, but they'd keep my 'resume' on file and be in touch if anything came up. I pointed to the number at the top of the page and made sure my phone was on loud.

After a few hours, I was exhausted. I went back to the hostel, made more food, and watched more reruns. America was meant to be an adventure, but somehow I'd travelled four thousand miles to end up in another dead-end routine, just as hopeless as I'd always been.

No calls came through. No texts. The lounge was empty today, but I didn't feel like talking to anyone anyway; my plan to make friends at the hostel seemed to have utterly failed. I shed frightened tears into my pillow that night. I thought about cutting, like I had done to cope with exams, but what was the point? What good would that do? In England I'd been trapped. Now I was free and alone, feebly attempting to fend for myself.

The next day I woke up, terrified of the world. Of that last free bowl of cereal. Of the empty inbox on my phone. I took a really long shower in the lukewarm water, trying to procrastinate the inevitable moment where I had to leave the hostel and go back to zero plans.

'Where to next?' asked the guy at reception as I checked out.

'Dunno. Here,' I said.

'You're not backpacking?'

'I've just moved here. Trying to find a job. Spent all day yesterday applying for stuff.'

'Nothing yet, huh?' He took my room key.

'Not yet,' I said, trying not to let my voice crack. I handed him my CV. 'You guys aren't hiring, are you?'

He glanced at the mostly blank piece of paper, then handed it back. 'We're all volunteers actually, working for accommodation. Except the owner.'

'I can't catch a break,' I said. 'I thought something entry-level would be easy, like a receptionist or assistant.'

'Oh, man, those are competitive. You gotta be a barista or a bartender first.' His words stung as they landed on my ear.

'I'd rather not do customer service,' I said. 'I'd rather do, like, an office job.'

The guy shrugged. 'Most people graduate from college and start working at McDonalds. You can't be too good for the crappy jobs.'

My face fell. Was he right? Was that the problem? That I was competing with people with degrees and internships for these supposedly entry-level positions? Was I really going to have to grind away at Starbucks before everything sorted itself out? Nothing was going to plan. Nothing was easier here.

I left the hostel, suitcase in hand, alone once more. So where does a girl go when she's lost in America with no plan, and she's definitely not too good for the crappy jobs? Back to the motel.

It was basically the same price as the hostel, and it had more privacy, so why not? Mr Baker didn't look too pleased to see me but led me back to the room all the same. Then I trundled across to the bar where I'd met Harry and begged the manager for a job. He said he could only do cash in hand and offered me a shift that night, choosing not to look at my ID since he probably suspected I wasn't twenty-one. I thanked him and went back to the motel room, then collapsed on the bed.

SCENE 14: MATT, 22

My twenty-second birthday began with two police officers on my doorstep.

It was a week after Brooke left. I had to keep up my attendance at uni, but I'd called in sick those first few days. Mum asked why I barely left the house, and I'd told her I had a cold, when really Amy and I had been playing detective over Facebook Messenger until the early hours. We researched all the Delta flights out of Bristol, trying to figure out where Brooke could have gone to. It felt like we were a team at the start, but we quickly realised our efforts were futile and ended up ruminating on *why* Brooke left. Neither of us knew the reason, and our guesses just seemed to depress us. Eventually, Amy stopped replying. I wondered if she'd come to blame me or felt like maybe I did something to drive Brooke away. Maybe I had, and we'd probably never see her again. As much as I was hurting, I couldn't imagine what it felt like to lose a sister.

I'd been catching up on the classes I'd missed when the doorbell rang, and I nearly shat myself when I saw them.

'Mr Williams?' the man said, flashing his badge at me. He introduced himself, then the woman, but my head was spinning, and I couldn't take in what they were saying until I heard the words '…disappearance of Brooke Tyler.'

'Have you found her?' I said, before I could stop myself.

'We just have a few questions. Can we come in?'

'Oh, okay. Sure, yeah, of course.'

I led them into the living room and ran my fingers through my uncombed hair, hoping it wasn't too obvious that I hadn't showered. They perched on the edge of the sofa, and the woman pointed to the banner on the wall that Mum had hung up reading *HAPPY BIRTHDAY*.

'Whose is it?'

'Mine. Twenty-two.'

'Happy birthday,' she said monotonously.

'Thanks. Um. Tea? Water?'

'No thank you, we won't be stopping long.' The man spoke politely, but had a stern look on his face. The woman turned to me.

'We heard from Brooke's sister that you were with her the night she disappeared, and as far as we're aware, you're the last person that knew her to have seen her.'

I mentally added the word 'alive' to the end of her sentence. Too many police dramas. I reminded myself that Brooke had left, she had chosen to leave. The note hadn't been a suicide note. She'd spent money on a plane ticket. She probably wasn't going to kill herself. 'Okay,' I said.

'We've just got a few questions about your relationship with her.'

'Sorry, um, am I in trouble?' As soon as I said it, I regretted it. Brooke had been my number one concern for days, and now, here I was, worrying about myself.

'We aren't interviewing you under caution. Just interested in what you can tell us as a witness, to track her movements.'

'Okay.' I sat opposite them, trying to ground myself in this surreal experience. I pressed my feet into the floor.

'How did you first meet Brooke Tyler?'

Shit. Was it all coming back to bite me? Part of me had a sinking feeling that *they know*. 'We went to the same am-dram-er, amateur dramatics group. Stagefright.'

'And how long have you known her?'

'Like, four, five years.'

'Okay. What were you two doing together, the evening of the twenty-eighth?'

I was relieved they didn't dwell on those early years. 'Um. Well. She had been at Prom. Her sixth form ball. And I went to pick her up. And we went to, um, it was The Botanist on Park Street. Then the Berkeley Suites hotel for drinks. Then the Travelodge near Millenium Square. Er...we stayed the night. Then the next day—'

'Just a moment. How did you get from Prom to the restaurant?'

'My car.'

'And the hotel?'

'We walked. I parked in Trenchard Street and then we walked everywhere.'

'Brooke's mother says that she took the family car to Prom.'

'I don't know. I didn't even think about her car.'

'Did either of you consume any alcohol that evening?'

'Yeah. At the hotel. We had a glass of champagne each.'

'Right. And what happened at the hotel? Did you share a room?'

'We didn't stay at that hotel, we went to the Travelodge. And yeah. We…like, we were romantic.'

'Did you and Brooke have sexual relations at the Travelodge?'

I'm sure I went red. 'Yes.'

'And Brooke consented to this?'

For a moment, I felt my stomach twist uncomfortably. But I'd offered, and asked, and said we could stop, or I could sleep next door, and she told me she wanted the room, wanted to stay, wanted…me.

'Yes, she consented,' I said.

'Were you in a relationship with Brooke?'

I sighed. 'Well, it was a date. I thought that was us getting together. Like, we spoke about it before. We'd gone for a drink after Stagefright and talked about it.'

'But you hadn't had sexual relations with her before the twenty-eighth.'

I felt a shiver down my back. 'That's correct,' I lied.

'Did she say anything about leaving?'

'No. I don't know if she planned it, or if…' I felt sick at the thought that she could've made the decision in that hotel room.

'Tell me what happened after you spent the night together.'

'Well, when I woke up, she was gone, and—'

'What time did you wake up?'

'Like, nine, nine-fifteen. And the receptionist told me she'd left at half five in the morning. I went back to the room to call her. And I saw she'd left me a note. It just said "sorry".'

'Right,' the woman said. 'Amelia said she rang you that morning.'

It took me a second to realise she meant Amy. 'Yeah. I started driving to Brooke's house. But Amy called me and told me about the note—not the one she left me but the one she left her mum—so I drove to the airport and made a bit of a dick of myself trying to see if I could find her there.'

'So you still had your car. Brooke's mother said that, when she went to bed on the twenty-eighth, Brooke's belongings were still in the house, and the note was not on the table. Brooke must have returned to the house after leaving the Travelodge. How did she get to the house and then back to the airport?'

I leaned back. 'I have no idea. Bus? Or taxi, maybe.'

'Do you know any of her friends who might've given her a lift?'

'No. Sorry. None that Amy won't have already told you about.'

'Okay. So why did you decide to drive to Brooke's home address when you read the note?'

'I don't know. I was worried about her.'

'Why were you worried about her?' the man piped up, his glare still unrelenting.

I paused. 'She was ill. She was depressed. Everyone knows that. And also, a few years back, she'd...it looked like she'd attempted suicide. Maybe.'

'This was before your relationship with Ms Tyler began.'

'Yes,' I said, a little too firmly.

'Her mother told us about the self-harm.' She flicked back a few pages in her notebook. 'Brooke Tyler was treated at hospital for deliberate self-injury in the early hours of January first, 2011.'

'Yeah, I heard about that. That's why I was scared when she vanished. I thought she might...hurt herself again.'

'So you went to her address.'

'I started to, but then Amy called. So I drove to the airport—Bristol airport—and they said her flight had left. They wouldn't tell me where it went. I mean, they probably shouldn't have been telling me anything. But they said she flew with Delta, and she's got dual citizenship, so we thought she might've gone to America.'

'That's corroborated by the information we received when we tracked her passport.'

I felt my heart thud. 'You know where she is?'

They hesitated. The man spoke first. 'Not exactly. We know where she flew to. She may have had an onward journey from there. We can't trace outside of the UK.'

'But you can still look for her?'

They paused again and glanced at each other. 'Unfortunately, Mr Williams, it seems she left of her own volition. Because of the note, and her travel documentation, we can only categorise her as a low-risk missing person.' The woman closed her notebook, and the man came to his feet.

'You're giving up? You're closing the case?'

'Her case will remain open until she is physically sighted by a police officer. But she is an adult, and it doesn't appear that any crime was committed here.'

'But what about how she got home? Don't you need to find a bus driver, or taxi driver?'

'Her mother's car was returned to the family home, probably at the same time the note was left. We know she was at the airport. She made her flight; she was seen by many airport staff. I'm sorry, sir, but there's nothing more we can really do.'

'But what if she hurts herself? What if she tried to kill herself again?'

'There's no evidence she would. She had depression, but her mother stated it had been under control.'

'But…can't you…can you tell me where her plane landed?'

'I'm not at liberty to discuss that.'

They made their way towards the hallway. I looked at the notebook in the woman's hand, and I couldn't believe that they knew where she had landed, that it was written somewhere on those pages a metre in front of me, and they still wouldn't tell me where she was.

'Isn't there anything else you can do? To try to find her?' I cried out after them.

The man opened the front door to leave. 'I'm sorry, Mr Williams, but some people just don't want to be found.'

SCENE 15: BROOKE, 18

Working at the bar was shit. The pay was shit. The regulars were shit. But it was money, and a couple of free meals, and I needed to survive. The days blurred into weeks and soon I was in the mindless routine of crossing the car park to make drinks and serve meals, then crossing back to my motel room and listening to the neighbours argue. I sank back into numbness. I would lie on my bed for hours and watch the sunlight move between the blinds, the shadows pass over my face. I scrolled through Reddit. I watched the cockroaches crawl across the carpet. July and August barely registered.

One afternoon at the bar, two guys came in and stood out. They were twenty years too young to be regulars and looked clean and bright against the dark wood and sticky floors. The brown-haired one had his car keys in hand, while the blond wheeled a small suitcase. 'Let's just go home, Pete,' he said.

'I'm starving, dude. Haven't eaten all day,' Pete replied.

'We can eat at my place,' the blond said.

'I'm not driving forty minutes on an empty stomach.' Pete put his keys away and grabbed two laminated menus. They took a seat at the bar.

After a minute, I went up to them. 'What can I get for you?'

'Whoa,' Pete said. 'English accent.' Which was most people's first reaction to me. I shrugged and half-smiled. 'What's your name?' Pete went on. He was skinny, with dark eyes and nice stubble, if a little patchy.

'Brooke,' I said.

He offered his hand. 'I'm Pete, this is Charlie.'

I shook Pete's hand. 'Hi, Pete. Hi, Charlie.'

Charlie smiled politely.

'Brooke, please can I get the dirty burger?' Pete asked.

'Sure. Charlie?'

'Mac and cheese, please,' Charlie said, rubbing his clean-shaven chin.

I put their orders through and got them their drinks. When I came back from wiping tables, Pete started talking to me again over his lunch.

'So Brooke,' he said, 'how long have you lived in Seattle?'

'Uh,' I counted in my head. 'Nearly two months.'

'And what brings you to the US of A?'

Christ, what a question. 'New start,' I said.

'So you're working here, and you live where?' he said.

'Here,' I said.

'You live in the bar?'

'No, I live in the motel. Across the lot.'

Pete swallowed his beer. 'You've been living in a *motel*? For two months?'

'That's no good,' Charlie said gently.

I'd told them too much, and instantly regretted it. 'I mean,' I cleared my throat, 'well, y'know, this place is cash in hand, so I can't get a flat.' They exchanged a look. I felt self-conscious, and quickly changed the subject. 'And what are you boys doing today?'

'I'm picking Charlie up from the airport. He goes to college in California and is back to visit his old high school friends, isn't that right?' Pete said, giving Charlie a slap on the back.

Charlie laughed but didn't engage. He looked at me seriously and said, 'What do you need to get an apartment? A job with a payroll?'

'Well…yeah,' I said.

'And what kind of job are you looking for?'

His interest in actually talking to me was surprising. 'I dunno. Something in an office, but that might not happen for a while.'

'Well, what would be ideal?'

'Hm…nothing too corporate. I'm good at science. And writing. I was good at English at school.'

'I could introduce you to my dad,' Charlie said. 'He owns a local paper, and a couple of trades.'

I felt a pang of sickness. The thought of meeting someone successful, someone who could see right through me, scared the shit out of me. I couldn't take another rejection. 'Oh, I don't know—'

'I'm an assistant manager in a bar downtown,' Pete cut in. 'I could get you a job. Proper payroll. Then you could get an apartment.'

'Really? I mean…I couldn't accept that.'

'You're working right now. I can see you could handle it. It's bigger and busier than this place, but it's nicer. You'll like it,' he said.

'I'm not twenty-one,' I said sheepishly.

'That's cool. You can waitress. Might have to do more cleaning too, if you can't make drinks.'

He seemed super keen to help me, and going from a shit bar to a better bar felt like a change I could handle. 'I mean, maybe I could come and check it out?'

Pete took my number and met me at his bar the next day. He showed me round before it opened and introduced me to the manager Steph, a young woman with arms covered in tattoos. She was happy to offer me a trial shift. Pete tried to argue that I didn't need one, but I told her it was fine. We booked it in for the following week. Pete took me to lunch at Chipotle and paid for my food. He reached over and kissed me, his stubble scraping against my skin, and I thought maybe, just maybe, he would help me.

*

I started working at the bar, and Pete would schedule the shifts so that we'd always be on at the same time. We started dating, and by 'dating' I meant smoking and eating DoorDash in front of Netflix. I stayed over a lot in the flat he shared with three guys, and unlike Harry and Brian, he was still there when I woke up in the morning. Pete was twenty-one but wanted to take me to clubs, so he sorted me a fake ID. We went out a lot, with his flatmates and the guys from the bar, and we'd come into work hungover the next day. Night was day and day was night for us. The alcohol and weed, legal here, helped when the intrusive thoughts came, and made the shifts go quicker. Pete never asked about England, or my family, so that helped me block them out, too.

He told me to ditch the motel and stay with him till I found a place, so I did, and it was convenient. Once I got my first pay cheque, I started browsing SpareRoom. Pete went with me to a few viewings but would point out how far it was from his place, or how the bed was just a single so he couldn't stay over, or how the woman showing me round was snooty to him, and we'd go back to his and have sex and forget all about it.

He would fuck me every day, and it became routine. It was less awkward than my first time, and less personal than the second. Matt had seemed to want to kiss me all over, to explore me, to memorise every inch of me. Pete was only really interested in two places. I looked into his eyes, but they were closed, concentrating on the rhythm of his hips. It always ended very quickly.

After a month at Steph's bar, I felt ready to give job hunting another go. 'But I got you a job,' Pete said.

'I don't want to work there forever.' I sat cross legged on the bed in front of his laptop. 'You know what? Can I have your friend's number? What was his name, Charlie? He mentioned a journalism thing.'

Pete unlocked his phone and chucked it onto the bed. I scrolled through his contacts to find someone called 'Charlie Young' and started copying the number into my mobile.

'I think he was just trying to flirt with you,' Pete said. 'His dad owns the newspaper, but I don't think they'll be able to just *give* you a job.' He grabbed the laptop and looked at the CV I was working on. He said I needed to stay at the bar for a year to look good for future employers. He said he could promote me to supervisor in six months, which would help. He handed me a joint. I took a drag and closed the laptop.

Pete's flatmate Wahid got a new girlfriend, Felicia. She was bubbly and full of life, the exact opposite of me. She joined in when we all smoked together, but she was always in yoga pants and going to the gym.

'I'm having a girls' night out,' she said one evening, as we watched the guys play video games. 'You should come, Brooke. Cocktails and then Baltic, Friday night.'

'We're closing on Friday,' Pete interjected, standing on a chair and putting a sock over the smoke detector. 'We could meet you at Baltic.'

'*Girls'* night out, Pete,' Felicia said.

'The cocktails will still be girly,' Pete said. 'We can't have a bunch of girls going to Baltic without us looking out for you. Y'know what the guys there are like.'

Wahid met us after close on Friday and the three of us started walking to the Baltic Rooms. He walked with tight shoulders and kept checking his phone.

'She was meant to text me when they left Heads and Tails,' he was saying. 'She hasn't replied to five messages. The last three didn't even get delivered.'

'They must be downstairs at Baltic,' Pete said.

'She should have told me when they were leaving!' Wahid snapped.

When we got to Baltic, Felicia was none-too-pleased to see Pete and Wahid. 'This is meant to be a GIRLS' night!' I heard her call out over the music.

Wahid didn't like what she was wearing, said it was too revealing. Felicia said he was ruining her night. They ended up having a fight and stormed off together. I told Pete we should leave too, since it was now just me and him and a bunch of girls we didn't know, and I was feeling awkward and shy. Pete told me to calm down, rubbed the last of his coke into his gums, and kissed me.

On nights out, Pete usually offered me some of whatever pill or powder he had. I was wary at first, but one time they were all taking ecstasy and he said I'd be a downer if I didn't take it too. He promised it would feel good, and he was right: I felt amazing, tingly and warm all over my body. I was so connected to him, to his flatmates, the lights and the music. I didn't want the night to end. We danced until the club closed, then went back to ours and smoked in the living room.

The next day I felt hungover and was relieved that the comedown had gone easy on me. But the day after that was horrendous. I couldn't stop crying; I couldn't get to work. Pete yelled at me that we'd be short staffed, but I couldn't get out of bed. In the end he left me and went to the bar while I fought off the strongest suicidal thoughts I'd had in years. The comedown threw into sharp focus how much I'd ruined my life, how shitty and awful it all was, how much I missed my mum. I cut up my legs with a razorblade and wore knee high socks for weeks so Pete wouldn't see. After that I stuck to weed and alcohol.

At the end of September, a woman called Lily started at work and Pete spent days training her behind the bar.

'But she's only twenty,' I said to him later, in bed.

'Her birthdays in two weeks,' he said, rolling a joint. 'No harm in training her now.'

'You didn't spend this long training me,' I said.

'Well, it takes longer to teach someone to make drinks than it does to teach them to clean toilets,' Pete snapped and lit up. When he saw the look on my face, he handed me the joint and said, 'Oh, c'mon, don't get upset. You're so sensitive. You need to relax more.'

'I'm not upset,' I lied, and smoked.

'By the way, I think I'll need you and Giulia to close on Saturday.'

'I thought we were going to open and go out for Alice's birthday in the evening?'

'Steph wasn't having it. She said Giulia can't close up alone.'

'Can't someone else close with Giulia?'

'No. I tried, babe, I swear. Couldn't work the schedule.'

It would be the first shift Pete and I didn't have together since I started. He went out for the work party, and I closed up the bar at three. When I got back to his place, the front door was locked, and of course, he had the key. It took ten minutes of me ringing the bell and crying while simultaneously phoning Wahid before he sleepily and wordlessly let me in. I fell asleep in Pete's bed, and when I woke up, he wasn't there. I met him at work for the evening shift, and he didn't even kiss me.

'You didn't come home,' I said to him.

'Stayed over at Lily's,' he said, without looking up from the drinks he was mixing.

'What?'

'Relax, Brooke. There were like, eight of us, we'd had a lot of E, okay? You're so uptight.'

'I got locked out,' I said. 'I thought you'd leave the door open for me.'

'I didn't realise you were treating my place like your home,' he said. 'If you're gonna do that, you could at least pay some rent.'

His coldness scared me, and I spent the next few hours working silently, racking my brain to figure out what I'd done to piss him off. Then, about halfway through the shift, he came up behind me and gave me a squeeze, and I was so relieved I didn't say anything about his mood earlier. We went home together, smoked, and had sex.

As October wore on, Pete and I were scheduled on separate shifts more and more. He complained that the Netflix shows we'd been watching for two months were now dull. He'd grab his phone quickly when it buzzed and turn away from me. I was sure something was going on with him and Lily, especially when he kept making me close up on a Saturday night and wouldn't come home till Monday morning.

'We crashed at Alice's,' he'd say bluntly, without looking at me. Another morning of worrying that I'd upset him. Another hug at lunchtime, another evening together as if nothing had happened. Maybe I was just being paranoid.

The following week he said he'd crashed at Lily's again, and I was careful not to show any reaction. 'Don't look at me like that,' he said anyway.

'Like what?' I said, using every effort to keep my voice toneless.

'Don't act like you're not weirdly jealous of Lily. Alice was with us the whole time. Chill the fuck out, I'm coming down. I can't deal with you today.'

'Jesus, sorry, I just thought my boyfriend might care if I—'

'I'm not your boyfriend,' he said.

I watched him mix the Bloody Mary, the stirrer clinking against the glass. 'But—you told me to come and stay at yours. You said—'

'I don't like labels,' he said, and walked off with the drink.

I felt the sting of his cold shoulder all morning. I had no idea what would happen to me if he decided he'd had enough of me, and I was panicking. But he'd told me to calm down. He'd said it was all in my head, so I tried to believe it, tried to believe nothing was going on with Lily.

Alice came in to start her shift at lunchtime. 'Hey, Brooke.'

'Hey, Alice,' I said as I shovelled down Chef's barbecue wings. 'How—how was Saturday?'

'Got sick. I was in bed by midnight. I thought someone spiked me, but I actually think it was stomach flu now.'

I froze and looked at her.

'What's up?'

'So was it just Lily and Pete?' I squeaked.

'Yeah. They're getting on well, if you know what I mean.' She winked at me.

I just stared at her.

'What's wrong?'

'Pete's my—' I stopped myself, remembering what he'd said earlier. 'We've been—we're a thing.'

'Oh,' Alice said, and her eyes widened. '*Oh*. God. Are you guys exclusive?'

'I've been living with—well, staying at his. But I guess we never...I just assumed...'

'Oh God, Brooke,' she said. 'He's not told anyone you two are together. Literally, no one knows you're together.'

'They're definitely hooking up?'

'I dunno, sis, you should talk to him yourself.'

I would, if he would tell me anything, I thought.

Pete was on a double, so I walked home alone, my heart pounding with every step. I sat on his bed and cried. When he got home, he rolled his eyes at the sight of me.

'Always crying, aren't you?' he said.

'I'm fine,' I lied.

'I don't like you treating my room like you live here. I think you should get your own place.'

'Well, that was the plan, remember?' I said to him. 'But we went to a bunch of viewings and you said, "Oh, no, these places are lousy, come and stay with me and suck my dick every morning."'

'Why are you being such a bitch?' he said.

'Because you're fucking Lily!' I yelled, getting up.

'And what if I am?' Pete said. 'We never said we were exclusive.'

'You asked me to live with you!'

'And now I'm asking you to give me some space,' he said. He laid diagonally across the bed and took a joint from his nightstand. He lit it. He didn't offer it to me.

'You're asking me to leave?' I said, the tears coming again.

'If you'd be so kind,' he said coldly.

I pathetically did as I was told and started putting my stuff back in my suitcase as tears streamed down my face. He didn't look up from his phone as I walked out. He didn't help me carry my bags down the stairs. I closed the front door behind me and found myself, once again, alone in Seattle. I knew there was only one place for me to go.

I cried the entire train ride there. I'd given Pete everything I had, and he still chose someone else over me. *If only I looked like her. If only I'd been more outgoing and fun. Maybe I should have done coke and E with him on nights out, and stopped complaining all the time. Stopped being so numb and down and empty. Maybe then he wouldn't have left me. Maybe then I wouldn't be alone now.*

Mr Baker didn't look best pleased to see me, but gave me my old room again. Once more I lay on those ugly brown sheets, staring at the ceiling, wondering what to do with myself. Back at the motel, nearly five months on, exactly where I'd started.

Had it really been five months? I checked the date on my phone. November tenth. My birthday. I was nineteen today, and I hadn't even remembered. I may not have been happy on my preceding birthdays, but at least I hadn't been alone. At least I'd had a cake baked for me. Candles to blow out. Someone there to sing to me.

Five months, and what did I have to show for it? A mobile, a bank account with a bit of money, and the menu at the bar memorised by heart. Nineteen numbers in my phone, one group chat for work. I flicked through the contacts, the entire inventory of everyone I knew in the world.

And there, right at the end, was Charlie Young's name. The guy who'd offered to help. Help was what I needed.

With trembling fingers, I pressed the 'call' button.

SCENE 16: MATT, 22

November tenth. Brooke's birthday. Almost five months after she left. By this point, the general pain had subsided to make way for a numb sensation that ran throughout my body. But I couldn't forget what today was.

Mum and Dad were at work and I was in the middle of an essay when the doorbell rang. I opened it and was mildly surprised to see a tall, thin man with significant grey in his slicked-back hair. He was fuming. This was how I met Brooke's father.

But of course, I'd never seen him before. 'Can I help you?' I said, when he said nothing.

'It's my daughter's birthday,' he said in his American accent, and the cogs started to turn in my brain. I realised who he was. He must've come over to shout at me.

'Mr Tyler,' I said politely, moving aside to let him in.

'Don't "Mr Tyler" me,' he snapped, stepping inside. He looked up at me and I could see it dawn on him that I was taller. Concern fell over the lines of his face, and in a hushed tone he added, 'Are we alone?'

'Yes,' I said.

His expression grew stern again, and he marched into the living room. 'I'm here for answers. You were the last person to see her. I want to know exactly what happened between my daughter and…and yourself.'

You really don't, I thought.

It was awkward because I stood between him and the door, yet he was trying to dominate me in my own home. His arms hung at his sides, like he wasn't sure what to do with them. It was clear he wanted to intimidate me, but things were not panning out as he'd imagined.

I sighed. 'What questions do you have, Mr Tyler?'

'What happened between you?' He folded his arms tightly.

'We went on a date. We'd been talking about getting together.'

'So…what, she had feelings for you?' he asked. The words sounded strange falling from his bitter lips.

'I guess not,' I said, and it hurt accepting the truth. I hadn't been enough for her. At least not enough to make her stay.

'How…how long were you…ugh.' He flopped down onto my sofa, weak and pained. For a second, I wondered who was hurting more, but really, he had the edge. What could losing a child feel like? I went to the sink to get a glass of water, and cautiously placed it on the coffee table in front of him. I took it as a good sign that he didn't throw it over me.

'And she was with you that night,' he breathed, barely a whisper. 'The night she left?'

I nodded.

'How old are you?' he said, peering at me. I saw the anger had gone, and now a broken man was looking through those dark eyes. That in itself was scarier than when he'd tried to be intimidating.

'Twenty-two,' I said.

'A fair bit older than her,' he observed, but didn't sound too judging. He took a long sip of water, then asked the same question I'd been asking myself every day and every night for months. 'Why did my baby girl leave me…?'

Wow. The man Brooke had always complained about, the one who'd left her feeling neglected and unloved, was a world away from this poor bloke on my sofa. *If only you could see him now*, I thought. *If you could see how much he loves you, even if he never showed it.*

I sat opposite him. 'Blame me, if you like.'

He stared at me, and I could see anger was growing behind his eyes again. 'Why? What did you do to her?'

I shrugged. 'I don't know. But she left anyway. Maybe it was what I didn't do.'

He swigged the water like it was vodka he could drown his sorrows in. As he put the glass down, I spoke. 'Look, I'm not really in a position to give you advice—'

'No, you're not,' he agreed, without looking at me.

'—but the truth is that you can go on blaming yourself and overthinking and playing the last time you saw her on repeat, but it won't bring her back and it'll make you miserable. So you may as well forget—'

'Don't you dare tell me to forget my daughter.' His eyes could have bored a hole in my head.

'I don't mean that,' I said. 'I mean, move on. Get closure. Not forget her, never that, just…forget the pain.'

He stared into space for a long time. When he finally broke the silence, he said, 'I can't do that. I'm moving back here. Just bought an apartment. Sold my place in London. I have to wait. Everything else is on hold till she comes back.'

He downed what was left of the water and put the glass on a coaster. Then he just left. Maybe leaving runs in their family.

SCENE 17: BROOKE, 19

'Hello?' a voice answered.

'Hi, Charlie,' I said. 'You won't remember me, but we met—'

'I remember you,' he cut in. 'Brooke, right?'

'Right. Hi. Sorry to call out of the blue.'

'I don't mind at all,' he said. His voice was like melted chocolate: warm and comforting, gentle with gravitas. I wanted to wrap myself up in that voice.

'How's…er…how's California?'

'It's alright, yeah, lots of assignments keeping me busy. How's Seattle? Did you take Pete up on that job?'

'Yeah, actually, yeah, he must've told you we were…um… togetherish.'

'Oh, right,' he said. Did he sound disappointed? 'No, actually, I don't really keep up with Pete.'

'We broke up,' I blurted out.

'Oh,' Charlie said. 'I'm sorry to hear that.'

'Yeah,' I said, 'it kind of sucks.'

'Yeah, though, I mean, Pete isn't the best.'

That was news to me. 'He's not?'

'Nah. I knew him at school but he's a bit of a deadbeat these days. I wouldn't exactly call him boyfriend material.'

It hadn't occurred to me that Pete might not be boyfriend material.

'Anyway—sorry, again—but you mentioned something about your dad owning a newspaper.'

'Oh, yeah, he owns the *Seattle Gazette*. That's the main one. There's a couple of trades and magazines as well.'

'Right, well, I was wondering…Pete got me this job, at the bar, but he's with someone else now, and I think my time there might be running out. And I was thinking, working in an office would be good, maybe something in journalism—'

'You want me to see if I can get you an interview?'

'Yes. Maybe. Please.'

I heard him smiling down the phone. 'Sure. I can do that. It won't be anything senior to start with, though.'

'No, honestly, I'll take anything. I'll clean the toilets. I've got loads of experience in that, actually.'

Charlie laughed. 'I think I can get you out of cleaning the toilets.'

He told me he would speak to his sister Marie, who worked there, and see if there was anything for me. He also promised to give me interview prep, and I ended the call feeling a little less alone.

I went back to work the next day, my head hanging low, dreading the sight of Pete with Lily. He looked kind of surprised to see me, like he thought I would've just quit. I would have, if I had that option. I swear, those were the longest eight hours of my life. Lily's shift started halfway through and Pete was all over her, publicly, in a way he'd never been with me. God, she was so pretty. No matter how cold it got, she only ever wore a leather jacket over her skinny jeans and crop top. I spent my lunch break crying and shivering in the empty beer garden as I stuffed another of Chef's cheeseburgers into my mouth.

Charlie called me again that night. 'Marie says you can email her your resume and she'll forward it to the sales manager. There's always room in ad sales. It's the very bottom, but you can move up from there.'

Charlie made me email him my CV for feedback, staying on the line while I forwarded it from my phone. He suggested edits and then made them himself when I told him I didn't have a laptop. He sent it back to me, with Marie's email address. And then, even when we were done, he kept chatting to me, making goofy jokes and sending me stupid videos to make me laugh. He made that motel room feel so much lighter.

The next day at work, Pete was ignoring me again. It broke my heart to see him with Lily, but today didn't feel as bad as the day before. I still cried at lunch in my big coat in the garden, but then I checked my phone and I had an email from the paper, inviting me to an interview.

Charlie prepped me over the phone. I scribbled down notes as he asked me practice questions and made suggestions for my answers. He made me go on video call to show him my interview clothes, which clearly didn't impress him because he offered to get Marie to take me shopping. I told him I'd take myself shopping.

'Wait—is this—are you still in that motel?' he said.

'Um.' I seized my phone and repositioned it so he was looking at the ceiling. 'Yes.'

'You've been in that motel since we met?'

'No, not for the most part. I was staying with Pete for a few months. He basically kicked me out on Monday.'

'Oh God, Brooke.' He sounded concerned.

'Yeah. So, I'm here.'

'You can't stay there forever.'

'No, I know. It's just, one thing at a time right now. I really want to change jobs, y'know. Stop seeing him and Lily every day.'

'Of course, you should get out of there.'

'Yeah. I think he'd just prefer it if I left so he didn't have to find a reason to fire me. I was always annoying him.'

'Were you, though?' Charlie said. He was looking kindly down the camera, lying on his bed, holding the phone above him. His blond curls fell towards the pillow.

'I guess so,' I said. 'He acted like I was.'

'I think you probably just saw right through him and he didn't like that.' I looked at my feet. When the silence dragged on, Charlie said, 'Okay, well, your job's basically in the bag, so why don't we start looking at apartments?'

I looked at the screen. He'd propped his phone up and was now opening his laptop and typing frantically.

'What are you doing?'

'Going onto SpareRoom,' he said. 'Let's see, within 2 miles of the office…'

He started sending me links to places. Nice places, too. I felt a bit more optimistic until I saw the price.

'Um. Charlie. Can we look a bit cheaper?'

'Hm? Oh sure, sure, of course.' He adjusted the budget and found some not-so-nice places further away. But at that point, I'd take whatever.

'Do you mind a twin size bed?' Charlie asked.

'Nope.'

'Do you mind sharing with five other people?'

'Nope.'

'Do you mind a tiny kitchen?'

'Anything I can cook food in will do.'

Charlie sent me a few links. They looked good, but the deposit was concerning. 'I don't know about these,' I said.

'Why not? You'll definitely be able to afford them on a sales salary.'

'Just the deposit. I didn't realise it'd be a whole month's rent.'

'Ah,' Charlie said. 'Okay. Well, let's lock down the job first, and then we'll get you an apartment.'

*

Being back at the motel made me feel uneasy, like when I first arrived in Seattle. Those last few months, Pete had been a comforting lead weight, giving me a place to sleep, a steady job, and people to talk to. With all that gone, I felt unanchored, like a balloon flying away in the wind. But it wasn't so scary this time. Not with Charlie at the other end of the phone.

A few days later, I swapped shifts with Alice and went to the interview in the new trousers and blazer I'd bought. Charlie's sister Marie met me for a coffee beforehand, by his arrangement.

'You've got nothing to worry about,' Marie said, stirring her latte. 'As long as you're enthusiastic, you've got it. Just act like you actually want this job.'

'I do want this job,' I said. 'Like, really super want it.'

Marie smiled. 'I'll be honest, I did it for six months and I hated every minute of it.'

'You did ad sales?'

'Oh, yeah. Being the daughter of the owner has basically zero benefit. Didn't want to be accused of nepotism, y'know? But now I'm a PA to one of the editors, so that's better. I'm gradually working my way across the office to the photographer's room.'

Marie was bubbly and friendly, as warm as her brother. She looked over my notes and said, 'Honestly, this is overkill. Just be enthusiastic. You'll need it.'

She walked me into the building and left me waiting outside the sales room with a quick squeeze of my arm. I tried to slow my breathing as I ran over my notes again, desperately trying to commit them all to memory.

The sales manager Liz showed me round the teensy office—the phones you use to cold-call businesses and persuade them to put an advert in the magazine, the bell you ring when you make a sale, the leaderboard for who was bringing in the most money. The people were older, and the room was stuffy, but to me it looked idyllic. So much better than a sticky bar with my ex.

After asking me a total of four questions, which I answered with expert precision, Liz shook my hand and told me she'd be in touch. I left the room smiling and Marie was waiting outside. 'How did it go?'

'Good, I think. I hope I hear back soon.'

'You'll be fine,' she said, walking me through the busy office to reception. 'Let me know when you've got a viewing and we'll meet up.'

'A viewing?'

'For apartments. Charlie told me you're house hunting. He said he'd go with you, but he's in Cali, so you get the superior sibling.'

'Oh, no, that's fine, you don't have to—'

'Honestly, Brooke, you'll get murdered if you go to viewings alone. Let me know when and we can grab some food too.'

With another beaming smile, Marie waved me off. I went home feeling weird. Why was she being so nice to me? Why was Charlie? I was basically a stranger and couldn't see what was in it for them.

But I gave up trying to figure it out when he texted that night. He asked how the interview went and insisted that I'd smashed it and definitely had the job. We started talking about his Medicine major, then veterinary school and then on to our favourite animals. He sent me videos of golden retrievers, and I smiled every time my phone buzzed.

The next day at work was lousy again, until Liz called on my break to offer me the job. After that, I couldn't stop smiling. I waited by the stairs for Steph to come in so I could hand in my notice.

Pete walked past. 'Brooke, you finished at five,' he said.

'I'm waiting for Steph,' I replied, and kept scrolling through Reddit.

'What for?' He sounded concerned.

I looked at him. 'Nothing about you.'

He seemed unconvinced. I don't know what he thought I'd say to get him in trouble. That he did a lot of drugs, just like everyone else here? That he kicked me out of his apartment when I wasn't paying rent and wasn't on the contract? As he sauntered off in Lily's wake, I caught a waft of his scent: sweat and weed. I stuck out my tongue. Had he always smelt like that? Is that what I'd smelt like, when I was living with him and getting high every night?

Steph came in at six, and I told her I'd been offered a job somewhere else. She promised to give me a good reference and said she could halve my two weeks' notice if I needed to start sooner. I left the office smiling, and Pete was looking expectantly at me as I passed him on my way out.

'What was—'

'See you tomorrow!' I said brightly.

Charlie rang me that night. When I answered the video call, he cheered down the phone, and I laughed, and fell onto my bed, looking through the screen at him. He asked about the contract and went through every minor detail with me. He started talking about his sister, how she could be fierce and focused at work, but how she'd melt the second she left the office and go back to being goofy and excitable. How their dad used to think about nothing but the business until their mum got sick, and then he started spending more time at home. He said they met at a hospital in the city. 'She was training to be a doctor, and he came in with a broken ankle from soccer. Mom wrote her number on his cast,' he chuckled, then went quiet for a moment. 'You don't expect doctors to get cancer.'

'So you've always lived here?' I quickly changed the subject. 'In Seattle, I mean?'

He nodded. 'Born and raised in Capitol Hill. Only moved for college. I'll be back, though. I can't deal with this heat. I mean, not right now, but in the summer.'

He smiled down the phone, and effortlessly, I smiled back, lost in the little screen in my hand. But then I remembered he could see me and sat back up.

'I've been talking too much about me,' he said, catching himself too. 'What about you? Where are you from?'

Shit. 'Uh,' I started, 'I'm from England.'

He laughed. 'Well, I could tell that much. But you'd only been here a couple of months, when we met. Wanted an adventure?'

I swallowed. My voice was suddenly very small. 'Something like that.'

'Your family must miss you,' he said.

'You don't even know me,' I breathed.

He stopped. 'Huh?'

'You don't know that they miss me,' I said, louder now.

'But of course they—'

'Stop talking like you know me. You don't know anything about me.'

He looked hurt. 'I know you,' he said.

'This is none of your business, okay?'

'Okay,' he said, looking strangely at me. 'I'm sorry. I didn't mean to upset you.'

'You didn't upset me,' I said bitterly, biting my lip. I didn't want him to see me cry.

'I just, Brooke, I was getting to know you—'

I hung up, and broke down in hot, shameful tears. He didn't call back.

The next morning, I lay in the motel room as usual, waiting for my shift to start and wallowing in my alone-ness. I guess I'd have to retract my notice from Steph and look for a different job, since I'd been stupid enough to yell at the son of my future employer, the only person who'd been nice to me.

An email came through from Marie. My heart dropped. *This will be it. This will be her withdrawing the job offer because I kicked off at Charlie.* I opened it, tears already queuing up behind my eyes.

> *Hey, Brooke, congrats on the new job! Very happy to have you starting soon. I meant what I said about the house viewings, so let me know when you have some lined up and we'll go together.*
>
> *Charlie mentioned you were worried about housing deposits. He told me a little about your current living situation (don't be mad at him), and Dad (Mr Young to you!) has agreed to give you an advance on your first paycheck. Hope that will be enough to sort you out?*
>
> *See ya soon,*
>
> *M*

I was shocked. How could these people be so nice to me? Charlie had got me a job and sent me adverts for flats and not told his sister how I yelled at him last night. Marie had bought me a coffee and promised to take me house hunting. And now their father, who I'd never met, had let his kids talk him into helping me out. I had done nothing to deserve this, could offer them nothing in return, yet they'd still gone out of their way for me. I felt warm and fuzzy for the first time in ages, and read the email three times. It wasn't the money that was overwhelming, it was the kindness of absolute strangers when I had no one else at all.

I scrolled down the email chain and saw a back and forth between Charlie and Marie. The earliest one was him asking if there were any jobs for me. Then her offer to talk to Liz. Him asking her to take me for coffee. Her agreeing, though a little reluctantly. *I don't want to be accused of giving anyone special treatment,* Marie wrote. I guess she took after her dad.

Then Charlie asked about the deposit: *Any chance of an advance on her paycheck, or a loan from the company?*

Marie bit back: *Are you giving this girl the world, Charlie? She's basically homeless, we've given her a job, I've offered to take her apartment hunting. Giving your latest charity project a paycheck before doing any work is overkill. Dad will never agree to that.*

The fuzzy feeling melted away. Was that all I was to Charlie? A charity project, something to make him feel good about himself?

He wrote back: *I'll talk to Dad myself if you'd rather not, just thought it might be better coming from you. I've talked to her on the phone, she's not a psycho, I promise. I just want to help her.*

Marie replied: *It's fine, I'll talk to Dad. This girl better be good though.*

Tears stung in my eyes. Marie didn't even want to be my friend. That coffee, that squeeze on the arm, was all fake. I started bawling. How had every single person I'd met in America turned out to not want anything to do with me? How had every single person been proof I should never have left England?

My phone started buzzing. It was Charlie, video calling again. I answered but turned off my camera. His face came through on the screen, again in his dorm room.

'Hey, Brooke,' he said a little stiffly. Then, 'Where are you?'

'Ch-Charlie,' was all I managed to get out.

He instantly looked concerned as he stared at my blank screen. 'Brooke, what's—'

'This is stupid, this whole thing is stupid. I should never have let you help me,' I sobbed into that ugly brown pillow.

'Brooke, what happened?'

'I should never have accepted help from you,' I said. 'It's wrong.'

'It's not wrong—'

'It's weird!' I cried. 'I'm just a project for you, I get it, you don't want to be my friend.'

'Of course I want to be your friend.'

'Marie doesn't!' I sobbed. 'She was being fake to me all this time. She forwarded me your emails. She's only being nice to me because you asked her to be.'

Charlie froze. 'What emails?'

'She just…emailed me, about…an advance on my payslip. And below it, I can see a thread from you to her…'

'Oh, fuck, Marie. Brooke, you've got to ignore that. She sent them to you by accident. She's just a tough girl at work, that's all. She's such a softie, of course she wants to be your friend. She just likes to snap at me sometimes. That was aimed at me, not you.'

'But you had to beg her to help me out! To have coffee with me! For the advance! I feel so—I don't want it anymore.'

'Brooke, c'mon—'

'It makes me feel shitty! To see you have to talk her into it. Talking about me like I'm…like I'm a charity case. I get that you've done a lot for me, but this doesn't make any sense.'

Charlie sighed. 'Brooke, you were never meant to see those emails. Okay. I'm really sorry. I never wanted to upset you. But I don't think of you as a charity case, you've got to believe me.'

'Well, that's all I am,' I sobbed. 'Worthless, and helpless—'

'Don't say that—'

'I am, though! I can't manage on my own! I've been surviving off the kindness of strangers, and guys who want to fuck me. I would've been homeless if it wasn't for Pete. I basically *am* homeless now…'

My sobs filled the silence. Charlie stared down the camera.

'Brooke,' he said gently, 'It's okay to let people help you. Okay. You're my friend. *That's* how I see you. And friends help each other.'

I sniffed.

'You'd help me, right?' he said.

'I mean, yeah. If I was in any position to do so.'

'I'm sorry you read those emails. And I'm sorry I upset you last night—'

'Don't be,' I interrupted him. 'I overreacted.'

'I was being nosy. Your family is none of my business.'

'Honestly, Charlie, you were being nice. It was my fault. I'm just sensitive about that stuff, I guess.'

'None of my business. I won't ask again.'

'Okay,' I gulped, wiping my tears and feeling very unworthy of this kindness. 'Thanks. Sorry.'

'You okay now? You feel better?'

I sniffed. 'A bit.'

'Okay, good. So, now you've got the job, and the advance, it must be time to start booking in apartment viewings?'

I giggled. 'You're relentless.'

'C'mon,' he said in a silly voice, and started sending me links to flats again. He helped me draft a message to introduce myself as the ideal roommate, and I sent it to a bunch of people. A few replied right away. We booked in viewings for the weekend.

'Okay, now don't be scared of Marie. Ignore all that other stuff, she wants to go with you. You can buy her a pizza after.'

I turned my camera back on and spent the rest of the afternoon letting him make me laugh. God, he was so warm, even from miles away. The one tether keeping me from freaking out.

'Shit,' I said, 'It's four already. I've got to get to work.'

'Okay,' he said, 'I'll speak to you soon.'

'Yeah, alright.' I thought of the emails again. 'But, er, I mean…don't feel you have to.'

He paused. 'Don't you want me to?'

'No, I do. I mean, I just don't want you to feel obliged, y'know.'

He hesitated for a second. 'Well, I guess you'll be busy with your new job soon.' My heart sank as he said it, but I'd felt like enough of an inconvenience to him already, as much as he insisted otherwise. I didn't want him to keep calling out of sympathy. He'd already done so much for me.

'And I bet you're kept busy with school,' I said. 'Studying. Partying. California girls.'

He laughed. 'Mostly just studying. Yeah. But soon you'll have loads of new friends, and roommates, and Marie will take you out all the time, that's for sure. You'll forget about me.'

'Oh, I couldn't forget you,' I said. 'You changed my life.'

He looked down the camera, and for a second I thought he was going to say something. He cleared his throat. 'Anyway, I don't want to make you late.'

'No, right,' I said, a little rushed. 'Okay. Bye, Charlie.'

'Bye, Brooke.' He smiled, and then he was gone.

Without Charlie, the room was darker, and I felt the hollowness inside me again. But I could keep going for a bit longer, with the resources he'd given me.

Marie did take me house hunting, and I got her that pizza. At first it was exhausting to pretend to be happy, to keep up the small talk when all I wanted to do was sleep all the time. But she helped me, and I laughed at her jokes and forced myself to make a couple of my own. She wouldn't let me choose the first two places we saw because of mould and, 'you don't wanna live with three guys,' even though I just wanted to get house hunting over with. She said I could take the third place. It was okay, a three-bedroom apartment with two other girls who seemed nice enough. The room was tiny, with a single bed and a broken chest of drawers which Marie looked sceptically at, but I reminded her it was all I could afford right now. She offered to help me move, but it didn't even take an Uber to carry all the things I owned in the world.

It felt amazing to walk away from my last shift at the bar, knowing I never had to serve food, clean toilets, or see Pete again. The new office felt like such a luxury by comparison: my own desk, a phone to myself, a drawer I could put anything in. The novelty quickly wore off, though, as I learned I wasn't much of a saleswoman.

'C'mon, Brooke, I want to hear your beautiful voice on the phone,' Liz would say.

'I'm just doing a bit of research on these guys before I call them,' I'd reply.

'That English accent is going to bring us big bucks,' she'd say, slapping me on the back. I would reach for the phone and practically beg these small businesses throughout the state to buy ad space in our magazine. On the rare occasion I got a sale, I had to ring the bell, which made me feel like an idiot, and write the profit on the whiteboard. My name was always at the bottom of the list, but I did okay.

The apartment was close to the office, but more than once I found myself legging it to work after waiting for one of my roommates to get out of the bathroom. I started showering at night and kept my toothpaste in my bedroom so I could brush my teeth over the kitchen sink. I had to learn how to cook too, since I only knew how to make a couple of things. Every time I used the oven the smoke alarm went off. I opened all the windows as wide as they would go until I was shivering, my bare feet against the cracked tile floor, but the alarm still went off, and I'd still end up standing on a chair flapping a tea towel at it. I burnt a lot of food, money straight in the trash.

The weekends were dedicated to survival: food shopping, laundry, doing my bits on the cleaning schedule to avoid passive-aggressive texts on the group chat. How anyone had time or energy to do anything else on the weekend was beyond me. I was still depressed and tired all the time, though I was certainly functioning better than I had done before, now that I had to survive on my own. I still had intrusive thoughts, but I didn't hurt myself anymore—I didn't want to worry about hiding my arms at work.

Marie was super nice to me. I forgot all about the emails. Charlie was right, she was a big softie, and I was grateful for her. She'd text me on the weekends to see if I wanted to go for a run or to the movies or out for drinks. Sometimes I forced myself to go, to try to have fun. But other times the thought of socialising was unbearable, and I'd be stuck in bed, listening to the sound of my roommates roaming around the apartment and waiting for it to get quiet so I could cook on my own. They would treat the kitchen like a lounge, moving the chairs around to watch movies on their laptop. I found myself hoarding popcorn and candy to avoid having to go in there when I was hungry. Sometimes Marie would come over, and she was like a catalyst between me and them. When she was there, I could have a normal conversation, all of us together, and I'd think *look! I can be normal! I have friends! This person likes me! I'm not just some weird British girl!*

Then Marie would see my room, see that I had washed the sheets but hadn't put new ones on. 'How long have you been sleeping like this?'

'Er,' I said, 'a week?'

She sighed, and started making the bed, despite my protestations. 'Look, I'll do this, you pick up your clothes.'

I was worried she was judging me. *But this is normal, right? This is what all nineteen-year-olds' bedrooms look like. I've just started living alone.* But she never said anything, just put on movies and bought us beer. She made the workdays go quicker too; even though she was in the main office and I was in the side room, she'd poke her head in a few times a day. I sat with her and her other friends at lunch, and we'd meet up at the coffee machine.

This was what being an adult was like. I hoped things would get easier, that I'd have some energy at the end of the day to do more than collapse into bed, but I was glad things weren't as bad as before. I could manage this. Everything was okay.

ACT 3: 22 | 25

2018

SCENE 1: BROOKE, 22

'I hate my job,' Katie said.

'To be fair, it's the worst job in the company,' Marie replied, joining us at our table.

I nodded in agreement. 'I hated it too. But look on the bright side, Katie—in four short years, you too could have the third worst job in the company instead.'

'Third worst?' Katie asked.

I nodded, swallowing a bite of my bagel. 'I went from ad sales to receptionist to PA. Worst to second worst to third worst. That's what they call career progression.'

'I started in ads too.' Marie ripped open the canteen's surprisingly okay sushi. 'Like, geez, Dad, I get you don't want to give me a leg up, but I didn't go to college for nothing.'

'At least you weren't stuck there for a year and a half,' I said.

'Should've gone to college,' Marie snorted.

'Your dad is scary,' Katie said.

'He is not,' Marie replied.

'He is,' I agreed.

'You guys just don't interact with him enough,' Marie said.

'Exactly,' Katie and I said in unison.

Marie licked the soy sauce off her chopsticks. 'Well, speaking of family, my brother's back in town.'

I nearly choked on my half-chewed bagel.

'He's transferred to the medical school here. We're going out tonight. You guys'll come, right?'

'Go out with your hot single doctor brother?' Katie said. 'Hell yeah.'

'We're going to Vick's. They card there.'

'Oh,' said Katie, who was nineteen.

'Come to pregame,' Marie offered, then nudged my arm cheekily and said, 'Though I think Brooke might have first dibs on the single doctor brother.'

'Fuck off,' I laughed, a little too hard.

'She actually met Charlie before she met me,' Marie explained to Katie.

'But I haven't spoken to him since, and I've had to put up with you on a daily basis for three years.'

Marie squeezed me affectionately. 'Yeah. I did win you.'

My phone buzzed. 'Uh oh, Yuko wants me back.'

'You've had fifteen minutes,' Marie said, 'you can absolutely push back on that.'

I shoved my Tupperware back into my rucksack. 'It's fine. I'll take another half-hour later. Maybe.'

I didn't get the rest of my break, but I didn't mind, because Yuko sent me down to the Federal Courthouse with the reporters to get quotes at a protest. Despite the January cold, it was fun to help the reporters, and to get some proper practice for when I'd hopefully become one of them. But I was distracted, thinking about how I'd be seeing Charlie later that night.

In the years that had passed, we hadn't called, emailed, or texted. I'd thought about it, but I didn't want to bother him. Marie had told me what he was up to and passed on the occasional 'hello' from him. He rarely came to Seattle, just for the holidays or special occasions I could never make, and I was glad. He'd seen me crying down the phone. He'd seen me at my worst. It was embarrassing. I was certainly better now than I had been then, but what had I made of myself? I was just a PA. I was in the same apartment, though I'd switched to a bigger room. Charlie would probably be expecting some transformation in me after all this time, but I still spent some Saturdays staring at my ceiling. I could still feel empty and numb.

At eight, I arrived at Marie's flat. Her girlfriend Lisa opened the door and gave me a hug and a bottle of red.

'I hope this isn't all for me,' I said, following her up the stairs.

'As if,' she replied.

'Is Charlie here?' I tried to sound nonchalant.

'Not yet,' Lisa said.

Marie came out of the bedroom. 'Hey B! You look nice.'

'Thanks,' I said, and adjusted my skirt. I'd spent a long time choosing what to wear.

Katie was in the living room, significantly less dolled-up than we were. She looked at my outfit and sipped her wine.

'Can you do my eyes?' I said, handing Marie a tube of eyeliner. She steered me into the bedroom and started to give me what she called, 'The Greatest Wings of All Time'. The doorbell rang between eyes, and before I could even register the sound, she had raced down the stairs with the tube.

I heard the door open and Marie squeal, 'CHARLIE!' Then there was laughter, and a pause for her to fling her arms around him. I heard their footsteps coming up the stairs, and I looked in the mirror. I mean, one eye looked great.

I saw the siblings appear at the top of the stairs and turn into the living room. 'Hey Lisa,' I heard Charlie's velvety voice say. I hovered in the bedroom, waiting for Marie to remember that my right eye existed. A good couple of minutes passed. *Fuck.* I didn't want the first time Charlie saw me in three years to be with one winged eye.

I edged towards the living room door. Charlie was knee-deep in introductions to Katie. Marie was staring at him like he was the best thing in the world, absent-mindedly holding my eyeliner as an extension of her hand. I cleared my throat. 'Marie,' I tried to say quietly.

Both siblings spun to look at me, four identical eyes peering at my uneven two.

'Oh crap, sorry, Brooke,' Marie said, looking at the tube in her hand.

'Brooke Tyler,' Charlie said.

'Hi, Charlie,' I said shyly. As he looked at me, he seemed just as awkward as I felt. I didn't know if a handshake or a hug would be more appropriate. In the end, we did neither. His arms hung inelegantly at his sides. Where had his confidence gone?

'Look at you!' he said, his hands indicating my general existence, but I wouldn't risk reaching out to him and second guessing the hug-or-handshake issue. I hadn't felt this self-conscious in years. 'Two promotions, I hear,' he added.

'It's true,' I shrugged, 'that personal assistant life is pretty sweet. Just like Yuko's coffee.' When nobody reacted, I added, 'That was a joke. She doesn't take sugar.'

'I'll finish your eyes,' Marie said, leading me back to her bedroom.

I breathed as she leaned over my face. 'That was awkward.'

'Seemed a bit,' Marie said, which didn't help. 'What's the deal? I thought you guys knew each other?'

'Kind of,' I said. 'We only met once, and I wasn't in a good place.'

'Well, it was years ago,' Marie said, flicking the wing. 'You guys will be fine after a drink.'

We went back into the living room and sat down. I didn't look at Charlie, but I saw Katie beaming at him. 'So you're like, an actual doctor?' she said. And I felt—*was that a twinge of jealousy?*

'Absolutely not,' Charlie said. 'But I will be, if all goes to plan.'

Marie plugged her phone into the aux and put on some awful house music. We drank and chatted, and I eased up. I looked at Charlie as he spoke to Lisa, and God, that man was handsome. His thick, golden hair, his dark brown eyes, the way his arms moved under that white buttoned shirt. I reached for my confidence, the one I'd developed cold-calling businesses from the sales room, and cracked a few jokes that made everyone laugh. Marie stuck some pizzas in the oven for our dinner, and when eleven o'clock crept round, she announced it was time to go. Katie looked disappointed, and headed home.

'Looks like we've got ourselves a double date!' Marie said, slipping her arm around Lisa as we put on our thick coats and made our way into the January night.

Vick's wasn't far, and it was nicer than the places that didn't card. It wasn't long before Marie dragged Lisa off to dance, leaving me alone with Charlie. We relaxed around each other—I mean, the drinks helped—and I ended up talking to him all night, like strangers meeting for the first time. We basically were. We caught up on the past few years: his studies, my job, our lives. His eyes seemed to glimmer with promise and maybe mine weren't quite so empty and dull anymore. Marie drank too much as usual, and Lisa took her home, but Charlie and I talked for another hour before calling it a night. We shared an Uber to mine; he said he'd walk from there. I wondered if he might make a move, but he was way out of my league.

'I'm glad you've done so well for yourself,' he said, 'since we met.'

'Oh, I…I'm doing okay,' I said. 'Thanks to you.'

'You got there on your own,' he said. 'I just gave you a nudge in the right direction.'

'You gave me a lot more than a nudge. You gave me a ladder. And a flashlight.'

He smiled. I looked down and reached for my courage again.

'I liked it.' I spoke tentatively. 'That week, when we were talking every day.'

'Yeah,' he said. 'I enjoyed it.'

I swallowed the lump in my throat. 'I wouldn't have minded if we'd kept talking.'

'I wanted to keep talking,' he said suddenly, which surprised me.

'Really?' I said. 'Why?'

He looked down, maybe a little embarrassed. 'I like talking to you.'

'No, I mean, why didn't you? Call.'

'Uh.' He searched for the words. 'I thought that maybe you didn't want me to. I didn't want to bother you.'

'I was afraid of bothering you too,' I rushed to say. 'You'd done so much for me; I didn't want to inconvenience you more.'

'I know, and I know you said you were worried about that. But after you said you thought I viewed you as a charity project, I just…' He drifted off.

'I get it,' I said. 'I guess we could have been talking this whole time.'

He smiled. 'Yeah. That would've been nice.'

'Though to be fair, you were in a different state, and I was a bit of a mess.'

He shrugged. 'Maybe it's better this way. I mean, now I can take you on a real date.'

I blinked.

'I mean,' he cleared his throat. 'Not if you don't want to. Obviously.'

'You're asking me on a date?'

'Um,' he said, 'not if you don't want me to.'

'No, I…it's not that.'

'What is it, then?' He gave me that killer smile, but some element of shyness in his gaze reminded me of Matt. Matt, England, and my family were just a memory now. Still painful when I was alone, feeling guilty, missing them, but I had learned to distract myself when something reminded me of them. Marie had brought up my home once, asking where I was from. 'I mean, England, obviously, but, like, where?' she'd said.

'I don't want to talk about it,' I'd said. I knew it was weird, knowing her history so intimately and her not knowing anything about my past.

She'd instantly dropped it. 'It doesn't matter where you've been,' she'd said. 'It's where you are now that matters. And where you're going. Though you're not going anywhere. Stay with me forever, best friend!'

I looked back at Charlie, his dark brown eyes kind and warm.

'I just…' The words were coming to me slowly. 'You remember what I was like, when we met, right?'

'Of course,' Charlie said.

'I mean, I was basically homeless. You do remember that part, don't you?'

'Do you remember the part where we fell asleep on video call every night?' he said, his cheeks a little red.

'You didn't…you didn't like me back then, did you?'

'Well, maybe a little,' he laughed nervously. 'I mean, I was in Cali, and I had to study and all. Plus, Marie had her eye on you. Professionally,' he added. 'She wanted you to settle into your job there. I didn't mean she had her eye on you, like, she's with Lisa. Well, she probably did have her eye on you a bit—you know what she's like—it's not like I haven't been on a date in years.

But I haven't been on loads.' He sighed and gave up, settling into his freshly-dug hole.

I couldn't help but laugh. He seemed more genuine now. 'You mean to tell me you've been on just the right number of dates? Not too many to freak me out, but enough so I don't think you're undateable?'

He laughed too. 'Yeah. I've been on the ideal number of dates. Whatever number you think is best. And they also went as well or as terribly as you like.'

I laughed but couldn't help but look sceptically at him. 'I haven't been asked out by someone like you before.'

I'd dated guys over the last few years, and had some short-lived almost-relationships. They were okay, these guys, people who'd swiped right on me or else started talking to me on a night out. But I usually caught feelings pretty fast, and probably slept with them too quickly. Then they'd tell me they weren't looking for anything serious, and I'd get upset, and Marie would tell me I needed to up my standards and order an at-home STI test. She told me they didn't treat me right, that they shouldn't be cancelling on me last minute. On the odd occasion I was with someone long enough for her to meet them, she'd roast the guy afterward, telling me he drank too much and that I could do better.

Charlie smirked. 'Tell me you haven't been stuck with guys like Pete this whole time?'

I shuddered. 'I've stepped up my game a tad. And thank you, for reminding me that I did, indeed, go out with him.' Time had made me wonder what I'd been thinking when I'd been with Pete. Well, to be fair, I hadn't been thinking. That was the worst period of my life, and he was like a big anaesthetic to all the pain I was in, handing me a joint and making me feel wanted. 'God, you're not still friends with him, are you?'

He shook his head. 'We weren't really friends when I met you. He only offered to pick me up from the airport that time so he could ask about pitching his app to my dad.'

'That guy? An app? Must've been like an Uber for drug dealers.'

Charlie laughed. 'I did tell you he wasn't boyfriend material.'

I laughed too. 'He couldn't even grow a beard.'

Charlie sat up and cleared his throat. 'Yeah, uh—I could definitely grow a beard if I wanted to,' he said sarcastically.

'So that makes you boyfriend material,' I laughed, and then heard myself.

Charlie was unfazed. 'I mean, let me have a shot at least.'

SCENE 2: MATT, 25

It took forever to get Brooke out of my head. But I did, because I had no other choice. Sometimes I felt angry that she'd spent the night with me, given me hope, and then left without explanation. Sometimes I felt guilty for what happened when she was fourteen. I had to remind myself that she had forgiven me. But I still didn't know why she left.

After everything that happened, I struggled to focus and ended up dropping out of my master's. I was living with Mum and Dad, desperate for a job, and had no idea what I wanted to do with my life, so I settled for getting a teaching qualification while working at my old secondary school. I rented a flat above the corner shop I used to work at, and Mum was thrilled that I'd moved barely a fifteen-minute walk away.

Teaching wasn't what I'd planned to do with my life but it was okay. It was weird working with my old teachers, but they hardly remembered me. I was okay with the kids, and the marking, and it wasn't like I was going out most nights anyway. A lot of my friends had moved away. I still saw Meg, though. She asked me to lead Stagefright with her.

'Pleeeeeaaaase?' she said on the phone. 'Stephen's moving to Wales with his fiancé. I can't do it by myself.'

'I don't know,' I said. 'I'm not staying in town for long.'

'Didn't you just rent a flat? And get a new job?'

'Yeah but…' I drifted off. 'The job is training at the same time. I'll probably move when it's over.'

'Just for the time being, then,' Meg said. 'Please, just Friday nights?'

I agreed to do it for a couple of weeks. That turned into a couple of months. Soon I was a fully qualified teacher, and I was still leading sessions. Meg talked about getting more people to join; it seemed to be an annual problem, when the eighteen-year-olds would go off to uni and suddenly our numbers were halved. But then one of my year tens, Louise, asked if I was going to see the school play.

'Oh, yeah, definitely,' I said. She looked surprised. She'd probably asked several teachers already who had all made vague excuses. 'Do you take Drama GCSE?' I asked.

She nodded.

'I run a drama club on Friday nights.'

'I thought Mr Singh ran the drama club.'

'This one's outside of school. It's called Stagefright. Do you want a leaflet?'

'Yes, please!' she said.

I went into my rucksack and found a business card for Stagefright. 'Well, there's a card, at least. Check it out.'

After that, Louise joined. Then she brought some friends. Then she told her GCSE class about it. Soon we had more than twenty regulars—far more people than we knew what to do with.

On Friday nights I'd walk into the rehearsal room, and there was always a part of me that hoped Brooke might show up. Might just walk up those stairs and pay her weekly fee, as if she'd never left. I couldn't find anything on the internet that even mentioned her disappearance, though I still checked, hoping for new information to come out. Nothing ever did. I assumed that people had heard I'd been with her the night she left, but no one ever brought it up. Meg told me that Amy was expecting a baby, and not on purpose. No mention of Brooke, as if Amy had never had a sister. It really was like the whole town had forgotten she'd ever been here.

SCENE 3: BROOKE, 22

Charlie called exactly when he said he would and suggested we get dinner on Friday. When the night came, he didn't let me down. At 7PM precisely, he buzzed on my door with a bunch of flowers in his hand.

'I thought you were joking,' I said.

'I was. It's funny, get it?'

I didn't.

'Marie said sunflowers were your favourite, but it's January, so you'll have to settle for yellow roses.' He grinned like a child and handed them to me.

'You're too kind,' I said, and it was true. I was ready to go with my massive puffy coat on, so I held the flowers awkwardly, unsure if I should bring them with me or stop and do the choppy thing. 'Er,' I said out loud, then elected to take them along and closed the door behind me. Charlie didn't say anything about it, and just started asking me about my week. We headed towards Elliot Bay and wound up at a place called Le Ciel de Paris. When I saw it, I panicked.

'We're going here?' I said.

He nodded, looking pleased with himself. He held the door open for me and I went in, not sure where to go or which direction to face. He steered me towards the doorman, who seemed to recognise him, and took our coats. The manager shook Charlie's hand and went to check on our table.

'Wow,' I said. 'You know everyone. Do you come here a lot?'

'Not a lot. Dad started as a food critic,' Charlie said.

'Huh.' I looked around the room, with its monochrome waiters and live pianist. 'I guess this place always got five stars.'

The manager returned and led us across the room, between diners in open-collared shirts and nice dresses. I pulled my short skirt lower and sat down at a table with a brilliant view of the bay, the lights of Bainbridge Island glittering against the darkness. He handed us menus and pointed out some bits inside, and I nodded and smiled, pretending to listen, hoping my hands wouldn't leave a smear of sweat on the leather binding. The flowers sat on the floor under the table, propped up against my worn-out handbag. Charlie chose some wine from memory, and the waiter left to get it.

I looked at the menu. Everything was so expensive. I really hoped Charlie was happy to pay. 'Please don't make me try snails,' I said.

Charlie laughed and poured water into my glass. 'I won't make you try snails.'

I excused myself to go to the bathroom and took my bag with me. I looked in the mirror and wished I'd worn more makeup. I'd left my lips colourless and now regretted it, so made do with tinted lip balm. I took out my mini hairbrush and tried to achieve anything at all with it. I felt so out of place here, I mean—this was the kind of place that had *hand cream* in the bathroom, for God's sake.

I sighed and went back to the table. The waiter had poured the wine.

'I won't have more than a glass,' I warned Charlie. 'I'm a lightweight.'

'That's fine. We can always take the bottle home.' He gave me that killer smile again, and I felt warmth spread across my chest.

Charlie was, once more, thoroughly charming, and quickly put me at ease. His laugh was as warm as his rosy cheeks, but this time I could make him laugh, too. I could smile and talk and actually contribute something to the conversation. He wasn't looking at me with sympathy anymore, but with something else entirely.

When dinner was over, he paid (thank fuck) and walked me home like a gentleman. At my door he leaned in to kiss me, and my stomach flipped, but then he chickened out and pecked me on the cheek instead. I was disappointed, but his shyness only added to his charm.

'Next Friday,' he said as he walked away, 'I'm taking you out.'

On Tuesday, he came into the office to see his dad. I hadn't realised until then that I was dating my boss' son, and, in this work environment, Charlie seemed so superior to me. I watched him chat to the guys at reception, then head off to his dad's office as I shrunk behind my computer. It was like he was one of the popular kids at school that I didn't feel cool enough to talk to. But on his way out, he knocked on my desk and said, 'Afternoon, Miss Tyler.'

'Afternoon, um, Charlie,' I said back.

'Still on for our second date?'

The sound of his voice made me smile. 'Yeah, course.'

'What do you want to do?'

'Well, you got dinner last time, so I thought maybe I could cook for you.'

'Sounds amazing. At your place?'

I blinked. 'Well, while I do have multiple kitchens at my disposal, that is the one I like best.'

He laughed. 'Okay. See you on Friday.'

And when I did see him on Friday, he was holding another bouquet.

'Oh,' I said, 'more flowers.'

'Don't sound so excited about it,' he said.

'Sorry, yes, sorry, thank you, it's just, I don't think last week's are dead yet. But they're lovely. Come in, come in.'

I had just started making dinner and had been freaking out about it, since I'd never cooked for someone else before. He came into the hallway (which I'd rushed home from work to vacuum) and followed me through to the kitchen.

'I thought, just steak and fries?' I said, as I stood on the table and wrapped a plastic bag around the smoke detector.

'Uh, yeah, yeah, sounds good.' He hovered by the laundry rack, looking at last week's flowers, which were sitting in a pint glass by the window.

'Have a seat,' I indicated one of the wooden chairs.

He hung his coat on the back of it. 'Actually, can I use your bathroom?' he said.

'Sure, sure,' I clambered off the table and hurried to my room, then came back with a roll of toilet paper. He looked at it, then back at me. 'Oh, I don't—won't there be—thanks.'

He left, and I unlocked my phone to bring up the recipe I'd googled earlier. *Oil in the pan, salt and pepper on a plate, press both sides of the steak into it.* I turned on the extractor fan and started frying.

'Where should I put this?' Charlie said, poking his head into the doorway and holding up the toilet paper.

The steaks caught on fire.

'Whoa,' I said, and turned the stove off. The flames went out. 'Jesus. Um, thanks, I'll take that.' I returned the roll to its rightful place on my nightstand, then went back to the stove as Charlie sat in the chair and watched my every move. *Okay, round two,* I thought as I turned the stove on again.

The steaks cooked fine, except for a little oil spitting, which had me running my fingers under the tap. I chatted to Charlie, and I could see his eyes flitting from me to the pans.

'How do you like your steak?' I said.

'Um,' Charlie said, 'medium.'

I prodded a steak. 'They're nearly done. Let's check the fries.' I opened the oven and a wall of smoke hit me in the face.

'Oh, that can't be good,' Charlie laughed.

'It's always like that, it just needs a clean.' I looked at the fries. 'Hm. Not much is happening here. I'll put it on higher.'

I put the fries back in, turned off the stove, and left the steaks sitting in the pans. I sat next to Charlie and we talked, our feet under the table, my leg leaning against his leg, almost forgetting about the food.

'Sorry, I should have got you a drink,' I realised, standing up. 'Is water okay? Or I've got a bit of apple juice.'

'I brought the leftover wine from last time,' Charlie said.

'Oh good, shit, I forgot about drinks.' I fished out two dusty wine glasses from the back of the cupboard and rinsed them under the tap before handing them to him. 'The fries are taking ages,' I said, returning to the oven to see that they still hadn't browned. 'Weird. I'll put the grill on for a bit.'

Charlie poured the wine and we chatted and drank. My flatmate Christina came in and started making pasta as we talked. Then, after a while, she said, 'Is something burning?'

'Crap, the fries.' I raced to the oven, which was full of black smoke. I took the fries out, a solid brown colour.

'I mean,' I said. 'These aren't too brown. They look okay. Do they look okay?'

I presented them to Charlie, who peered at them and said, 'They look okay.'

'They look okay,' Christina repeated on her way out, a successful bowl of ravioli in hand. I put the stove back on to reheat the steaks and dished out the fries onto two almost-matching plates.

I picked up one of the pans and turned to Charlie. 'Did I tell you I'm really good at flipping pancakes?'

'You realise those aren't pancakes,' he said.

'Anything's a pancake if you make it a pancake,' I said, and flipped the steak with expert precision.

Charlie applauded me, and I smiled, and curtseyed, and as I did, the steak slid from the pan straight onto the floor.

'Nooooo,' I said, kneeling down to examine the casualty. Was it salvageable? I mean, it had some dust clumps on it, and a long hair…

'Maybe rinse it and give it another…' Charlie was suggesting, but I dumped the fifteen-dollar hunk of cow in the garbage. I looked at him, disappointed and embarrassed. 'It'll be fine,' he said.

We ended up splitting the surviving steak, which was more medium-rare than medium, but close enough. The fries weren't crazy brown, but they were solid as a rock.

'Why aren't the fries soft on the inside?' I asked.

'Did you boil the potatoes first?' Charlie said, squeezing ketchup all over his.

'Are you meant to?'

'I mean,' Charlie forced the tough sticks onto his fork. 'Maybe. I don't know.'

'I think you do know.' I peered at my plate. *Mum never boiled the potatoes first*, I thought, then pushed it away.

He seemed to find it funny. After we'd eaten, he started washing up without me asking him to, and suggested we watch something "in the lounge."

'Um,' I said, 'me and Marie use my bed as a sofa when she comes over.'

'That could work,' he said. 'Oh, um, unless you don't—I mean—want me in your room.'

'It's fine,' I shrugged. He followed me into my bedroom, and I nervously said, 'Ta-da,' as I opened the door.

I immediately wished I'd lit a scented candle and rushed to open the window. *Does the room smell? Do I smell? I mean, I assume not, if he's here, on a second date, but maybe I smell right now—shit—I should have showered after work.*

I hadn't really been expecting him to make it into my room, so it was a bit of a mess. Luckily, the floordrobe wasn't currently in use, but the dresser was littered with makeup and tissues and an open packet of cookies. I expected Charlie to be unimpressed, and I was embarrassed again—he'd taken me to a fancy-ass restaurant and here I was, burning dinner and showing him my mess. He didn't bat an eye, though; he just jumped on the bed, propped a pillow behind him, and said, 'Alright, what are we watching?'

I opened my work laptop and clicked onto Christina's Netflix. We ended up choosing *Queer Eye*, which Charlie had seen a bit of but I hadn't, and we freaked out at the haircuts, pointed out our favourite bits of the home makeovers, and cried at the transformations. We watched three in a row back-to-back, giggling like children, sitting cross-legged on the bed and eating the last of my cookies. Eventually, Charlie's arm crept around my shoulders and pulled me closer. I looked at him and smiled.

'Whatcha looking at me like that for?' he grinned.

'Nothing,' I smiled back.

'Is this okay?' he said, nodding towards the arm.

'That's okay.'

'Is this okay?' he reached over and took my hand in his free one.

'That's okay,' I said.

He looked at me a bit longer, then interlinked my fingers with his and pulled me in towards him. 'Is this okay?' he said, his lips an inch from mine.

'That's definitely okay,' I said. He finally kissed me with those lips I had been staring at all night, and oh my god, fireworks.

He didn't stay long after that; we watched a bit more *Queer Eye* and then he headed home.

'This was fun,' he said, clearly ignoring dinner.

'Yeah, it was,' I agreed.

'Next Friday? Make the most of it before I start nightshifts. It's my turn to plan a date, isn't it?'

'Please, nothing too fancy this time,' I said, feeling a little more open now he'd seen my house and not screamed. 'Something more McDonalds than Parisian cuisine?'

He laughed. 'How about I cook, then?'

'Okay,' I said, and once more, he leaned in and kissed me.

I thought about that kiss the entire week that followed. Those were the longest seven days of my life. I watched the reception desk like a hawk, hoping he'd come in to see his dad again, preferably in a lab coat with a stethoscope round his neck. Didn't happen. I tried to memorise the way his lips had felt against mine, his warm arm around my shoulder, his fingers brushing my thigh as they reached for my hand. Even picturing his face made me breathless.

'Does it turn you on?' Marie said, sticking her face in front of my computer screen.

'Can you not,' I said.

'We share half our genes, you know. But lesbians are always better in bed, it's a scientific fact.'

'Don't you have some lenses to clean?'

'I'm just saying, now that you're fucking my brother—'

'I am not fucking your brother.'

'—which I'm totally cool with, by the way, I just find it strange, how the heterosexual woman can look at me, an image of perfection, and settle for some hairy-ass dude who picks his nose when he thinks no one's watching. C'mon, you've got to admit, we look similar.'

'Marie, when I look at you, all I see is you drunkenly crying because you realised your tenancy said you can't get a cat.'

'That was a very hard time for me!' Marie snapped, and marched back to the photographer's room, all the while pointing at her bum and saying, 'Better than his.'

When Friday came around, I was nervous. I walked to Charlie's place and got more and more anxious with every step I took, especially when the neighbourhoods got posher and posher as I approached Volunteer Park. Surely a twenty-four-year-old med student didn't live here.

Turns out he did. He lived in an unassuming redbrick building surrounded by frost-tipped trees. He greeted me a little awkwardly, unsure if he should touch me (so he didn't) and showed me round his enormous open-plan apartment, with hardwood floors, plush furniture, and a kitchen that looked brand new. He'd set the dining table with candles and a bottle of wine and two places for dinner.

I knew his dad was rich, and had probably got him this place, but I couldn't believe this was Charlie's apartment. I mean, Marie's place was nice too, and presumably also funded by their father, but she shared it with Lisa, and they didn't live right by the park. I guess I always saw her room when it'd been ransacked for Saturday night clothes, and her lounge when it was full of pizza and wine. Charlie's place must've cost a fortune.

'Sorry I didn't get you flowers. I was so busy cooking all day I completely forgot,' he said, pulling out a chair for me.

'That's very okay,' I said, and sat down.

'First,' he said, opening the wine and pouring two glasses, 'we have tomato soup with fresh sourdough. And then we have goats' cheese on grilled bread with cherry tomatoes, golden pancetta, and parmesan shavings. For our main course, we've got chicken Milanese with spaghetti, and for dessert, I've made a chocolate cheesecake.'

I looked at him, stunned. He'd listed it all off as he arranged the table, all the while glancing back at me to gauge my reaction. 'How did you—memorise all that?' I asked.

'I was a server through college.' A timer dinged, and he dashed back to the kitchen. When he opened the oven, smoke did not come pouring out. Suddenly, I was even more embarrassed about my steak.

'When you said you were going to cook,' I said, 'I didn't realise you were going to show me how it's done.'

The meal was delicious, even though I was full after the first course, but something about the evening felt false. He was being smooth and charming again; he suddenly seemed far too good for me. Where had laughing-at-*Queer-Eye*-and-eating-cookies Charlie gone? When he was slicing up the divine-looking cheesecake, I finally brought it up.

'Charlie—'

'Miss Tyler?'

'I—this was delicious—'

'Oh no,' he said, sensing my tone, 'did you not like it?'

'Oh my god, no, it was to die for, all of it was so good. But the fancy restaurant, and the flowers, and the meal that looks like you've been cooking all day it's so perfect—is it not, well, a bit much?'

He put the knife down and sat in his chair. 'Have I come on too strong?'

'No, that's not it—I just feel like you're trying too hard to impress me.'

Charlie stared at the cheesecake. 'Ah.'

'It's really flattering, it really is. It's lovely. But I just can't compete, like—my apartment is half the size of yours, I don't live alone, we've learned that I can't really cook—'

'You can cook—'

'—and to be honest, places like The Sealion of Paris freak me out a bit. The prices, the guests, I mean they've all got Burberry coats and—I dunno—Louis Vuitton handbags and all. I really don't mean to sound ungrateful, you've been so sweet, but I can't keep up like this. I'd like to go somewhere where I can pay for half.'

Charlie processed this, twirling his fork around in his hand. 'I wanted to show you that I was different. To Pete, and, y'know—I don't know. I wanted to show you I wouldn't treat you like that.'

My chest glowed with warmth. 'That's so lovely. And it's worked. You're not like Pete. I get it, you can stop now. If we're going to keep seeing each other—and I want to—then I've got to get to know you properly. Like when we were watching *Queer Eye,* it felt like you weren't, y'know, trying to impress me. I mean, I was trying to impress you, and it was such a flop. I can't believe you wanted another date, especially now I've seen this place and how well you can cook. But what I'm trying to say is, I want to see more than just the best of you. I just want to see—well—Charlie.'

He leaned back. 'Okay, deal.'

'Deal?' I said.

He nodded. 'We'll go to cheaper places. And you can get your own flowers.'

I smiled. 'Yes. Great. Awesome.'

He smiled too and pointed at the cheesecake. 'How about we eat this on the couch in front of a movie?'

I grinned as he took our plates and led me over to the TV. As we ate, he put his arm around my shoulders and I reached up and interlinked my fingers with his. We watched *Her* and chatted and laughed and kissed until I melted.

SCENE 4: MATT, 25

'I'm done with Liverpool,' Simon said. 'Finished. Complete. Bada bing, bada boom.'

We were in The Anchor, one of the pubs we'd frequented as sixth formers, only now it was swarming with *my* sixth formers. I hadn't been here in so long, it hadn't occurred to me it'd be full of students, grown up into the shadows of me and my friends.

'We should have gone to The Shakespeare,' I said, peering over my shoulder at a table of year thirteens. 'Bit quieter.'

'Bit older, you mean,' Simon said, following my gaze. 'Though we're not ready to join the bald beer-bellied bowls players yet.'

'Sorry.' I turned back to him. 'Liverpool.'

'I'm back in with Mum and Drew. Saving up. I've been working so hard, y'know? It's time for a break. Reckon I'll go to Australia.'

'And would this have anything to do with the fact that Shauna dumped you?'

'She didn't dump me, dude, it was mutual—'

'I'm winding you up, mate.'

He smirked. 'You can only do the Australia working holiday thing until thirty-one. After that, you're too old. And I'm already old for a backpacker in a hostel. I'm gonna work with Drew for three months and then go.'

'That'll kill you, working for your stepdad.'

'Don't I know it,' he said over his pint.

'What does Fliss think of this?' I asked. 'I've been meaning to call her.'

'She's down for it, y'know. Thinks it'd be good for me to see the world. She never liked Shauna.'

'She never does,' I said, taking a sip of my cider.

'What about you, eh?' Simon asked. 'I mean, mate, living above the shop you used to work in is a bit tragic.'

'You don't think it's a metaphor for success?' I laughed.

'And teaching at our old school, with all our old teachers—'

'I'm not staying,' I said, then turned round to check my students hadn't heard me. 'It's all temporary. I'm just figuring out what I want to do.'

'Figure it out in Aus with me,' Simon said.

'I dunno, man. I worry about Mum, y'know.'

'You worry about your mum?'

'Yeah, she's getting on a bit…'

'Getting on—mate, sixty is the new forty, okay? She's fine. She's got your dad.'

'I've got a job interview in London next week. I'll move, if I get that. It'll start right when term ends.'

'And what do they do?'

'They make materials—'

'Ooh, materials,' Simon said. 'That's a lot better than surfing.'

I'd told work that I had some ambiguous health appointment to get the morning off for the interview. I drove to London the night before and stopped over in a shared house that I found on Airbnb. A stern woman opened the door when I rang the bell. 'Yes?' she said in an Italian accent.

'Um, I'm looking for Gabriella.'

'That's me,' she said.

'Hi, I'm Airbnb-ing Rich's room?'

'Rich has been—we told him to stop doing that. He told you to ask for me?'

I nodded tentatively.

'Fine, okay, come in,' she said, and ushered me inside.

She tapped her long nails on a door at the top of the stairs. 'This is Rich's room,' she said, then disappeared behind another door.

I went into the room. It was alright, a bit small; the double bed took up most of the space. It was clean, though there were some cigarette burns on top of the dresser. When I explored the rest of the flat, I found a bathroom full of empty shampoo bottles, and a kitchen with some dirty dishes in the sink. Thankfully, I'd already eaten.

I barely slept. Gabriella was on the phone until two, and some dude in another room was clearly getting lucky. Doors were banging, the toilet was flushing, and I could hear sirens whizzing down the road all night—were we near a hospital, or was crime in London as bad as everyone said it was?

The next morning, I walked to the tube station in my suit and headed into central London. I kept checking my watch, crushed between the other commuters and anxious I'd miss my slot. I changed trains at Bond Street Station, and so did everyone else. My eyes darted around at the signs for the Central Line, keen to keep up with the vacant crowd as they pushed on through the claustrophobic tunnels. It took three trains before I managed to squeeze onto one, securing a spot by the doors. I looked back through the glass, and over the rows of heads I saw an advert on the wall: *Romeo and Juliet* at Shakespeare's Globe.

I looked around the tube carriage. People were squeezed together, a short woman facing the wrath of a tall guy's armpit as he held on to the bar above him. Some expert in the middle, surfing hands-free while holding a book to their nose. Kids in school uniform, chatting away. No sign of her.

The interview was fine, and as soon as it ended, I jumped back on the tube to get to my car and drive the two hours back to school. I made it to my two o'clock lesson and powered through the afternoon without lunch. By the time I got home, I was knackered.

The next day I checked my email at breaktime and saw I'd been invited for a second interview. I groaned. I hadn't realised there'd be more than one interview. A second trip to London, a second lie to my department head, and a second sleepless night in a tiny flat. I deleted the email.

SCENE 5: BROOKE, 22

'Happy six-month anniversary!' Charlie said, when he opened the door to me. He was holding a bouquet of sunflowers. 'Don't be mad, it's a special occasion.' I laughed. 'I'm not mad. Thank you. And a happy six-month anniversary to you too.'

Dating Charlie had been a dream. No drama, no jealousy, just falling in love, plain and simple. He'd gone back to California that March to finish his exams and now was studying at the med school in town, often training at the hospital where his parents met.

He'd made me a better person, too—made me *want* to be a better person. He went out running a lot, so I would run with him, and I felt fitter and stronger. We cooked together, and I made new meals, healthy stuff I could reheat for lunch rather than just having a bagel and a bag of potato chips. I slept at his most nights. We'd spend Saturdays with Marie and Lisa, and Sundays volunteering at the foodbank or watching films. I never spent the weekend staring at my ceiling anymore.

Everyone had seen a change in me. Yuko had noticed my energy and motivation, and sent me out with the reporters more. Mr Young had taken to walking past my desk on the way to his office and smiling at me, which had first made me uncomfortable, but eventually I started smiling back and asking how he was. His PA Henry would complain to me about his bad mood, but I never saw it.

I snipped the bottom of the flowers over Charlie's sink. 'Are you all set for tonight?'

He handed me a vase. 'Dinners in the oven and your gift's on the table. You?'

'I've got your present, I'm wearing very small underwear, and I'm starving. I think we're sorted.'

It was fine until, during dinner, Charlie said, 'Brooke, I want to know about your family.'

My heart stopped. Everything—*everything*—had been perfect up till then. I knew I could try to put the question off for another six months, but I couldn't put it off forever. Things were going so well with Charlie. He'd have to find out eventually. And when the time came, when I told him the truth, he would undoubtedly leave me, and I would be alone again. For a long time, we sat in silence.

'You have parents?' he asked.

I nodded.

'And siblings?'

My voice cracked when I spoke. 'A sister.'

'Okay,' he said, putting down his bread. 'Why did you leave England?'

'I had to leave…my…past…behind.' The words came to me one by one, strung together clumsily.

'And what was that past?' he asked.

I stared at my empty plate, remnants of hummus still smeared across it. 'I was unhappy,' I said. 'Really unhappy.'

The silence dragged on. Eventually, 'I don't want to live in the past,' made it out of my mouth.

I could see he wanted to talk more about it, and he could see that I didn't. He dropped it and changed the subject, but I knew it was just a matter of time. I couldn't keep my secrets forever.

Later that night, when dessert had been eaten and presents had been opened and the tiny underwear was on the bedroom floor, I whispered, 'I'm a bad person,' into the darkness.

'You're wrong,' Charlie said emphatically.

'No, I am.'

'How are you a bad person?'

I gulped. Tears stung my eyes as I felt the confession swell up in my throat. 'I stole from my family. To come to America. They gave me money for university, and I used it to leave them.'

I listened to his breathing, clinging to it, the proof that he was still there, that he hadn't disappeared. 'Didn't they wonder where you were getting the money to move?' he asked.

My stomach knotted tightly, and the tears spilled over. 'They didn't know I was going,' I whispered. I buried my head in his chest, wanting to crawl inside it and hide from his eyes. *This is it. This is the moment he leaves you. He hates you now.*

After a long silence—I wondered if he'd fallen asleep—he said, 'So you just left them? They woke up one day and you were gone?'

There was an ache I felt somewhere, some piece of me that had broken off and got left behind when I got on that plane. I nodded and he felt it on his chest. He must've felt the tears, too.

'That's a lot, Brooke. I mean, no wonder...' He sat up and looked at me through the darkness. 'No wonder, when I met you, you were living out of a motel. That must've been really hard for you.'

'For me?' I repeated in disbelief. Charlie was always so kind to me, and I felt guilty for it.

'Yeah, I mean, to leave your home, everyone you knew. To start over.'

I stared at the ceiling. 'It was hard,' I said, 'but I can't imagine…'

'Can't imagine what?'

'What it felt like. For them. My family.'

'They must've treated you badly,' Charlie said.

I shook my head, my eyes fixed on his lampshade, a shape on the ceiling darker than the rest, a black hole ready to consume me. 'They were good people.'

'They weren't abusive?'

I shook my head.

'They weren't—huh.' He cut himself off.

Neither of us said anything for a long time. *He's going to break up with you. He's going to leave and you'll be alone again. And you deserve it. Look what you did to your family.*

'Have you ever told anyone this?' Charlie said eventually.

I shook my head again.

'Geez. That's a lot for you to deal with on your own. Do you ever want to talk to someone about it?'

I shook my head frantically and sat up too. 'I can't—I can't tell anyone—it's the worst thing I've ever done. I just told you, and that was—this is—' I broke down crying again. Charlie hesitated, but then he wrapped his arms around me and pulled me into him. *He's not leaving. Why isn't he leaving?*

'What if there was someone who wouldn't judge you? Someone who was paid to listen to anything you say. Someone who wasn't allowed to tell anyone else.'

'You mean a therapist,' I said.

'Yeah,' Charlie said, 'a therapist.'

I'd had counselling before, and Carrie had been okay, though I'd never got very far with her. But I hadn't really told her much. I'd struggled to open up.

'I saw someone after Mom died,' Charlie went on. 'Dad made us. I was young, but it really helped.'

That surprised me. Someone as well-put-together as Charlie could need the same help as the broken mess of fragments I was.

'It's covered by your health insurance. Dad made a point of it. That and cancer care.'

I sniffed. Charlie was usually right. He'd been right about running making me feel better. He'd been right about all this healthy food being good for me. Maybe if I tried, and actually opened up to someone, things could get easier. Maybe I could end up as whole and complete as him, and forget all about England, and my family, and the permanent underlying guilt that was like a stone in the sole of my shoe. My voice cracked when I said, 'Okay.'

'If you feel bad about the money, maybe you could find a way to send some back to them. That might make you feel better.'

'Okay,' I repeated. I sniffed and pulled away from him. Now he was the one staring into space.

'Are you okay?' I asked.

'Mm hm,' he nodded, but still looked ahead.

'What are you…is there something you want to say?' I asked.

He lay back and turned to me. 'Will there ever be some morning when I wake up and you're gone?'

I only thought about it for a second. 'No.'

'Good. I love you.'

'I love you too.'

He kissed me on the top of my head and we fell asleep.

The next morning, we went back to normal. Charlie didn't bring up the previous night, and I didn't either. But after he left for work, he texted me the number of someone he recommended. I rang up and booked a free consultation with a therapist called Sanjay. I told Yuko I had a doctor's appointment and didn't go into detail, though if I started having to miss work every week for it, I'd have to tell her the truth.

That first session, Sanjay suggested I draw a map of the important friends and family in my life, and I started bawling my eyes out. I had to explain to him about leaving England. That took up most of the time. It felt horrible to admit this stuff, but Sanjay didn't judge me, just as Charlie had said. He asked about my relationships with my parents; it was the first time I'd really let myself think about them since I'd left. We never did draw the map.

'There's a lot to unpack here, and I think I could help you in the long term. If you want to have a weekly session, we can do that, though if you don't think we're a great fit, then I can recommend some of my colleagues for you.'

'I'd like a weekly appointment,' I blubbered.

'Alright. And I want to be clear, you are in the driver's seat and I'm here to help you. I'm not going to make you do anything you aren't ready to do, like reach out to your family—'

I looked at him in horror at the suggestion.

'I'm *not* going to make you do that. But I hear that you're feeling a lot of shame about what happened. I know you feel guilty about leaving, and about the money, and for not saying goodbye. You said you really struggled to tell your partner about this, what was his name—'

'Charlie,' I said, like it was the most important thing in the world.

'Charlie. Right. I would like us to try to deal with this guilt, and remove its grip on you, if we can.'

I nodded and wiped my nose with the last tissue in the box.

Immediately after the session, I went to the bank to send a shamefully expensive cashier's check to my mother in the name of removing guilt's grip on me. I crossed my fingers that her address was still the same, and felt a little weight lift from my shoulders as I left the bank and headed to the office.

I sat with Yuko and told her I was dealing with some stuff and needed to come in late on Thursdays to go to these appointments. I offered to stay late to make up the hours, but she told me not to worry. She didn't ask too many questions but said I could talk to her anytime, which was nice, if a little awkward. She was usually so fierce, and her softer side was slightly unnerving.

I had another couple of sessions with Sanjay. It felt good to finally be talking about this stuff, even if it was hard and even if I cried out my daily two litres of water in every session. We talked about my relationships with my parents, and with Charlie, and also about Matt. I wasn't sure which direction we were going in, but I trusted Sanjay.

One Tuesday morning, I got into the office as usual and started making Yuko her coffee in the kitchen.

'Morning, Dan,' I said, as the receptionist came to my side.

'Hey, Brooke,' he said. 'There's a detective waiting in Yuko's office.' Being the city editor meant she covered crime, and I would sometimes schedule meetings with detectives so she could get the story.

'I didn't book anyone in for this morning,' I said. 'Bit rude of them to just show up. She won't be in for ten minutes.'

'Yeah, I couldn't see him on the calendar, but he asked for you by name, so I let him in.'

'He asked for me?' I said. Sometimes people would find my name on the company website, and decode our formulaic email addresses to contact me directly, knowing that PAs were the best way to get to editors. But to just show up was a first.

I headed to the city editor's office and saw an East Asian man sat in front of the desk. 'Hi,' I said, closing the door and feeling weird as I sat in Yuko's seat, though I had pre-interviewed people for her before. 'I'm Brooke, PA to the city editor.'

'Jamie Higa,' he said, in a thick Scottish accent. 'Thanks for meeting with me.'

'Are you from Scotland?' I asked.

'I grew up there, but I live in London now.'

'Oh, right.' So he wasn't a local detective. 'I must apologise, I'm not sure what we're covering here.'

'Well, firstly, I'll tell you that I work as a private investigator.'

'Private. Ah.' Private detectives sometimes tried to sell us stories, but usually they weren't worth printing. Yuko had asked me not to accept meetings with them. I leant back. 'What've you got for us, then?'

'Well, Brooke. I've been employed by a private family for about a month, for the purpose of finding out what happened to a low-risk missing person.'

'Right,' I said, jotting it down. Low-risk was hardly going to make a headline.

'And I believe you are that missing person.'

I looked up at him. 'Huh, sorry?'

'An eighteen-year-old woman named Brooke Tyler went missing from the Bristol area about four years ago. It's believed she left the UK of her own volition. I've been employed by the family to try to find her.'

I froze, mouth open and heart pounding, as it slowly sank in. *He's looking for you.*

'I believe you are that missing person,' he said again.

My hands were sweaty, and my stomach had knotted. I tried hard to keep my breathing calm, but my worst fear had been realised: *they can find you. This safe little space you've made for yourself is in danger. Your separate worlds can bleed together. All that hurt, pain, and sadness from your past can wash in through the cracks in the walls you've built and get to you.*

I swallowed and looked down. 'Um, I think, Mr Higa, that you must have me mistaken for someone else.'

'I'm afraid I find that difficult to believe, Brooke. I've seen photographs of you. Your family was very distressed by your disappearance and misses you very much.'

I stood up. 'I'm going to have to ask you to leave now, Mr Higa.'

'Your mother thanks you for the money you sent. It was that check that allowed me to trace your whereabouts. When I saw you worked at this paper—'

'Mr Higa, please—'

'They just want to know that you are alright, and safe. A little contact would go a long way—'

'STOP IT!' I yelled. He fell silent. I opened the office door and saw a dozen faces staring at me as people filed in. I had to hold back tears. 'Dan, please see this gentleman out.'

Jamie Higa looked at me. 'Just my card—'

'Please leave,' I said, stifling a sob.

'Just my business card. If you want to—'

'Okay, I get it.'

'—call me anytime.'

'Okay! I know! *Now please get out of my office!*'

Dan was at my side, looking thoroughly guilty. He must have tried to turn this PI away, and Jamie Higa must have argued, and told him he was investigating *me* rather than selling a story. Dan took the man out towards the elevators, and I slammed the door to Yuko's office and succumbed to tears.

SCENE 6: MATT, 26

'Hey stranger,' Fliss said, as she opened the door to her mum's house.

'Flisstopher!' I pulled her into a hug. 'God, I haven't seen you since...since...'

'Since Christmas, I reckon,' she said, letting me inside. 'You need to come to London more.'

'Oh, yeah,' I said. 'I was there a few months ago, actually. Briefly, for a job interview.'

'And you didn't tell me!' she cried. 'I would've let you camp out on my floor.'

'That would probably have been a better night's sleep than the one I got.'

Simon came into the hall and pulled me into a bear hug. 'Duuude!'

I handed him the present I'd brought. 'Just something for down under.'

He opened it and chucked the wrapping paper on the floor. 'Awh, shit, a compass and a box of condoms. Very funny.'

Fliss didn't look impressed.

'I...he gave me a condom for uni,' I explained. 'This is just the circle of life.'

'I actually hope these condoms will prevent the circle of life,' Simon said.

'GROSS! Stop it,' Fliss snapped, and led us into the living room.

Simon's parents and stepparents were all there, and a dozen aunts, uncles, and cousins I might've seen before. A few of his friends from Liverpool had made it down, ones I'd met a couple of times when I'd visited for his birthday. A *BON VOYAGE* sign was Blu-tacked to the wall. Simon's dad and stepdad were both attempting to dominate the barbecue, and his mum was visibly stifling a sob every time someone mentioned him leaving. We had beers and burgers and polite conversation as the afternoon waned into evening.

'How did that job thing go?' Simon said.

'In London? That was ages ago, I told you—'

'Not that one. The job in Cardiff. You said you were head-hunted.'

'Headhunted?' I repeated.

'You said your old supervisor knew somebody, who knew somebody...'

'Oh,' I said. 'Yeah. I told him I'd think about it. That was a few weeks back. They've probably got someone else by now.'

Simon's mum made a speech, and cried, and he hugged her tipsily, and his family started leaving. He was ordered to bed before his flight the next day, and I hugged him hard as we said goodbye.

'When you see my pics on Instagram and die of jealousy,' he said to me, 'fly out and join me, 'kay?'

Fliss offered me a lift home, insisting on seeing my flat. 'It's nothing special,' I said.

She parked outside the shop and followed me up the stairs to my front door. I let her in and she looked around. 'It's nice,' she said half-heartedly.

'It's temporary,' I said quickly.

It was a studio flat, with a kitchenette and Mum and Dad's old TV propped at the end of my bed. Fliss sat on the old leather couch.

'Tea?' I said.

'Nah, I should head back in a minute. I'm driving him to Heathrow in the morning.'

'Your mum looked heartbroken,' I said, putting the kettle on for me anyway.

'Yeah,' she laughed. 'How long have you been here?'

'Um. Two, three years?'

'I thought you said it was temporary?'

'Well, yeah, but I had to qualify first.'

'You qualified ages ago.'

'Well,' I said, 'yeah.'

'So, you're going to leave? Are you going to keep teaching?'

'Uh. I don't know. I don't really like teaching. But I'm still figuring out what I want to do.'

She pointed at my framed picture of the Space Needle that was leaning against the wall. 'You've been here three years and you haven't put your pictures up?'

'I'm not staying,' I said, 'I'm not staying.'

I took the tea and sat next to her on the sofa. She was still looking around the room. 'Do you spend your weekends here?' she asked.

'Um,' I said. 'I'll go round and see Mum and Dad. Catch up on work, marking, y'know. Hang out with Simon, though that's over now, I guess. I dunno. Just chill, really.'

'You spend it alone?'

'Not completely. But I like doing things on my own.'

'You never used to. Well, maybe you did, but you also went out a lot.'

I shrugged, feeling my cheeks flush. 'Just getting older, aren't we? Well, it's probably different in London, isn't it?'

'You should come down one weekend. We'll go out. I think you and my flatmate will get on. Speaking of, have you done any dating?'

'Not really. Not since my master's, actually. And those were nothing to write home about.'

Fliss pulled up the Bumble app on her mobile, showed me her profile and how you have to answer questions about yourself. She took a decent photo of me on her posh phone and left me with an instruction to set up an account.

'Promise you'll send me screenshots, so I can critique it for you,' she said, as I walked her to her car. 'Every single guy says the most spontaneous thing they've ever done is quit their job and go travelling. Though I guess that's more true for Simon than for you. Anyway, get yourself a nice girlfriend for the summer.'

I watched Fliss drive off and went back inside. I looked at the picture of the Space Needle, then at the stack of exercise books next to it. I knew I wasn't meant to be here, but I didn't know where else to go.

SCENE 7: BROOKE, 22

Jamie Higa's visit shook me to my core. Who else had he researched in my life? Who else had he talked to? Had he spoken to anyone at work? Had he found Charlie? My colleagues had seen me scream at him, thankfully, before Yuko got in. She didn't say anything, so hopefully no one had told her about it. Dan told Marie, though, and she took me to a burrito place for lunch. My eyes darted around the streets, looking for a sign of the detective. Surely he wouldn't give up that easily.

'I really don't want to talk about it,' I said to Marie.

'I'm not gonna make you talk about it,' she said, as she ordered for both of us. 'I'm just gonna make you tell me if you're okay or not.'

'I'm okay,' I said, though my hands hadn't stopped shaking.

'Do you need to go home early?'

'No,' I said, though when I did go home, I went to my flat instead of Charlie's place like I usually did. I got into my bed and stared at the ceiling and cried.

Charlie called me at ten, when he got back from work. 'Brooke, where are you?'

'Charlie,' I blubbered, 'I'm at home.'

'Did you not want to come over?' he said. 'You've got my keys, remember?'

'Oh, God, I'm s-sorry, Charlie, I f-forgot,' I said.

'It's okay, the super has a spare—what happened, Brooke?'

'I h-had a r-really bad day,' I said.

'Okay. I'm coming over. Give me an hour.'

He was forty minutes. When he rang the bell, I was too exhausted to get up, so Christina let him in, and he came into my room and kicked off his shoes and crawled into bed with me.

'What happened today, Brooke?' he said into the back of my head.

'Ch-Charlie,' I said, looking at the wall, 'Has anyone asked you any w-weird questions lately?'

'Weird?' he repeated. 'I don't think so.'

'An E-East Asian man with a S-Scottish accent?'

'Um,' he said. 'Not that I can think of? I see a lot of patients, but I don't remember anyone Scottish.'

'Jamie Higa,' I said. 'He's a p-private investigator.'

'What did he do, then?'

'My m-mother sent him to f-find me.'

'Oh,' Charlie said, 'Brooke.'

'And he f-found me. Because of that stupid check, which I ch-checked, and they haven't even c-cashed it.'

'What did you tell him?'

'I d-denied it and asked him to leave.'

'Did he say anything?'

'He said my mum th-thanked me for the money. And he said they missed me, which…which…maybe my mum does, but my dad doesn't. He forgot I existed a l-long time ago.'

'If your mom hired someone,' Charlie said softly, 'when you sent the check, maybe …maybe she just wants to reach out, Brooke.'

'I can't, Charlie!' I howled at the wall. 'I can't, I did something awful to her. I can't face it, I can't face her. I've built my own life here and I can't go back to how shitty and awful everything was in England.'

Charlie didn't say anything. He held me for a long time, then got up and ran me a bath. He got in with me and washed my skin gently. The warm water, his warm arms, calmed my tears.

'What if he talked to Sanjay?' I whispered.

'That won't have happened,' Charlie said, 'I promise you.'

'I thought I was safe here,' I said.

'You are safe.'

'I don't feel safe,' I said. Charlie slept at mine that night.

For the rest of that week I was hypervigilant, but no Jamie Higa appeared. When I went to see Sanjay on Thursday, he assured me that no one had talked to him, and he wouldn't have told them anything if they had. He taught me some breathing techniques to calm myself down if I panicked like that again. God, that was a session, and the light blazed through the windows the whole time. I'd tried to fix this by switching my appointment slot, but as the seasons changed, I'd successfully lined myself up with the sun's fiercest hour. *Good job, Brooke.*

But the months passed, and I didn't see Jamie Higa again. Fall came to Seattle, and it got colder, and I started wearing my coat again. I stopped worrying.

Charlie invited me to his dad's 60th, and I was shit scared. Mr Young was my boss, and I'd never been to his house before. But Charlie assured me that he wanted me there, and Sanjay helped to challenge some of my anxieties. 'Brooke, what evidence is there that you'll wet yourself in front of everyone?'

When Charlie and I entered the enormous house on Broadmoor, Mr Young hugged me for the first time. Lisa was there, and Charlie introduced me to countless aunts, uncles, and cousins, who all hugged me like they'd known me forever. I'd bought Mr Young a scarf and he said he loved it. He wore it to work every day after that.

Charlie really made me feel like I had a family. He introduced me to all his Seattle friends. He started to get to know his doctor friends, too, and occasionally they'd go out for drinks after work.

'Can't I come?' I said, when he told me one morning.

'Some time, for sure,' Charlie said, shaving his face. 'I'm still getting to know them myself.'

'I've met all your other friends,' I said. 'It feels weird that I don't know these guys. You talk about them all the time.'

'They're my work friends though,' Charlie said. 'They're not like those high school geeks. I can't goof around with these guys.'

'You know all my work friends,' I said.

'That's different. It's Dad's—I know everyone there. I'd rather bring you when they're all bringing their partners.'

'So you can hang out with all of my friends, but I can't hang out with yours?'

'It's not about keeping score, Brooke, they're just different. I have to be professional around them.'

'So you think I'm unprofessional?'

'No.' He kept shaving his face.

'You think I'm going to embarrass you?'

'No. I just want to get to know them more.'

'I'm going to be on my own tonight.'

'Only until, like, eleven. You're welcome to hang out here until I get home.'

'I'd rather go back to my place,' I said bitterly.

'Okie dokie,' he said, and kissed me on the nose.

Spending time without Charlie was just a waiting game for when he came back. I could handle being on my own for a bit here and there, watching Netflix to pass the time or having girly nights with Marie and Lisa, but I didn't enjoy doing stuff without him. This felt like a rejection. I made a lonely dinner that night, and when Christina saw me in the kitchen, she was surprised.

'Oh, you're here,' she said. 'Is everything alright with Charlie?'

'Yeah, he's just out with some friends tonight.'

'Oh, okay. You just spend so much time at his, I was like, "Oh my god, they must've split up!"' she laughed.

I slept badly that night without him and yawned as I made my way into work the next day, knowing full well I could've had a decent eight hours if I hadn't been so stubborn. It was Halloween, and all the storefronts were dressed up with pumpkins and fake cobwebs. My phone buzzed.

> *Charlie Young: Morning babe, I missed sleeping next to you last night. See you later?*

I smiled, my stubbornness thawed by his name on the screen.

> *Brooke Tyler: Missed you too ☺ I'll come over after work.*

It buzzed again.

> *Charlie Young: Can't wait. And happy Halloween! Love you.*

When I got into the office, Dan ran up and grabbed my wrist.

'Don't be mad,' he said, which made me instantly scared. 'A woman showed up asking for you.'

'That's not funny, Dan,' I said, looking at the plastic spiders he'd spread all over the reception desk.

'I'm being serious, Brooke. Marie started talking to her, they're in the photographer's room.'

I felt my breath hitch. I exhaled for a long time, like Sanjay had taught me. *This must be Jamie Higa's colleague. I'm sure of it.*

'Who is this person?'

'She didn't say her name. But she's tall, white, middle aged, curly hair.' My heart dropped. I saw Dan was reluctant to keep talking. 'British accent,' he said finally.

Mum.

The door to the photographer's room opened and both Dan and I jumped. It was Marie. She hurried over to the reception desk. 'Brooke,' she said in a low voice.

'Hide me,' I said desperately.

'Is that your mom?'

'Yes. Please, quickly, hide me.'

Marie took my hand and looked at Dan. 'Dan, please, can you stall Yuko a minute?'

Dan nodded, and Marie steered me towards the bathroom. Katie was in there, washing her hands.

'What's going on, B?' Marie asked.

'Katie, can I have a cigarette?' My voice shook as I spoke. Katie handed me one from her pocket and I took it with trembling fingers. 'And a light?' I added.

She looked at Marie, who nodded, and opened the window. Katie lit my cig and left.

'I left home when I was eighteen,' I said.

Marie nodded.

'Moved to America. Cut off all contact. Haven't been in touch. Haven't seen her since.'

Marie blinked as she took in my words. 'Why...why did you leave?'

I shrugged.

'Well...was she abusive?'

I shook my head. 'No. She was a good mum. She tried really hard to…' My voice cracked. 'To make me happy.'

Marie swallowed the lump that rose in her throat, and I was sure it was the same one that rose in Charlie's. That their mother had been taken away from them, and I'd left mine voluntarily.

'It's the worst thing I've ever done,' I said.

'I'm not judging you,' she said, but I didn't believe her.

'Please—can you ask her to leave? Tell her I don't work here anymore. Changed jobs. Moved out of state, no forwarding address.'

'I don't know, Brooke,' Marie said.

'Please, Marie…'

'She cares about you.'

'I don't need to know that!' I cried. 'I don't need evidence that people care about me. If there's evidence, then it makes me feel worse. For leaving.'

Marie gave me a long look.

'Please, Marie,' I begged. 'I'm so sorry to ask, I swear, but I just can't—I'm not ready—I just can't.' The cigarette was shaking in my hand.

Marie sighed. 'You're asking me to break her heart, you know.'

'I know.'

She gave me a really sad look, and she left. I stubbed the cigarette out. It hadn't helped.

I looked in the mirror and saw my makeup was streaked with tears that I hadn't realised I'd been crying. I splashed my face with water and went into a stall to catch my breath.

Seattle wasn't safe for me anymore. Ghosts from my past kept coming back to haunt me. I couldn't escape them, no matter how hard I tried. I balled up toilet paper in my hand to catch the tears. *Marie must hate you now. Charlie probably hates you secretly too, he just won't leave because he feels bad for you and knows—*

I caught myself before I spiralled. Sanjay had taught me what this type of anxious thinking was: catastrophising. I was meant to counter it with evidence. *I don't mean that,* came the counterthought. *And I could never leave Charlie. He loves me.*

I calmed my breathing the way I'd practised, and I felt my pulse slow down. My racing thoughts steadied themselves. *Of course Charlie still loves me, Marie too. She's just a little shocked. I don't need to leave Seattle. I'm safe here.*

I heard the bathroom door open, and I held my breath. I knew who it was instantly, recognised the pace and pitch of those footsteps. I checked my stall was locked, and then lifted my feet silently off the floor, hugging my knees into my chest.

Of all six stalls, Mum chose the one right next to me. She sat in there silently for a long time, and after a minute, I realised she was crying. Me too, Mum, me too.

SCENE 8: MATT, 26

I'm running through the airport. I'm running, but my legs are so slow and my feet are so heavy and I barely move. A mass of people flood against me, forcing me back with their bags and suitcases. Over their heads I glimpse a woman in a prom dress. She is moving and her dark hair is flying everywhere and she isn't looking back. I try to scream her name, but no noise comes out. I can't speak, she can't hear me.

I weave through the crowd and get to the other side just as she disappears through a door. I run towards it and I am so close to it and it's right in front of me but it takes ages, I can only move slowly, I can't get to it. When I finally do, when my hand finally lands on the cool metal, I tear it open and there she is, bleeding on the bathroom floor. Her naked body is covered in cuts and scars and she's not moving, her eyes won't open. I take out my phone to call 999, but every time I type in the numbers, I look at the screen and it's got different numbers, random numbers, and I clear the screen and type again, but it's not 999, it's some other numbers, and it makes no sense because I just pressed the "9" button three times but nothing works, she's bleeding and nothing works, she's dying and nothing works and it's my fault my fault my fault—

I woke with a jolt. My breathing was hard and the back of my neck was sweaty. I darted for the light switch to wake myself up, to prove to myself that it was just a dream, that it wasn't real, that there was nobody lying on my floor.

I took a deep breath and picked up my phone. I tapped on Instagram, wanting to remind myself what the real world was, what real life looked like. Simon had posted yet another picture of a beach against a clear blue sky. I double tapped, and the heart appeared in its centre.

I clicked on his profile and saw pictures of him surfing, drinking in bars, his arms always around a group of friends. He was tanned. He'd got a tattoo of a turtle on his thigh. I wondered if he'd regret it.

I scrolled further and saw an old photo of him with Fliss in a restaurant. It was a few months old, and the caption read *Happy joint birthday to my oldest friend.* I clicked on Fliss' profile.

Her photos had much less sun, sea, and sand, but still looked happy. Holiday pictures. A few smiling selfies. Black and white photos of her and her friends laughing over brunch. Staged, I was sure, but still it displayed a life that lacked no richness.

I opened Bumble. I'd given it a go, back when Fliss had made me download it, but I hadn't made it beyond a bit of small talk with a couple of women who eventually stopped replying. Then school had started again, and I'd gone back to work, and been too busy to think about it.

I checked my location settings. I couldn't be stingy on the outskirts of a city, so I set them to maximum. Minimum age, twenty-two; max, twenty-seven. I started swiping. It was weird, and unnatural, to be judging people on their looks, the way we'd always been told was shallow. I scrolled down and read the little bios, the Spotify favourites. I got a couple of matches, but I didn't swipe fast. Just in case I spotted her.

The next morning, one of my matches had messaged: *Hey, you were up late. Big night?*

I typed back: *If playing Skyrim till 2am counts, then yes.* I sent it, and instantly regretted it. *God, what if she thinks I'm some kind of video game nerd?*

She did reply, though, and we got chatting. Her name was Sophie. She was twenty-five and lived halfway between here and Bristol. She was funny. She worked in a GP's office.

Sophie Bumble: I've literally been scanning pictures of colonoscopies all day. It's not pretty.

Eventually she asked when I was going to invite her for a drink. I typed back: *I was just getting to that,* though I hadn't been. She suggested we go to the ice rink that they'd just opened at the mall for the run up to Christmas. Every time I thought about it, I felt a pang of nausea. I hadn't been on a date in more than a year. During my master's I'd gone out with a couple of women who'd approached me in bars, and another from my course who'd asked me out, but I'd never made it past a second date. They all lost interest, I guess.

I showered, shaved, and brushed my teeth. I wondered if I should shake her hand, or hug her, or kiss her on the cheek when I saw her. It was different, going on a date with someone you'd never met before. The fact I'd had to swipe on her and she'd had to swipe on me took away some fear of rejection. But what if I couldn't recognise her? What if she was disappointed by how I looked in real life?

I drove to the mall and parked up, my hands shaking as I did. *For fuck's sake, you're a twenty-six-year-old man.* She'd told me she'd be wearing a big red coat and jeans, and when I spotted her, she greeted me with a hug before I could worry about whether to shake her hand or whatever.

I was stumbling over my words for the first few sentences, but she was warm and nice and didn't look horrified by my appearance, so we started chatting and got into the swing of it. We went to get our skates and I quickly regretted choosing to go out early on a Saturday night. The rink was teeming with my students.

'Hey Mr Wills!' one of my year tens, Izzy, skated up to me as I pretended to help Sophie onto the ice, desperately clutching at her gloved hand and trying to keep myself upright.

'Oh, hi, girls,' I said, spotting Louise following in suit.

'Are you on a date?' Izzy asked.

'Um, yes, in fact, I am.' I hoped she would react maturely. At the sight of some year-eight boys behind her, I realised that was a mistake.

'Er—Sophie, these are some of my students. They also go to the drama group I run.'

'Hi,' Sophie smiled at them before returning her attention to her feet.

'See you, Mr Wills,' Izzy skated off happily with Louise. The year-eights were pointing and sniggering at us.

'Ignore them,' Sophie smiled, but the boys made that difficult. They skated right behind us, whispering fiercely.

'Is that Mr Williams?'

'The science teacher?'

'Is that his wife?'

'That's got to be his girlfriend. He's too young to be married.'

'How old do you reckon he is? Twenty? Forty?'

'Oooh, Mr Williams has a giiiirlfrieeend.'

At least Sophie seemed to find it funny. She definitely found it funny when I slipped and fell on my face (the year-eight boys dissolved into hysterics).

After forty-five minutes, we sat down for mulled wine. Sophie told me how she wanted to be an actress and was doing a musical theatre course that finished in August. She was hoping to get an agent. She was going to try children's TV, and some theatre work. She was nice. Nice, nice, nice.

But when I said I'd text her, I wasn't certain I would.

SCENE 9: BROOKE, 22

My next session with Sanjay was a blast. 'If you thought the PI was bad,' I said as I walked in, 'then you're in for a treat today.'

'Oh no,' he said from his usual seat in front of the window. 'What happened?'

Of course, I was crying within the first five minutes. 'And then I just waited for her to leave the b-bathroom, and Marie came to get me, she told me that she'd said she would just fly back to England, and I asked my boss if I could go h-home, and I just cried in bed all day.'

'Okay. I'd like to revisit that moment in the bathroom, so let's do it from a calmer place first.' Sanjay had me close my eyes and relax my muscles as much as possible. He did a guided meditation to slow my breathing, and when I was calmer, he began.

'Let's go back to that moment. You are in the bathroom, standing and watching yourself through the cubicle door. You're looking at your past self. What do you see?'

I took a deep breath. 'I see myself sat on the toilet lid. Crying.'

'Alright. Can you go up and talk to her?'

In my mind's eye, I walked through the cubicle door and put my hand on Past Brooke's shoulder.

'Ask her if she has a message for you,' Sanjay said.

I listened. 'She says, "I'm sorry for everything."'

'Okay,' Sanjay said. 'Can you ask her if she's in pain?'

'She says "yes."'

'Okay. What happens next?'

I pictured Mum, walking through the bathroom and sitting on the toilet lid in the next cubicle along.

'My—my mum comes in.'

'What's she doing?'

'She's crying,' I said.

'Okay. Can you ask your mom if she has a message for you?'

In my head, I walked up to Mum, whose face I hadn't dared to picture in years. 'She said, "I came because I love you, Brooke."'

'Good. Okay. So is your mom someone to be scared of in this scenario?'

'No,' I said, tearing up.

'And if the Brooke in the room with me now could say something to her, what would you say?'

Through the tears I said, 'I'm sorry, Mum.'

'Good. Is there anything else?'

'I miss you, Mum.'

'Good. Is there anything more that needs to happen between you?'

In my head, Mum hugged me, like I'd never been hugged before.

'She's hugging me,' I said.

'Good,' Sanjay said. 'Okay, when you're ready, open your eyes.'

The image in my head disappeared. The sun was burning. I squinted towards Sanjay, wiping my tears.

'How do you feel?' he said.

'Sad,' I breathed.

'What's making you sad?' he said softly.

'I miss my mum,' I said, like a child.

He left that hanging in the air for a long time. Eventually, he said, 'Did part of you want to speak to her when she came to your office?'

'Yes,' I said.

'Can you tell me why you chose not to?'

I sniffed loudly. 'I felt too guilty. I know I hurt her when I left. I was so unhappy in England; I couldn't let my two worlds touch.'

'Okay. Brooke, can you tell me why you left England?'

'I don't know,' I said. 'I can't remember.'

'There were a lot of different people you left behind. Your family, and this guy Matt we've been talking about. Let's break it down person by person. Why did you leave your sister?'

'I thought she'd be happier without me,' I said.

'Is there evidence for that?'

'No.'

'Why did you leave your dad?'

'Because he didn't love me anyway.'

'Is there evidence for that?'

'Some,' I said.

'Why did you leave your mom?'

I sobbed. 'Because I thought I made her so sad, and I was such a failure, because she was a good person and I was sad all the time. Who would want a daughter like that?'

Sanjay paused, and let my sobs fill the silence for a moment. 'Do you think she loved you?'

'Yes,' I said.

'Do you think she wanted you to leave?'

'No. But at the time, I thought everyone would be better off without me.'

'Was there evidence that they would be?'

'I guess not,' I said.

'Okay. As you said before, you spent your last night in England with Matt. Why did you leave him?'

'Because I couldn't let him break my heart again,' I said.

'Is there evidence that he would?'

'Based on the past,' I said, 'yes.'

'Maybe you expect to be disappointed. Do you think maybe a part of you felt undeserving of love? Of being treated well?'

'Maybe,' I said. The light through the windows was blinding, and I was blinking fast.

'Previously, we talked about your first few dates with Charlie, and how his attempts to spoil you made you uncomfortable.'

'I wasn't used to, y'know…' I looked at my shoes. 'Being treated like that.'

'It makes sense that, with an absent father, poor treatment from men might feel like love.'

I kept staring at my feet. I guess he was right.

'And when Matt discussed a relationship with you, just before you left, you said it was something that you wanted. Yet you still took yourself away from him. You've been hurt in the past, so naturally you want to protect yourself.'

I pressed my feet together, the toe of one shoe sitting on top of the other.

'Our early relationships can be really formative,' Sanjay went on. 'Especially after your dad. It makes sense that this relationship with Matt had a profound effect on you. Do you see how your self-image was dependent on his actions towards you? How he was the dictator of whether or not you felt loved?'

'He wasn't a dictator,' I said. 'He wasn't a bad guy.'

'But he did become the master of your emotions, your decisions. Whether to get on that plane or not depended on if he made you feel wanted. Subconsciously, you gave him a power over your happiness that he never asked for. And when you put your self-esteem in the hands of something you can't control, that's when it's a danger to your wellbeing. Does that make sense?' he said.

'Sort of?' I replied.

'If you think of yourself as leaning on a pillar. You take the pillar away, and you fall. That's kind of what it was like with Matt, when you were fourteen. He was the only pillar you were leaning on, the source of all your love. When he didn't make you feel wanted, like when you saw him kissing someone else, you collapsed.'

I looked at my hands, my fingers twisting up in each other. I guess it made sense, the pillar thing.

'This is what codependency does. It makes you give your partner power that they never asked for. Which puts you in a vulnerable position. And you were already in a vulnerable position, simply because you were so young and he was older.'

'I guess,' I said. 'I would've done anything for him.'

'Exactly.' Sanjay nodded.

'But that's on me, like you said. I put him in that position. Matt didn't ask for that.'

'That's true. But he did ask you to do things that weren't reasonable. Things that aren't normal in a relationship.'

I shrugged. 'That's because it was secret.'

'Well, there's a good example. Matt asked you to keep the relationship a secret. Did you understand why he wanted that?'

'I do now,' I said. 'I didn't really get it at the time. Not fully.'

'Would Charlie ask you to do something like that? To keep your relationship secret?'

'No,' I said.

'Matt wouldn't introduce you to the people in his life—'

'But he couldn't. He would've got into trouble.'

'Matt had his reasons, but I'm not interested in those. I'm interested in how it made you feel when he wouldn't introduce you to the people closest to him.'

I thought about this, about seeing his friends and his parents at *Romeo and Juliet* and having to act like we weren't something special to each other. 'Weird. It wasn't a great feeling.'

'Right. And do you feel that way with Charlie?'

'No. I've met his friends.'

'And how does that feel?'

I hesitated. 'Good. Like he's proud to be with me.'

'Right. When you were in a relationship with Matt, who was in control?'

'Matt wasn't controlling—'

'You might not describe him that way, and that's fine. But bringing it back to the relationship you had with him. Who was in control of it? Who got to make the decisions about what it looked like, about its parameters?'

'I guess,' I felt a lump in my throat. 'I guess Matt was—was in control.'

'And with Charlie?'

'We both are,' I swallowed. 'I feel like…I feel like there's negotiation. And communication.'

'Right.' Sanjay nodded gently. He lowered his voice and spoke slowly. 'And when it comes to physical intimacy. How does that compare?'

'With…with Charlie, we talked about it beforehand, y'know, we talked a *lot*. We took it pretty slow, I'd say. He cares about me, like, not just making me feel comfortable, but making sure

I'm actually enjoying it. And we always check in with each other. Even though we've been together for months.'

'And with Matt?' Sanjay nudged.

I felt my body tense up, though I didn't know why. 'The second time was fine. But the first, I—I don't think either of us knew it was going to happen. We didn't take it slow. We didn't talk about it. Maybe if we'd spoken about it, we'd've…we'd've actually thought about it. And realised it was a bad idea. But he didn't ask. I mean, neither of us asked.'

'Right,' Sanjay said softly. 'Neither of you asked. Do you feel he had the same responsibility to ask as you did?'

'Moreso,' I said, 'because he was older.'

'Right,' Sanjay said again, 'he was an adult. You were underage. What happened between you was illegal.'

'Right,' I said, my voice cracking.

'So compared to the relationship you're in now. How does the relationship you had with Matt feel, looking back on it?'

I swallowed. 'Like…like it probably wasn't very good. And maybe…maybe it was, um. Toxic.'

I saw Sanjay's silhouette nod, his head moving the smallest amount, though I felt like this was where he'd been trying to get me all along.

'I don't think he was trying to be toxic.'

'Probably not,' Sanjay said. 'But intention doesn't matter here so much as the real effect it had on you. He may not have intended to be manipulative, but that doesn't mean he wasn't. We know you were probably already vulnerable to depression, but having a relationship like this certainly didn't help, and maybe it was a catalyst. I'm not saying Matt was responsible for your mental health. But I do think he acted irresponsibly, and you got hurt.'

I looked down at my fingers.

'I got hurt,' I said back.

Sanjay let the silence drag on.

'But I wanted to be with him.'

'Do you feel like your fourteen-year-old self knew what was best for her?'

'No,' I said. 'I hardly know what's best for me now.'

'Would you choose that relationship for your younger self now?'

'No,' I said.

Sanjay nodded again. I felt something heavy in the pit of my stomach, a nauseating feeling hard as a rock. But weirdly I also felt lighter, in my chest, in my shoulders.

'I think I should talk to Charlie about this.'

'Talking to someone close to you could be helpful if you think he would be supportive.'

'He would be,' I said. 'He will be.'

Sanjay looked at the clock, a subtle way of signalling our time was up. 'How are you now?'

'I'm okay,' I said, taking a deep breath. 'I'm okay, just… thinking. Realising, maybe.'

Sanjay nodded again. 'Call me if you need an extra session this week.'

'Thanks. I think I'm okay.' I stood and picked up my bag. 'By the way. The light, through the window behind you? Blinding in the mornings. It might be worth moving the chairs.' I left through the doors and went to work.

When Charlie got home, I'd made dinner.

'Babe, thanks for cooking,' he said, dumping his bag and coming over to kiss me. 'How was your day?'

'Yeah,' I said a little cautiously, putting the steaming plates on the table. 'How was yours?'

'It was okay. Messy. Had to change my scrubs because—well, I'll tell you after. Good session today?'

'Yeah, actually, there was something I wanted to talk to you about.'

Charlie tucked in, but kept his eyes locked on mine.

'Something…something happened to me. When I was fourteen. There was this guy. Matt.'

I told him. I told him everything that happened from audition day to that night in the auditorium to the fight on the roadside to New Year's Eve. I left out the part about Prom; it was too close to what happened the next day and I wasn't ready to talk about that yet.

'This-this guy was eighteen? When you were fourteen,' Charlie said.

'Yeah.'

'And what he—what he did to you was…'

I nodded. 'Yeah.'

'That's…that's kinda fucked up.'

'It was,' I said. 'But he was young. Eighteen-year-olds make stupid decisions.' *I certainly did.*

'I don't buy that. I wouldn't have made that choice when I was eighteen.'

'Well, you're a better man than him.' I stood up and he mirrored me, coming to his feet as I wrapped my arms around his waist. He put his around me too, but he couldn't look at me. His eyes weren't warm and chocolatey like they usually were; they were stony, cold, looking past me. For a second, I thought his anger was directed at me.

'I fucking hate this guy,' Charlie said.

'I know.'

'They wouldn't let me be a doctor if I did the things I want to do to him.'

'He doesn't matter,' I said. 'Me and you are what matters. That's all in the past. You're my present.'

He looked down at me and pressed his nose against mine. 'And your future?'

I smiled. 'And my future.'

SCENE 10: MATT, 26

'I thought this group was for fourteen to twenty-five-year-olds?' I said to Meg.

'It is,' she said, flicking through her notebook.

I looked at the kids, devising scenes in small groups. 'We've got no one over eighteen.'

Meg shrugged. 'I'm always worried about numbers, Matt. We need to do something to rope in new members. Preferably older members. I can't think what, though.'

I looked at Izzy, directing her friends happily, steering them about. *Did Brooke look that young when she was fourteen?* 'Maybe it's not a good idea to have anyone older. There could be a separate group for adults. Fourteen to eighteen is a good range. Or even fourteen to sixteen, and then the sixth formers separately.'

'You're talking about running three drama groups, Matt. Don't you think we have enough work with one?'

I looked at my shoes. 'Sometimes they have parties, though. Surely fourteen-year-olds shouldn't be at the same party as eighteen, nineteen, and twenty-year-olds.'

Meg shrugged. 'I'd discourage it, Matt, but after a point, it's really up to the parents.'

I heard footsteps coming up the stairs and my head turned instinctively, hopefully, as it always did. How clearly I could picture her, with that baggy hoodie and her long brown hair. Walking up the stairs like she'd never left, walking into my arms and telling me she missed me and she was sorry she went away—

When Louise appeared at the top of the stairs, I felt disappointment, as I always did.

At noon the next day, my phone vibrated: a video call from Simon.

I answered. 'Hey, man.'

It took a few seconds for the audio to come through, and the image was pixelated. 'Matt? Can you hear me, mate?'

'Yeah, I can,' I said, getting up and moving closer to the router. 'Can you hear me?'

He was in a lounge that was teeming with people. He tried to talk to me, but his new friends would come up behind him and say hello, or grab the phone and start barking in-jokes I didn't get. He went to his bedroom and put his headphones in to hear me better.

Simon was ten hours ahead. He'd flown into Cairns and moved down the East Coast, stopping now in Brisbane for a couple of months. He'd got an Airbnb with some friends, and a job in a bar. He looked so happy, so relaxed.

'Yeah, that's what not having any responsibilities for four months will do for you,' he said, when I told him. 'I did some work for accommodation, but that was it. Spent most of my time on the beach. I'm really good at surfing, now, even if I have no money.'

'You've got *no* money?'

'Well, now, that was an exaggeration. I'm doing okay. I'm actually thinking of staying a second year. I have to do farm work, though, so I'll probably do that next. Go to the Northern Territory and harvest watermelons, or something.'

'Cool, man. I'm jealous, it looks like fun.'

'Dude, you should come out here. I'm serious. It's kind of like being a student again.'

'I've told you, mate, I can't.'

'Why not? You said you'd quit once you qualified.'

'Yeah, but—'

'But what? You've gotta stop letting opportunities pass you by.'

'I don't—'

'Yes, you do. What about those nice girls you dated during your master's? Or on your app?'

'They stopped replying—'

'Did they, or did you? Because I remember you making excuses to not text them back.'

I didn't say anything.

'What about that job in Cardiff they basically begged you to take? Or the one in London?'

'They didn't want me.'

'They didn't want you, or you couldn't be bothered to go back for a second interview?'

'I mean—London was nasty, mate, the tube, the crime—'

'You're not moving to London because of the *tube?*'

'—it's noisy, the place I stayed was grim, I got no sleep.'

'Not all of London is like that, dude. Fliss' flat is nice. You could've got a decent place on the fat fucking salary they advertised. Way better than a teacher's.'

'There's nothing wrong with teaching,' I said.

'Of course not, if it's what you actually want to do. Is it what you want to do?'

I didn't say anything again. Simon didn't either, he just looked at me. He knew me too well not to see through my bullshit.

Eventually I admitted, 'I don't know what I want to do. Or where I want to be.'

'Neither do I,' Simon said encouragingly. 'Come and figure it out here with me. Or in Bali on your own, or Thailand, or Peru. Just get off your arse. What's stopping you?'

I swallowed the lump in my throat. 'I don't know,' I said, though I probably did.

SCENE 11: BROOKE, 23

I came into the kitchen and saw Charlie keeled over the frying pan. He looked at me and smirked. 'Babe, surprise breakfast in bed only works if you stay *in bed*.'

'It was never going to be a surprise. I could smell it.' I came up behind him and wrapped my arms around him, burying my face in the back of his T-shirt. He'd slept in it, so it smelt of him, which made it all the more wonderful.

'Happy birthday, B,' he said.

'Happy my birthday to you,' I replied.

'We'll eat in here, anyway. You always get crumbs on the sheets.'

I went and sat at the table and saw a couple of gift-wrapped parcels leaning against a vase. 'Where did you get sunflowers in November?'

'Got connections, haven't I?' he joked. Soon we were eating scrambled egg and pancakes together.

I opened my gifts: a ring from Marie, a shirt from Lisa, a book from Mr Young, and some new running shoes from Charlie. I recognised them as the expensive ones.

'Oh, thank you, honey,' I said, kissing him. 'These are so great, mine were wearing out.'

'There was something else that I wanted to talk to you about,' Charlie said, speaking with a seriousness that arrested my attention. I always dreaded bad news—like he'd been transferred out of state, or he didn't want to be my boyfriend anymore and was dumping me right here on my twenty-third birthday.

'What,' I said. 'What, whatwhatwhatisit?'

'No, I just got you another present.'

'Oh,' I said. That did make me feel better.

He went into the bedroom and came out with a small draw-string bag. He looked nervous as he gave it to me. I opened it, and a little key fell on to my palm. 'The key to here?'

Charlie nodded.

'That's so lovely! Thanks,' I kissed him again. 'Makes sense. I'm over all the time—now I can sleep here when you're on nightshift.'

'That's the thing,' Charlie said, following me as I got up to add it to my keychain. 'You *are* here all the time. It doesn't really make sense for you to keep paying rent on another place.'

I spun round to face him.

'We've been together nearly a year, and you barely use your apartment, and I just…' He wrapped his arms around me and put his hands on the small of my back. 'I like it better when you're here.'

'You want me to move in?' I said.

'I want you to move in,' he repeated.

'Wow,' I smiled, warmth flooding my chest. 'But I don't think I could swing half the mortgage.'

'That's okay, I mean, Dad takes care of that since I'm still studying.'

'Hm,' I said, 'I'd want to make *some* contribution.'

'I don't see the point of you worrying about that. I mean, I've got this place. It's big enough for the both of us, so you may as well stay here.'

'I feel weird about it,' I said. 'Your dad pays my salary.'

'So why would you give that money back to him?' Charlie said. 'Just consider this place a raise.'

I looked around the apartment, at the big kitchen and the plush couch. 'Does your dad pay for Marie's place, too?'

'For some of it. For all of it when she was at college, though. He's happy to, as long as we're studying and not just sitting around. Lisa doesn't contribute to their place.'

'Lisa doesn't work for your dad.'

'But Brooke, if you're saving your rent every month, we can put that towards something else in the future. A place we can pay for on our own. Dad would want us to save up. He doesn't need that money, and he'd end up giving it back to us later. He likes to help out.'

'It feels like a handout,' I said.

'Can't you just accept a little help, Brooke?' Charlie smiled. 'I want you to live here. Do you want to live here?'

My mouth gave in to the smile. 'Yes.'

'Okay. Awesome.' He kissed me. 'Let's do it.'

We'd both booked the day off work to do nothing but lie in bed and watch Disney films. We stuffed our faces with candy for lunch, then finally got dressed at seven o'clock for dinner. Charlie took me to my favourite restaurant. It was more *Lady and the Tramp* than lady and gentleman: casual dress, candlelit tables, and amazing pizza.

When two pepperonis and a bottle of wine had appeared and then promptly disappeared, the server brought us the check. Charlie stood up and chucked his Amex on the little silver plate. 'Would you mind? I really need a number two, might take a while.'

'I didn't ask for a number, Charlie.'

'Well, you'd better get used to it. When we live together, I'll be keeping you posted on all my bodily functions.'

'I'd really be very okay if you didn't,' I smirked. 'God, you love gross stuff.'

He shrugged. 'I'm a doctor.'

'Not yet, you're not,' I teased.

He left, returning just as I was punching his PIN into the card machine, and we walked home hand in hand.

'I can't wait to live with you,' I said.

'I can't wait to live with you too.' He kissed the top of my head.

SCENE 12: MATT, 26

'I've had an idea to get more members,' Meg said. 'We need to pick a show for next term, I can't believe it's already December. I'm thinking we should do *Romeo and Juliet* again...'

The hair on the back of my neck stood up.

'...it's not too long, it's easy to produce and we can—'

'Wait—*Romeo and Juliet?*'

'Yeah,' Meg said, barrelling on. 'If we advertise auditions, hopefully some older members will join, ones who aren't about to disappear off to uni. We can put it on at Easter—'

'Wait—just a second—I think the kids would get bored of that, y'know. Shakespeare. They're all doing it for GCSE.'

'Yeah, so they'll be really good at it,' Meg said.

'Is there another show we could do?' I tried to ground myself, to keep the desperation out of my voice. Too many memories were attached to that play.

Meg flicked through her notes. 'I can get copies of *James and the Giant Peach* from school, but that's aimed at young kids. The whole point was to get older members to join.'

'Oh, but they'll prefer that one, surely. It's got great characters, y'know, fun...er...costumes.'

Meg looked at me sceptically. 'You were in *Romeo and Juliet*. Why have you suddenly got a huge problem with Shakespeare?' Her gaze was fierce, like she knew I wasn't telling her something. Anything she'd heard about me and Brooke the night before she disappeared were rumours, if true ones. She'd never asked me, though.

'I don't have a problem with him,' I said. 'I just think he's got—y'know—less depressing stuff. Like *Twelfth Night*, that's a better one. Or *A Midsummer Night's Dream*, everyone loves that.'

'Well, I already have twenty-five copies of *Romeo and Juliet* in my attic, so it's that or the enormous paper mâché project, okay? We'll let the group choose.'

The kids started rolling in, and I swallowed the bad taste in my mouth. *If Romeo and Juliet wins, I'm leaving. I can't teach that play for three months. I can't.* The kids handed me their fees, and I smiled and chatted as usual, but the whole time it felt like something was burning in my chest.

'Matt, can you start the session?' Meg asked, turning back to her notebook.

'Okay, so, um, everybody, before we start,' I said, pulling up a chair into the usual circle. 'We want to know…um…want to discuss…options for a play next term. We're asking what you guys want to do.'

'Mr Williams?'

'We're not in school, Izzy. You can call me "Matt".'

'Mr Williams, can we do a musical?'

'Not really,' Meg chipped in. 'It's quite difficult to get a musical director. We can put some songs in a play, though. We've got two options that would be easy to do—Matt, do you want to tell everybody?'

'Um…okay, so we've been thinking about *James and the Giant Peach*, and, um, *Romeo and Juliet.*'

'I'd prefer to do a proper play,' said Louise, who clearly considered herself a serious actor. 'I think Shakespeare could be good.'

'Shakespeare?' Mateo said. 'Bleugh.' *Good job, Mateo.*

Izzy's hand went up. 'I did *James and the Giant Peach* in year six. I don't really want to do it again.'

The conversation went on, and Meg came over and took charge. She put it to a vote. Six hands went up for *James and the Giant Peach.* Thirteen for Shakespeare. *Shit.*

Meg started the session, just some games and exercises in the run up to Christmas. Mateo went to the bathroom. My mind was racing. *How can I stay here and direct that show? How can I relive the worst choice I ever made? How can I go downstairs to the*

*auditorium and sit through it? I've got to leave. I've got to leave
Stagefright. Meg will have to find someone else to help her. I can't
stay here—I can't.*

I heard footsteps coming up the stairs, and my heart stopped,
and my head turned. It was just Mateo. I stared at the door long
after he'd passed through it, the door that never closed, and I
knew I couldn't leave.

I went through the motions of the session, half-present. Meg
talked about auditions. The kids went home. 'Lift?' she offered
as usual, though she wasn't looking at me.

'Yeah, thanks.'

She drove me home, apparently in a bad mood about something.
I let the silence drag on for a long time. My stomach was still in
knots. Finally I said, 'Meg, I can't direct that play.'

'Why not?' she asked.

I didn't say anything. How was I supposed to begin to explain
everything that'd happened?

She looked at me, then looked back at the road. Without
warning, she swerved and pulled over, not bothering to turn the
engine off.

'When did you and Brooke become friends?' she demanded.
Her eyes were livid. My heart started racing.

'When we did that bloody play,' I said quietly.

'And when did you start whatever fucked up relationship you
had?'

My jaw dropped. No one had actually asked me about this
before. In my shock, all I managed was, 'It wasn't fucked up.'

'So there was one!' she cried.

'Yes,' I said, looking at her like she was stupid. 'Everyone
knows that, don't they? I was with her the night before she...'
Surely everyone had heard the rumours. They all looked at me
sympathetically: the abandoned boyfriend. *Why is Meg freaking
out?*

'You were *with her* the night before she *vanished?*'

'Yes! This is common knowledge! We went on a date, we
were talking about picking things back up, I thought it was—'

'*Back* up? Picking things *back* up? From when?'

I didn't say anything. I was breathing hard. Had I given too much away? I looked at Meg and saw her piece the puzzle together in her head.

'You fucking *idiot*, Matt,' she said slowly.

'What?'

'You think I don't have eyes? You two were all over each other during *Romeo and Juliet*.'

'Yes, because that's what William Shakespeare scripted, Meg. We were friends.'

'You weren't after you left for uni,' Meg said. 'I never saw you talking. So when else could you have been together?'

Fuckfuckfuck.

'I mean,' I tried to backtrack, but knew it was no good. 'We weren't really together.'

'You *idiot*, Matt, you mother. Fucking. *Idiot*. Are you seriously telling me you had a relationship with a teenage girl when you were an adult?'

'It wasn't a real relationship!' I cried. 'I was eighteen, I was a teenager, I was still at school.'

She rubbed her eyes. 'And worse, I was fucking accommodating this. I can't believe I cast you against her. Oh, Christ, Matt, you've really thrown us in it, you know that?'

'What are you talking about?'

'Do I have to spell it out for you?' I had never seen her like this, and it frightened me. 'You're a *teacher*, Matt. And so am I. If I have to tell your school, I will.'

My mouth went dry. *I could lose my job?*

'Did you?' she asked.

'Did I what?' I snapped.

Meg looked at me.

'No!' I lied magnificently. 'Of course not!'

'If you had—'

'We didn't have—'

'—if you had, you know what that would make you—'

'—I know—'

'—a rapist.'

Hearing someone else say it, out loud, rather than just in my head, made my throat freeze up. Words weren't rising to my defence. I didn't have a defence. So I lied. 'I'm not. I never did.'

'Never?'

'Well, when she was eighteen…' I expected Meg to interrupt me, but she didn't. 'We had one night. She definitely consented. She was eighteen,' I said again.

'And this was the only time?'

'Yes,' I lied.

'And in between those times?'

'We weren't together.'

'You weren't.'

'We never really were.' For a second the image of fourteen-year-old Brooke flashed in my mind, and how her bright young heart would break if she heard me say that. Meg turned her head away, but the onslaught continued.

'When did this happen, when she was eighteen? Specifically?'

'The night before she left. When she'd finished school.'

'Are you just trying to sound less like a pervy teacher—'

'No!' I said. 'I swear it was just that she *had* finished school, and that's the truth.' That last part made everything else I'd said sound like not-the-truth. I wanted to kick myself.

'So this was before she left?' Meg asked.

'Of course,' I hissed. 'If it was *after* she disappeared, don't you think I might have *some* idea where she is, or if she's even still alive?'

Meg looked horrified.

'I DIDN'T KILL HER!' I roared. I couldn't believe this was happening to me. Extremely ordinary, school teacher, am-dram me. 'We had one night, and I thought it was the start of something real, and when I woke up, she'd gone and nobody knew where she was and that was the last time I ever saw her.'

'You were the last person to see her,' Meg said.

'No,' I spoke through gritted teeth. 'The police said she went to the airport.'

'You talked to the police!'

'For fuck's sake, Meg, this is none of your business!'

My pulse was thumping. I was angry but had no right to be—I was the bad guy. I had…I had done…

'They asked me some questions as a witness, to trace her movements, and that's all. Because I never hurt her.' The lie burnt my throat as it came up.

Meg looked pensive. She was my judge and jury, deciding my fate right there in the car on the roadside. 'What was the nature of your relationship when she was fourteen?'

I sighed. I hated laying this stuff out for Meg to look at, the little fragments of our relationship. Tiny broken pieces that were all I had left of her. 'We just—we kind of liked each other. And we told each other that.'

'Physical?'

'Just kissed, once or twice,' I lied again. Would I ever tell anyone the truth? Would I ever trust someone enough to? Would I ever meet a woman and get married, and tell her? Would she leave me when she found out?

'How did it end?'

'Uni.'

Pause.

'Brooke was ill,' Meg said.

'What?'

'She had depression.'

'I know that.'

'Didn't you think it was a bad idea to mess with the head of a depressed, vulnerable teenage girl?'

'She wasn't ill at the time.' I tried to think back to that night at The Anchor, to Brooke telling me it wasn't my fault she'd got sick, but it felt like a memory I'd invented to make myself feel better. 'But yes, I am sorry for what happened.'

'For what you did,' Meg corrected me.

'For…for what I did,' I admitted.

Meg took a breath. She was quiet for a long time, the hum of the engine filling the silence. Finally she said, 'I'm not going to tell the school.'

I tried to hide my relief. I'd spent this whole conversation lying about what I had done, pretending to seem disgusted by the things Meg was suggesting. But *I had done those things.*

'I'm not sure you should stay at Stagefright,' she said.

My heart stopped. 'I can't leave, Meg.'

'Now I see why you don't want to do *Romeo and Juliet.*'

'Please don't make me leave, Meg. It was a one-time thing. I was basically a kid—'

'Not legally—'

'—it would never happen again—'

'—paedophilia is a sexual disorder—'

'I am not a paedophile!' I cried. That, at least, sounded true. 'I have no interest in young girls, okay? Not in the slightest.'

'Swear to God?' Meg said.

'Yes,' I hissed.

'You're telling me this was a one-time thing, that it was just a few kisses, and that it's water under the bridge?'

'Of course, Meg.'

'Do I need to be worried about the kids? About your students?'

'No.' I felt disgusted at the suggestion. 'Of course not.'

The silence dragged on.

'You can stay,' she said eventually.

I was unsure of what to say back so I just said, 'Thanks.'

'Can you borrow copies of *Twelfth Night* from your school?'

'Yes.'

'Okay,' she said. 'If there's one tiny thing—'

'There won't be,' I assured her.

'Because I would hate to be responsible for allowing you—'

'There won't be, Meg,' I said.

'If you never let yourself be alone with a young person, then you're protected from—'

'I know, Meg, I know.'

After a long while, she said, 'Okay.' She flipped the indicator and pulled onto the road.

She drove me home in silence. I thanked her for the lift and went inside. Finally, in the safety of my own flat, I bent over the sink, feeling nauseous and breathing hard. I looked in the mirror. Beads of sweat were on my forehead, the bags under my eyes looked huge. A string of saliva hung from my top lip. I looked at my reflection and hated it, hated it, hated it. I threw my fist into the glass until it shattered.

SCENE 13: BROOKE, 23

When I walked into Sanjay's office for our next session, he'd rearranged the room.

'Morning, Brooke,' he said from his seat, which was now perpendicular to the window.

'You moved the chairs,' I said warmly, like I was walking into my friend's lounge.

'I moved the chairs,' he repeated. 'Thanks for telling me. Now do say if the sun is in your eyes, or if you don't like the air freshener, or if you are in any way uncomfortable. Alright?'

'Alright,' I said, and sat opposite him.

'Good. How was your week?'

'It was good. It was my birthday—'

'Happy birthday,' he interrupted.

'—thanks. And Charlie asked me to move in with him.'

'Ooh,' Sanjay said, like Marie, Katie, and Dan had done when I'd told them. 'And do you want to?'

'Yes,' I said.

'You're smiling.'

I laughed, a little uncomfortably, as I always did when he commented on my body language. 'I'm so excited. I just love him so much. I want to spend all my time with him.'

'All of it?' Sanjay said.

'All of it,' I repeated.

'Okay. So you'd get rid of your place and move into his, when?'

'Well, my contract ends in a couple of months. I've renewed it for a few years running, but I guess this time I just won't.'

'And you'll take over half the rent?'

'Oh—he doesn't rent his apartment. Um.' I felt a little embarrassed to admit it. 'His dad owns it. He told me not to worry about paying anything.'

'Right,' Sanjay said, and I could tell he was sceptical. 'And how do you feel about that?'

'Conflicted. I mean, I feel I should contribute something.'

'Why do you feel that way?'

'Because I don't like being given a handout. Like when I first moved to Seattle, and he helped me out so much. Marie, too, and their dad.'

'So there's a part of you that wants to feel like you can support yourself?'

'Yeah,' I said. 'It wasn't a good feeling to be at the mercy of the people around me when I first got here. I wasn't paying rent on Pete's place, so he was able to kick me out whenever he wanted. Charlie wouldn't kick me out, but still. I didn't feel safe.'

'And cultivating your independence has been something we've been talking about, as a means of moving away from codependency,' Sanjay said. I felt him urging me with his eyes.

'You think this is a bad idea,' I said.

'I don't. But I do think you might be taking a step towards greater dependency on Charlie. Financially, with the rent, and also emotionally, since you say you want to spend all your time with him. You've told me before that when you were younger and going out with Matt, you wanted to spend all your time with him, too. There's a little bit of a pattern going on. Do you remember when we talked about the pillars in your life, and having enough of them so that if the Charlie pillar was to ever go away, you wouldn't crumble?'

I looked at my hands, at the ring Marie had given me for my birthday. I twisted it round. 'The trouble is, I don't have enough of the other pillars. I don't have a family, and all my friends I've met through Charlie. My job was through him and now my home.'

'Everyone needs pillars, because we all go through times where we have to rely on the support systems in our lives. But when you only have one pillar, it's easy to put too much pressure on it, and hope that it's going to have all the answers. When you first got to Seattle, you were looking for a man to solve your problems for you, and Charlie did just that. I want you to have the ability to solve your own problems.'

I ran my finger around the ring. 'So maybe I'm becoming too dependent on Charlie.'

'All relationships have a little dependency. And relationships progress naturally. I'm not encouraging you to fight that. I'm just encouraging you to be aware.' Sanjay adjusted his posture. It was different, being able to see his face. 'I want you to feel like a complete human being. Rather than having your identity enmeshed with someone else.'

'Charlie isn't enmeshed with me,' I said. 'He's a whole person on his own.'

'That probably indicates that he's good at setting boundaries, between what's yours and what's his.'

'But we'll live together soon,' I said.

'Boundaries can be material, about space, belongings, and finance, but they can also be in other areas of life. There might be things Charlie keeps to himself, certain activities, or friends that are just his. It can be hard for codependent people to respect boundaries, because you struggle to set your own.'

I thought back to Charlie's work drinks, and how I'd felt left out. I could remember thinking if I was willing to share my friends with him, but he wasn't willing to do the same, he must love me less than I loved him. But maybe work friends were just one of his boundaries.

'Setting your own boundaries can help draw a line between where you leave off and where Charlie begins. Do you know who you are without him?'

Boy, what a question. I dug deep, reached through the darkness for my own edges, for the outline of me. It felt void, hollow, like I was only half a person. 'Maybe not,' I said.

'Perhaps you're a little enmeshed with him,' Sanjay said gently. 'I want to encourage you to do more things that make you feel like an individual.'

I looked down. 'You mean doing things on my own?'

'Some things. Doing things with friends, too. Maybe some of your own hobbies. Things you can enjoy without Charlie.'

I couldn't see the appeal of doing anything without Charlie.

'Do you have friends you could spend time with? Friends who are just yours?'

I had to think. 'My roommates, I guess. I never really got to know them that well. But I barely spend any time there anymore.'

'Are they nice?'

'Yeah, they're nice,' I said. 'I'd just rather spend my time at Charlie's.'

'You met him at a pivotal moment, when you'd just got to Seattle. He was formative in creating the woman you are today. There are, of course, parts of you that existed before you met him. Parts you created in England.'

'I didn't like myself in England,' I said quickly.

'What didn't you like about yourself?'

I felt my voice tremble as I said, 'I don't know.'

Sanjay left me to fill the silence.

'I felt worthless. I thought I wasn't going anywhere. I thought I was a burden to everyone around me. I thought everyone hated me.' Tears were welling up in my eyes.

'Was there evidence for those things?'

'No,' I sobbed.

'Do you like yourself now?'

I hesitated. 'Maybe. I don't know.'

'What parts about yourself do you like?' Sanjay said.

'Charlie says—'

'I'm not interested in what Charlie thinks of you right now. I'm interested in what *you* think of you. What are you good at?'

I shrugged. 'I'm good at my job.'

'Okay, that's great,' Sanjay said. 'What else?'

'I do some volunteering,' I said, but wondered if that would be true if Charlie hadn't introduced me to it.

'Good, so you think of others.'

I bit my lip. 'I can't think of anything else.' I was shocked that I couldn't remember what I was good at. I could remember what I *used* to be good at. Singing. Acting. School. Math. Science.

'Okay,' Sanjay said. 'And what things about yourself don't you like?'

'I don't like...' I drifted off. 'I don't like what I did to my family.'

Sanjay left the silence again.

'And I don't like that I ran away from my problems. I didn't hold myself accountable. I wasn't an adult about it.'

'Have those things changed? Are you an adult about things now?'

'Moreso,' I said. 'Not completely.'

'Do you think, maybe you let Charlie parent you sometimes?'

I was surprised at the suggestion of my boyfriend 'parenting' me. But then I thought of how I got into bed after the private investigator came, and I cried all day. I couldn't move. I couldn't do anything. I would probably have laid there forever if Charlie hadn't come to comfort me. Bathe me. Cook for me.

'Maybe,' I sniffed.

'And that's okay. In relationships, we parent each other from time to time. My concern is if this is a recurring dynamic. Are you able to be the adult for Charlie when he needs it? Would you be able to parent yourself if you had to?'

'If Charlie needs me, I can be there for him.' I wiped my nose. 'But if *I* need me...'

'I want you to have the skills you need to soothe yourself when you're upset, or anxious. So you aren't leaning on the Charlie pillar quite so often.'

I felt the weight of Sanjay's words crushing my chest, making it hard for me to breathe. *Am I really that fucked up? Is my relationship really this unhealthy? Does Sanjay really think I shouldn't move in with Charlie? I have to move in with Charlie. I can't not move in with Charlie.*

'You said you were interested in "being an adult about things,"' Sanjay interrupted the panic brewing in my brain. 'If that would help you to like yourself more, what would that look like?'

I considered this. 'I'd be able to calm myself down when I'm upset, if Charlie's not there. I wouldn't rely on him so much to do that for me. Or to do anything for me. I guess maybe I could do stuff on the weekends without him. With my own friends.'

Sanjay was nodding encouragingly. 'What about taking accountability? Do you think you'd like yourself more if you were able to hold yourself accountable?'

I nodded slowly.

'What would that look like?'

I stiffened. 'Um. Well. Owning up for mistakes at work, if I get something wrong. Apologising to Charlie if something was my fault, or if maybe I've been snappy with him.'

Sanjay was looking at me encouragingly. 'Okay. Good. And what about things in the past? Actions you haven't forgiven yourself for?'

I didn't move. I barely breathed. He was looking at me, and we both knew what I had to do. But I couldn't bring myself to say it out loud. *Go back. Apologise. Make amends.*

'I'm not,' I stuttered. 'I'm not…ready.'

'You're not ready to talk about that?'

I nodded.

'That's okay. But it keeps coming up for you. It would be a struggle to ignore it forever.'

I didn't say anything.

'I can't help but feel that the decision you made to leave at eighteen has been like an anchor, weighing you down. As much as you try to push the past away, it follows you, because it's unresolved.'

I knew all those damn certificates on his wall meant he'd figured out what I had to do weeks ago, and I knew in my gut he was right.

'I'm not here to tell you to do anything. That's not what therapy is about. But I'm listening to what you're telling *yourself* you need to do. If these feelings of guilt aren't going away, if they're demanding your attention, maybe it's because that's what they need. When we did the visualisation of sitting in the bathroom at work, your unconscious told you that talking to your mom was nothing to be scared of. Your unconscious wanted to apologise. Your unconscious wants to reach out.'

How was I supposed to reach out? How could I do that? Not only had I abandoned everyone I knew, I'd let Mum come all the way to Seattle only to fly back empty-handed. I *chose* to let that happen. If they hadn't hated me before I left, they'd all hate me now.

'Facing this stuff is scary,' Sanjay said, as if reading my mind. 'And maybe that's why you've been avoiding it for so long. But you say you don't like yourself because you didn't hold yourself accountable. I'm just asking what it would take, now, four years later, to address that?'

It would take booking a flight and making a hell of a lot of apologies—

'Maybe,' I suggested, 'maybe I could contribute the rent I already pay towards Charlie's flat?'

'That's an idea,' Sanjay said neutrally. 'Would that make you feel more independent?'

'Yes,' I said unconvincingly.

SCENE 14: MATT, 26

I rubbed my eyes and reached for a tube of Pringles. I grabbed a six pack of Stella too, for good measure, though my knuckles stung as I did. The dressing I'd slapped over the cuts was peeling off.

I went up to the till and dumped the beer and crisps on the checkout. Meg's words had been ringing in my ear for the last hour. *Rapist. I'd have to tell the school. I don't think you should stay.* I prodded at the dressing and wished I'd punched with my left hand.

'Hi, Mr Wills,' I heard.

I looked at the shop assistant and was surprised to see one of my year thirteens looking back at me.

'Oh, hi, Marcus. I didn't know you worked here.'

'Just started. Had to wait till I turned eighteen.' He looked at the items I'd chosen. 'Big Friday night in?'

'Uh…yeah.' I watched him scan the beer.

'I didn't know you lived near here, sir.'

'Yeah,' I said, 'upstairs, actually.'

He looked surprised. 'You're the flat upstairs?'

I kicked myself for oversharing with a student, and not just any student, but a student who now worked underneath my flat. 'It's temporary,' I said quickly.

'Huh. But you didn't grow up in town.'

'No, I did,' I said. 'I actually used to work here.'

'Oh, wow,' Marcus said, as if it was actually impressive. 'Did you go to our school?'

I nodded, a little uncomfortable.

'This is that kind of town, I guess.' He jammed his finger into the till keys. 'You either get out at eighteen, or never leave.'

'I am leaving,' I said, before I could stop myself.

'Oh, really? Going to another school?'

Idiot. Now there'll be a rumour that reaches all the staff before you've even handed in your notice. 'Nah, I—to be honest, I have no plans. I don't know what I want to do.'

Marcus looked at me. 'But you're a teacher,' he said. I saw him processing my words and how they didn't fit into his understanding of the world. I looked back at the boy, all young and hormonal. This boy who still had options. I'd used up so many of mine and was stuck right where I'd started.

'Are you going to university, Marcus?' I asked.

He nodded. 'Manchester, hopefully.'

'Good, okay, good.' I tapped my card against the machine and heard the beep. Manchester was a proper city, built for young people. It was hard to experience a place like that and then come back and get stuck in this tiny town.

I put my wallet away and my eyes slid back onto him. They hadn't updated the polo shirts in eight years. 'Do you have a girlfriend, Marcus?'

He blinked. 'Um, yeah, Erin…'

'Erin, yes, I know Erin,' I said, remembering how she often waited outside my classroom for him. 'She's your year, isn't she?'

'Yeah,' Marcus said, a little uneasily.

'Good.' I scooped up my stuff. 'Okay. Well. Have a good night.'

'You too,' he said, watching me as I went.

SCENE 15: BROOKE, 23

Charlie and I got an Uber to grab the last of my things, though I barely had anything left at my place anyway. Christina gave me a hug and a box of cookies to send me off. I felt a rush of affection for her, and wished I'd gotten to know her better while I had the chance. We'd probably lose touch, now.

But it was okay, because I was officially moving into Charlie's place. When we got back to his, armed with boxes, he'd put flowers and wine on the kitchen table.

'Right, what pictures do you have? We can put them on the walls.'

'I've only got one,' I said. It was a frame Lisa had given me, and I'd put a picture of the four of us in there. 'It can just go on the sideboard.'

'Okay. What about your kitchen stuff? I'll make room in the cupboards.'

'I've only got one plate,' I said.

'*One* plate?' Charlie repeated.

'Well, I had two, till I smashed one. You've got enough plates.'

'Put that one in, at least.'

'It won't match all your others.'

Charlie shrugged. 'Alright. What about your clothes?'

'Um,' I followed him into the bedroom. 'Well, all of my underwear fits in that bottom drawer,' I pointed to his dresser. 'And you already gave me a rail in your closet.'

He opened his closet and flicked through the clothes on my side. 'These are your clothes?'

I nodded.

'Where's the rest of them?'

'That's all of them,' I said.

'What about the ones from your place?'

I shrugged. 'There wasn't anything left, nothing I'd actually wear.'

'Huh,' Charlie said, closing the door.

We sat on the couch, his arm around me, sipping wine. He looked around the room.

'It looks the same,' he said.

'What does?'

'The apartment.'

I looked around. 'I've added my books to the bookcase.'

'And you've left the boxes in the doorway.'

'I'll clean them up tomorrow.'

'I'm serious, Brooke,' he said, standing up. He looked at the room: the flowers in a vase on the table; the kitchen, pristine as ever. 'I can't see any of you in here.'

I looked around too, at his limited-edition art prints on the walls, his duck-egg-blue kitchenware. 'I like your place.'

'I want this to be *our* place,' Charlie perched next to me. 'I want to see both of us here. What about the table? Do you want us to move it?'

I looked at it. 'It's fine there. Where else would it go?'

'Okay,' Charlie said. 'What about the sideboard? Shall we upcycle it?'

'What's wrong with it?' I protested.

'Nothing, I'm just saying…' He got up and touched the cream walls. 'Shall we repaint it? Go for a different colour scheme?'

'I like the colour scheme,' I said. 'Why are you being weird?'

'It's just *my* apartment,' Charlie said. 'It's too much of me.'

'There's no such thing as too much of you.'

'But Brooke—' He sat on the arm of the couch and put his feet on the cushions. '—isn't there anything you want? A plant? Or a rug? What do you like?'

I like what you like, I thought, and felt my breath hitch. *This is what Sanjay has been talking about. I don't know what I like. I don't know what I'm good at. I don't know where I leave off and Charlie begins.*

'I'm paying rent,' I blurted out.

He looked at me. 'Babe, I already told you that you don't have to do that.'

'I'm doing it. It's decided. Me and Sanjay—he thinks it's a good idea. The same amount I paid on my last place, at minimum.'

Charlie digested this. 'Okay. If you really want to. As long as you know you don't have to.'

'I know,' I smiled, and kissed him.

Living together wasn't too different from before, since I'd been round most nights anyway. I thought I might see more of Charlie, but he got super busy at work in those first few weeks and would come home late and collapse. To help out, I'd run him a bath or put on his favourite shows, but I drew the line at cooking.

'I'm not cooking,' Charlie said one night. 'I'm exhausted.'

'It's your turn to cook,' I said.

'No way in high holy hell am I cooking tonight, babe.'

'I cooked last night *and* was smart enough to freeze half for tomorrow,' I said.

'Fine. Takeout? Let's get Chinese?'

I nodded.

He sniffed his own armpit. 'God, I've never needed a shower more in my life. Will you order?'

'The usual?' I asked, as he nodded and disappeared into the bedroom.

I opened UberEats on my phone and re-ordered the same as last time. When it asked for the credit card details, I fished Charlie's wallet out of his bag and typed in the Amex numbers.

'Is it on the way?' He emerged in a fresh T-shirt and shorts.

I nodded. 'Twenty minutes.'

'Thank God.' He collapsed on the sofa. 'How much do I owe you? I was meant to cook, so I'll pay.'

'I used your card,' I said, pointing at the Amex that was still laying on the table.

He looked at me. 'You used my credit card?'

I nodded.

'I mean, I'd rather you didn't,' he said.

'What do you mean? I use it all the time.'

'Yeah, when I'm with you.' He sat up. 'But I'd rather you didn't use it without my permission.'

'Permission?' I repeated. 'I just…I assumed that you'd want to pay for it. And I was right. It is your night to cook.'

'I'm happy to pay for it,' he said. 'I just wish you'd asked first.'

I crossed my arms over myself. 'I wouldn't mind if you used my card without asking, as long as you told me after.'

'Well, that's you,' he said, 'but I'm not okay with it. Alright?'

I remembered what Sanjay had said about boundaries, and how they could be financial. I knew that I was meant to respect Charlie's when I came up against one, but it felt like a rejection. A fence between us. 'Don't you trust me?' I asked.

'Of course I trust you. I just want to be in control of my own money.'

'I'll pay you back.'

'You don't have to pay me back, okay,' he said. 'I'm happy to pay, it's fine. I just want to be aware of what my card's being used for in future.'

'I thought you'd want the air miles,' I mumbled. The sound of the TV filled the silence, and then the sound of eating Chinese food that didn't taste as good as usual.

The weekend before Christmas was the anniversary of Charlie's mum's birthday. He'd told me about it months before; he had plane tickets to visit his grandparents in Minnesota, with Marie and their dad. They went every year, and he'd warned me that it was usually a tough weekend.

I decided to be the best girlfriend ever. Charlie was always there for me when I needed him, so I was going to make this weekend as easy for him as possible. I'd sleep with the phone on loud in case he called. I'd reply to his texts instantly. And I'd do all the chores, so that when he came back on Sunday night, he wouldn't have to lift a finger.

He kissed me goodbye on Friday morning and flew out that afternoon with Marie and Mr Young, who both left the office at lunchtime. I texted him ten minutes before he took off.

Brooke Tyler: Have a good flight. I love you.

When I got home from work that night, the apartment seemed huge without him. *This is quite nice,* I thought, *a night to myself.* I looked at the chores I'd listed on my phone: *laundry, grocery shopping, have dinner ready for when he gets back.* Those could wait.

I ran myself a bath and lit the fancy candles. After five minutes, I was hot, sweaty, and bored. I stepped out of the tub to grab the book Mr Young had got me for my birthday, but I couldn't concentrate on it and just re-read the same page without taking it in for fifteen minutes. My skin was pruney and I got out again.

I laid on the sofa in one of Charlie's T-shirts that I fished from the wash basket. It smelled of him, and maybe not in the best way, but I didn't care. I stuck on a Netflix film and scrolled through my phone until it was time to fall asleep, alone in that massive bed without him.

When I woke up, he had already sent me a 'good morning' text, being two hours ahead. I typed back.

Brooke Tyler: Morning babe! Sending you lots of love today. Call or text anytime.

I knew that today was going to be hard for him: he was visiting his mother's grave and then going to celebrate her birthday with a special dinner. I didn't expect to hear from him but I checked my phone volume was up, just in case.

I looked at the empty weekend ahead of me. Usually, if Charlie didn't have to work, we would make a nice cooked breakfast on a Saturday and go for a run. Then we'd clean the flat and go to the supermarket. In the evening, we might go out with Marie and Lisa and our other friends. And on Sundays we'd go to the foodbank to help sort donations, then watch movies until it was time for bed. The foodbank was expecting me tomorrow, but for today I could have some fun.

Instead of cooking breakfast, I found a massive bar of chocolate at the back of the fridge. I stuck on *Modern Family*, picking up where Charlie and I had left off, but then I realised we were watching that show together and he probably wouldn't want me to cut ahead. *That's not very best-girlfriend-in-the-world of you,* I thought. I scrolled through Netflix, but nothing took my fancy. I ended up resorting to *Friends*, even though I'd watched all ten seasons multiple times.

When the chocolate was gone, and five episodes had played out, I really couldn't think of anything to do with my day. *What do I usually do when Charlie's not here?* If he had a weekend shift, he was usually only gone for half a day. I'd just watch movies or start on the chores, and wait for him to come back. But the cleaning could wait till tomorrow. Today was meant to be my day off.

I thought about taking myself to a gallery, but I couldn't picture it being fun without Charlie there to joke with and compare our favourite pieces. I thought about calling Katie and Dan, but I worried they wouldn't want to hang out with just me. I could try that restaurant Marie had told me about, but it felt like going there wouldn't really count until I was doing it with Charlie. I didn't want to experience it without him.

What did other people do on the weekends, normal people, single people? What did I do before I moved to America? Hadn't I ever had hobbies? I couldn't remember what they were. I couldn't remember what made me 'me'.

I know what made me 'me'. I was the drama kid.

I had been, before everything got twisted and broken. Brooke, who loved to be the centre of attention. She spent her weekends singing, painting, or with her best friend, Lucy.

I'd barely allowed myself to think about those times, about *before,* about England. I realised I was crying. This was what Sanjay had been getting at: I'd left a part of myself behind in England, along with all the people I'd left. I missed them and I missed who I used to be.

I laid on the sofa and stared at the ceiling. All of my pillars in Seattle—friends, the flat, even volunteering—were tied to Charlie. I felt a black hole inside me, a bottomless ache that said I was half a person, that I didn't know who I was or what I was good at or what I liked or disliked. I was nothing without Charlie.

I must've drifted off, and when I woke up, it was too dark to go for a run, so I thought I might as well skip the shower too. I let the *Friends* episodes keep playing in the background as I wallowed in my misery. *Is Charlie really the only thing that makes me happy? Am I as dependent on him as Sanjay seems to think?*

I realised I hadn't eaten since that bar of chocolate. I didn't feel hungry, but I could tell that my stomach was empty. I ordered a burger and chips on UberEats and opened the door to the delivery guy, still in Charlie's shirt. I scoffed it down, barely tasting the food on my tongue.

The nap had thrown my sleep pattern off and I ended up mindlessly scrolling through Reddit till 3AM, like I had done when I'd first got to Seattle, when I'd been with Pete, during the worst time of my life. When I woke up Sunday morning (still on the sofa, still in Charlie's shirt) I felt awful. I had to call the foodbank and tell them I couldn't make it in. I'd been planning to surprise Charlie at the airport by picking him up, but that wasn't going to happen. *Just get through the day*, I thought, *six more hours till he's back.*

I ordered more takeout. I drank all the cola. I couldn't stand *Friends* anymore and went back to *Modern Family*. When I watched it with Charlie, we both cackled out loud. Without him, nothing. *Four-and-a-half hours. When he's back, I'll be fine. He'll make everything okay.*

Having fucked up my sleep pattern, I failed to fight off another nap. I woke up to the sound of the front door and leapt off the couch.

'Charlie!' I cried, and jumped on him happily.

He hugged me, but looked drained. 'Hi, Brooke,' he said.

'Are you okay?' I asked, suddenly concerned.

'Yeah. I'm fine. It's just been heavy. Are you okay? Is that my shirt?'

'Oh.' I looked down at myself. 'Yeah. I missed you.'

'I jogged in that shirt, y'know. It probably smells.' He looked at the coffee table, littered with wrappers and crumbs. I suddenly felt guilty. 'Did you vacuum?' he asked.

'Um,' I said, 'no.'

He sighed. 'I'll do it in the morning, before work.'

'Oh,' I said, quickly remembering the laundry. 'I'd better put a wash on then.' I raced into the bedroom to grab the basket, shovelling the clothes into the washing machine.

'You haven't done the laundry? I thought you said you were gonna do all the chores this weekend.'

'I'm sorry, I'm sorry!' I said frantically.

'It's fine if you haven't done them,' he said. 'I just wish you hadn't said you would. They won't be dry by the time I need them.'

'I'll—I'll leave your work shirt in the airing cupboard overnight. I'm sorry, I had a bad weekend. I felt really awful without you. I missed you so much.'

He didn't say it back, because of course it hadn't been me that he'd been missing all weekend. I could see that he really needed me now, needed me not to need him, but there I was, needing him.

'I'll make dinner,' I said quickly.

'We can order takeout.'

'I've ordered enough,' I said, picking up the boxes that were on the table and trying to stuff them in the trash can. I had to leave them sitting on top.

'Did you just leave Netflix playing all weekend?'

'Yeah, sorry, I just felt so lonely without you.' *You've really fucked up this time.*

I filled a pan with water, then took out some mushrooms from the almost-empty fridge and started chopping them. Tears stung in my eyes. I had failed to act like an adult, actually be independent, and be the one he leans on.

'Brooke, you're upset,' Charlie said.

'I'm fine,' I said, tears spilling onto the chopping board as I did.

'You're not fine, you're crying.'

'I can do this! You're the one who's meant to be sad. You had your big weekend, and I couldn't even…' I nicked my finger with the tip of the blade.

'Let me do that,' Charlie said.

'I can do it.' Blood trickled onto a mushroom slice.

'Brooke, come on, you just hurt yourself, let me make dinner.'

I abandoned the knife and marched into the bathroom to grab a band-aid. I looked in the mirror and couldn't bear the sight of myself: unwashed, red-eyed, chocolate on my chin that'd been there for God knows how long. I sat on the toilet lid and hid my shameful tears from both him and myself. I didn't come out for fifteen minutes, and when I did, he'd nearly finished cooking. He'd also wiped down the surfaces and taken out the trash.

I walked over to him and he opened his arms for me. I buried myself into his chest and he held me tight.

'I'm sorry,' I said.

'It's okay.' He stroked my hair.

'I really wanted to be there for you this weekend when you needed me. But I ended up needing you.'

'It's okay,' he repeated.

'It's not okay.' I moved out of his hug. 'Sanjay's been talking to me about this. I mean, how do you feel about it? Do you think I'm too dependent on you? Be honest.'

Charlie took a deep breath, and I could see him choosing his words. See him preparing to admit what he'd never admitted before, see the cracks between us for the first time. 'I feel like you always need me, Brooke,' he said. 'Sometimes I come home and you've fallen apart, like you've randomly got depressed for an hour, or you haven't eaten all day because you thought you looked fat. Though it's never been as bad as this. I guess you haven't been alone for a whole weekend before.'

His words were like knives in me, and I could feel my insides twisting as he said them, because I knew he was right. I knew our relationship was too good to be true. I was the fragile pieces of a woman held together with sticky tape, and now I was scared these cracks in me would be enough for him to leave.

'It's tiring, sometimes,' he finished. 'Worrying about you, having to keep you happy.'

'I'm always happy when I'm with you,' I said.

'But what about when you're not with me?'

I felt my lip tremble and bit down on it. 'I'm getting better,' I said shakily. 'Me and Sanjay—we've got a plan. Things I can do. To be more independent.'

'That's great, baby,' he said, but it was perfunctory. He rubbed his eyes and the guilt washed over me. There he was, exhausted and emotionally drained, serving us dinner when I'd spent all weekend on the sofa. My only pillar had gone away for two days and, once again, I'd collapsed.

SCENE 16: MATT, 26

It was December 31st, and The Shakespeare was full. We'd always gone to the pub for New Year's, the annual reunion of our lunch table with Simon and Ellie and even Georgia, but over time our numbers had dwindled, and now it was just me and Fliss. We used to go to The Anchor, which would be bursting with everyone we'd gone to school with, but lots of them were now spending New Year's in different cities with different people, and The Anchor was full of teenagers.

As I waited for our drinks, I looked around the room. There were some people's parents I recognised, and a couple of washed-up guys from school who'd never left town. Was I one of them?

Fliss sourced an unused stool from one corner and a chair from another and propped them near the wall. 'No tables, but at least we're not standing,' she said. I crouched onto the tiny stool, my knees up to my chest. Fliss and I talked in the way that old friends do, when you know it's not quite the same anymore, but you're two people who've had each other all along.

'Drew got Mum an Apple watch for Christmas. He's got this private healthcare thing, which means if she hits ten thousand steps a day, she gets a free Starbucks.'

The sound of the door went, and every head in the pub turned to see if it was someone they knew. The bald and vaguely familiar face of someone's dad came in and went straight to the smoking area. Heads turned back.

'All that data they'd have would freak me out,' Fliss said, leaning her red wine on her lap. 'And seeing every notification on your wrist, instantly. I think people are forgetting to live in the moment. He just wants her to exercise more. He's all about appearances.'

The door went again. This time it was Lucy, who I'd been at Stagefright with for a bit. I'd said hi to her brother Callum already, leaning over the pool table with his school mates. He was living in Bristol and came home every now and then to see his parents, so I'd run into him at the pubs from time to time. He'd told me Lucy was now working in Sheffield. She must've been back for the holidays, too.

She was taller now, her hair shorter, and sort of glowing with the confidence that came with adulthood. She was wearing black jeans with heeled boots and a jumper. It was so strange, seeing someone who was so blatantly the same person yet looked so different, so clearly a woman now rather than a girl. She went and sat at a table with her friends and didn't see me.

Fliss had started talking to a woman at the table behind us. I looked at the door and, for a moment, I allowed myself to wonder what it'd be like if Brooke walked in. If she wandered in right now, would she still be that dull, faded girl I knew? Would her skin still be dry, her hair still unkempt, her eyes still as sad as they always were? Would she still have on that massive hoodie, hiding God knows what beneath the sleeves?

Would she walk in, moving as if her blood had turned to lead? Would she sit down with Lucy like she hoped her friends wouldn't even notice she'd arrived? After all these years, would she have picked herself up off the bathroom floor?

Would she see me? Would she say anything? Would she apologise for leaving? Would she tell me she still—she still—

'Matt, this is Mary. She goes to Zumba with Mum,' Fliss said.

I politely offered my hand to the middle-aged woman who smiled back. 'You two make a lovely couple.'

'We're not a couple,' Fliss said, at the same time as I said, 'We're just friends.'

'Oh, well. Never mind then.'

The door clattered again, and I tried to resist the instinct to turn my head, but I couldn't.

It wasn't Brooke, but it was the closest thing to her. Amy had come in through the door, followed by her six-foot-something boyfriend. My stomach dropped. We hadn't crossed paths since those nights just after Brooke left, staying up till the early hours doing research online. I'd always felt she'd come to blame me after that, and her dad's appearance on my doorstep only strengthened my theory. She scanned the room and looked at me, then quickly looked away.

I held my breath as I watched her walk across the floor. She reached Lucy's table, then touched her shoulder, and I saw Lucy stand up and hug both Amy and the boyfriend. I hadn't known they were friends. Lucy had saved them seats, and they all sat down together.

'Don't you hate that?' Fliss' voice came through. 'When people just *assume* that a man and a woman have to be a couple. People can be friends.'

'Yeah,' I said, half listening.

I tried to engage in conversation with Fliss, tried to forget Amy was there, but *there she was* in my peripheral, side by side with Brooke's best friend. I wondered if we were the only three people in the town to remember her.

Eventually, Lucy went up to the bar. I asked Fliss if she wanted another drink and she drained her glass. 'Just a lemonade.'

I came and stood next to Lucy. 'Hey,' I said.

She turned and smiled at me. 'Oh. Hi, Matt.'

'How—how are you?'

'Yes, I'm okay,' she said brightly. She'd always been bright. 'How about you?'

'I'm alright, I'm alright. I teach, actually, at our old school.'

'Oh, cool,' she said, and I was sure she was feigning interest. 'Do you enjoy it?'

'Um,' I said, 'a bit.'

'Nice, that's good.' She was so damn polite.

I cleared my throat. 'Callum told me you're in Sheffield?'

'Yeah, generic English grad. I'm at a creative agency. We do marketing stuff.'

'Cool, do you like it there?'

'Yeah, I'm learning a lot.' She smiled again.

The barman took her order. I cleared my throat. When she turned back to me, I said, 'I didn't know you and Amy were friends.'

'Yeah, we got close, after—y'know, what happened. We talked a lot at the time, trying to figure out where she—what happened.'

'Yeah, I spoke to Amy too, at the time,' I said. 'Looking at all the flights and stuff.'

Lucy nodded diplomatically. 'Yeah. Hard thing to go through, for her.'

'I—yeah, I—yeah.'

'You were with her, weren't you?' she said. 'Prom night.'

'Yeah, we,' I swallowed. 'We went on a date.'

'She seemed so excited.' Lucy tapped her card against the machine. 'When you showed up.'

'Really?' My stomach flipped.

'Yeah. She was really happy you'd surprised her. It's mad that she left the next day. But she must've had it planned for months. She took all her things with her. She had money and stuff. Her bank statement said she'd bought the plane ticket like, three months before.'

Three months? That was news to me. I thought I'd driven her away, that night in the Travelodge. I thought I'd done something to make her go. There had been bank statements, and Amy hadn't told me. I started to feel sick. The barman turned to me. 'Um, a lemonade and a water, please,' I said.

'Anyway…' Lucy picked up her drinks. 'It was good to see you.'

'Yeah,' I said, 'yeah, good to see you too.'

I went back to Fliss and nodded and mm-ed my way through the conversation. A lot of people recognised her and stopped to chat, which made it easier for me to think. *She'd planned to leave. She didn't decide that night. She'd been planning it for months. Maybe that was why she'd said we couldn't have a future. Maybe it wasn't my fault.*

Midnight approached. Amy's boyfriend got up and headed out the door, clutching his vape and looking worse for wear. She hurried after him, leaving her bag at the table. Fliss was chatting to some women from her old hockey team. I excused myself and followed Amy out the front.

Her boyfriend was keeled over, puking round the corner of the pub. 'Ryan, I told you not to pre-drink,' she was saying, rubbing his back at arms' length.

'You alright?' I asked her, as a cheer of 'Three, two, one!' rang out from inside.

She glanced back at me. 'Yeah, thanks.'

'Does he want the rest of my water?' I offered my half-drunk pint.

'No thanks, Matt.' She spoke without looking at me. I looked at the ground.

'Actually—go on,' she said, reaching over. I gave her the pint and she spun Ryan round. 'Drink this, babe,' she said. He leaned against the wall, pale and sweaty, and sipped. His heavy breathing filled the silence.

'Congrats on your baby,' I said eventually. 'Boy or girl?'

'Boy. Freddie. He's not really a baby anymore, he's almost two.'

'Jesus,' I said. 'Time—time flies.'

Amy didn't reply, just kept rubbing Ryan's arm.

'You haven't...have you...heard from...'

Amy shook her head, then finally looked at me. 'She sent— she took money when she left, and in the summer she sent a cheque. Mum got a private detective to look at it. He traced it and found where she worked. Said he spoke to her, face to face.'

An unbelievable sense of relief flooded me. *She's alive.* The police had said she probably wasn't suicidal when she left, but I'd always worried.

'Mum flew there to find her. But it was a few months later, and they said she didn't work there anymore. She'd moved away.'

'Where was it that they thought she worked?'

'Some newspaper, in Seattle.'

My thundering heart was audible in the silence. I had spent the last four years waiting for a clue, and now I finally had one. Adrenaline rushed through me. I could go to the airport right away, get on the next plane to Seattle, beg Amy for the name of that newspaper and question her old boss and trace her payslips and show up on her doorstep.

But if her own mother, armed with a private detective, couldn't find her—then how could I? Where could she be? What could she be like? What if she was with someone else? Married? Oh God, she could have kids. She could be a lawyer, a doctor, or a vet on safari in Africa. What if she hated me for what I did to her all those years ago? I tried to control my breathing. The pub and Amy and her barfing boyfriend faded away.

Why did you leave? Why did you leave? Why did you leave…

And then my own little grudge against her rose up, resentful that she had run away from me like that. Even if what I did to her was so much worse. She had forgiven me. She had told me not to be sorry. Then she had spent the night with me, given me hope, and broken my heart. Worst of all, she'd *planned* it, and never said a word. I'd been killing myself over the idea that the night with me had driven her away. I'd been suffering, wallowing in guilt, and *she'd let me*. I'd been stuck in that shitty flat, teaching at our old school, staring at the rehearsal room door every Friday night. She'd been in Seattle. She didn't give a shit about me.

Fuck that, I thought. *Fuck. That.*

SCENE 17: BROOKE, 23

'Happy New Year!' Marie and Lisa yelled. Our arms were round each other and the crowds cheered and fireworks exploded into 2019.

Marie pulled Lisa into a kiss. I watched them and smiled, only a teensy bit jealous that Charlie was on a nightshift, and I was third wheeling. But when they broke apart, they put their arms back round me, and we watched the Space Needle glow against the sky, sipping from cans in our coats and scarves.

The holidays ended as quickly as they'd started. I was used to spending them on my own, when the office closed and everyone flew back to their families and I was alone in my apartment. Marie had invited me to her dad's for Thanksgiving and Christmas in the years prior, but I'd felt too guilty to say yes. This time I felt okay accepting the invitation as Charlie's (now) live-in girlfriend. We had my first ever Thanksgiving, eating at the random hour of four o'clock. A month later was Christmas, which struck me as all wrong. They had the wrong foods, even if Charlie had cooked it all to perfection, and they opened their presents at the wrong time, and the movies on TV were different and unfamiliar. I tried and tried to push away my thoughts, but vivid memories of Christmases from my past were swallowing me whole. I remembered waking up early with Amy to stockings filled with mints and nail varnish. I remembered Dad being there for some of them, and others when he'd have us for Boxing Day. I remembered watching *The Snowman* on repeat. I remembered being sad when it was all over. I could barely feel Charlie's arm around me as we sat in front of the fireplace, chatting over wine and cheese. My head was oceans away, back in England several years earlier, playing CDs too loudly and refusing to get out of my pyjamas. I wondered how Amy and Mum were spending the day.

It was the first time I'd really allowed myself to think about my family, friends, Bristol, everything I'd left behind. I felt an ache for it all, one that persisted for days. I couldn't see Sanjay as he was on vacation, but I thought about what he'd said. *Your unconscious told you there's nothing to be scared of in talking to your mom. Your unconscious wants to apologise to her. Your unconscious wants to reach out.*

'You're quiet,' Marie said, when we went back to work on the second of January.

'Hm?' I'd been lost in thought as I made Yuko's coffee.

'Are you okay? January blues getting you down?'

'Um.' I picked up the mug. 'I'm okay. Just got a lot on my mind.'

'No rest for the PAs,' Marie said.

I gave Yuko her coffee and sat at my desk. I worked through my inbox and checked the calendar, then traced the edge of the laptop with my fingers. *Do I want to reach out?*

I looked at my cell. I knew the number for the landline off by heart. I could just type it in and speak to Mum. Tear down these walls I'd been building for years, protecting this world from the reach of my past. I touched my phone, then retracted my finger as if burned, scared of how easily I could do it, how quickly I could destroy everything I'd worked for in just a matter of seconds.

I caught my breath and shoved my cell in the desk drawer, slamming it shut. Calling would be too huge. I wasn't ready for that.

But I could look at Facebook. Mum, Amy—I could look them up on social media. They'd be none the wiser, and I'd be able to gauge how I felt about contacting them. It was a reversible decision. If I reacted badly, I could push it away and never think of them again.

As I typed the letters 'fb' into the search bar, Yuko appeared behind me. 'Brooke, can you go down to City Hall?'

I was on my own all day, waiting around in the freezing cold to see what the mayor had to say for one square inch of a page. My mind whirred the whole time. How easy would it be to log in again? How quick would it be to send a message?

When I got home, I put spaghetti on the stove, then sat on the couch in front of Netflix. My MacBook was on the coffee table. The ache was still in my chest.

I opened the laptop and unlocked it. My heart rate had picked up. I typed 'fb' into the search bar again and navigated to Facebook. The blue homepage stared back at me, inviting me to create an account. I tapped my fingers against the cool silver metal next to the keyboard, breathing in through my nose, out through my mouth, like Sanjay had taught me.

I typed my old email address into the white box. Baby steps. I was not committed, not yet. Just seeing how far I was willing to go. The cursor flashed at me, demanding my password. My finger typed the first letter. Then the second. The black dots were waiting. My mouse hovered over the 'Log In' button. I held my breath and clicked.

Fifty-eight messages. Eleven friend requests. One hundred and one notifications.

I looked at my profile. The layout had been updated since I had last logged on. A photo of eighteen-year-old me on the sixth form field dominated the page. Dozens and dozens of posts from friends and family telling me they missed me, and asking me to come home. Tears prickled in my eyes. That was all I would've needed at the airport that day: someone to ask me to stay.

Lucy's picture appeared on the side of my profile, among a list of friends. In the photograph she looked beautiful, holding a massive cocktail against a sunny background.

Amy—*fuck*—Amy was holding a kid. A little boy. Was he hers? Did I have a nephew? Had she got married to some faceless brother-in-law I'd never met? Had I missed my sister's wedding?

Mum, what have I done to you? In her picture she was lined beyond her years, with streaks of premature grey in her hair. An ache in my chest missed her so, so much.

These faces, I hadn't seen in years, had been imperfect and faded in my mind. I'd forgotten the colour of Lucy's eyes, the freckles on Callum's nose. Each memory hit me with a pang of familiar unfamiliarity. How much had changed. How life had gone on without me.

I started bawling pathetically on the couch. I couldn't force these people from my head. They were real, and I still loved them. I missed them all so much.

Charlie came home, dumping his coat and work bag on the floor. He came over and pressed my snotty wet face into his chest until my sobs slowed.

'What's wrong, Brooke?'

I pulled away and turned the laptop to face him. 'This is my mum,' I said.

He looked at the screen, at the Facebook profile staring back at him. 'This is your mom?' he repeated. 'But this is—I didn't even know you had a Facebook account.'

'I did,' I sniffed, 'in England. I just logged in.'

Charlie looked from me to the screen. He clicked on my profile and saw the picture of me.

'So this…' he said, '…was you.'

I watched as he clicked through the profile pictures of a grey, lifeless girl at the back of the party, photographed only reluctantly as she tugged down her sleeves.

'You looked so different,' Charlie said. 'You looked…'

'Miserable,' I finished.

'But you logged in?' He turned back to me. 'What made you log in?'

I sniffed, and half-shrugged. 'I dunno, I—I miss them.'

Charlie closed the laptop. 'Brooke, why did you leave England?'

I had told Charlie about Matt, after that therapy session. I had told him I'd been ill, that I'd self-harmed. And I'd told him about my dad. But I'd never told him about the day I left.

'Huh,' he said, when I'd finished. He wouldn't look at me. He hadn't looked at me for the last ten minutes. 'So when you said you left, without telling anyone, without saying goodbye…you really did.'

'Did what?'

'Leave. Without a word.'

'Yeah, I—I told you that.'

'But I hadn't realised—I hadn't pictured—they woke up, and you had literally vanished, and they never saw you again.'

'But you knew that,' I said defensively.

'But just a note,' he went on. 'You left a note and then they never saw you again. I mean, that's…' He came to his feet.

'Charlie, what's going on?'

'I don't get it, Brooke.' He was pacing in front of me now. 'You had a mom that loved you, that would have done anything for you, who gave you everything—'

'I don't need to hear this—'

'How could you do that to her, Brooke?'

'I told you, it's the worst thing I've ever—'

'How could you not speak to her when she came here looking for you? Who could do that to a person?'

'You think I don't know that? You think I don't know how selfish and horrible—'

'You're so fucked up, Brooke! Everything about you is fucked up! How can you be such a mess? How can there not be one normal thing in your life?'

I'd never seen him like this. His mother's death and the abandonment of mine had connected, the dots finally joined up, and he resented me. I'd tiptoed around it before, waiting for the judgement, the explosion, and he'd always done well to keep a lid on it, but now his patience had reached its limit. A mixture of guilt and defensiveness swelled in my stomach.

'I'm sorry, Charlie, what gave you the idea that I wasn't a fucking chore? Was it meeting me in that goddamn motel when I was too depressed to remember my own birthday?'

Charlie caught himself and cleared his throat.

'I'm trying to be better,' I said. 'I *want* to be a whole person. I don't want to be so needy all the time. In order to do that, I think I need to start taking accountability.'

Charlie leant on the wall, still quietly burning. 'Okay, so, what now? You want to fly back to England and give them all a twelve-step apology?'

'No, I—I don't know. Maybe.'

'*Maybe?*'

'I haven't thought that far ahead, but…' I swallowed. 'Maybe that's what I need to do.'

'You need to…okay.' He rubbed his eyes. Poor bloke had just done twelve hours at the hospital and come home to this. 'I expect you'll be patching things up with that piece of shit ex too, huh? Are there unresolved feelings there?'

'Of course not,' I said. 'I never think about him, outside of therapy. God, is that what you're worried about?'

He didn't answer. He just turned away from me, shaking his head. 'Don't I get a say in this, Brooke? Don't you care what I think?'

'Of course—'

'I asked you to move in with me. I begged my father to let you come for Christmas. I was serious about us, Brooke.'

'I'm serious, too,' I said quietly. He was staring at the floor. 'I'm serious, and I don't think things can carry on like this if we're going to have a future. I don't think this is sustainable, me being the way I am.'

Charlie sighed heavily, but still would not look at me.

'I feel so dependent on you,' I went on. 'For everything in my life. And I'm grateful for what you've given me. You helped me when I was in no position to help myself. But I'm not in that position anymore. I want to be my own person.'

Charlie marched into the kitchen. He grabbed a glass and filled it from the tap. I came to my feet and went on.

'Sometimes I feel like I don't have my own personality. My own friends, or hobbies. I just copied you for all that. I want to know what I like and what I don't like. I want to have opinions about your apartment.' I wasn't sure where I was going with this, but something inside me felt solid. 'I don't want to crumble at the slightest touch. I want to be able to look after myself and not constantly burst into tears and need your help. I want to be an adult. I need to hold myself accountable. I need to take responsibility for the past.'

'Ow!' I heard Charlie say, followed by the tap again. 'You left the fucking stove on.'

'Sorry,' I said.

'I'm going for a run.' He disappeared into the bedroom. I went to the stove and opened the lid to the pot. All the water had evaporated, and the spaghetti was now a sticky brown lump at the bottom. I binned the pasta and put the pot in the sink to soak.

For once, I didn't care that Charlie was upset. I mean, I did care. Of course I cared, but I felt like I could tolerate it. I felt like the earth would not shatter if I didn't make things okay between us immediately. Something was telling me that what I was saying was right.

Charlie came out in his running clothes and left without a word. When the door closed behind him, I opened the laptop. This was something I'd been ignoring for the longest time, but there was a feeling in my gut that this was what I had to do.

I went onto SkyScanner and started looking at flights to England. They all landed in London, and the cheapest ones were in a couple of weeks' time. I checked my bank account. It would cost most of my savings, but there was no question about it. I bookmarked the flights and closed the laptop.

I went into the kitchen for my second attempt at spag bol, eager to keep my hands busy. Charlie came in when I was dishing up dinner. He was sweaty, but calmer. 'Hey, babe,' he said, walking back into the bedroom.

'Hey,' I replied.

'I'm sorry I got upset earlier,' he called out. 'It wasn't cool.' He came back into the kitchen in a fresh T-shirt, mopping his face with a towel. 'Thanks for cooking.' He kissed my cheek, then grabbed his plate and sat on the couch, eating off his lap. 'If you want to talk about all that stuff, we can. We can talk about going to England.'

'Maybe another time,' I said, curling up next to him with my spaghetti. 'Let's just watch *Modern Family*.'

I wasn't ready to tell Charlie. Not yet. He'd want to take the time to really think about it, or come with me, or suggest I go later in the year and make a vacation out of it. I had already decided. I needed to do this on my own; for once in my life, I needed to do something for myself.

The next day at work, I emailed Yuko to book off two weeks' vacation in mid-January. She poked her head out of her office door to approve it. 'Going somewhere nice?'

'Er, kinda,' was my reply.

I spent my lunch break on SkyScanner and paid a lot of money for a return flight. I figured I'd best get a flexi ticket, in case I was hounded out of Britain and had to fly back to Seattle the next day. I pre-booked a taxi to pick me up in London. I even looked up a hotel near my hometown, just in case I found myself with nowhere to sleep.

Once that was all done, I could barely concentrate on my work. *I'm going, I'm going, oh God, I'm going back to England.* Just for two weeks, I told myself. Just for a visit. Just to make amends. *What will I say to them? How will I explain myself?* I started visualising the scene in my head, me getting off the plane and driving back to Bristol and walking up that driveway and knocking on my old front door. I considered every scenario: that Mum had moved, that she'd slam the door in my face, that she'd punch me, or just stand there and look at me blankly. That was as far as it would play out in my head. I couldn't find the words, couldn't picture the scene once the door opened and my stomach hit the floor.

I sent Sanjay an email to tell him my plan, since I felt I needed his blessing. He shouldn't have replied because he was on vacation, but he did anyway: *You have my full support in going back. I think it's a good decision, though it's important to be aware that things might not turn out as you hope, and you cannot control other people's reactions. You can only control you. Let me know if you want to set up a video session while you're over there.*

I found myself checking Facebook, scared that I'd only imagined the profiles, worried that I'd glance away and find they'd disappeared when I looked back. Amy had been tagged at a restaurant with someone called Ryan, who I figured wasn't her husband since there were no wedding photos, and Mum had been tagged in a photograph at her office Christmas dinner.

Seeing the pictures of them warmed my chest, gave me a rush of affection and a pang of anxiety.

Charlie was working late all week, and always came home grumpy and exhausted and usually covered in someone else's bodily fluids, so I figured it wasn't the best time to tell him. On Sunday he was finally off, and I cooked a really nice breakfast to butter him up. I was so nervous to actually start the conversation, and I exhaled for a long, long time. *Oxygen fuels anxiety*, I remembered Sanjay telling me. *Breathe out.*

'Charlie,' I said.

'Yes, Brooke?'

'I need to tell you something.'

He put his knife and fork down. I'd read that the best thing was to tell someone the truth immediately rather than drag it out, because the longer you took, the more time they had to imagine the worst.

'I've decided to take a trip back to England.' Those were the words I'd been practising all week.

'Okay,' he said.

'I think I need to go back and try to…reconnect, and apologise to my family. To make amends.'

'Okay,' he said.

'Sanjay thinks it's a good idea,' I added hastily.

Charlie took a second to digest this. 'Well, great, then. It sounds like a smart decision.'

'Do *you* think it's a smart decision?' I asked.

'Yeah,' he said. 'I think reconnecting with your family would be good for you. But, of course, we need to bear in mind that they might…'

'…react badly, yeah,' I finished for him. 'Don't worry, I've imagined every possible outcome. I couldn't be more ready to get punched in the face.'

He laughed, though I wasn't joking. 'When do you think we should go?'

'Oh, um,' I said, 'I've booked to go a week on Monday.'

'You booked already?' Charlie looked surprised. 'I don't think I can take vacation on this short notice.'

'To be honest, I—I think this is something I should do alone.' I corrected myself, 'I have to do this alone.'

Charlie hesitated. 'You don't want me to come?'

'It's not that,' I said, and was reminded of when I'd asked him that exact question, when I hadn't been invited to his work drinks. 'You remember Sanjay and I have been talking about me becoming more independent.'

'I thought you meant hobbies and stuff. This is like a big thing, Brooke. Don't you want some support?'

'It does mean hobbies too. But I feel like retracing my steps is…I don't know. It's something I think I should do for myself. Without help. With support, but without help.'

Charlie leaned back. 'So you've taken time off work?'

'Two weeks.'

'That doesn't leave many vacation days for us to go away later in the year, y'know.'

'I know. I'm sorry, Charlie. This just feels really important.'

'It is important,' he agreed. 'You're right. You should go. And then I'll be able to meet your mom over Skype.'

'Let's not get ahead of ourselves,' I said. 'I might be back in Seattle by Tuesday.'

'You're definitely not going back to talk to that…that Matt guy? I don't like him. I don't want you going near him.'

'Oh no,' I said. 'I'm sure he won't even be there anymore.'

Marie insisted that we go out on the Saturday before my flight. Since talking to Charlie, I'd managed to open up to her about my past, and she knew this was a big deal. She took us to a very expensive bar and bought champagne.

'To Brooke's homecoming,' she said.

'To Brooke's homecoming!' Charlie and Lisa echoed.

'We wish you luck, because you'll need it, and we remind you that you have a family right here waiting for you, no matter how it turns out.' Marie grinned at me and sipped from her glass.

'Though, it's not *really* a homecoming, since your home is here,' Lisa said.

'You can have two homes,' Charlie said, giving me a squeeze. 'I think of Minnesota as my second home.'

'But we didn't grow up there,' Marie said. 'Brooke's whole life was in England.'

'Thanks guys,' I cut in, 'but please, can we talk about anything else? I'm shitting myself.'

'We could talk about Dan's promotion, as your replacement,' Marie teased.

'Replacement?' Charlie looked worried.

'Ignore her,' I kissed him. 'He's covering my desk while I'm gone.'

Charlie offered to switch shifts so he could drive me to the airport, but I insisted on taking an Uber. 'Retracing steps,' I said. 'Gotta do this on my own.'

On Sunday night, I could hardly eat. My stomach was in knots and my head was spinning. Charlie put on a movie and rubbed my feet, then ran me a bath, and then we had sex. The next morning, he left at five to get to work. Through the darkness he kissed me hard, and I sleepily took in the feel of him, the sight of his dim figure as he left the bedroom.

When I woke up, I double checked my bags, my passports, everything I needed. I'd only packed a small suitcase, not wanting to seem presumptive by showing up at Mum's front door with a big one. I blew air out of my lungs as I got in the Uber, and arrived at Sea-Tac, which I hadn't been back to since I first got to America. I looked at all the different check-in desks and felt overwhelmed for a second. I didn't really know how this worked, having only flown alone once in my life. I felt the urge to turn to Charlie and wait for his lead, wait for how he always knew which bus was ours or where we were going. But he wasn't here, and I had to do this alone. The only way was through.

It was easier than I thought to find my desk and hand over my bags. The attendant saw my American passport but heard my British accent and asked, 'Are you leaving home, or going home?'

'That's actually a difficult question,' I joked.

Security wasn't hard. Neither was finding my gate. I didn't struggle to get on the plane or find my seat, watching the airport shrink into a tiny dot and then vanish from view. What was hard lay ahead, across the Atlantic. But I told myself I had ten hours until that time, so I wrapped myself up in a blanket and tried to drift off.

SCENE 18: MATT, 26

'But this is where you've always lived,' Mum was whining. 'You've never left this town—except for uni.'

'Exactly,' I said. 'All my friends live in the city, or London. They got big jobs, and what have I got? There's nothing for me here.'

She turned to look at me, and said, 'Gee, thanks, Matt.'

We were in her kitchen, and she was sawing at a loaf of bread with such force that the slice snapped in half. Clearly, this conversation about me moving wasn't going down well.

'You know I didn't mean you, Mum. But I'm not talking far—just further into Bristol. It'll be a forty-minute drive, max.'

'When you said you wanted to spend your lunch break here, I didn't think you were going to drop this bomb on me.'

'It's not a bomb, Mum, everyone moves.'

'What's wrong with your current place?'

'A one-bed, above a shop? I want a mortgage. I've got savings. I'm looking for a two-bed at least.'

'What do you need a two-bed for?' she whined again, now buttering the bread. Crumbs were flying everywhere. 'There's only one of you.'

'Yeah, that's my point. I'm twenty-six. I want to start thinking about, y'know, the future. I'm sick of being stuck here, and never meeting anyone new. I'm bored of waiting around.'

'Waiting for what?' Mum said, slamming a plate down in front of me.

I didn't look at her, just bit into the sandwich.

'Well, I can't say I'm happy about this, and your father won't be, either,' she went on, sitting opposite me and folding her arms.

'Mum, please try to be understanding about this. Either I can stay here, and teach, and never really progress, or I could move away and have a shot at something bigger.'

'Next you'll go travelling, meet some Australian lass, and never come back.' Mum bit into her sandwich.

'I've got some free periods tomorrow afternoon. I'm gonna look at this place in Henleaze. You can come, if you want.'

'I can't, I'm seeing Helen.'

'Fine.'

We ate in silence. Just as I thought the tantrum was over, she tried again.

'But you were born here!' she cried, both angry and pleading.

I put down my sandwich. 'Yes, Mum, I was born here, and I went to school here, and now I work here, but you're going to have to accept that this place has no future for me.'

SCENE 19: BROOKE, 23

I woke up on the plane. One hour left. I felt nauseous. Fifty minutes left. I started shaking. Forty minutes left.

My hands were sweaty and fidgety and I couldn't sit still. My eyes darted around the cabin. A teenage girl across the aisle was peeling off some plasticky face mask. A weary air hostess wandered by with her trolley. The bloke next to me was snoring, drool trailing from his lips. I could smell peanuts on his breath and hoped his head wouldn't roll onto my shoulder. The teenage girl was now applying moisturiser. I touched my own eyes and could feel the bags beneath them.

Suddenly self-conscious, I squeezed past the snoring bloke and made my way to the bathroom. My head was fuzzy. How long ago had it been when everything was fine, before I logged on to Facebook, before I got on this plane? What was I wearing? I had to look down to remind myself.

In the mirror I saw my puffy eyes, my dry lips, my hair dulled by a thin layer of grease. I put on some deodorant and smeared Chapstick on my lips. I gripped onto the sink, feeling more nauseous with every second that went by. I tied my hair back with an elastic, just in case.

The seatbelt sign flashed and an announcement from the captain rang out, alerting us that we were going to land soon. I took another glance at my reflection before returning to my seat. My thoughts felt so muddled and all I wanted to do was call Charlie. But I knew I couldn't do that, and I knew I had no alternative than to get off the plane and keep going.

The doors opened, people raced to grab bags from the overhead lockers, and eventually we started filing out. I went through passport control, and baggage claim, and finally out of arrivals.

The taxi driver was waiting for me, holding up an iPad with my name on it. 'Brooke Tyler?' he said as I approached him. 'Going to Bristol?' I nodded and walked out with him.

London's wintry sunshine fell on my face, and I could smell the rain in the air. It was all so different from Seattle. I felt alien. I had gotten so used to the American accent; the English accent seemed so jarring.

I'd already given him the address, Mum's address, in the small town just outside the city. I hadn't seen any signs on Facebook that she'd moved. But what happened to my room after I left? What if Dad had died, or Grandma? When was the last time I pictured her face?

Off we went, driving on the 'wrong' side. The roads were different, the street signs were different. We passed a university. Did Amy teach Archaeology there? Or was she off doing something abroad? Had that really been her kid in the picture, or someone else's? What about Lucy? Where was she now? It was a mission to keep myself from panicking, and I figured it might help to call ahead, rather than just show up. My cell would work here, but would be really expensive, I was sure. My hands shook as I typed in the number. I wiped them on my jeans.

'Hello?' came my mother's timid voice. I froze at the sound. There was a long silence.

'Hello?' she said again. I inhaled deeply, trying to speak, but she hung up.

I considered not calling back, taking this as a sign that I should turn back now, but even as I thought it I found my fingers dialling, just as I had once found myself putting a razor to my skin.

'Hello?' Mum said again, more impatiently this time.

'Hi, Mum.' My voice came as a whimper.

Silence.

'Brooke?'

'Yeah,' I said, 'it's me.'

'Oh my god,' she said, and I couldn't tell if she was excited or angry. 'Oh my god, Brooke! Thank God—what—where are you?'

'I'm-I'm on the M4.'

'I'm coming to get you, stay where you are—' I guess she was excited, then.

'No, it's fine—'

'Don't move—'

'I'll drive up to you.'

After a pause, she said, 'But will you?'

'Yes.'

'…Okay.'

'Give me a couple of hours.'

'Okay, love, I'll be here.'

'Okay,' I sniffed. I was so relieved she wasn't angry. 'Bye.'

'Okay, uh, bye, darling.'

After that call, I put my face in my hands and cried thick tears of relief. *I'm okay,* I thought. *I'm going to be okay.*

As I got closer and closer to home, I saw more and more things I remembered. The big white letters on the grass outside the spa; the roundabout with the sculpture on top; the little muddy patch on the roadside where a man, known only as 'The A38 Guy', would stand and whip a lamppost with skipping ropes while wearing lab goggles. No one ever knew why he did it. I even had a sideways glance to see if he was still there, waiting for the school buses full of teenagers to wave at him as they went past.

Then the church where my parents got married and the rugby club and down the twisty hill where all the sixth formers would drive into trees. Then the car dealership, the pub (renamed), and the sports centre with its new paint job. It was all so horribly familiar, each memory giving me a pang of anxiety in my stomach that ached for minutes afterwards.

By the time I saw the sports centre, the pangs had been too frequent for me to recover between, and the nausea was too hard to hold in. I asked the driver to pull into the car park, threw open the door, and puked my guts onto the ground.

Ugh. I needed that. I went into the building to wash my mouth out with water from the sink, half-expecting to see the kids I went to school with still walking around in their lifeguard uniforms. The toilets weren't where they used to be, and it took me a while to find them. My reflection above the sink had depleted even more. I left the building and wandered back across the car park towards the taxi.

'Brooke?'

I spun round, and I could hardly believe I was looking at Callum, my Callum, who had been at Stagefright. Callum, whose sister was Lucy and whose mother was friends with mine; Callum, who I'd known since I was five; Callum, who had kissed me in Spin the Bottle and hugged me when I cried because the boy I fancied liked someone else. My friend Callum.

'Hi, Callum,' I said with a nervous smile.

He stared at me in shock, his tennis racket loose in his hand. For a second, I thought he was going to walk away, to refuse to speak to me for what I did to him, what I did to my family.

'Fucking hell, Brooke,' he said and stormed off. I felt my lip tremble as I watched the retreating figure of one of my favourite people in the world.

The driver must've missed that. 'Nearly home then, love,' I heard him say behind me.

I blinked rapidly and turned back to the car.

SCENE 20: MATT, 26

'And this is the largest bedroom,' the estate agent said, propping the door open for me.

I went inside. The room was big, spacious, dominated by a bed in flowery sheets. Framing the top and sides of it were ornate white cupboards that stretched into wardrobes. There was a dressing table, the current owner's perfume bottles and makeup spread all over it. The room was so feminine. *I suppose this would be good for my wife.*

It felt ridiculous, thinking about a wife, as if I'd even met someone. I was trying to imagine the figure of a woman, trying to guess if this would be the kind of place she'd want to live. I suppose you usually meet someone first before buying a place.

'This is the perfect starter home for families,' the agent said, as if reading my mind.

'Are there any good schools in the area?'

'Loads. There's a preschool just round the corner, and two primary schools that have scored highly with Ofsted.'

'What about secondary?'

She looked at me as if to say I was getting ahead of myself.

'I'm a teacher,' I explained.

'Oh. Right. Yes, there's one nearby, and a private school a bit of a further drive away.'

I looked out the window. The garden had a swing in it. That really brought me down to earth. I couldn't imagine bringing a woman back here after a date and having a swing in my garden. I may as well buy a cot.

'The current owners will take that with them,' the agent said, following my gaze.

'Yeah, I don't have much need for a swing just yet.'

She smiled politely. 'So why the change then, if you don't mind me asking?'

I sighed. 'It's just time to move on.'

SCENE 21: BROOKE, 23

The taxi pulled up at the bottom of the drive and with trembling hands I undid my seatbelt. Mum must've been waiting for me because she hurried out the front door and towards the car. I could see she was trying to stop her legs from running. I tried to stop my legs from running away.

When she got to me, she stopped and blinked. 'Brooke?'

'Hi Mum,' I mumbled.

She was crying and smiling at the same time, and I was relieved to see she didn't look as aged as she had done in her Facebook picture. She threw her arms around me. 'Brooke, oh, Brooke, thank God, are you—did you—how are—oh, thank God.'

I wrapped my arms around her too, more tentatively than she was. 'I'm sorry, Mum.'

The driver clearly hadn't heard this exchange in full because he popped my suitcase down and cheerily said, 'Surprised your mum with a visit, did you?'

'A very big surprise,' Mum said, seizing my suitcase and pulling me inside.

The house smelled the same. It looked mostly the same. Mum wouldn't let me go. She hugged me on the sofa for at least an hour, crying and smiling and asking me how I was and telling me how much she loved me. I told her I was sorry and that I loved her too and that I was glad she looked well and that I was so, so sorry.

She managed to tell me that Amy had moved into the city and was working at the museum but was back all the time, dropping her toddler—*toddler*—off to be babysat. I had seen the picture on Facebook, but still couldn't believe it: I was an aunt…Mum was a grandma…

She went on about the things that had changed in this tiny little town. She told me how much she had missed me and how she'd looked for me and how she had tried to get the police to find me, but they couldn't do anything if I'd wanted to disappear. She had saved mail for me and kept my stuff in my room and had apparently never given up hope that, one day, I would come back.

Her tears subsided into smiles and we both relaxed. It was strange to see someone I knew so well asking all these questions about me, as if we had just met. She put the kettle on and made tea in her posh teapot, something she saved for special occasions. I obediently drank it, choosing not to mention that I now preferred coffee.

I told her what I had been doing in America and the people I'd met and what brought me home. I told her about Charlie, Marie, and Lisa, and the newspaper, and the apartment. And she smiled and listened as if I was telling her about something my school friends had done, nodding as if she recognised the names of the people she would never meet.

I was relieved at how happy she was to see me, and I felt stupid for being surprised. Just because I had been depressed didn't make all the bad things I'd thought about myself true. Just because I was scared everyone would hate me didn't mean that it was real. Just because I had felt unloved didn't mean Mum had stopped loving me. And just because I hadn't forgiven myself for what I did to my family didn't mean they hadn't forgiven me. Or so I thought, until Amy came in.

Apparently, she'd left work to come and see me, but was not happy about it. When she came into the living room, she didn't miss a beat in marching over to me and slapping me hard across the face. 'You *bitch*, you fucking *bitch, Brooke!*'

'Amy, stop!' Mum shrieked, pushing her away from me. 'What are you doing?'

Amy ignored this. 'You fucking *abandon* us, fuck off to America or God knows where, and come sweeping back in whenever you feel like it? Ran out of money, did you? Came crawling back to the bank of Mum and Dad?'

'Amy,' I began, my hand on my face, but no words followed. I'd expected this and knew I deserved worse.

'Stop it, Amy, *now*,' Mum said, standing between us and trying to assume her stern parent voice that we hadn't heard since our teens. It had no effect on Amy, now nearly twenty-five and living alone and raising her own kid.

'You made her fucking *tea?*' Amy roared at Mum, seizing the cup and throwing the contents over me. It was cold, so I just got wet. She shook the empty cup in Mum's face. '*Tea?* After she kept you up crying every night for *years?* You treat her like the prodigal fucking daughter after she ruined your life?' This confirmed my worst fear: leaving Mum had caused her agony. Guilt rose like nausea in my stomach and I rushed to the bathroom to vomit up the tea. *Can I please keep something down?*

Through the door I could hear more shouting, but knew that Amy would never hit Mum like she'd hit me, so I stayed hidden. Mum was crying. 'I've waited for this day for so long and you're ruining it!'

'You expect me to play happy families after what she did to you? To us? And now she's hiding in that bloody toilet playing victim again. Fuck this. I'm going to pick Freddie up.'

Eventually, I heard the front door slam and the house fell silent. After a pause, Mum spoke through the door in her let's-pretend-everything's-fine voice. 'Brooke, everything okay in there?'

'Yup,' I said, rinsing my mouth with tap water, and opened the door.

She looked worried, as if she was afraid I'd have somehow vanished again, but then she put on a big fake smile, and I realised she was hiding her fear by pretending everything was fine. She was frightened I'd leave and was trying to make it as appealing as possible to stay.

I sat down with her and promised I wasn't going to disappear again without a trace. A lump rose in my throat when I started trying to explain why I left, but I did it because she deserved an answer. I wasn't very sure of the reasons myself, but I tried my best to articulate them: depression, stubbornness, ingratitude. Mum's face fell the more I went on, but we had to talk about the hard stuff. The only way was through.

'Why couldn't you have called…' she asked, her voice barely above a whisper.

'I should have,' I said. 'I'm sorry. I was too scared. I felt too guilty. Those are selfish reasons, though. I should have.'

'I came to America. I came to Seattle. We hired a private detective.'

'I know, Mum. I'm sorry.' I took a deep breath. 'I was there that day, when you came to my office. I hid from you. I got my friend to lie to you. I'm so sorry.' I could see the injury on her face as I said this, could see how it hurt to hear the truth: that we'd been in the same room and I had let her go home heartbroken. But I had to tell the truth. I had to hold myself accountable.

'You seem better,' she said, looking at me. 'You seem happier. More yourself, than when…than before.'

I smiled gently and pushed my hair behind my ear. At least four years hadn't been for nothing.

The doorbell rang, and Mum rushed to answer it. 'Who's…' I said, standing up, and in came my father. I had to blink a few times.

Mum closed the door behind him. 'I phoned him when you called.'

'I just got out of work,' Dad said in his warm American accent. We stared at each other, both incredulous.

'Dad?' I heard myself say.

'Brooke,' he said, and came towards me, arms outstretched.

I backed away instinctively. His happy expression fell into surprise, hurt, confusion. He looked from me to Mum and back to me. 'Why did you leave, honey?' he asked. 'Why did you go without saying goodbye?'

I opened my mouth but didn't know what to say. I hadn't expected to see him, today, here, now.

Dad stared at me. 'Honey, you just upped and left.'

'You upped and left,' I said.

He didn't say anything, just kept staring at me.

'You were never there.' My words were lined with an anger I didn't know I still felt. 'You were never there when I needed you.'

He looked down. 'I'm sorry. I'm here now.'

'It's a bit late,' I said.

'Brooke,' Mum interjected, with a look that told me I wasn't one to talk. 'Your dad moved back after you—four years ago. He wanted to be here for when you came home.'

I looked back at my father. 'You don't live in London anymore?'

'I live three streets down.'

I stared at him as he exchanged a glance with Mum again.

'I had to be here, Brooke. I had to wait for you.'

I couldn't believe it. Dad, who'd missed all my plays, who called once in a blue moon, who'd felt more like a stranger than a father. That same man was standing before me, telling me he'd uprooted his entire life in London to come back to his ex-wife's town, to wait and see if his daughter would come home. He crossed the room and wrapped his arms around me, and I felt myself give in as my face met his shoulder. He held me for a long time, and when he stepped back, I saw his eyes were wet.

'Cam, why don't you put the kettle on,' Mum said, even though we'd just had tea.

'Right, yes,' he said, rubbing his forehead as he went into the kitchen.

I turned to Mum. 'He moved back.'

She nodded.

'But he was never…he was never…'

'He's a really good grandfather, Brooke,' she said softly. 'Very involved with Freddie. He's over all the time.'

'How do you have it, Brooke?' I heard Dad call from the kitchen. When I imagined coming back to England, he hadn't even been part of it—now he was asking how many sugars I wanted.

'I hope you'll be able to give him a second chance,' Mum said. And we both knew she was giving me one.

I called back, a little uneasily, 'Nothing for me, thanks.'

He came in with two mugs, gave one to Mum, and then hugged me again as if he'd only gone a week since seeing me. I regarded him with scepticism, but Mum smiled encouragingly. He sat in his old armchair and asked how I'd been. It was how I imagined fathers would politely ask their daughters how university was going, pretending that alcohol, sex, and drugs didn't exist. I guess he didn't know how he was meant to handle this situation. None of us did.

I spent the afternoon with Mum and Dad in the house where I grew up. They got on so well, even better than when they'd been together. Mum made dinner for us and didn't let me out of her sight all day. Amy texted her to say she wouldn't be coming back that night. Mum gave my shoulder a squeeze and said, 'She'll come around.'

My bedroom was practically untouched. The duvet cover was different, but that was really it. My books were still in the bookcase, my pictures on the walls. It was bittersweet to see how much hope they had that I'd return, how they hadn't moved on. They said over and over, 'We *knew* you would come home,' and it scared me because I hadn't even known I would come home.

Now officially back, I logged into Facebook on my cell to flick through Messenger. I had messages from aunts, cousins, people from school. I had loads from Lucy, including one dated today.

Lucy Haines: CAL SAYS HE SAW YOU TODAY!! IS IT TRUE? ARE YOU BACK???

I couldn't tell if Lucy's capitals were happy or angry, but remembering the look on Callum's face that morning made me wince. I typed back.

Brooke Tyler: Yeah, it's true. Hey stranger.

Lucy Haines: YAAAAAAAAY!

A second after that, she was video calling me. I nervously answered and her face appeared on the screen.

'BROOKEIAMSOHAPPYTOSEEYOU!' she yelled before I could say anything.

I laughed. 'I'm so happy to see you too, Luce.'

'When did you get back? Are you at your mum's?'

'Yeah, I'm with Mum, and er, I just got back today, actually.'

'Where've you been? I missed you. We were so worried about you. Amy and I tried to find you. We were looking at all the flights and trying to figure out where you could have gone—I'm just so relieved and happy you're back! Tell me everything.'

Lucy's enthusiasm flooded me with warmth, even if I felt undeserving of it. I spent the next two hours laying on my bed, catching up with her. Mum kept coming up to check I was still there, so I ended up leaving the door open so she could hear my voice from downstairs.

'You know who was asking after you?' Lucy said. 'Matt. Mr Prom Night.'

'Matt?' I said.

'Yeah, I ran into him at the pub on New Year's. I think he was with his girlfriend.'

'But he was asking after me?'

'It was just small talk. I guess you're the only thing we have in common.'

I laughed. 'Luce, I'm so glad you're not mad at me.'

'Why would I be mad at you?'

'Because of what I did. Because I abandoned you. My family. Everyone.'

'Oh, Brooke, I wouldn't get angry about that. You were ill.'

'Callum was mad,' I said, and my voice cracked.

'You know him, he's just moody. I don't blame you at all, Brooke. You weren't well. I always…I always wished I did more for you.'

'Are you kidding?' I said. 'You tried, Luce. You invited me to everything, you tried to talk to me. I wouldn't let anyone in. That wasn't your fault.'

Lucy wasn't looking at the screen anymore. 'I was always worried I was a bad friend to you.'

'You were never a bad friend, Luce.' I sat up. 'I was a bad friend. I mean, I wasn't in a position to be a good friend. I was so caught up in me. You were always so nice. We used to be best mates.'

She smiled. 'Maybe we still are.'

SCENE 22: MATT, 26

I was in Tesco when I saw her.

It was a Tuesday, a little after Valentine's. It was around four, and it was raining. She was wearing a navy waterproof over her green jumper and blue jeans. She was in the produce aisle. Her skin was warm and rosy, her lips pink. She was leaning over the vegetables, a basket on the crook of her arm, her chestnut hair dangling down as she picked up an onion and peered at it.

I had to blink, three times over, before I was sure I wasn't imagining it. Even then I stared at her, edging closer, to be sure I wasn't mistaking someone else for her, but it was her, it was really her.

'Brooke?'

She looked up and her dark eyes met my gaze. Her eyelids fluttered, her lashes stretching up towards her brows, and at first her mouth looked surprised, then she summoned a polite smile. 'Hi, Matt,' she said, a little tentatively.

I went numb, my heart silent. All I could hear was her voice. Brooke Tyler was in front of me and I was actually looking at her and she was actually looking at me. Photons of light were bouncing off her skin and entering my eyes, hitting my retina and producing an image in my brain. *She's here. Oh, shit. She actually came back.*

Without noticing that my arms were moving, I reached out and pulled her into a hug. I was drowning in disbelief. I had longed for this moment, for her to show up and tell me she was sorry she ever left. Every time I heard footsteps coming up to the rehearsal room, I had turned to see if it was her. I had imagined her blurry silhouette passing on the street outside my window a million times before I fell asleep. And now she was actually here.

I was hyperaware of her presence, the warmth of her in my arms, the feel of her head against my shoulder. For once, it wasn't a memory, and it wasn't a dream. It was real and present and actually happening. She was here.

She laughed politely and I felt her pulling away from me. I didn't want to, but I let her go and she stepped back, giving me a friendly smile. I looked at her face: that same, achingly beautiful face, now older, and happier than I'd ever seen before.

Despite all the times I'd imagined her returning, I had no idea what to say. She broke the silence. 'How are you?'

'I—' I stumbled. 'I'm fine. How are you?'

She replied, but I barely registered the response. My head was spinning with a million questions all more pressing than 'How are you?'

'When—when did you get back?' I managed.

'Oh, um, I've been home for about a month.'

'You—you've been back a month?' I repeated, and she nodded. 'Cool,' I said. *She's been home a month, and nobody told me? She's been home a month and hasn't reached out? We have so much to talk about. Why hasn't she—*

'I've been in Seattle,' she said, when I didn't say anything.

'I know,' I said. 'I saw your sister, at New Year's, and she said something about—about Seattle.'

'Oh, you ran into Amy?'

'Yeah. Hasn't she…didn't she say?'

'Nah, she's not mentioned it,' Brooke said casually, like it made sense, except it made no sense at all. She brushed her hair behind her ear. 'I didn't think you'd still be here.'

I ignored this. 'I really want to talk to you.'

'Oh yeah?' she said. 'What do you want to talk about?'

What kind of question was that? 'Everything—everything that happened.'

'Oh, er, well maybe not today,' she said, indicating to her basket. 'Got chilli con carne to make.'

We agreed to get dinner at the Italian place on the High Street on Thursday. Two nights felt like a long time to wait, but I didn't want to be pushy. I told myself she had her family to spend time with, and that was important, but still I had a million unanswered questions and came away from Tesco with a sour taste on my tongue. *Isn't it obvious that we have loads to talk about? Why didn't Amy say I'd been asking after her? Why did no one tell me she was back?*

It was strange, moving through the world knowing she was here, in town, she was back, she'd been back a month and I may have seen her in a coat on a rainy day with the hood up, none the wiser that we'd crossed paths. That night, my legs wouldn't rest; they were trying to pull me out of my bed and walk to her house and maybe even toss pebbles again just so I could see her, so I could ask her all the questions I'd been ruminating on for four years. And I'll admit, something hurt about the fact she hadn't come straight to me once she landed back in England, or at least in the first few days. Why hadn't she asked to meet up already? Hadn't she wanted to?

Maybe she didn't come back for you. The thought crossed my mind, and I shoved it down. I couldn't let myself believe it.

On Thursday, I couldn't sit still, and could barely concentrate on my lessons. I willed seven o'clock to come round faster, and was showered and dressed by six, staring at my watch. I'd offered her a lift, but she said she'd meet me at the restaurant. I thought about getting her flowers, but decided that would be too much. I'd only hugged her that one time in Tesco, but the conversation had been too polite, too scripted, to feel like I could hug her again. I'd said goodbye and continued up the aisles, stealing glances as she followed a hundred metres behind, wondering why this air, this distance between us, seemed to have appeared.

I got to the restaurant ten minutes early. She was five minutes early. When I saw her walking up in her coat and umbrella, I couldn't help but hug her tightly. Again, she laughed politely and hugged me back, but broke off the contact far sooner than I would've.

We sat down to dinner and we talked. I kept blinking, staring at her, trying to remind myself that this was real, that she was actually sat opposite me in her spotty blue blouse and ripped jeans. After a bit of small talk, she asked what I was up to.

'Well, I teach. At our old school.'

'You're a teacher? That's cool. Do you enjoy it?'

'Yeah,' I said, and then realised I was lying. 'Yeah, it's good. I actually live in town, above the corner shop.'

'You don't live in the city?' She sounded surprised.

'No, I mean, work is here, Mum and Dad are here, and Stagefright—'

'Stagefright's still going?' she said.

'Yes,' I said. I had to stop myself saying, *of course it is. Of course I'm still here. Of course I've been waiting…waiting for…*

The waiter took our orders. I watched her as she smiled at him, running her finger over the menu, laughing as he made a joke about the salmon and her eyes creased and her hair shook. When he walked away, I said, 'I've really missed you.'

She smiled politely, and looked down at her cutlery, but said nothing.

'But what about you?' I asked, quick to change the subject. 'Tell me everything.'

She told me about Seattle and how she'd been messed up and worked in a bar and lived in a motel. A man named Charlie. A job he'd helped her with. A woman called Marie. A lot of secrets she kept from them. A bunch of sunflowers. An apartment they shared. A plane ticket.

'Do you love him?' I asked.

'Yeah, he's my boyfriend,' she said, like it was obvious, which I guess it was.

My stupid dream shattered. Her coming back and telling me she still loved me. Her asking us to give it another shot. I'd always pictured her as I'd seen her that last night we had together—excited and happy, looking at me with bright eyes. Maybe a little unsure, and sad behind it all, in a way I'd be able to fix if I could just love her enough. This woman sat opposite me was not that eighteen-year-old girl anymore. She was confident and together and she didn't need fixing at all.

'Then why did you come back?' I said, biting my lip to keep it steady.

'Because…well…I need to try to take accountability for all the damage I caused back then.'

'You didn't…' I looked at my drink, ashamed of the question I knew I shouldn't ask. 'You didn't come back for us to start again.'

Brooke looked surprised that I'd even said that. She shook her head slowly. 'We're different people, Matt. To how we were back then.'

'I'm not,' I said.

'I am,' she said.

Silence.

'I'm with Charlie.'

I sighed. I hadn't expected her to come back, but I *really* hadn't expected her to come back and break my heart.

'I'm sorry if you…if I made you think…we could pick things up…' She drifted off. I looked at her, at real, living, breathing Brooke. Brooke who had left, who had vanished, who I had thought about every night and every single morning for the past four years. But I hadn't thought about her, about her being *alive,* living her life and doing things and falling asleep next to somebody else. Time may have stopped for me when she left, but it hadn't for her. She'd moved on.

'Seeing you…knowing you're okay…that's enough for me,' I said, and maybe it would become true.

She smiled shyly, poking her fish with her fork.

'Are you staying?' I asked suddenly. When I'd seen her, I'd been so sure she was back for good, but I wasn't certain now that things weren't working out the way I'd hoped.

'I'm not sure yet,' she said. *More disappointment.* 'I originally just took two weeks' vacation, so since then I've been working from home. But I don't know how much longer I can keep doing that, with the time difference and all.'

'Please come to Stagefright,' I said. 'Maybe—we could be— friends.' It was a desperate plea to keep her in my life in some form, to have some sense of resolution. She looked down.

'I feel like,' she said, 'you had a way you wanted this—me coming back—to pan out.'

'But can you blame me?' Suddenly I was defensive. 'Can you blame me for having wished that you'd come back, having imagined how this would go? You left! You just left without a word, so how was I supposed to negotiate that in my head? Do you realise what that was like for me?'

Her blank stare made me realise that she didn't. She had no clue. She has just flown away and got on with her life without any concern for what it was like for the people she left behind. Now I was angry with her.

'Do you realise your family blamed me for driving you away? Do you realise I blamed myself! I thought we were getting back together that night, *I was in love with you*, and then you just vanish, so what other conclusion could I come to?'

She said nothing. Heads were turning to look at us, but that didn't stop me.

'I thought what happened in that hotel was unwanted. I thought you were scared of me. I thought you were dead! No one ever told me you'd been planning to leave months beforehand. How do you think I'm supposed to deal with that? Did you think things were easy here without you?'

'I thought everyone would be happier without me,' she said quietly.

'Well, everything was shit, Brooke! I felt so *fucking* guilty every *fucking* day, so maybe that's why I needed you to come back. Maybe that's why I needed to hope you'd say you still loved me and that all that shit had happened for a reason and it wasn't just a mess of mistakes. That night, I wanted to fix all the shit from before, and then right as I think I've got the chance to, right as I think we're getting back together, you just vanish! How am I supposed to move on from that? How am I supposed to get over you and meet someone new when I'm worrying that you've offed yourself and I'm the reason why?'

I didn't care that the other diners were staring. She had to know what she'd done to me.

'I never moved away,' I said. 'Four years—my life was on hold.'

'I'm sorry,' she said.

I sipped my drink. I couldn't bear to look at her, at the mix of shock and sympathy in her eyes.

'I didn't know things were like that for you,' she said. 'I had no idea you'd even be here. I thought you would've moved on. You were always the first to move on.'

'Didn't Amy tell you I was asking after you? At the pub on New Year's? Lucy, too, I spoke to her.'

'Lucy mentioned it. She thought you were just checking in. She thought you were with your girlfriend.'

'Fliss isn't my girlfriend.' I sounded so bitter. 'Lucy surely knew that I hadn't moved away. I see Callum at the pub all the time. I even told her I worked at school. Didn't she say?'

Brooke shook her head, and I was astounded. I couldn't believe how the six degrees of separation, the lines of communication stretching from me to her, had so spectacularly failed.

'Did Amy even tell you that I chased you to the airport? The day you left?'

'She did,' Brooke said. 'But she phrased it like you were doing her a favour, because we'd just spent the night and you were already in the city, so could get to the airport fast.'

'A *favour*?' I repeated. 'So that night together, that night, what was it to you? What was I? A one-night stand? A hook up?'

She looked down. 'It was goodbye.'

I scoffed.

'I'd told you we didn't have a future. At Prom, I said one date. That was all I said.'

I downed my drink even though it was only cola. It was clear that I had overestimated how important I was to Brooke. I had not been afforded entry into the inner circle, not deemed worthy of knowing that she had returned, that a PI had spoken to her, that there was a bank statement with a transaction for a plane ticket three months before she disappeared. Her sister, her best friend, and even Brooke herself clearly didn't view me as her abandoned boyfriend, her ex, her anything at all.

After some silence, she said, 'Nothing in that hotel was unwanted,' and I did feel a rush of relief. 'Part of me wanted to get back together with you that night. I had planned to leave for so long and when you showed up at my Prom, I didn't want to go anymore.'

'Then why did you?' I finally asked the question, the question I'd been ruminating on for four years. 'Why did you leave?'

She sighed. 'Stubbornness? Self-destruction? I don't know. It was my only plan. I was depressed.'

'So are a lot of people, Brooke. They don't do things like that. They don't hurt other people, their families.'

'I know. It was wrong. And I didn't realise how…things were for you.'

'Since you left, you didn't once put yourself in my shoes? You didn't wonder where I was, how I was doing?'

She shook her head, and it stung me to see. 'When I left, I—I didn't…let myself,' I could hear her choosing her words carefully. 'I didn't let myself think of what I left behind. That was the whole point of going. To start fresh. Block that all out.'

It looked like she had more to say, but I didn't care. 'Starting fresh is a privilege I didn't get to enjoy, Brooke. I couldn't block stuff out. I was here, driving myself crazy with guilt, hoping you would come back to relieve me of it. I would have *loved* to skip town. I would have *loved* to move somewhere where nobody knew me. But I couldn't because I have a conscience, and I would have *carried that guilt with me*. I can't just leave it all behind like you can.'

'I couldn't,' she said slowly. 'I tried to run away from all my problems. It didn't work. Look, here I am, four years later, right back where I started, doing the actual work I should have done then. Taking accountability. Resolving things.'

'That's what we're doing now, then? Resolving things?'

'Well…I hope so.'

I looked down at my empty plate. She went on. 'In the state I was in, it was hard to imagine anyone could care about me. I felt so worthless. I really thought everyone would be better off without me. Now I can see clearly and think soberly, and I know I was wrong. We hurt each other a lot over the years and I think we need to talk about that. And maybe by working through that, we can help each other to—you know—move on.'

I looked at her. Something had broken. I reached for the pull she used to have on me, but it was gone. I didn't feel about her the way I thought I would.

'You want me to help you work through what happened between us? So that you can get closure and move on with your life and fly back to your boyfriend?'

'Well...yes,' she said.

I looked down again. I guessed I owed her that.

'Closure for you too,' she said, 'so that you can move on.'

Moving on felt like an enormous task. I thought back to that empty house that I'd looked at a few days before. I'd found it hard to picture a wife or a girlfriend or any kind of future for myself that didn't rely on Brooke coming back. Now she had done, and none of it had gone to plan. But something in me did feel lighter. Something felt freer to picture a future for myself.

I looked up at Brooke, twenty-three-year-old Brooke, so different yet the same, so utterly familiar, yet also a complete stranger. She gave me a small smile, and I knew she was right: we had hurt each other—we were both still hurting—but that didn't make us right for each other. That didn't mean we had to be together to heal.

'You think we...you think we need to talk,' I said.

She nodded. 'Not tonight, though, I mean, emotions are running high. But we do need to talk about it. Everything. Not just Prom, but what happened before.'

My whole body stiffened. 'We already talked about that stuff. In the pub. When you were eighteen.'

'But we didn't really *talk* about it, did we? I mean, I was really ill at the time. I think we need to face what happened.'

I felt a bolt of fear run through me, like an electric shock. The task that had seemed so impossible. But Brooke was back. Everything was different now.

'Yes. Let's face what happened.'

I drove her home in silence, trying to take the whole night in. Brooke sat next to me in the passenger seat as I pulled up near her house, just like we had done a million years ago. Her mother was at the top of the driveway, clearly anxious that her daughter wouldn't come home. Brooke got out of the car and told me she would text. I watched her walk up the drive, watched her mother put her arm around her, watched the light from the hallway disappear as the door closed behind them.

My fantasy of her return had been destroyed, only to make way for reality. A reality in which I could see that I'd idealised the idea of us, as if that would justify all that'd happened between us. But this was okay. She was alive, and okay, and so was I. For the first time in a long time, I felt hopeful. I felt like I could face my guilt, face what I'd done, and take responsibility. I could finally start to work on myself, to stop acting like a coward, to become somebody I could respect. For the first time in my life, I could see a future for myself beyond the edges of this town.

Without realising, I wound up not at my flat, but at my old house, Mum's house. She saw my car pull up from the kitchen window and came to the door.

'Matt? What are you doing here?'

'Can I stay here tonight?' I asked, getting out of the car.

For a moment, she looked surprised. 'Of course you can, Matty.'

I bent down to hug her small frame and she kissed me on the cheek. She spoke over my shoulder as she held me. 'You can stay here any time you want.'

Even though I was a head taller than her, I still felt she was holding me, like mothers are supposed to hold their sons. I fought off the tears that prickled in my eyes.

'Now, I've calmed down and I've talked to Dad, and I'll say that if you want to buy a house, you should.'

'I don't want to buy a house,' I said quickly, pulling back from her. I didn't even have to think about it. I'd been tied down to one place long enough; I didn't want that again.

'Okay,' Mum said. 'Well, whatever you want. Wherever you go,' she patted me on the arm as she led me inside. 'You can always come back home.'

SCENE 23: BROOKE, 23

'Auntie Bwooke,' Freddie said, pouring air into my plastic cup.

'Mmm, yum,' I said, pretending to sip from it. 'Thank you, Freddie.'

It was a Sunday. I'd been home for six weeks. Mum was cooking a roast dinner and Dad was going to join us, like when we were kids. Amy and I were on the sofa. It had taken a couple of weeks for her to come round. She didn't hug me, but she let me hug Freddie, and play with him. I wasn't working so I helped Mum babysit; we would go to pick him up from pre-school and he'd get so excited when he saw me, running into my arms and stumbling as he did.

'I keep the tea set here, I don't bring it home,' Amy said, as the toddler trotted over to fill the cups of various teddy bears. 'Otherwise, I'd never get anything done. It's his favourite thing in the world.'

I'd texted Matt, like I said I would, and we met up again for a coffee. It'd been more sombre this time, less warm, and Matt didn't hug me like he had done before. He seemed calmer this time, stiffer. 'This is going to be a difficult conversation,' he said.

I nodded. He didn't quite know where to look. Nor did I.

'Matt,' I said, 'I know that I hurt you, when I left. I get why that was confusing, leaving you with unanswered questions. I understand why you felt guilty, like you might've driven me away. You weren't responsible for the decision I made to leave.

'But I didn't say we were getting back together that night. I said one date. And I said that we didn't have a future. I'm not responsible for the version of me you made up in your mind.'

Matt nodded. 'You're not,' he said quietly.

'And…what happened between us, when I was fourteen. That was pretty fucked up.' I saw him try to hide the sting in his face as I said it, but he needed to hear it. This needed to be acknowledged. 'Yes, I wanted to be in the relationship, but I was fourteen. I didn't know what was best for me. I didn't make decisions that were in my own interest. I'm not saying you weren't stupid and immature too, but you were older. You had more of a responsibility to stop it. Not just that one night, but the whole thing, asking me to keep secrets, to lie. I got hurt. It wasn't okay.'

He was looking at me steadily as I spoke, hardly breathing.

'But I'm okay now. And so are you,' I finished.

Matt blinked and looked down at his cup. He breathed silently for several seconds. Then he finally opened his mouth. 'I did have the responsibility,' he said. 'I wish I'd acted differently. I wish I could undo it.' He looked up and met my eyes. 'I am very sorry for all the hurt I have caused you.'

I took a deep breath as we held each other's gaze. 'Thank you,' I said.

'I hope…' I could see he was choosing his words carefully. 'I hope that helps.'

'It does.'

'If there's anything else I can do for you. If you want to talk more—'

'I think this should be the last time we talk,' I said.

Matt looked disappointed, then nodded, and I came home feeling like I'd put down a weight I hadn't realised I was carrying.

Freddie seized another cup. 'Gwanma, it's time for tea!' he called out.

'Grandma's cooking, Fredster,' Amy said. 'But Mummy and Auntie Brooke will have tea with you.'

'Can I have a refill, please, Freddie?' I asked, and he seized the teapot, keen to oblige.

I'd been home for longer than planned, and my flexi return flight was about to expire. My first two weeks here had been paid vacation. After that, I was able to work from home in the dining room for another two weeks. After a month, Yuko told me I'd have to take an indefinite leave of absence.

'Indefinite?' Charlie had said on the phone. 'So, like, you might never come back?'

'I will come back,' I insisted. 'I just don't know when.'

'Two weeks,' Charlie said. 'That's how long you said you'd be.'

'I know, but things are going really great here. I couldn't have predicted how much I…how much longer I needed to stay.'

'How much longer, Brooke?'

I didn't say anything.

'Are you sure you're gonna come back?'

Freddie handed me a plastic cupcake. 'Ooh, thank you,' I said, and mimed eating it.

My cell buzzed.

Charlie Young: How's it going?

I snapped a picture of Freddie, wielding the plastic teapot like a weapon, and sent it to him.

'You must miss him,' Amy said, glancing at my phone. 'It must be hard—not knowing when you'll see him next.'

This was progress: Amy trying to empathise with me. 'Yeah, it is a bit.'

'He seems like a good guy. Unlike my baby daddy. But no biggie.' Freddie picked up a teacup and handed it to Amy, and she ruffled his hair. 'Who needs him when I have this handsome fella?'

My phone buzzed again.

Charlie Young: Adorable
    The foodbank is having a fundraiser on the 15th. If you're home by then we could steward it.

I leaned back. Amy had come to her feet now and had Freddie in her arms. She was swinging him round and he was giggling manically. Mum came in and asked Amy something about the gravy, grabbing Freddie's toes and wiggling his feet about as she did.

Brooke Tyler: I don't think I'll be back by then, sorry. I have to stay here for at least a while longer.

'Brooke, can you set the table?' Mum said. I followed her back into the kitchen and took the placemats from the cupboard.

My phone buzzed again.

Charlie Young: I don't know how much longer I can go on not knowing when you'll be home.

I looked at the message, staring at me from my lock screen. I was starting to wonder if Charlie had been right when he suggested I might not come back. I still wasn't sure, but I felt another night of arguing down the phone coming on.

I ignored it for now, putting my cell in my pocket, and went into the kitchen. Mum had her back to me, her hands in oven gloves, sloshing hot oil over potatoes in a baking tray. I snuck up behind her and looped my arms around her shoulders.

She jumped in surprise, but then patted my arms with the big mitt. 'You alright, love?'

'Yeah,' I smiled, and released her. 'Yeah, it's just good to be home.'

SCENE 24: MATT, 26

I picked up my rucksack as the taxi drove off. I walked into the airport and scanned the orange signs until I saw my flight: Bristol to Brisbane, via Doha.

After my coffee with Brooke, I felt like she'd handed me a weight, and I knew I would carry it forever. It was heavy, but I could lift it. I sat with it for a few days, and things became clear to me. I didn't want to buy a house. I didn't want to stay in town. Four days after we spoke, I handed in my notice at work. I took out all my savings. I ended my contract with my landlady and put my stuff into Mum and Dad's attic, until I was left with just my rucksack, my passport, and a plane ticket.

'Text me every day,' Mum had said tearfully when we'd said goodbye that morning. Dad had been more stoic. 'Have fun, but not too much fun,' was his advice.

I wasn't just going for fun, though. I was going to shake myself out of self-pity and take responsibility for my life. I needed to be true to myself and think about the kind of man I wanted to be, and do whatever it took to become him.

And now I was at the airport. Simon would pick me up when I landed. Together, we were going to drive down to Sydney, Canberra, and Melbourne. After that was anyone's guess. Maybe we'd head to Tasmania for a bit or we'd go our separate ways and I'd end up in Bali or Vietnam and he'd go to Thailand or South Korea. It didn't matter where we went. What mattered was that I was going somewhere. The weight would come with me, but I knew I could carry it.

I put my phone away and took my small bag out of the big one. I left the rucksack with the man behind the desk and headed to security. It was a bit cold for the shorts I was wearing, but I knew it wouldn't be cold where I landed. I took off my belt and shoes and put them in a plastic tray.

The last time I'd been at this airport, I'd been running after a girl who'd already left on a plane. I'd spent years unable to move on, stuck in a holding pattern until she came back and showed me that the love I held for her was nothing but guilt. I might never see her again, and that was okay. Our lives were not entwined, our paths were not destined together. She wasn't thinking about me. And I wasn't thinking about her, not in the same way. I was thinking about my choices. I was thinking about Australia. I was thinking about putting one foot in front of the other and pushing ahead, towards something new.

My phone buzzed.

Simon Hughes: Have a good flight dude, see you on the other side

SCENE 25: BROOKE, 23

'That's the ugliest sofa I've ever seen,' Amy said.
'It's lovely,' Mum counteracted, even though neither of us believed her.

'It's ugly,' I said, 'but it's mine.'

I looked around the flat. I'd found it on SpareRoom, and I shared it with a woman called Rosie, who seemed nice. It was a small place in Bristol, a bus ride from Mum's house. I'd paid for it with the deposit I'd saved from my old apartment in Seattle.

I'd been home for a few months, and America felt so far away now. Yuko couldn't hold my job any longer, and Charlie said he couldn't wait forever. I came to realise he was right, that I wasn't going to come back. Breaking up had been painful, but rediscovering my roots made me realise that I needed to be here, to start over and do it right this time.

I'd managed to get an assistant job at the *Bristol Post*, and still had a little money left from my American account. I was texting Lucy in Sheffield and Marie in America. Callum hadn't come round. Amy had. I'd looked at some clubs I could join, choirs or dance classes where I might be able to make friends. I'd also found a therapist, since I still had work to do. All these things I should have done at eighteen. I should have built a life for myself here with the support of people who loved me. But I'd had to learn that.

'I think you need a couple of lamps,' Amy said. 'It's quite dark in here.'

'We could take you to IKEA,' Mum suggested.

'That's okay,' I shrugged. 'I'm sure I'll find some in a charity shop.'

My heart still ached for Charlie. The first man who ever truly loved me, kindly and unconditionally. It hurt to know that he was so far away, and that he was destined for some other woman. I could picture Marie giving this faceless person a hard time, telling her she had some big shoes to fill. But that wasn't for me to worry about. I knew where I needed to be.

The doorbell rang. 'Pizza's here,' Amy said, shooting off to answer it.

'I'll get some plates.' Mum disappeared into the kitchen.

'We don't need plates, it comes in a box,' Amy called back. I followed her into the hall and stood in the doorway to my bedroom. A double bed that took up most of the space, a wardrobe with a crooked door, a little nightstand. It was small and it was shabby, but it was mine. Found by me, paid for by me, owned—well, rented—by me. It finally felt like I had some of my own territory on this earth, like I knew how much space my body took up and where all of my edges were. I had something that was truly mine. For the first time in my life.

'What shall we watch, Brooke?' Mum called from the lounge.

I smiled, closed the door, and followed the scent of pizza.

BOOK CLUB QUESTIONS

Where do you stand on the age difference at the beginning of the book? Did the way you feel about it change by the end of the book?

The theme of consent features heavily in *Can I Stray*. There is one scene where the characters seem to view consent as something of a grey area. In your opinion, how complicated is the issue of consent actually?

Brooke's mental health is connected to her codependency. What effect do you think this has on her, and do you relate in any way to her character?

In therapy with Sanjay, Brooke describes some of Matt's behaviour in their relationship as 'toxic'. Do you think Matt is a toxic person? What are some of the traits of a toxic relationship?

At various points in the book, Brooke is involved in relationships with Matt, Pete, and Charlie. What do you believe each of them represent?

Matt has very different sexual relationships with Georgia, Brooke, and Kayleigh. What do each of these reveal about his relationship with women and sex, and how do they reflect society's wider attitudes to sex?

When Brooke returns to the UK, Lucy, Amy, and Callum have contrasting reactions to her return. Why do you think that is? How would you react in their position?

At the end of the book, the characters talk a lot about accountability. Why is it important for both of them to take accountability for their actions? Do you think Brooke and Matt are held accountable for their actions? Do you think one has to take more accountability than the other?

Can I Stray is a work of fiction but it draws on real-world experiences. How has this story informed or even challenged your understandings of victimhood, agency, and consent? Do you consider Brooke a victim? Is Matt also a victim or not?

There are many adults that could have intervened in the relationship between Brooke and Matt, but don't. How responsible as a society are we in creating the sorts of conditions that create boys/men like Matt and girls/women like Brooke?

ACKNOWLEDGEMENTS

Firstly, a huge thank you to my publisher Archna and, of course, the wonderful Jade at Neem Tree Press. You two have made this book a reality and I will never be able to thank you both enough. Thank you also to Sofia, Lisa, and Misha at Neem Tree Press. You guys are legends.

Thank you, Michael, for being the world's greatest writing partner, and for Caitlin, who saw so much in the book that I didn't even see. Thank you to Erin and PQ for the beautiful cover design, and to Bee for always saving me a space on the couch.

An enormous thank you to all my beta readers whose feedback made the book just so much better. Thank you to Phil for all your support and guidance.

Thank you to my mum, my dad, and my sister for giving me a million opportunities. Thank you to all my friends and family for the unwavering support and the jokes about how long this book was taking. Got there in the end, eh?

If you have been affected by the issues raised in this book, such as mental health, codependency, unhealthy relationships, and sexual assault, I urge you to reach out to loved ones, professionals, or charities for support:

MENTAL HEALTH:

Mind
Mind provides advice and support on a range of topics including types of mental health problems, self-harm, legislation and details of local help and support in England and Wales.
Phone: 0300 123 3393 (weekdays 9am - 6pm)
Website: https://www.mind.org.uk/information-support

YoungMinds

YoungMinds offers information, support and advice for children and young people on mental health, wellbeing, racism and self-harm. Help for concerned parents of those under 25 is offered by phone.

Crisis Messenger for young people: text YM to 85258.
Helpline for parents: 0808 802 5544 (Mon–Fri 9.30am-4pm)
Website: https://www.youngminds.org.uk

Rethink Mental Illness

Rethink Mental Illness advice offers practical help and information for anyone affected by mental illness on a wide range of topics such as The Mental Health Act, living with mental illness, medication and care.

Website:https://www.rethink.org/aboutus/what-we-do/advice-and-information-service/get-help-now

SANE

SANE provides confidential emotional support and information to anyone affected by mental illness. It also provides a resource for anyone affected by suicide.

Leave a message at: 07984 967 708
Website: https://www.sane.org.uk/how-we-help/emotional-support

The Mix

The Mix provide non-judgmental support and information for young people under 25 on a variety of issues including mental wellbeing, sex & relationships, exam stress, money, drugs and self-harm.

Phone: 0808 808 4994 (4pm-11pm daily)
Website: https://www.themix.org.uk/get-support/speak-to-our-team

Codependents Anonymous

Codependents Anonymous is a fellowship of men and women whose common purpose is to develop healthy relationships.

Website: https://codauk.org

SEXUAL HEALTH:

Brook

Brook operates a number of sexual health and wellbeing services across the UK.

Brook is committed to supporting young people and the majority of services are for people under 25. However, in December 2019 they began running all-age sexual health services in parts of the country. They also provide outreach and education services for young people and training for professionals across the UK.

Website: https://www.brook.org.uk/find-a-service/

UNHEALTHY RELATIONSHIPS:

Love Is Respect

Love Is Respect is the US's national resource to disrupt and prevent unhealthy relationships and intimate partner violence by empowering young people through inclusive and equitable education, support, and resources.

Website: https://www.loveisrespect.org/get-relation-ship-help

Act On It Now

We help teens & young people, parents & carers and professionals to better understand why young people are more vulnerable to unhealthy or toxic relationships.

Website: https://www.actonitnow.org.uk/resources-teens

The National Domestic Abuse Helpline

The 24 hour National Domestic Abuse Helpline, run by Refuge is for women experiencing domestic abuse, their family, friends and others calling on their behalf.

Phone: 0808 2000 247 (24 hour)

Web chat: https://www.nationaldahelpline.org.uk/en/Chat-to-us-online

BSL interpretation service: https://www.nationaldahelpline.org.uk/en/bsl

Men's Advice Line

Men's Advice Line is a confidential service for male victims of domestic abuse offering support help men keep themselves (and their children) safe.

Phone: 0808 801 0327 (Mon-Fri, 10am-8pm)

Website: https://mensadviceline.org.uk/contact-us/

Galop

Galop are trans inclusive and are welcoming of anyone from the LGBT+ community (including those who are questioning their identity). Contact them to receive support if you are a victim of sexual violence, hate crime, or domestic abuse.

Email: help@galop.org.uk

National LGBT domestic violence helpline: 0800 999 5428 (Mon-Fri 10am-5pm, Wed & Thurs 10am-8pm)

Website & webchat: https://galop.org.uk/get-help

SEXUAL ASSAULT:

Rape Crisis England & Wales

Rape Crisis England & Wales offers confidential support and information to women in England and Wales who have survived any form of sexual violence, no matter how long ago. Also provides immediate support to friends and family on how to support female survivors of sexual violence.

Phone: 0808 802 9999 (12-2:30pm & 7-9:30pm daily)

Website: https://rapecrisis.org.uk/get-help

Rape Crisis Scotland

Rape Crisis Scotland provides confidential support for anyone affected by sexual violence, no matter when or how it happened. They can also put you in touch with local rape crisis centres.

Phone: 08088 010 302 (5pm-midnight daily)

Website: https://www.rapecrisisscotland.org.uk/help

NHS Sexual Assault Referral Centres
England & Wales: https://www.nhs.uk/live-well/sexual-health/
help-after-rape-and-sexual-assault
   Scotland: https://www.nhsinform.scot/turn-to-sarcs

The Survivors Trust
The Survivors Trust provides support and signposting for
women, men and children who are survivors of rape, sexual
violence or childhood sexual abuse.
   Phone: 0808 801 0818 (Mon-Thurs 10am-12.30pm,
1.30pm-5.30pm & 6pm-8pm; Fri 10am-12.30pm &
1.30pm-5.30pm; Sat 10am-1pm; Sun 5pm-8pm)
   Website & live chat: https://www.thesurvivorstrust.org

Victim Support
Victim Support provides emotional and practical help to victims
or witnesses of any crime, whether or not it has been reported
to the police.
   Phone: 0808 16 89 111 (24/7)
   Website: https://www.victimsupport.org.uk